NOIRE

VOLUMES ONE AND TWO

EMMANUELLE DE MAUPASSANT

Edited by
ADREA KORE

'The Gentlemen's Club' was first published in 2014, and
'Italian Sonata' in 2017.

www.emmanuelledemaupassant.com

Cover design by Victoria Cooper
Cover image : Sarah Bernhardt (1871)
painted by Georges Clairin
reproduced courtesy of Wikipedia Commons

My greatest thanks go to my dear friend, and developmental editor, Adrea Kore, for her work in helping bring my stories to the page.

THE GENTLEMEN'S CLUB

VOLUME ONE - NOIRE

We live in the wondrous here and now and it's here that our flesh must take its pleasure. Your body is yours and yours alone, but not for long, and never long enough.

Mademoiselle Noire

FOREWORD

VICTORIAN LONDON

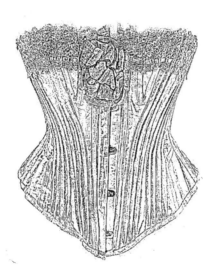

The nineteenth century was a time of prudery and hypocrisy. While it was expected that men would indulge their sexual impulses widely, regardless of marital status, it was unthinkable for a 'genteel' woman to admit even to enjoyment of her marriage bed.

For her to express undue interest in sexual matters was a sign of wantonness and questionable moral character. More ominously, it could inspire diagnosis of hysteria.

In extreme cases, a woman might be referred to an asylum for treatment of this perversion. Engaging in sex outside of marriage made her a 'fallen woman'.

Although sheaths, made from animal gut, had been in use for some time, the use of rubber caps (womb veils) allowed women to gain greater control over pregnancy, and, thereby, over some of their choices.

MAUD

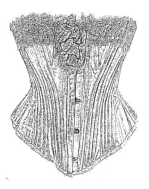

With thinly veiled intentions, Great-aunt Isabella has presented Maud with a series of hand-tinted stereographs, entitled 'Twenty-Five Stages from Courtship to Marriage'. There are nineteen stages before the suitor lowers his lips chastely to his beloved's hand. The innocent maiden, so wooed, turns her face away coyly.

Perusing them in the privacy of her room, Maud smiles. The final image is risqué indeed. The couple, attired neck to toe, retire to bed, the man closing the curtains against prying eyes. The twenty-sixth stage is left to her imagination. In this, her inventiveness is better suited than Isabella can conceive.

She secretes them carefully away in the wooden travelling chest at the end of her bed, opening its heavy lock with the key she keeps always in the pocket of her dress. All her treasures are there: mementoes of her past, keepsakes and souvenirs, and the curios which amuse her, though Isabella would surely not consider them appropriate for one of her years and unwedded state.

From within, she draws out her new novel, hot from France. Its yellow cover denotes its content of 'dubious morality'. She secures such luxuries, wearing her heaviest veil, from a bookshop whose owner cares not about the corruption of young ladies, as long as their coin is good.

Her first book, purchased last winter, was a copy of Mr. Stoker's *Dracula*; what dreams she has enjoyed since reading those pages. Is there anything more delicious than such a book, read by the flicker of lamplight, in the comfort of one's bed?

Maud's imagination takes her to the snow-peaked wilds of the Carpathians, and the jagged Borgo Pass. Creatures of the night, eyes blazing, run through the twilight, their agonized howls stilled only by the sweep of the mysterious Count's arm, bringing them under his bidding.

She pictures herself in place of Jonathan Harker, imprisoned against her will within the broken battlements of Castle Dracula. The three vampire brides descend upon her, closer, closer. She feels the tingling sweetness of their breath, tinged with the bitter smell of blood. Their tongues lick crimson lips in greedy anticipation as they lower their mouths upon her skin, intent on sating their lust.

She is keen to lose herself in the delicious carnality of the narrative, that it might inspire sweet dreams for the coming night. However, thoughts of Lorenzo intrude upon her enjoyment.

To her chagrin, Isabella clearly presents him in the guise of a suitor, as if Maud might be tempted into wedlock with the son Isabella has, with regularity, disparaged for his 'wicked ways'.

His carriage has delivered the latest recipient of the title of Conte di Cavour the previous morning. Though his arrival from Siena pertains to business, he has some time in which to visit Isabella and become acquainted with this distant cousin, for whom his mother has such praise.

Over the ritual of afternoon tea, Maud has endured the torment of being inspected. Dainty sandwiches of cucumber were consumed as his eyes, dark and heavy-lidded, gazed upon her as a wolf might survey its prey. His hungry appraisal, of her waist, her hips, her bust, is familiar. He looks at her through a veneer of civility; she sees this trait in most of his species.

Meanwhile, Isabella enumerated her talents as one might list the saleable qualities of a prize heifer.

He is not unhandsome, his stature upright though his hair is silver-threaded. It is his presumption of her compliance that riles her.

Later, Isabella bid her show him to his room. As he followed Maud upstairs, she paused, and felt his hand slip beneath her hem. Circling her ankle, he held her firm, fingers squeezing a bruise against the jut of bone.

She feels that grasp upon her ankle, as if it were a circlet of iron. To be married would be to be pinned, like a museum butterfly, or to placed under the wolf's paw. He would remain free to prowl. She stepped back to free herself, clipped his face with her heel, leaving him with a split lip and the taste of blood.

Tomorrow, he will find syrup of figs in his morning coffee, and a menu unvaried in its repulsiveness: sautéed tripe with lentils, braised liver and cabbage soup.

Isabella's cat, Satan, is a superb catcher of vermin. Maud will collect his daily victims from the bucket beside the kitchen door; downstairs staff have a weekly wager on the headcount.

She'll place them in Lorenzo's chamber: one little mouse snuggled prettily in a sock, as if sleeping; another perched upon his shaving brush, in mock coitus with its prickly mate; several sprinkled liberally in the pockets of his smoking jacket; and a particularly fine specimen upon his pillow, eyes beady and mouth slightly frothing.

THE CLUB

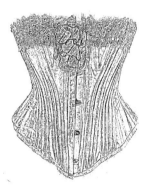

Those in the upper echelons of society alone know what lies beyond certain doors. Where membership is exclusive, the rules may be as strict as required to keep it that way.

To all intents, the club is a modest refuge from the bustle of business: a place where a chap might read the papers in peace, over coffee or brandy. A fair steak, pea soup and apricot tart can be had: adequate for those worshipping at the temple of the stomach.

However, on passing through a certain curtain, pleasure, pain and humiliation may be enjoyed in the company of ladies who return the virile salute of desire with the same enthusiasm in which it is given. They welcome the bounteous gifts bestowed upon them and, in catering to such whims, are well remunerated.

Nevertheless, financial reward is far from their only incentive. Without exception, the ladies of this harem remain at the establishment longer than is necessary to amass a goodly amount of capital (such as is sufficient to open a millinery or haberdashery).

In most cases, personal interest in the pursuit of pleasure keeps them in continued service. They delight in wielding power over men, whether in domination or in sweet surrender, and their thirst thrills to the added knowledge of being watched by many eyes.

A FIRM HAND

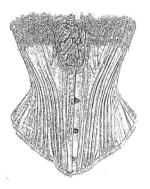

As London sits damp under autumn drizzle and all respectable gentlefolk are either before their fires or in their beds, Lord McCaulay, handsome in full evening dress, is leaving his fashionable residence on Eaton Square, Belgravia, for the five-minute carriage journey to his club. He has endured a dull few hours in the company of the great and the good, including his uncle, the Duke of Mornemouth. McCaulay enjoys a good income and his responsibilities are few, but humouring his relatives remains a duty he must endure.

The only conversation worth his breath was with a fellow member of the British Ornithological Union, discussing the good work of the ladies of the Society for the Protection of Birds, who are rightly intent on discouraging the wearing of plumage in hats.

Lord McCaulay does not generally encourage women to voice an opinion on any matter. However, his own love of birds, to which he devotes many hours of study, moves him to hold the Society's dedication in high regard. He accedes that their efforts in deterring the destruction of almost a million birds annually, merely to provide plumage for the headdresses of the feather-brained, are more worthwhile than those of the uncouth suffragists.

Duties done for the day, it is now time to indulge his pleasures. Replete with the usual dinner conversation denouncing the moral decline of the working classes, Lord McCaulay is ready to fulfil his own hunger for vice.

The luxurious salon on the second floor of the club, furnished in plush velvets and damasks, the floor spread with Persian rugs, is lit by a chandelier of black glass and by the dim glimmer of lamplight. A dozen men are seated in a semi-circle of armchairs; despite their half-moon masks, he recognizes them all.

Lord McCaulay orders a large whisky and settles himself comfortably. The Master of Ceremonies enters and bows, bidding those gathered welcome and assuring them that tonight will be particularly memorable. They are honoured to present Mademoiselle Noire, who will be gracing the club over coming weeks, orchestrating a variety of entertainments for their amusement.

The lady in question enters, walking the outer circumference of the room, where the shadows cling thickest, so that her visage is not immediately apparent. Her skirts brush the back of chairs and she pauses behind each, as if to stroke the nape of a neck with her gloved hand; yet, she does not. Her scent trails behind: heavy with wood and musk, and bergamot.

An unusual choice for a woman, muses McCaulay.

Her circuit complete, she steps forward, and McCaulay sees that her costume is modest: a black taffeta gown, revealing shoulders and a little décolletage. Her waist is cinched tightly, as is the fashion, and her skirts are abundant. Black evening gloves cover most of her arm, and, in one hand, she carries a riding crop. The swell of her form beneath the silk indicates a full figure.

Her skin is luminous in the lamplight. Auburn hair is pinned high, every lock precisely placed. Her eyes, framed within guipure lace, glitter darkly.

A clap of her hands brings forward a statuesque African, from behind the drapes, clad in a leather hood. His muscular body is naked and oiled, and every hair has been removed from his body, so that the muscles in his chest stand boldly and his generous member is proudly unveiled. Its full length and girth are visible, hanging heavily between his thighs.

Mademoiselle Noire's eyes wander over this godlike creature. McCaulay flinches as she flicks her crop lightly at the ebony giant's phallus, the smallest smile upon her lips. The fringed tail end makes contact with the tender skin, but the giant's face remains immobile. She wields the crop a little harder, catching him full along the length of the shaft. The African stands firm, unmoving, his dark truncheon engorging. The crop strikes twice more, each time raising the beast between his legs. McCaulay is aware of a twitch within his own groin.

Mademoiselle Noire bids the giant turn. His buttocks bring to mind a midnight shadow of Michelangelo's David. She commands him to bend and part his legs, so that his testicles hang, huge and low.

A view at once familiar yet disturbing, thinks McCaulay, his finger to his lips.

She reaches down and grasps them gently in her silk-gloved hand, kneading them like the dough of bread rolls ready for the oven. Having uttered no sound until this moment, he now groans, in undoubtable pleasure. Men about the room shift in their seats.

Her gaze scans the assembled faces, seeking out their eyes, ensuring that she has their full attention before she proceeds.

Lord McCaulay lights a cigar, reclines within his armchair and inhales deeply. He returns her stare, which has settled upon him. He imagines that she is admiring the plane of his jaw and his shoulders' breadth, and the bronzed-gold of his hair. He is used to the admiration of women. Resolutely, her eyes remain on his and she presses the African's treasures harder, until the effort shows in the small sliver of flesh at the top of her arm, above her evening glove.

The recipient's moan grows more audible. She keeps her hand clenched for what seems an eternity, every man in the room now squirming.

At last, she lets those ripe and heavy plums swing free and, keeping McCaulay in her vision, flexes her crop, switching it once through the air before bringing it across the tight flesh of black buttocks. Twice more she delivers her whip to its target. Dark muscles contract in response but he offers no cry of pain, not until the next strike catches him partially on the testicles.

Her scrutiny upon McCaulay, Mademoiselle Noire flicks her crop lightly against the man's inner thigh, so that he might open his legs further, leaving his most tender parts vulnerable to her ministrations.

Another sharp crack of exquisite torture conjures a collective intake of breath. The African's knees bend but resume their stance.

Lord McCaulay swallows, his interest piqued, despite his discomfort. Mademoiselle Noire laughs and, at the click of her fingers, the African stands to one side.

A BLOSSOM YET UNFURLED

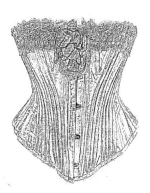

From between the curtains emerges a slight young girl, blindfolded. Mademoiselle Noire leads her to the centre of the room before speaking, her voice a distillation of seduction.

'Daisy, you're in the salon. About you are gathered several gentlemen.'

The girl turns her head.

'I don't understand, Ma'am.'

'You're here because your behaviour upstairs has been inappropriate to your position as chambermaid. We must reach an understanding if you're to stay in service here.'

Daisy nods.

'You must know to what I'm referring. The offence occurred yesterday evening, at around six o'clock. Tell the gentlemen in this room what happened.'

The chambermaid is trembling. 'I approached a guest in his bedroom, Ma'am. I asked him if he'd like me to pleasure him, in return for a small payment.'

Mademoiselle continues, her voice low and steady. 'And what did you have in mind, Daisy? Are you a woman of the world?'

A blush suffuses the poor girl's cheek.

'Come now. You must be honest with us.'

Daisy drops her head in shame.

'I thought that I might rub the gentleman, Ma'am. I know that men like to touch, and to have their places touched. I have my own young man. We're set to marry, in the spring. He says it's a long time to wait, so I let him take some liberties.'

Smiling, Mademoiselle places her hand gently on Daisy's arm.

'Thank you for your candour. Our gentlemen may do as they please upstairs, but not with chambermaids.'

Mademoiselle Noire adds curtly, 'Unless through prior notice with the management. There are rules. If you wish to sport with our guests, rather than make their beds, that can be arranged. You might find such new duties preferable, and they would pay a great deal more. It would, no doubt, make a handsome purse to bring to your marriage, and your young man need never know.'

She pauses. 'Is that what you'd like?'

The girl whispers her reply, her head bowed. 'I think I might, Ma'am.'

'That being the case, I think it best that we discover if you are truly suited for such an occupation. Those who come here are discerning. Let's waste no time,' continues Mademoiselle.

She circles the young girl, and casts her gaze, as before, over the gentlemen seated, observing their expression as she speaks.

'You must do as I say. Your hands are free, so you may remove your bloomers.'

The girl looks up in bewilderment. Her lips part, as if to remonstrate. Hesitantly, she reaches under her skirt and petticoat. Fumbling, relying on her fingers' familiarity, she unties the ribbon at the top of her undergarment. The bloomers drop.

'Our gentlemen, like bees gathering at the lip of a succulent lily, are keen to assess the succulence within,' Mademoiselle coaxes.

The girl takes the hem of her skirts and raises them to her knee, then higher, until the top of her thick worsted stockings is visible and a small section of pale thigh above.

Someone coughs. There is an atmosphere of impatience. Mademoiselle Noire is taking her time. McCaulay is not alone in wishing she would speed up proceedings.

'We must see more, Daisy.' Mademoiselle's fingers stroke a curl of hair at the nape of the girl's neck.

'Take off your stockings, and raise your skirts fully, so that they're about your waist.'

'Oh Ma'am,' mumbles Daisy, her lips quivering now, close to tears.

'You may leave, now, or at any time you choose; it is a freedom all ladies of this establishment enjoy. Only those who wish to be here stay,' answers Mademoiselle. 'If this is your calling, you must prove yourself.'

So it is that the girl, flustered but willing, holds the rough fabric high. The cleft between her legs is revealed: two slivers of pink protruding from a bush of dark hair.

Brava, thinks McCaulay. *This little show is becoming more diverting.*

Mademoiselle bids the girl turn, to show her rump. The girl obliges, letting her skirts drop to the front, and raising them instead at the back. Her behind is a fleshy peach. Mademoiselle instructs her to bend further and, as she tilts, the young maid reveals more than she might imagine.

'You're quite delightful,' Mademoiselle Noire assures her. 'Now, stay just as you are. A test lies before you and the end result will be worth any small discomfort. In truth, modesty is an obstacle easily surmounted.'

Mademoiselle gestures forward the African, of whom Daisy, being blindfolded, is unaware. The giant's erection has eased a little over the passing minutes, but what next ensues restores its prowess.

With surprising gentleness, he rests his palms upon the girl's buttocks, so that she might feel their heat. This startles her, but his tender touch quickly reassures. One hand moves to cup her sweet cunny. She is surprisingly still, pushing back against the pressure of its warmth. The dark Adonis moves his finger, finding her, pressing lightly, until the girl's breath comes more rapidly.

Mademoiselle Noire observes closely, asking Daisy if she wishes to drop her skirts and leave. The girl shakes her head. Her virgin cleft welcomes the African's caressing finger. There is no hint of struggle.

Mademoiselle watches with genuine satisfaction. 'The last test,' she announces, 'is one which you may perform for us yourself.'

She motions for the African to remove his hand and Mademoiselle helps the girl, she being without her sight, to a chair. So light-headed is the maid that she can barely stand. Mademoiselle sits her to the edge, her buttocks perched, and lifts the girl's skirts. She eases her legs apart.

McCaulay licks his lips at this stirring sight.

Mademoiselle Noire removes her evening glove, to reveal a delicate wrist and fingers long and elegant.

'Our gentlemen, like good worker bees, are watching, Daisy,' she murmurs to her ear. 'Be their Queen. Let your beauty bloom for them, nourish them.'

She guides Daisy's hand to her sex, her own fingers in parallel with the maid's. Mademoiselle locates the waiting nub and, through the pressure of her own hand, caresses the chambermaid to the final pulsing, gasping moments of feminine fulfilment.

It is a sight to behold: the previously timid and intimidated girl, legs spread wide, pleasuring herself to such an audience. McCaulay is inspired to applaud the maid, and Mademoiselle, the others soon following in signifying their admiration.

Mademoiselle Noire inclines her head in recognition. Her satisfaction is evident.

'Gentlemen, our young chambermaid was a blossom yet unfurled; now, the garden of delights is open to her. Daisy has proven herself highly suitable for the labours commensurate with her new position. She will come to revel in the activities of the bed chamber.'

Lowering the girl's skirts, and raising her to her feet, Mademoiselle's voice is gentle.

'Daisy, you'll go upstairs now, to bathe, and to wait in our finest bedroom, ready for your first lover. The bestowing of maidenhood is rare, so your price will be high: a worthy contribution to your dowry. I'll select your lover myself and will see to it that he makes this night one of sweet and shuddering pleasure. There's no need for fear. You're right that men will like to feel your hand upon them and will touch you in return. They'll do a great many things that may surprise you. Allow your body to respond as it wishes, and all will be well.'

She rubs Daisy's shoulder companionably.

'If, after tonight, you decide that these duties are not to your taste, we'll send you on your way with all that you need to find employment elsewhere. Nevertheless, I believe that you'll enjoy the amours which await.'

The notion holds some appeal to McCaulay, who can see what Mademoiselle's keen eye had penetrated far earlier: that Daisy is a girl of unfulfilled passion, shy and inexperienced, but wonderfully responsive. He sits up a little in his chair, attempting to catch Mademoiselle's gaze once more.

However, she avoids his look of eagerness, searching the room for another: a man whose hair is tinged with silver. She glides her ungloved hand across his cheek, allowing his nose to catch the girl's scent, and tilting his head that she might whisper into his ear. All seriousness, he listens to her instructions, nodding in assent before removing himself to the outer chamber. Daisy's lover has been chosen.

DEBASEMENT

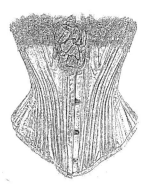

For the final performance of the evening, Mademoiselle Noire requests a volunteer. Resolving that he will not be deprived of any pleasure on offer, Lord McCaulay chooses not to dilly-dally, immediately standing to present his services. She laughs at his impatience and motions him forward, requesting that he remove his clothing. This he does without embarrassment, being proud of his strong body. His chest, legs, arms and groin are abundant in hair, and his phallus is of good size; he does not fear it appearing unworthy, despite the proximity of the ebony giant.

Once naked, he stands expectantly. 'And you, Mademoiselle, might you remove some of your garments? he asks.

She appears nothing but amused.

'Tonight, it is I who give the commands, Sir, not you. Some other time, you may have the gratification of reversing our roles. Do you consent to place yourself at my bidding, to undertake any action I see fit?'

He replies with alacrity. 'You may do with me as you wish; my body is at your disposal, and I vouch it will not disappoint.' He gives a mock bow.

Mademoiselle Noire is accustomed to such airs of hauteur; those of his upbringing and education rarely fail to surprise her.

From a trunk placed to one side, she fetches an item unfamiliar to McCaulay: a leg spreader. This she places between his ankles, fixing them apart, so that he stands not uncomfortably, but rather self-consciously, his genitalia swinging free.

She binds his wrists in front of his body with a sash of velvet. His anticipation causes his penis to leap. With a smile of satisfaction, he hopes that the other gentlemen feel some envy at him being the first to perform with Mademoiselle.

However, Lord McCaulay's expectations are soon thwarted.

'Have you ever felt the touch of a man, gentle Sir?' the seductress enquires.

'Of course, during my school days, there were some minor dalliances, prompted by boyish dares or pranks, but not for some twelve years.'

In fact, McCaulay's tastes are various, but his private indulgences are not for present ears.

'I'm sure you speak the truth but perhaps we may be permitted to awaken a memory for you.'

Mademoiselle gives McCaulay the most charming of smiles.

'We are apt to unduly set aside some pleasures, seeking to create an image of which we feel our peers would approve.'

The challenge is unmistakable. Lord McCaulay becomes at once aware of the black mountain of a man and his body stiffens in alarm.

It's not the performance he had in mind and he curses her, and himself, for having been tricked so easily. Nevertheless, he feels a surge of arousal at the control she exerts over him; she is a woman to be admired.

Barely concealed laughter ripples through the assembled gentlemen, determining him to steel himself for whatever Mademoiselle has in mind. He won't allow his 'colleagues' or this wily vamp the pleasure of seeing him discomfited.

Mademoiselle Noire asks him once more, 'Sir, you need not prove yourself to any man here. Do you wish to return to your chair and allow another to take your place?'

The lady is all outward civility, but McCaulay feels the impudence of her tone. Whatever she might proclaim, his manhood is in question. He resolves to stand firm.

At this, she bids the African step forward. His mighty hands grasp McCaulay's buttocks, allowing a draught of cool air to move between them. As his anus is exposed, he clenches his cheeks, inspiring a firmer grip from the giant. McCaulay hopes that his face betrays none of his trepidation.

'Our friend will place his phallus between your cheeks, there to pleasure himself in whatever motion most satisfies him. He may knock at your door a little, but he will not enter... yet.'

With his legs apart, McCaulay's nether regions are entirely undefended. The giant locks McCaulay's pelvis in a firm grip and begins the slow rubbing of his shaft along the crease of our Lord's buttocks. The African's heavy testicles bump against McCaulay's own with each motion.

Despite his fear, his heart's rapid beat fuels an erection, as cannot fail to be noted by his seated colleagues.

Damn the woman, he curses.

Reminding himself to breathe slowly and keep his head, he takes solace in the principle by which he aspires to live: the enjoyment of experiences new and unexpected. He can hardly argue that the evening has been a bore. Whatever transpires in the following minutes, he doubts he might describe it later as having been dull.

Mademoiselle Noire touches his cheek and leans in to his ear, so close that her hair brushes his lobe.

'Are you quite sure you are the adventurer you believe yourself to be? Do you wish me to end this?' she whispers, without hint of mockery.

He considers for a moment, before hissing a curse.

'My Lord,' she proclaims, loud enough for all to hear now. 'I detect some apprehension. Let us relax you.'

She pulls over a padded stool, placing it before him, and drops to her knees, settling herself into a comfortable position. To McCaulay's surprise, she takes his cock into the velvet of her mouth. As the African continues his labours behind, she begins her feast.

In light of her antagonistic tone, McCaulay has not expected such an intimacy as this. Her devouring of him belies the taunting of her previous discourse, being most expertly and enthusiastically given. Many a whore has performed a similar service upon his Lordship, but never with such vigour. The soft caress of her tongue and the suction of her mouth are executed as if entirely for her own pleasure. Her skill, combined with the rhythmic grinding between his cheeks, sends McCaulay quickly to the edge of his control.

There can be no doubt that Mademoiselle's enjoyment matches his own. She grasps the back of his thighs, pulling him deeper into her throat.

Meanwhile, the African's movements have inspired viscous emanations, which allow his dark phallus to move more easily, lubricated in its confinement.

McCaulay is discovering that rear stimulation, notwithstanding from a huge black penis rather than the dainty fingers of a girl, is a heady combination in conjunction with a cock-suck fit for royalty.

Mademoiselle Noire's hands move from the back of his thighs to his balls, cupping them tightly as her mouth plunges. His natural inclination is to thrust forward, matching her movements, and, within moments, he feels that his climax may be upon him.

His hands, though bound, weave into Mademoiselle's auburn locks, so carefully arranged atop her elegant head. He yanks her by the hair, so that he might see her eyes and witness the expression in them as he comes deeply, her mouth wrapped around him, lips plump and red.

He sees pure lust: pupils dilated and the glazed immersion of desire – but only for a moment. He holds her fast, her head at an awkward angle, his organ pushed fully to the back of her throat, preventing her from withdrawing, or taking breath. This presumption brings forth her anger, and a spike of malice.

Digging her nails into his testicles, she elicits her release from his grasp, retracting her mouth to the head of his organ and biting down upon it, casting away the power of his imminent eruption and replacing it with pain.

She stands, smoothing her skirt and her hair. 'Why, gentle Sir,' she reprimands, her voice steely, 'you misunderstand your role. Let me remind you.'

McCaulay's cock remains purple, full-veined and potent before him, a little tender from her attack, but still at near full extension. He grinds his teeth in frustration.

At a nod from Mademoiselle Noire, the black Adonis wraps one mighty arm around his captive's abdomen, drawing him close to his own, and reaches around with the other hand, taking the root of the Lord's penis in his grip. Thumb and forefinger form a tight circum-navigation of its girth, while the giant's remaining fingers brush the front of McCaulay's testicles.

To McCaulay's shame, the African begins a slow massage of the base of his shaft. He realises that he will soon be powerless to control his ejaculation, before this room of men. McCaulay's arousal, though unwilling, is obvious. No matter his finer feelings, his body responds fiercely to the grasp of his assailant. His audience is no longer chuck-ling. Their gaze is fixed upon his member. Some lick their lips and shift in their seats; others adjust themselves discreetly.

With expert co-ordination, the giant resumes his grinding against McCaulay's rear, juices flowing freely, so that he is able to reach some speed. As promised, he hasn't penetrated McCaulay's person, merely gratifying himself in rubbing between the gentleman's cheeks.

Another nod from Mademoiselle Noire commands the African to alter the angle of his thrust, so that his phallus no longer slips innocently between McCaulay's buttocks but begins pressing more insistently, the bulbous helmet probing the outer rim of the Lord's anus, seeking entry.

At this, McCaulay attempts to struggle, but the creature's grip on his member and torso holds him firm. His legs he cannot move, since they remain pinned awkwardly by the spreader. Despite himself, McCaulay is edging dangerously close to the precipice. He feels the wet penis behind him gain some foothold in its quest, pressing solidly at his door.

'Do you wish us to close the performance early, dear Sir?' enquires Mademoiselle, the casualness of her question at odds with the chill in her voice. 'I see that you strive to free yourself, despite being evidently stirred. It may be that you do not know your true carnal nature, but I have no wish to force this upon you if you're unwilling to welcome such desires.'

McCaulay knows that he might cry out in indignation, ending the assault upon his person in an instant. Yet, he does not. He is a man used to his own way in all things. That another might gain the better of him is inconceivable. He won't give this woman the satisfaction of seeing him squirm.

In truth, McCaulay had forgotten the illicit thrill of a man's hands upon his private parts and the charge of a hot organ nudging at his rear: pleasures enjoyed on many cold nights in his college days. That this woman, in no more than an instant, has surmised his hidden inclinations fills him with both horror and begrudging admiration.

Gritting his teeth, he nods his assent.

'I'm sufficiently confident in my masculinity to withstand any task you might set.'

Thus it is that he surrenders himself, allows this forbidden pleasure. At a final nod from Mademoiselle, the Adonis inches within. McCaulay stifles a groan of arousal.

Meanwhile, the giant's masturbation of McCaulay's cock is

reaching its final pitch: his great hand working faster now. The lord's member glistens with excitement.

As McCaulay's ejaculate arches through the air, the African steadies his grip on the base of that organ and thrusts his own impressive phallus deeper, shooting his abundance.

McCaulay slumps forward, his knees weak, held up by the man behind him.

Those gathered betray not a smile nor snigger. In the silence of the room, the voice of Mademoiselle Noire rings out. 'It seems that our guest was mistaken in his preferences. His pleasure is evident, lying here upon the rug for all to see.'

McCaulay lifts his head and shifts upright as best as he is able, too ashamed to fully meet her eye but wishing at least to appear master of himself.

She continues. 'If it is a path he chooses to pursue, gentlemen, perhaps you may lend a hand, or whatever else is necessary, to help him in his endeavours. Our noble giant, being prodigious in size and considerate of bearing, has bequeathed merely a fraction of his length to our gentle Sir; perhaps, if there is another occasion, our guest might like to try the full sample.'

At this, the tension in the room is broken, and those assembled guffaw openly, rising to slap one another on the back and make lewd jokes. McCaulay, aware now that he has laid himself bare, shrinks back in mortification, desiring to cover himself and leave.

'Feel free to join our eager harem in the adjoining room, gentlemen,' concludes Mademoiselle Noire. 'Remember, their desire is beyond that of most women. Their pleasure is to honour yours, fulfilling every caprice, without reservation. To deprive them of your complete dedication would be a disservice. Those who wish to take a lady, or two or three, to the upper rooms may do so. For the rest, we trust that you will enjoy your own performances in the adjoining salon, giving encouragement to one another in your exertions, and to your hostesses. Remember the rule of the house, that no woman may be obliged against her will. You all know the 'safe' word.'

She sweeps from the room, disappearing beyond the drapes, and the gentlemen drift off, turning their backs on the stage, thinking now of what is to come.

The African unlocks McCaulay's spreaders and unties the velvet sash. Silently, he too, departs. McCaulay gathers his clothes, wiping the worst excesses from his body with his handkerchief, dressing hastily. He leaves without a word.

ENTOMOLOGY

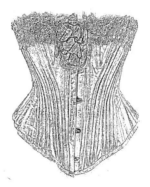

M aud, though a young woman of wit and intelligence, has received a sparse education: several years under governesses of modest abilities, some tutelage with her grandmother, in Italy, and a single year at the Beaulieu Academy for Ladies, where dancing and music, and the art of genteel conversation, comprised the lion's share of instruction.

She is familiar with the basics of mathematics, has a smattering of geographical knowledge, and rather more of history (mostly gleaned from the shelves of her grandmother, who has a penchant for the biographies of great men's mistresses). She plays the pianoforte, and sings, though not well. She can embroider, but has vowed never again to do so of her own free will.

She reads and speaks French moderately but is far more proficient in Italian, having been raised for many years on those heavenly shores. In fact, she has only recently come from her grandmother's residence, where wisteria fragrance seems always to fill the air, blended with the sea-salted scent of the Mediterranean.

Of her parents, she knows little; they cast her upon the goodwill of others when she was no more than seven years old. Having conquered various summits in the name of mountaineering, they swung their last hook over an icy crag and the Hereafter abruptly conquered them.

Maud's academic achievements are just as they should be, since what husband wishes a wife to be better informed than him or, Heaven forbid, to shape such knowledge into opinions; better that she should be ignorant and sweet-natured.

However, despite the best efforts of the world at large, Maud has found herself an interest, for which she has a natural capacity and a memory quite excellent: the study of entomology.

Having begun with a single tattered volume, faded pages depicting Coleoptera, Lepidoptera and Hymenoptera, she is now a regular visitor to the Waterhouse Building, on Cromwell Road in South Kensington.

She first peered into its fascinating cases of beetles and butterflies at the age of six, in the company of her father. She recalls her pity for each occupant, pinned for display. It was no great leap to draw the same conclusion of ladies: similarly bound and trussed, pinned and constrained, with the objective of being admired, in all their gaudy beauty.

The huge elephants and stuffed tigers left the greatest impression on her young imagination. The galleries of corals, minerals, meteorites and fossils were of lesser fascination, though compelling in their way.

Her familiarity with the small creatures of the Natural History

Museum is growing, but her studies extend beyond these husks, taking her into Hyde Park and St. James' with equal regularity.

Those who notice her peering intently at leaf mold think she has dropped an earring or a glove. Who among them would guess that Maud is taking note of the social order between ants? Or analysing wasps' exploration of leaf tips in search of their prey? Or inspecting the manner in which a ladybird eats an aphid?

She is still forming her conclusions but, above all, is convinced that their actions are borne of instinct: fixed patterns that take them to their source of food, to their safe havens, to their mates, and, ultimately, to their death, since their predators learn these patterns as surely as if they had read an encyclopedia on the matter.

Her great-aunt's coachman is complicit in keeping secret the truth of many of her excursions. Supposedly, these are often to the Ritz or the Savoy, to take tea with an old friend. In actuality, she does so once weekly, spending most of her afternoons observing diminutive, six-legged life forms.

While Isabella would take a dim view of her great-niece scrabbling under bushes, she is content to permit Maud's attendance at the Museum's lectures. Maud has discovered these to be both stimulating events and indispensable excuses, on evenings when she desires to steal away for her own amusement. Ever under scrutiny, she is adept at contriving such pretexts.

Maud's exposition of meticulous scientific detail has been sufficient to convince Isabella, and deter her from pursuing investigation into her great-niece's 'hobbies'.

On this day, one of many on which Maud has left Isabella dozing before a warm fire, and has slipped out into the world, she finds herself viewing not merely the inhabitants of museum cases but those on two-legs, engaged in surveying them. She muses on what lives they lead when they scurry back to their nests across the city.

The insect rooms gradually grow quiet, leading her through into the gallery of birds. She tends to avoid this place, feeling sad that these creatures, once so free, are now forever fixed. Beautiful they may be, in their colour and variety, but the extinguishing of their life force, more than any other in this building of corpses, imprints and bones, inspires her deepest empathy.

It is here, among the brilliant parakeets and delicate humming-birds, the owls, the ducks, and all feathered inmates, that Maud spies a certain fellow.

His nose is pressed close upon the glass of a case containing an adult ostrich, brought to London from the furthest and most exotic reaches of the Empire. The specimen has been posed in an aspect of surprise, as if the final thought to have passed its mind was one of incredulity; that the obviously inferior biped before it was more deserving of having become its victim than the other way about.

Maud watches as the man descends into a crouch, to better inspect the great bird's peculiar two-toed feet, each with its long claw. She approaches closer and leans over him, reading from the information card: *Alpha males maintain their herd, mating first with the dominant hen and then with others in the group. Wandering males may later be permitted to mate with lesser hens. In defending against rivals and predators, the ostrich may use its formidable legs as weapons, being able to kill a lion with a single kick.*

An urge comes over her to press the toe of her boot into the gentleman's rear, her own modest kick being sure to send him sprawling. Her foot itches to perform its wickedness. Really! What has come over her?

In truth, the fellow is, probably, no better or worse than the rest of his gender and class: proud, egotistical and pompous but easily humbled when shown his limitations.

It is only then that she recognizes him.

Her boot hovers in mid-air before being retracted beneath her skirts. Quietly, she exits the room.

THOUGHTS OF REVENGE

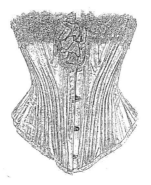

M cCaulay has endured a week of near sleeplessness, tormented as he is by the memory of his illicit consummation before a roomful of men, orchestrated by that woman.

His consent was irrelevant, he being no more than a puppet. In fact, he rather wonders if something might have been put into his drink. A return to the club is out of the question. He keeps a low profile from his usual haunts, being unwilling to cross paths with any of those fellows: those who have watched his shame; first, with glee, then sexual interest, then mockery. The thought sickens him.

He broods at home, takes more than his usual number of baths, smokes and drinks excessively, paces and glowers out of the window. His sister, Cecile, with whom he shares his apartments, puts his sulkiness down to an unfulfilled love affair, and leaves him to himself. She has plenty of distractions of her own and no need to be under his feet.

McCaulay's desire for revenge simmers steadily. Neither his perusal of a fascinating article on the birdlife of the Cape Verde islands in *Ibis*, the ornithologists' journal, nor time spent with his extensive collection of pornographic literature has the power to calm him.

Having studied zoology in his Oxford years, he has often reflected upon man's failure to rise much above the condition of his fellow creatures, driven largely by the desire to feed and procreate. It is only in his ponderings of the melodious and colourful avian world, with its beauty and diversity, and its embodiment of freedom, through flight, that he finds the finger of the Divine.

On the subject of pornography, Lord McCaulay believes that term suited alone to material lacking artistic merit. His own collection of books, sketches and cards (some more dog-eared than others) he deems akin to the Venus de Milo, rising above the common fodder of aids to 'relief'.

Nevertheless, he recalls with some fondness his youthful glimpses at the penny illustrated weeklies, discovered by his thirteen year old self, hidden behind greenhouse begonias by the estate's under-gardener. A series of thirty-six poses by a certain lady on a swing and trapeze continue to hold power over him and are brought to mind with more regularity than he would care to admit.

McCaulay's advanced sexual education began, aged seventeen, with his reading of *My Secret Life,* by Henry Spencer Ashbee: memoirs of experience, detailing every activity a man and woman might indulge in involving their genitals. The edition was thoughtfully given to him by his father, to enlighten young Henry before his ascent to the dreaming spires of his chosen college.

He urged his son to remember the wisdom of Albert Sidebottom: 'Love between the sexes is based upon sexual passion and this instinct is neither coarse nor degrading, unless it exists in a coarse or degraded individual.'

That he retains a much-thumbed copy of *Lady BumTickler's Revels*, a joyful romp through the pleasures of flagellation and spanking, he commends to his tendency to nostalgia, the volume having been a twenty-first birthday gift most jovially bestowed by his Oxford chums.

Naturally, his editions are not left in plain sight on his library shelves; they are under lock and key. The idea of Cecile laying eyes upon them fills him with horror. His duty is to ensure that no maggot defiles the pure bud of her innocent youth. Until she is delivered into the arms of a suitable husband, he cannot conceive of her having the slightest knowledge of what occurs in the marriage bed.

In fact, her unwedded state has been plaguing him of late, since she is already a little beyond the usual age. His parents, God rest them, would surely chastise him. He has been negligent in his duties as guardian: far too caught up in his own pleasures, and his personal desire to avoid betrothal.

Their aunt presented Cecile at court three summers ago, and McCaulay spared no expense, in her wardrobe, or in her 'coming-out' ball. There were suitors, but Cecile, in her innocence, seemed not at all to comprehend the ways of love.

In truth, McCaulay had been loathe to encourage a match, wishing not yet to lose his sister to another man.

Selfish of me, he realizes. *I must remedy the situation. Next season, we shall do better. I shall make it my mission to find a man worthy of her: to secure her happiness.*

His own happiness he can barely think on. As the days pass and McCaulay's remembrance of that night loses some of its harder edge, he is left not only with feelings of abasement, but of unmistakable arousal. He recalls the commanding grip of the African upon his penis and the intrusion from behind: at once repugnant yet stimulating. The excitement catches in his throat.

No less rousing is the image of that she-devil, with her harpy mouth around his cock. How he'd like to choke her, or take that crop of hers and thrash her senseless. This leads to thoughts of the figure beneath her costume. He imagines full breasts with dark nipples, the whip leaving livid marks against the tender flesh. It would be no less than she deserves.

To appease the strange desire evoked by these memories and to soothe his injured ego, he seeks out a street prostitute, intending to take her roughly, against a wall, releasing some of his anger and frustration.

To his discomfort, he is unable to raise an adequate erection, despite the darkness of the alley. The trollop laughs in his face, shaking down her skirts and strutting off with a toss of the head, as well as his shilling in her pocket.

FORBIDDEN PLEASURES

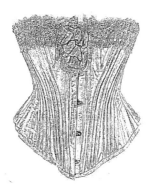

The confectioner's shop Maud most often frequents, located close upon St. James' Park, is first-class: quite as good as anyone might find in Paris. Its crème tarts topped with strawberries, thickly coated éclairs and pastel macaroons are, truly, too pretty to crush between the teeth, yet she does so with relish.

Often, she takes her purchases no further than a bench in the park, sitting quite alone and savouring every bite. She first removes her gloves, lifting her veil to allow the morsels to slip into her waiting mouth, finally making sure that she licks each finger of its sugary coating.

This particular day, she has brought a box home with her, to share with Great-aunt Isabella. Her residence in the house is not long-standing, but suits both parties well. The grand dame, younger sister to Maud's long-departed grandfather, while still sprightly, isn't able to go into the world as often as she once did. Her pleasure now is to recall the scandals of the past and to pronounce on those of the present. She takes all the fashionable journals and, of course, *The Times*, which can be relied upon to keep her informed of the death of her former rivals, and lovers.

Her drinking of sweet sherry begins early in the afternoon and continues steadily enough to see her to her bed as soon as a light supper has been eaten, around half past seven. Ever at her side is her beloved Persian, Satan, whose fluffy demeanour belies a vicious streak. His mistress alone is immune to his claws, since the creature is wise enough to know whose hand supplies its daily dish of salmon.

Maud wishes Isabella a good morning (although the hour is close enough upon midday). Her great-aunt has dressed but recently, and her costume is rather deshabillé, but her hair, as ever, is beautifully coiffed and jewels adorn her ears, throat and fingers. Satan, nestled in his mistress' lap, hisses at Maud as she leans to kiss Isabella upon the forehead.

'A marvelous sensation today, my dear,' Isabella declares, pointing to her newspaper. Lord Sebastian Biddulph, whom I remember most distinctly from my younger years, the rogue, has left a significant fortune on his passing. However, the chief benefactor is neither his wife, nor his adult offspring!'

Maud raises an eyebrow. The story is *scandaloso* indeed.

'A modest allowance is endowed on Lady Biddulph, alongside a portrait of her husband upon his prize filly, Matilda, as won the Grand National last season.'

Isabella is positively gleeful.

'Lady Biddulph has never liked to ride, so I hear, and has always resented her husband's pursuit of the pastime. Meanwhile, Sebastian and Archibald are cast entirely upon their own initiative, which I would assume to be in limited supply.'

'Lord Biddulph?' muses Maud. 'I don't think I've been formally introduced, although his name sounds familiar.'

'The recipient is, would you believe, a young woman of dubious background,' continues Isabella. 'In fact, it's rumoured that she works at a high-class brothel! Some place between Belgravia and Mayfair, though the newspaper is irritatingly vague.'

Isabella dashes down the pages in a fit of pique, her desire for details disappointed.

'It wouldn't surprise me if this mysterious, debauched establishment hadn't paid to have this thinly-veiled mention,' she sighs. 'No doubt, there will be a stampede for its doors.'

Maud thinks it best to deflect the conversation, opening the patisserie box and inviting Isabella to make first selection.

'*Buon appetito!*' says Maud, and the two sit in contemplative appreciation of so much raspberry glaze, vanilla custard and light choux pastry. Upon such moments is the bond between them most strongly forged: in the shared enjoyment of the forbidden.

'Have I ever told you of Lady Montgomery, my dear?' asks Isabella, dipping in to lift an éclair. 'Her pleasure in sweet pastries was only surpassed by her passion for taxidermy.' Isabella's tongue flicks to catch a dollop of escaping cream

Maud knows her great-aunt's wild and wicked reminiscences well, and waits patiently, content in the knowledge that the account will be adequately ridiculous or salacious, or both.

'It began with her desire to immortalise her pets, which were great in number, and much beloved. They always shared her bed you know, after her husband died. It's no bad thing in a British winter. Far more effective than blankets, as long as one doesn't mind bad breath and intrusive little bottoms.'

She pauses for a bite of meringue.

'Each time one passed away she'd grieve for months: quite inconsolable. Her solution was to fill her drawing room with her dearly departed and to move them, daily, into new tableaux. Some were fixed with the most alarming grimaces, teeth bared. You'd pop in for a cup of tea and slice of seed cake and find them in unexpected poses: an ancient Pekinese attacking a startled guinea pig, or a bedraggled feline. One day, I took Satan with me and he set about 'deflowering' each and every one of her stuffed treasures, much accelerating their decrepitude.'

Isabella chuckles to herself and strokes Satan fondly.

'Perhaps,' interjects Maud, 'I'll be like Lady Montgomery, kept cosy by fond canine companions. I might try it sooner than your friend. I have no plans to install a husband.'

The old lady splutters on a profiterole.

'Preposterous!' she declares. 'A young girl like you, with such conversation, good health and elegant manners: a loss to humanity if you don't propagate!'

She gives a sniff of disapproval.

'You were certainly not short of suitors during your "coming out" season. If you hadn't returned to your grandmother's villa in Italy, I'm quite sure we'd have secured a proposal for you.'

Maud chooses merely to lower her eyes. She won't contradict Isabella, whose opinions, she believes, reflect her genuine concern for her great-niece's happiness. However, the elderly dowager is from another age. Maud is more than happy to disregard suggestions she deems unsuited to her disposition.

'Not that I'll be content to see you with just any husband, my dear,' adds Isabella. 'You need a man to match you in intelligence, as well as social rank, and with a satisfactory pocketbook. Many a love has languished for want of adequate funds to enjoy life.'

Isabella sets aside her lemon mousse tart and clasps Satan in her arms. The cat struggles momentarily against the embrace but the old lady's grasp is firm. She is about to impart serious advice.

'There is much to be said for a man with a quiet disposition, dear one: a man ready to devote himself to an occupation, and to his wife. Of all my suitors, and I can assure you that there were many, I chose badly. I allowed a flirtation to go to my head and, before I knew it, I was married to Conte Camillo Benito di Cavour: the most notorious playboy of his age, just as his father was before him. Half of Tuscany is probably descended from those loins. God rest his soul.'

Maud, having spent much time in Italy, with her grandmother, has some knowledge of the ways of men. She knows that where the eye roams, the hand has a tendency to follow. Her grandmother has ensured that Maud is not entirely ignorant, for her own safety.

Isabella continues to chatter.

'Your cousin Lorenzo is the same. My darling boy is too handsome and rich for his own good. I hardly dare wish him upon any woman as a husband, although he has reached an age at which the wedded state is the preferable course.'

Isabella fondles the frill at the neck of her gown.

'No doubt, there are offspring aplenty, but a legitimate heir is paramount.'

Maud passes the last cake to Isabella in heartfelt sympathy, inspiring the lady to pinch her cheek in fondness.

Such a sweet, gentle and generous girl! thinks Isabella. *Perhaps, all Lorenzo needs is a wife of more authentic character, yet one also charming enough to bring him to the marital bed each night.*

Isabella tucks a stray curl behind her great-niece's ear.

Maud, meanwhile, has intentions of her own.

'Aunt, I wondered if you'd mind my attending a new series of evening lectures, on the work of the late Mr. Darwin, as it applies to natural selection in the insect world?' she enquires. 'Of course, you might accompany me, if the subject is of interest...'

She knows that Isabella would rather invite the inmates of Newgate Prison to afternoon tea than do any such thing. Maud seeks her blessing, though she has set her heart on attending, regardless of what her great-aunt proposes.

However, Isabella is lost in pleasant reverie.

An elegant wedding, at the family castello, on the coast. Maud in ivory lace, carrying a bouquet of orchids. With her unusual colouring, she'll make a beautiful bride.

'In fact,' says Maud, 'I've been looking into a course of instruction, being offered to women, in the natural sciences.'

A select guest list, of the oldest, and wealthiest, families, muses Isabella, looking no longer at her great-niece, but through her. *I'll commission a portrait of the happy couple, to hang in my salon.*

'I have sufficient funds to pay my own expenses,' adds Maud.

How beautiful my grandchildren will be, sighs Isabella, hearing not a word Maud has spoken. *Lorenzo might yet learn to behave himself.*

'And I may return to Italy,' says Maud. 'I miss the sunshine and the gardens at the Villa Scogliera.'

In truth, she is eager to make a comparative study between her London research subjects and those of the Mediterranean. Does the heat alter their predatory inclinations, their mating rituals, their eternal search for what sustains them?

Isabella, at the mention of Italy, returns to the moment and, to Maud's surprise, declares, 'Splendid, my dear. I approve heartily.'

Perhaps Italy will be a more suitable place for them to meet, thinks Isabella, with a blaze of triumph, *'And conduct a proper courtship.'*

FIT FOR ROYALTY

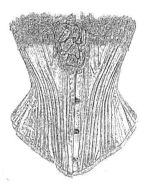

McCaulay realizes that any regaining of his peace of mind relies upon revisiting the scene of his degradation. He must achieve a private audience with that Queen of the Night, so that he may humble her as she has him, by whatever means presented.

He enters his carriage in a state of agitation, with a feeling more of compulsion, of inevitability, than of considered action. As he enters the salon, he finds there is no seat to be had. Mademoiselle Noire's performances have gained acclaim and all are eager to witness her invention. He is obliged to stand at the back of the room, near the door, but is in time to see Mademoiselle enter, leading a girl by the hand.

She, whom he has come to think of as Medusa, wears a dress in deepest violet: a shade complimenting her auburn hair. The curve of her breasts is more apparent, her neckline sweeping low from shoulder to shoulder. As before, her face is half-masked.

The sight of her stirs rage within him, but he will bide his time, waiting for the right moment.

Beside her, the girl, eyes covered by a sash, stands meekly, fairest blonde hair piled upon her dainty head, caped in cornflower blue silk. She grips the cloak tightly about her.

'Tonight,' begins Mademoiselle, her voice dripping with promise, 'I am delighted to introduce Hetty, making her first appearance, in honour of a special guest who will soon join us.'

She removes the cape from the girl's shoulders with a flourish, to reveal her pale nakedness. The girl lowers a hand to cover her pubis; the other clasps to her chest.

She is in the bloom of youth, without need of embellishment. Her skin is luminous and her breasts pert, offering an adequate handful, each topped with a rosebud almost indiscernible from the milky flesh. Her figure is slight, though generous at the hip. Her legs, though not long, are sculpted as they should be.

A worthy addition indeed, thinks McCaulay.

'Hetty is aware of the distinction of being chosen this night and, though a little shy, is delighted to know that her first performance is to be with a guest so illustrious; we might even say regal.'

It seems that a member of the royal family will be taking his pleasure.

She guides Hetty to a padded divan and bids her lie back in comfort. The girl's hand continues to cover her sweet cunny, adorned in the palest nimbus of gold.

'Hide not your treasure,' Mademoiselle urges her. 'The candlelight is illuminating you beautifully and it is fitting that the many eyes tonight upon you be allowed to devour your most charming aspect.'

She takes a long ostrich feather and runs its tantalising blade from

Hetty's ankle, to the top of her inner thigh, lightly up her torso and across her breasts. The girl shivers and forgets her shyness, dropping her hands to either side.

Mademoiselle lifts a decanter of claret over her and pours the liquid, darkest red. The droplets contrast with her pale skin, pooling between her orbs, and upon her stomach.

Replacing the decanter, Mademoiselle lowers her mouth, her licks claiming each bead before suckling at the maiden's nipple.

McCaulay's groin twitches. He notes the girl's parted lips, her soft moans and the arch of her back.

Mademoiselle moves to the end of the divan and pours claret onto the girl's pubis. The wine clings between the golden hairs and drips; rivulets run between her thighs. Mademoiselle draws up a footstool, to kneel between Hetty's legs.

As she inserts her tongue, Hetty wriggles and lifts her legs, so that she is better placed to accept the ministrations of that kindly mouth, which sips so attentively at her secret place.

It's not long before Hetty is full and open, revealing the slick nub of her pleasure. She sighs, and cups her cunny as the warm tongue completes its duties. Never was a girl more ready for plucking than this ripe fruit.

'I have tasted the eternal fountain, gentlemen.'

Mademoiselle's words are like fingers about the neck of a lover.

The crimson drapes at the end of the room part, to reveal the waiting guest. His costume is nothing if not theatrical: scarlet velvet britches to the knee, with legs and feet bare, as is his chest. A swathe of fabric has been removed from the front of his trousers, so that his genitals are visible.

In some degree of excitement, his organ is almost fully erect, bobbing before him as he walks. Besides an open waistcoat of red velvet, trimmed in ermine, he wears short black leather gloves and a black hood. It covers his head, with openings for his nose, mouth and eyes.

McCaulay peruses the size of the man's phallus, commending its shape and inclination to memory. In the event that he encounters it in one of London's bathhouses, he shall be able to identify the owner.

Approaching the girl, the royal guest claims a pot of honey from beside the claret and drizzles the viscous sweetness upon each rosy areola before lowering his mouth to the task of suckling, like a hungry infant, greedily seeking its mother's breast. As he does so, one leather-gloved hand holds her belly and the other the girl's forehead.

He brings Hetty to delightful squirms of pleasure. The royal guest places more honey upon the girl's lips and bestows gentle kisses, until it is all but gone and she has only to lick the remainder for herself. The atmosphere is one of strange intimacy.

McCaulay watches as leather fingers find the girl's cunt and it's not long before she is brought to a familiar state, sighing and lifting herself to his touch. As she approaches her crisis, rubbing against his hand, he removes his fingers and lifts her buttocks high, one hand firmly under each. Her juices glisten upon her sex.

There is a collective sigh of commendation from the gathered audience as his phallus enters, and he commences his pumping in worthy fashion. His prowess meets with the girl's approval, she giving full voice to her fulfillment: a melody echoed by her lover's roar of release.

At this, the company, one man and all, stands to applaud the girl – and her suitor – for their inspiring performance. The hooded guest bends once more to kiss Hetty upon the lips and departs.

PUNISHMENT

In his enthrallment with the arousing scene before him, Lord McCaulay has failed to notice Mademoiselle Noire's departure from the room. It's with some surprise that he now receives an invitation, via the Master of Ceremonies, informing him that the lady seeks his company for a private audience. Consenting readily, and wondering if his chance for retribution is to be presented so easily, McCaulay is led not upstairs but down, towards the cellars.

In a room so dark that it's some moments before his eyes adjust, he becomes aware of Mademoiselle, reposed upon a chaise. Her hair remains pinned, but she's no longer in her evening gown, nor wearing her long, satin gloves. Her robe is of finest gossamer silk, tied by a single ribbon. As he approaches, she stands, lifting a lamp, so that its glow illuminates her features. The flicker of the flame reveals the curves of her upper body, in silhouette beneath the flimsy material.

When she speaks, it's with her usual taunting.

'I'd begun to think you'd never dare return,' she reproaches.

He's within two paces of being able to grasp her about the throat, his eyes glinting with suppressed fury.

'Do you harbour some resentment from our last meeting?' she enquires, the habitual smirk upon her lips. 'In truth, you deserve compensation for your humiliation, do you not?'

He remains silent, allowing the Medusa to speak.

'It's said that all is fair in love and war.'

Reaching behind her, Mademoiselle brings forth her crop and places it in McCaulay's hands. It's a fair length but light. She watches him turn it in his hands, feeling its suppleness.

'I grant you permission to use it against me, but for ten strokes, no more.'

He'd not imagined her placing herself at his mercy so willingly, and his suspicions are raised, but she makes no move to run or evade him. He can smell the musk of her skin and see the pulse at her throat. Her décolletage is barely covered by the flimsy silk, breasts rising with each breath.

He touches the end of the crop to the fabric, brushing her delicate nipple, and pulls the ribbon, so that the silk falls away to each side, revealing the bare flesh: her belly, dark bush and legs. He has thought of little else but exacting his retribution upon this siren but, now, as she stands before him, so vulnerable, he's uncertain. His tongue grows dry in his mouth as he looks upon her.

Hands clenched upon the crop, he battles his compulsion to thrust his mouth at the abundant camber of her breasts, to devour them, to bite until she cries for his mercy. He would graze down her belly and bury his face in her bush, his tongue seeking its plump wetness. His desire to consume her near chokes him.

'I'm waiting,' she prompts, her voice silken. 'You see me before you. I'm unprotected against your wrath. Remember, ten strokes.'

His eyes search her face, seeking there some softness. If her lips were upward cast and parted, he'd fling aside the crop and crush his own upon them. However, her mouth, though full and sensual, betrays its usual subtle sneer. He sees derision and disdain, which steels his heart to raise the cruel whip against her.

The first stroke catches her stomach with a light flick, such as would sting, but not greatly hurt. Her face remains still.

'I believe you can do better,' she states, in that tone which seems ever to mock him.

He raises the crop higher and brings it to bear against her upper thigh, stippling the silk, leaving a tear through the fabric. Her breath catches. Then, she exhales, languorously.

At once, he realizes that he is no more than a pawn in her game and the knowledge brings a flood of ire, making him brandish the crop with more force, sending its tail across the bounty of her breasts, leaving a welt.

She gasps audibly, and throws back her head, an auburn curl escaping to her cheek. Her body unfurls under the pain, resonating with new vibrancy.

The sight of her stirs his blood and his thoughts are again distracted. His tongue might trace the line of the weal, warm saliva removing the bite of the lash, but anger wins out, and he spins her round so that her back is to him. He sends three swift strokes to her buttocks, the whip making light work of her robe. The silk shreds at its touch.

She sighs, and lets the gown fall from her shoulders, so that nothing stands between her and the remaining lashes.

McCaulay hesitates again, observing the stripes rising on her tender skin: faultless, but for the injuries he has inflicted.

Coquettishly, she glances over her shoulder.

He suspects he is merely her instrument.

Flourishing the crop against the underside of her cheeks, where he knows it will be felt most keenly, he follows with another, and two more to the middle of those lush fruits.

He raises the whip again but a voice from the shadows interrupts, commanding, 'No more!'

It is the African, all the while hidden from view.

McCaulay drops back, frozen in terror, reminded immediately of their last encounter. He releases the crop and turns to flee but a firm hand stays his arm. Her face is without rebuke.

'You've nothing to fear,' she assures him. 'Our noble friend won't harm you. He's here for me, not for you.'

She beckons Lord McCaulay to the chaise upon which she first sat. The lamp is beside them, the dancing flame illuminating her skin.

Mademoiselle lowers herself over the taller end of the seat and, extending her arms, bids McCaulay take her bare hands. She stretches taut through her spine.

'My ebony god, having suffered at my hand, deserves also to punish me. Forty lashes, but not from the whip.'

She parts her legs as the giant emerges from the inky shadows, naked, his organ at full fortitude, its tip wet in readiness. She keeps her eyes on those of Lord McCaulay as the African takes his position.

'I deserve punishment for my wicked ways, do I not? I've caused pain, and only pain will suffice in return. Forty lashes, each one deeper and harder than the last. Offer me no respite or pity, no matter how I might plead.'

The African grasps his phallus. To his surprise, McCaulay sees in that face tenderness, as well as lust. The giant hesitates, before entering her, slowly, allowing her flesh to accommodate him.

Her eyes are darker than ever, glittering in an otherworldly fashion. Her mouth is open, forming words she cannot utter.

At last, he has embedded most of his length. Her lover savours the moment before easing back, his shaft releasing her. McCaulay is transfixed by each measured penetration and withdrawal. The African is coated clearly with the glistening of her desire.

Then, with a motion unexpectedly swift, the colossus pulls her pelvis back resolutely against his, so that her cheeks slap hard against his abdomen. Her face contorts in anguish, her eyes close and her wrists flex within McCaulay's grasp.

The African holds her there, against his stomach, relishing his fleshy burial. Slowly, he again withdraws, pausing before plunging into her once more, hauling her hips towards him. She cries out again, but less acutely now, accompanied by a gasp and sigh.

She opens her eyes, staring McCaulay full in the face as she beseeches him, 'Count for me.'

The giant holds her to his torso, grinding against her. This brings forth another cry, soon transformed into a low groan. McCaulay wonders that any woman can endure that dark weapon without injury, but Mademoiselle's pain is also her pleasure.

His voice trembles as he iterates the numbers, the African delivering several full-bodied piston strokes. Each sends a shudder the length of her body, evoking her song of suffering and bliss.

McCaulay stumbles in his counting as the giant's pace quickens, thrusts coming one upon the other.

Her curls are shaken loose and her cries become indistinguishable from sobs.

McCaulay's head grows light, his body present, but his limbs numb. He has reached a count of twenty-five and can no longer speak.

As Mademoiselle Noire submits, McCaulay's own desire grows, imagining that it is he administering those brutal strokes.

The giant lashes harder, lifting her rump to allow the deepest angle of entry. His hands imprison her hips, as he hammers with energy indefatigable. Her hair tumbles in every direction. Her breasts jump and fall with each thrust.

Pulling her fully onto his groin, his jet sears her. McCaulay can barely keep his hold. She writhes, her face transformed, lost in her own world: one in which McCaulay has played but a minor part.

Breathless, the giant steps back. McCaulay lets loose her hands, so that she slumps exhausted over the divan of the chaise, her hair in disarray, face flushed and pupils dilated. She looks him once more fully in the face. She says nothing; no words are needed.

He has fantasized about chastising her but her own enactment far surpasses anything his imagination might conjure. Once more, she has outplayed him, demonstrating to McCaulay that her sexuality is not to be categorized or anticipated. For him to judge would be obscene, since every aspect of her behaviour rouses his own appetite.

He knows, without question, that acquaintance with her will prove his undoing.

TORMENT

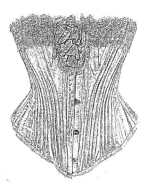

McCaulay blunders blindly up the stairs, arriving back upon the street, where the rain-spitted night brings him partially to his senses. Grim horror beats within his chest, knowing that he has crossed a threshold from which there is no return. He cannot escape her image: mouth contorted in gasps of torture and exaltation, body convulsed in euphoria, eyes fevered.

He waves off his carriage, needing to feel the chill air on his cheek and shake off the power of the memories assailing him.

His feet take him where they might, past the homes of men of breeding and fashion: Devonshire House, where the Cavendish family reside behind forbidding brick walls; Stafford House, which is more a palace than St. James' and has hosted some of the most glittering gatherings of the century; Holland House, headquarters to the most brilliant men of the age and celebrated for its library; Bridgewater House, with its fine frontage onto Green Park; and Grosvenor House, with its distinguished colonnades and priceless gallery.

The exercise serves to remind him of the Society to which he should be keeping. Despite this, his thoughts remain with her.

McCaulay spends the darkest hours of night swollen with passion no self-fornication can ease. He finally succumbs to sleep, but wakes soon after, feeling great mental discomfort and a penetrating ache in his loins.

Such is his frustration and wretchedness over the following days that nothing can divert him. The hours stretch, banal and meaningless. It is intolerable. By night, his dreams leave him exhausted and unfulfilled. By day, his misery plunges him into a chasm of despair.

He seeks understanding of his feelings. Is this pure lust, a desire to possess and conquer, to bring this woman beneath his heel? In part, this is true; he yearns to claim her body and consume it, until nothing remains. He will take her at every orifice, so that his body becomes hers, welded in a fiery explosion of heat and light.

The thought leaves him reeling. Her power over him is a diabolic contagion. Yet, there is something else. He feels her exhibition of her basest animal impulses as a revelation: a miracle of honesty, against which the rest of his life stands in counterfeit. It is as if she has been sent to awaken him to his true self and to lead him on some previously unconsidered path.

He knows that his infatuation is inspired not just by physical need but by something deeper. He hungers for her body, in all its sensual perfection, but also thirsts for the essence of her marrow, to consume the flame of her. He feels compelled to humble himself before her honesty, that he might realize greater honesty of his own. It cannot be love: a condition he holds in contempt. He knows it can only be obsession.

Nevertheless, he cannot escape his conviction that, with her, his life will be glorious: an exploration of uncharted waters. Without her, he will desiccate to dust.

RIDING INTO THE NEW WORLD

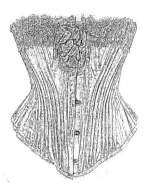

I sabella likes to take her breakfast in bed, with Satan by her pillow, ready to lick her fingers: a pot of Assam tea, three boiled eggs, two slices of ham, and several of thinly cut bread, generously buttered. It's a hearty meal for one her age. She savours each bite, as she peruses the more provocative pieces in the newspaper.

It is the best time of day to ask a favour of her great-aunt, so Maud has crept in, wearing her night attire, long hair plaited, to perch on the coverlet.

'Such stories today, my dear,' proclaims the old lady, indicating the fifth page of the newspaper. 'The Reverend Huntsworthy, of Smedley Maltings, in the County of Buckinghamshire, has been found to have been warming not only his marital bed, but, in most generous fashion, those of several of his flock.'

She wields her scissors, cutting out the column for her scrapbook, into which she pastes the most salacious snippets. 'He is, apparently, liberal in his love, serving no less than seven households!'

Maud is intent, however, on deflecting Isabella's attention from the fruitful exertions of the Reverend Huntsworthy. She wishes to purchase a bicycle, with which to ride in Hyde Park. It's all the rage in certain circles. She wants a steed upon which to ride into the new world. It will be more than a toy to her; it will be a passport to freedom.

Isabella, though well-versed in the benefits of fresh air and moderate exercise, isn't inclined to give her approval. Times are changing, it's true, but she believes a young lady of breeding should never appear without her chaperone.

She has already been more than indulgent, permitting Maud's attendance at her Museum lectures, and her taking of afternoon tea with an old school friend, in public, although only at the best hotels. Isabella allows this because she knows the eyes of a dozen respectable duchesses will be upon her charge at all times. The carriage takes her there and returns her safely. There is no opportunity for mischief.

'My darling,' Isabella soothes. 'You are of the modern age, I know, but you must remember what is important. How can a lady sit upon such a machine? It's undignified!'

A sliver of ham disappears into Satan's little pussycat mouth.

'I could wear 'rational' dress,' offers Maud, careful to keep the tone of her voice sweet and her face most open in expression.

Isabella knows the meaning of the term: no corset and a skirt reduced in volume and length, to balloon somewhere below the knee; the ankles and calves encased in no more than thick stockings. Indecent! She's read about it in the *Literary Digest*.

Maud has read this, too. Apparently, the weight of a woman's undergarments is reduced to no more than seven pounds. Think of that! There's good reason why Isabella likes to stay late in her bed. It delays the donning of layer after layer and, most abhorrent in Maud's eyes, the restrictive lacing of a foundation bodice: a torture instrument of whalebone and ribbons. How much more comfortable it is to lounge in one's night-shift and dressing gown.

'I don't think so, dear,' answers Isabella. It's her duty to be firm. Maud has no mother to set her on the right path, and her grandmother is hundreds of miles away, reclining in respectable inertia, warmed by the Italian sun.

'Besides which,' she continues, letting golden yolk ooze into a finger of bread, 'all that exertion is dangerous. Such women end up with bicycle face from concentrating on keeping their balance. You wouldn't want to end up with a clenched jaw and bulging eyes, my darling.'

Utter rubbish, thinks Maud, lips pursing. *I'm more likely to end up with frown lines from a life of perpetual frustration.*

The women she's seen on their bicycles appear anything but clenched; they look liberated. Maud is convinced that, were her grandmother sitting before her, she would suggest purchase of a bicycle not only for Maud but for herself too. She does not share Isabella's overbearing sense of propriety.

Isabella glances up from her tray and addresses her great-niece more directly. 'What if you should forget yourself in the excitement and just peddle straight through the park and out the other end?' she warns. 'If you keep your feet on the pedals and don't stop, where might you end up?'

The idea appeals to Maud more than she can say.

DIVINE COUPLINGS

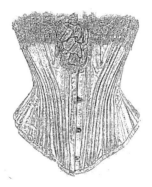

E leven days and nights pass. McCaulay is confounded as to what action to take: whether to pack his bags and remove himself from temptation, or to fling himself at the seductress' feet. He knows now why men join monasteries perched on remote mountain outcrops, or the French Foreign Legion, to sweat away their vitality in the harsh desert climate of North Africa. They seek oblivion.

Heart heavy, he finally shaves the stubble from his weary face and allows his feet to take him where they will and where they must: once more, to the crimson salon.

It appears that every member has gathered. Chairs have been brought from the dining room and placed about the circumference, nestled in niches and tucked right up to the tapestries about the walls.

The seating is arranged in a full circle around the space of a central stage. There, a bed has been placed upon a raised dais, scattered with rich fabrics and plush cushions, but open on all sides, so that no view is obscured.

A bell rings to call attention, so that the theatre may begin. McCaulay's heart is beating rapidly, wondering when 'she' may appear.

Two women enter, identical in stature and physique, with well-proportioned hips and buttocks, full of breast and slender of waist. Besides their masks of white lace, they wear simple dresses, Grecian in style, from the lightest, diaphanous muslin. The pair hold hands, fingers clasped in friendship, leading one another. The skin of one is the colour of coffee when milk has been added, and her hair is dark, hanging straight and lustrous. The other is palest alabaster, her hair a luxuriant copper, falling in loose curls about her shoulders.

Both are beautiful but McCaulay's disappointment is palpable. Where is she? It is only when one of the women speaks that McCaulay's consciousness is jolted. There, before him, stands the woman who haunts his days and nights. It is the first time that he has seen her in the salon without the formality of her evening gown and with her hair liberated from the confines of a multitude of pins.

He recognizes now its rich threads of auburn and gold. Moreover, he detects the faint bloom of bruising on her body, though the marks are not obvious in the subtle illumination of the room.

Her voice offers its customary silken seduction. 'Tonight, my gentle sirs, I am Thetis, the sea nymph of ancient Greek mythology, and this is Semele, the Theban princess. Once lovers of mighty Zeus, we stand before you as distilled vials of feminine sensuality. We were born to love: to give and receive pleasure. We shall prepare each other's bodies, to welcome the king of all gods. He shall come to us not as the Zeus of later days, replete with having fathered so many offspring by mortal women, but as his younger self, barely matured, new to feelings of passion. We shall initiate him in the ways of love.'

The two turn to one another and kiss: a caress sweet in its gentleness, lingering and true, as if they are alone and unwatched.

Semele takes a pitcher from beside the bed, while Thetis draws away her hair, allowing her breasts to rise. The Theban pours water across her partner's gown, so that the fabric becomes translucent and clinging, revealing the raspberry areola of her nipples, pushed tight against the muslin, and the dark triangle below her belly. Semele bends her head to Thetis' collarbone, while letting her hand travel down.

McCaulay wets his lips, a flame kindling within him at the sight of Mademoiselle, his eyes drinking her form. His eager anxiety to observe constricts his chest, as if a steel band were placed about it.

As Thetis, she shrugs the wet robe from her shoulders, so that it falls to the floor, and the beauty of her body is fully displayed, droplets of water adorning her curves. Her noble head is raised; her hair shimmers.

Semele raises the pitcher again. Rivulets of water cascade over Thetis' porcelain landscape: across her abundant hills and downwards, to the mysterious valley between her legs. They kiss languorously once more, without sense of time or, seemingly, their audience, Thetis pressing her damp body against that of Semele, still clad.

The Theban princess permits her gown to be pushed from her shoulders, so that she stands before Thetis as a dark mirror: breast to breast, belly to belly.

McCaulay has never witnessed any sight more beautiful.

Thetis anoints Semele with oil of orange blossom, warming it in her hands, so that the sweet scent fills the room. She kneads thighs and belly, and satin spheres, lingering, taking delight in the curves beneath her palm, her hands slipping easily over silken flesh.

Thetis reaches down to the precipice of Semele's secret garden, cupping its warmth; the maiden rocks against the pressure of her touch.

The gentlemen of the room sit silent, eyes drawn irresistibly to the wonderous sight before them.

The sea nymph caresses, reaching every crevice, stroking between her lover's cleft as she steals another kiss. The pair drink deeply of one another, until they fall upon the waiting bed, their legs entwined. Fingers wrap into hair and Semele's kisses travel at last to Thetis' velvet grotto.

McCaulay's lips part, seeing Mademoiselle's legs agape, revealing her plump centre, awaiting exploration. Semele's tongue probes and licks, until the sea nymph is tossed in passion, waves mounting within her. Head cast back, her face shows delicious delight, her pearly teeth biting in concentration.

McCaulay imagines the sweet nectar exploding within her, and her consciousness flying beyond the room, out into the dark skies, transported. A rush of tenderness comes upon him, watching Mademoiselle's mouth open in ecstasy, thinking of how he would love to place his lips upon hers.

As the two lie resplendent, the drapes part to reveal Zeus: a young man whose angelic face is framed with curls of blonde. He is slight but muscular.

The two beauties upon the bed draw him down, that he might lie between them. In turn, they receive his kisses, upon breasts and belly, and give kisses in return. Their hands stroke his limbs, his buttocks and his cock.

Zeus' caresses become more urgent, his hands grasping the shapely Semele, ready to impale her with his divine spear. She meets his long strokes with her own, hips rising to meet him, until she cries out, her legs clinging, as Zeus' seed travels deep, with each throbbing pulse.

Thetis, hungry for her turn with the king of the gods, kisses his member back to life, so that Zeus might mount her with the same ardour.

Clasping her slender waist, he guides her upon his lap, exulting in the delight with which she shares her flesh. Her belly undulates as she encircles him. The divinity suckles like a babe at her breasts, until Thetis' shrine aches for the final lash of the god's thunderbolt.

Zeus bites down upon her nipple, and his juices spring forth, his crescendo inspiring her own song of jubilation.

They fall, entwined, with Semele joining them in their slumber, her legs about those of golden Zeus, her breasts pressed lovingly at his back. Like a painting by Titian come to life, the three curve their bodies one about the other, so that it is hard to tell where one ends and another begins.

So concludes the tableau, and the gathered assembly gives its applause with enthusiasm, some standing to offer their ovation. The play has been presented with utmost delicacy, so that each kiss has appeared to fly on wings from Heaven and each thrust has been delivered with ease, as if truly bestowed by a god.

McCaulay has watched enraptured, gratified to see the serenity with which the object of his affections has conducted herself. Each movement has been lithe, performed with the grace of a ballerina. From the tilt of her head to the pointing of her toes, her body is a thing of beauty, a ship gliding across an ocean of pleasure. How ready she is to lay bare her inner self: showing her soul in its utmost bliss.

As the gentlemen begin to drum their feet upon the floor, shouting for an encore, the three young players rise from their slumber to bow in thanks, honoured to receive such approbation. The approval and admiration of the crowd brings a new flush to the performers' cheeks and they exit the stage with lightness in their step.

THE BATH

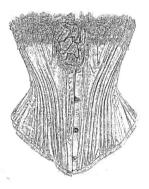

The gentlemen drift into the adjoining room: the assembly hall in which they might act out their own scenes, with the ready participation of the waiting harem. The performance inspires a great use of perfumed oil that night: the better for the massaging of tender flesh and the slip-sliding of bodies one against the other.

McCaulay remains in the salon until quite alone, ordering his customary whisky and waiting, in expectation that Thetis might reappear. An hour passes in solitude, so that he has almost given up hope, until the Master of Ceremonies enters, to inform him that Mademoiselle awaits his pleasure. He leads McCaulay through the drapes to a corridor beyond. There are several doors but from behind one can be heard feminine laughter and the splashing of water.

There is a huge bath, above the rim of which three graceful necks are visible, crowned by pinned locks: one dark, one palest blonde and one richly red. To the rear of the room is a large bed.

Mademoiselle Noire turns on hearing his step, her face flushed rosily from the steam. She appears younger than he has seen her thus far, her face stripped of any embellishment at the lip or cheek. Moreover, she is without her mask. She holds his gaze for some moments, her head tilted to one side, chin raised, taking stock of him.

She is the first to speak, catching him off guard by addressing him by name. 'Lord McCaulay, you remember Daisy and Hetty, I think?'

The girls turn their heads, looking at him over their shoulders, as demure as he remembers them, but with something worldly about their eyes. They are also without any mask of concealment.

'Our bath is very warm,' Mademoiselle calls to him. 'It would be a shame for you to miss the opportunity to join us, would it not?'

He desires so very much to be near her. McCaulay removes all items of his evening dress, placing them neatly upon a chair. He takes pains to ensure that his actions are without undue haste, sliding into the comfortable embrace of the water, placing himself at one end, so that the three women face him at the other, all but their shoulders hidden.

'So, you discovered my name,' he says at last, his eyes searching, keen to detect any nuance of feeling. 'You know that anonymity is one of the club's watchwords.'

'I thought it only proper,' she reproaches playfully. 'A lady requires a formal introduction in polite Society and this is not, after all, our first meeting.'

Her tone, as ever, is mocking. Her self-possession is without question, but her finer emotions remain a mystery to him.

'As you can see, I, too, have laid myself bare before you. If you were to pass me on the street, you would know me at once. My own anonymity is now also compromised.'

'It is,' he replies. 'Although the secret of your true name remains to be disclosed, so your advantage over me continues.'

At this, she laughs in genuine merriment. 'Of course it does, Lord McCaulay, and the revelation of my name would perhaps hardly change that, since I appear to control the outcome of all our encounters.'

Her face assumes a more serious expression. 'I invited you here being desirous of better acquaintance,' she admits. 'Since the time of my arrival, you haven't once followed the other gentlemen into the hall of games, to sport gaily with the majestic ladies of this establishment. Had you done so, I would have observed you at play, seeing the cut of your cloth. I know but little of your tastes. Perhaps you have few, being content to follow the whims of others?'

He begins to remonstrate but she moves at once closer, placing a single finger upon his lips. Her proximity serves to quiet him. He feels the smooth skin of her leg brush his below the surface and her hand rests lightly upon his thigh. Water glistens at her throat and at the inviting parting of her cleavage, but her body remains concealed, the suds of the bath preventing him from seeing her form.

He has beheld her nakedness more than once, but those images are as from a dream. At this moment, she is real, close enough that he might feel her breath upon his cheek.

She allows him to search her face, with softness new to his experience. Her features are noble: her nose slender, her forehead high, her bearing imperial. It would never occur to her to consider herself inferior to another being, much less any man. In others, this would irritate him as pure arrogance; in her, it inspires his admiration.

He is swallowed by the predatory, feline green of her eyes. Then, she breaks the enchantment.

'I rather wonder if you attempt to woo me, so intense is your gaze. Of course, that wouldn't do at all, and is assuredly not my desire. I wish merely to conduct a more thorough assessment of you, Lord McCaulay.'

He feels the retort but allows her to reprimand him. For the moment, he is content to be near her. Whatever game she has in mind, he will do his best not to disappoint.

Mademoiselle's young assistants lather their soap and commence their washing, of themselves, and one another. They stroke foam over their shoulders, squeezing water from their sponges. Their heads, one dark and one fair, they hold close, alternately lowering their lashes in modesty, before meeting McCaulay's eye, as if to say: 'Be good enough to look upon us and say what you think of us, my Lord.'

To his knowledge, both are unsophisticated in their knowledge of men, although he doubts not that a week or two in the playrooms of this establishment will have opened their minds considerably. At any rate, the adventure seems to have agreed with them, since their eyes glitter most mirthfully. They have learnt quickly how to trifle and flirt. Nevertheless, they retain some degree of naïve ingenuousness.

They sit now a little higher in the water, so that their breasts are revealed: Hetty's modestly full, with their girlish rosebuds; Daisy's smaller, with dark nipples placed high on the crown.

They cast glances at McCaulay, seeking out his expression, eager to stir him as they soap each other's dainty peaks. Content that her audience is attentive, Daisy lowers her head to the coral of her friend's orb, Hetty twining her arms about her companion's neck and shoulders.

The pair rise to their knees, so that the peaches of their buttocks come into view and the down of their sex: one dark, one golden. Their mouths come together in a light kiss, as if testing how this might be done.

Their antics are rousing, but McCaulay's thoughts remain foremost with Mademoiselle. Her body, naked and alluring, is within arm's reach.

Hetty turns her back, so that Daisy might soap the graceful arch of her spine. The sponge slips and glides, reaching to the under-crease of buttocks and between ample cheeks, water squeezed and replenished, suds dripping. Hetty bends, parting her thighs, so that her friend might probe as she dares. The sight brings a small leap to McCaulay's cock.

Mademoiselle detects the change in his face and draws close; he feels her breast brush his arm.

Her voice is no more than a whisper, her breath catching at the hairs of his neck.

'What is your command?'

He licks his lips and turns to look at Mademoiselle. In leaning towards him, her breasts are almost clear of the water: damp and full, nipples upward curving. How he longs to lower his lips to their perfection. However, he senses that she wishes him to wait, that her interest lies in his interaction with the young women before them.

Daisy squeezes her sponge over the golden down of her friend's labia, then allows it to drop, placing instead two fingers at that ready place, sliding within. Hetty pushes eagerly against the caress.

Eyes wide with feigned innocence, Daisy enquires, 'Shall I, Sir?'

McCaulay nods, watching this pretty scene, but is distracted by Mademoiselle's hand moving between his legs, seeking out his member. She encircles him, squeezing. Her breasts press to his arm, her chin at his shoulder, her lips almost touching his throat. Her fingers reach down further, between his anus and his testicles. The sensation is delicious. He parts his legs that she might cradle him more easily.

Of a sudden, he is aware that her touch may bring upon him an untimely release, but she takes her hand upwards again, massaging his shaft. Her hand moves in synchronisation with that of Daisy, all the while pleasuring her friend. Hetty is gasping, as the flames grow tall.

Mademoiselle scrapes her teeth against the skin of McCaulay's neck, and he can contain himself no more. She wraps her hand firmly about his cock as he pulses, spending his semen into the warm waters of the bath.

When his orgasm has subsided, she shifts to straddle his right thigh, her cunt pushing against him. Her hand remains loosely upon his member.

Her eyes are liquid now, soft and deep. He feels safe, comforted, loved. Her embrace is everything to him.

'Daisy, sit upon the side of the bath and open your legs. It is Hetty's turn to caress you,' Mademoiselle suggests.

Soon, it is all Daisy can do to sit still. She grasps the rim of the tub and lifts her cheeks, urging her friend deeper.

Mademoiselle is pressed against McCaulay's leg, stroking his growing organ with her expert touch, sending his heart soaring, his balls aching again for release.

Lightheaded, he watches as Hetty penetrates devotedly with her tongue, lapping Daisy to the brink. As she tumbles over, giving voice to each wave of wonder, Mademoiselle straddles McCaulay, her sex pounding, insistent.

She slides, warm and tight, rocking against his hardness, drawing him into her. Her soapy breasts crush against his chest and her fingers twine in his hair, pulling back his head. Seeking his open lips, she covers them with her own hungry kisses. Her desire overpowers him, his mouth finding her breast, clasping to her nipple, biting upon the tender areola.

Taking the curve of her buttocks, he feels her shudder and his cock is lifted upon the ripples of her orgasm. She struggles to breathe against the ferocity of the tempest and his rod, fulfilled in its duty, shoots into her.

At last, sighs alone remain, and she holds his head to her chest.

A CLOSE SHAVE

They remain clasped together, neither wishing to relinquish their hold. At last, it is the impatient murmurings of Hetty and Daisy that rouse them.

Mademoiselle is languorous as she rises, droplets shimmering from her body. She steps from the bath, McCaulay's eyes following her all the while, feasting. She beckons, and he follows, allows her to steer him towards the bed, his head growing sleepy now that his body is spent.

He dozes for a few minutes, and when he wakens, it is to find her tying his legs and arms, in the manner of Da Vinci's Vitruvian Man, fastened securely to the corners of the solid wooden bed frame. His penis looms large, already reviving. She places a cushion beneath his buttocks and he closes his eyes, waiting for her mouth to close around his member.

However, the sound of a razor being sharpened against leather jolts him to his senses. There she sits, neatly between his legs.

Seeing the horror upon his face, she cannot help but laugh.

'*Mio Dio, charisma!*' she cries, wiping a tear of merriment from her eye. 'How brave you are! *Quanto coraggiosa, mio piccolo!*'

She lathers soap from a bowl, in readiness to shave him.

The shame of it; how will he enter his regular bathhouse with naked cock and balls? He'll be a laughing stock.

'What an accent you have,' he remarks, gulping as she daubs the brush around the base of his shaft. His own Italian lacks such melody, despite his having spent several months in Florence in his younger years.

She is hesitant in answering.

'My first lover was Italian,' she says at last, taking the bristles downwards, over his testicles.

'He shared his tongue with you,' nods McCaulay, and then blushes at his own pun.

'Indeed!' she replies.

The soap is cold and his erection is fading fast, prompting her to reproach him. 'This will be much easier done if you remain upright, my Lord.'

Grasping his trunk, she delivers slow strokes, the soap offering pleasant lubrication for the job.

'Hold still,' she warns. 'It's not my intention to injure you.'

She proves adept, holding his skin taut, manipulating the razor effectively. Finally, wiping away soap and hair with a sponge, she sits back to admire her handiwork.

'You see, now we can more easily admire you.'

She calls Daisy and Hetty to sit a little closer and explains to McCaulay that, as part of their ongoing instruction in how best to please themselves and, thereby, the gentlemen they may encounter, she would appreciate his assistance. As he is already placed so fortuitously upon the bed, it would be a shame to forsake the opportunity.

He recognizes the small bottle she holds, the fragrance of orange oil, which she pours liberally onto her breasts, squeezing and kneading, pressing and releasing. Touching where he cannot, inflaming him. She slides her nipples between her fingers, hands moving fluidly. In the gentle lamplight of the room, her skin gleams.

McCaulay admires once more the desire she so readily exhibits, without shame or inhibition. Her hands move to her thighs, and to her private self, fingers pulling open her lips, displaying, taunting.

Her pupils are wide as she lowers her body upon his, thighs, breasts and belly slippery with oil, flesh touching flesh. She presses against his smooth upper groin, grasping his engorgement between her legs, rocking, slithering, pleasuring herself. Her teeth are sharp against his nipples, her cunt hot upon his cock. He can barely endure more of her use of him.

She is close to her peak when she stops, saying, with a smile, 'Allow me to dismount.'

Changing direction, she turns to sit astride his chest, facing his feet. Bending, she shows him her coppered moss, and the cleft of her buttocks. Her heated aroma reaches his nostrils, her salted-musk cave overlaid with orange blossom.

Her oily hands minister to his phallus, caressing its delicate skin, and she calls to Hetty and Daisy. One upon each leg, they kiss McCaulay's inner thighs, up, up, until they take his aching sacks, one each, into their mouths, sucking lightly, then harder, responding to his groans of anguished delight.

Mademoiselle takes his member between her lips, her nipples brushing back and forth upon his belly with each stroke. Even in his most debauched fantasies, he has never imagined three mouths applied to his private parts, each offering its own rhythm of attention.

Mademoiselle lowers herself, so that, at last, he might reach her moist slit with the flick of his tongue. He ventures deeper, bringing forth a purr of appreciation. Her frenzy grows, so that his face is soon full of her.

She sucks down harder upon his shaft, and the sensation across his balls and cock overwhelms him. Hetty and Daisy's dainty lips remain firmly about his testicles as he gives forth.

His erection bursts into Mademoiselle's mouth, and she allows her own spasm to bubble over, sending a spurt of juices, so that each enjoys the taste of the other.

OBSESSION

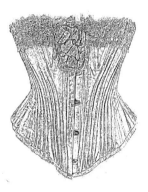

The girls depart, leaving her alone with McCaulay, to sponge and dry him, to untie him, kissing each wrist and ankle. Then, she dons a silken kimono and leaves.

Reeling, he dresses. It is as if a lifetime has passed since his arrival at the club that evening. He doesn't take his carriage straight home, but rather through the empty streets of Belgravia and Knightsbridge, wishing to gather his thoughts. He passes the homes of those he knows and those he does not; families sleep behind darkened windows, concealed by veils tangible and imperceptible. The world he believes he has understood, and belonged to, now seems false.

As dawn breaks, he turns homeward and finds oblivion in his bed, waking long after noon, to a head hot with fever and a chest of uncomfortable constriction. He is strong of constitution, but is out of sorts. His valet, George, brings a solution of Epsom Salts, a pot of peppermint tea and a tray from the kitchen: sparsely buttered white bread toast and two lightly boiled eggs.

His Lordship will surely feel more himself after eating, and might take a turn in Kensington Gardens; fresh air is known for its restorative powers.

McCaulay is somewhat revived by early evening, although his head continues to plague him, struggling with a confluence of conflicting ideas. Such images assail him from the previous night, bringing a rush of blood not just to his head but to his groin.

His siren remains a mystery, though he has no sense that she truly seeks to entrap him; she takes her pleasure, desiring no promises or declarations of love. He imagines that professions of devotion will repulse her. She will laugh or revile him, denouncing romantic conventions.

She continues to fascinate him, because she continues to elude him, in mind and spirit. Her touch lingers upon his flesh.

He has long held the state of matrimony to be undesirable, since it places irrevocable constraints upon a man. Women, he finds, lack vigour, for all their accomplishments. Meanwhile, most feminine opinions are best left unheard. Even his sister, of whom he is inordinately fond, tries his patience.

Dear Cecile, hearing that he isn't himself, insists that she will remain at home until he is quite well, setting aside an invitation from their aunt in Oxfordshire for a few days' visit. The railway line from Paddington is so convenient that she might easily defer her trip another week.

McCaulay strokes her cheek fondly and removes himself to his library. Her affection is welcome; her continual company is not.

He can think only of his seductress: a woman so in contrast with his sister. Although their ages are probably much the same, their attitude couldn't differ more. Cecile likes to embroider linens, paint portraits, and take afternoon tea with friends and family. She chats endlessly to her little terrier and her exercise comprises a twice-weekly turn through Hyde Park upon her mare, in company with other ladies of equestrian persuasion.

Mademoiselle Noire's exercise, he imagines, is rarely performed out of doors.

The solution, to his mind, is to persuade her to become his mistress.

SCULPTED FLESH

M aud, after much cajoling, has persuaded Isabella to
accompany her to see the great Sandow. The queue is so long
that many are turned away at the door. Fortunately, their coachman,
sent ahead, has secured tickets for an upper box. Great-aunt Isabella is
in good humour, but she stands in early winter drizzle for no one.

As they rattle through the cobbled streets to the theatre, Isabella's
eye is caught by the gaiety of a purple and white striped awning on a
new millinery shop. The window is filled with the latest fashions:

wide brimmed hats abundant in ribbons, roses and peonies, and slender evening headdresses, topped stylishly with single plumes.

'This is the shop Lady Fortiscue was telling me about,' declares Isabella, craning her neck. 'We must pay a visit, my dear. *The Lady* ran an article on the proprietess last week: a Ms. Tarbuck, I recall.'

Isabella gives a small sniff.

'Such a common name, though the picture of her was becoming. She is young, and of no notable family, I'm certain. One wonders how on Earth she has financed the venture. However, Ms. Tarbuck's hats are the talk of all fashionable circles.'

Maud's ears have pricked up at the mention of the name.

'These are modern times, aunt,' she comments. 'With a little capital, a woman may make her way. Clearly, she has business acumen and is making the best of her talents. I wish her every success.'

'You're right, of course, my dearest,' answers Isabella. 'We will support her with our purses.'

She muses for a moment.

'Ms.Tarbuck, I'm told, even offers a Devonshire cream tea as one waits. A delightful notion!'

~

THE STALLS ARE FILLED with men and women, equally inclined to admire the mighty Sandow, this modern personification of the Greek and Roman sculptures. The curtains part and the bodybuilder takes the stage. The very sight of him, torso firm and wearing no more than tights and a fig leaf, has several ladies swooning on the spot.

As he performs his routine of classical poses, sighs ripple through the rows. Ladies lean forward, entranced; their noses twitch, eager to inhale this virile specimen. Men of their acquaintance are flabby of belly. Few have defined musculature, unless they undertake a daily regime of sport, or are of the working classes.

Sandow snaps a chain with his bare hands, holding it aloft, biceps bulging. Maud is enjoying the show immensely, but even more so the audience's reaction. They are like the crickets in Hyde Park, swiveling their antenna, rubbing their legs together and clicking their approval.

Isabella is peering through her lorgnettes with more attention than she gave to the opera on her last outing. Several times she begins to exclaim disapproval, then claps her mouth shut. She's not leaving until she sees what comes next.

Finally, Sandow lifts a platform on which a man is playing the piano. He strains so hard that it's a wonder the fig leaf stays in place. Two hundred and fifty pairs of eyes are fixed upon its fate.

In this age of physical and moral degeneration, he is a paragon of health and strength, an antidote to the sedentary lifestyle of the leisured classes. Females left and right squawk with delight: parrots overcome by the sight of a preening male. Gloved hands beat in applause with more fury than can be considered genteel.

Isabella makes a mental note to locate the reviews in the following day's papers and, if there are photographs, to cut these out, for addition to her scrapbook.

DISGUISES

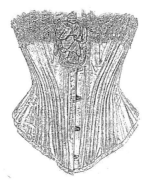

After some hours spent in deep melancholy, closeted in his library, while reading nothing, McCaulay accompanies Cecile, at her request, to the newly reopened Claridge's Hotel in Mayfair. Desirous of seeing the grandeur of the décor, and of sampling the sweet pastries so praised by her friends, she coaxes him into the carriage. They enter the grand hall at four in the afternoon.

Cecile exclaims on the beautiful marble of the flooring and the sweep of the grand staircase, as they walk through to the dining room in which tea is served. McCaulay eyes the finger sandwiches, éclairs and cream tarts with little appetite, although Cecile is all praise and clearly enjoying their outing. He smiles fondly, happy at least that she is so easily contented.

His sister isn't the only female in London eager to see the hotel in its refurbished state. The central court is brimming with frivolous simpletons and superfluous piffle. Fortunately, the orchestra is excellent, so he is spared the pain of eavesdropping on the conversations about him.

He finds himself seeking out hair colour. Two ladies boast locks approximate in shade to those of Mademoiselle Noire, but neither has the same rich luster, and their skin lacks luminosity. In fact, there isn't a woman here whom he would call beautiful (apart from his darling Cecile). Several are pretty, but simpering; most are decidedly plain, in his opinion. Has he always been so choosy?

He recalls an amour he entertained here a few seasons past: an actress lesser known at the time, but now making her name on the New York stages, he is told. She would order caviar, oysters and champagne.

The affair amused him well enough, until he discovered that he wasn't the only suitor paying handsomely for her company. She is the last woman to have extracted from him the purchase of jewellery. Of course, it hardly matters now. Many a man has lost his head between flattery and a smutty suggestion.

It is the hope of success that leads men to this end, although the wisest of women know that the chase is more profitable, on both sides, if prolonged. Like military generals, women understand that, once a castle's gates are unlocked, there is no need for further siege.

Their tea drunk, and Cecile happy at having exchanged pleasantries with several ladies of note, the siblings return to their carriage. They have hardly reached Grosvenor Square before an upturned face catches McCaulay's attention, in the crowd, upon the pavement.

Banging on the ceiling, so that their coachman might stop, he kisses Cecile upon the brow, offers profuse apologies, and leaps down, adeptly avoiding the collected filth of the gutter.

He looks about him, certain that he has recognized her, but no lady visible meets her description. Then, he sees the familiar figure, with distinctive hair tucked under a cap, just a few locks escaping. She's wearing trousers of rough cloth, heavy boots, waistcoat, jacket, and a scarf closely about her neck, so that her face is barely visible. Disappearing down Audley Street, she weaves between pedestrians, obliging him to quicken his pace.

He's almost upon her when she turns and sees him, surprise and irritation crossing her face. She begins to run, dodging down Mount Street and almost knocking into the flower sellers, who deliver ripe rebuke.

McCaulay keeps her in sight, though with difficulty. She turns left into Park Street, runs a few paces more, and disappears into a narrow opening. He's somewhat familiar with these streets; the Dorchester Hotel is nearby, as is the entrance to Hyde Park, off Park Lane.

Entering the alleyway, carefully avoiding curds of vomit, he's unable to spot her, and wonders if she has already exited at the other end, back onto Audley Street. He takes a few steps more, drawing level with barrels of ale stacked against the wall, and discovers her, crouched among foul-smelling refuse.

Her beauty is all the more dazzling in this low and dirty place, nauseating in its odour, habituated more often by the beer-bloated and sodden-eyed.

She's soon on her feet, making to flee, but he grabs her shoulder, holding her fast. The material of her jacket is so very coarse that he wonders how she can bear it. She turns from him, refusing to meet his eye, clearly unhappy that he has come upon her.

'My dear Mademoiselle,' he begins, curiosity in his voice, and the softness of one who cares. 'Why are you dressed this way? What can be the reason? And why must you run from me?'

She makes no further attempt to bolt. However, her voice is full of annoyance.

'Lord McCaulay, it may surprise you to discover that some like to wander London without being recognized. My costume is surely evidence that I'm not taking the air as a genteel young woman, for which I would require a chaperone. I prefer to walk alone, being of independent mind. Let me be, and I shall continue.'

Her demeanour is so earnest that he cannot help but laugh. Irked that her fancy dress provides him with such amusement, she eyes him with petulance.

'Of course,' he replies, steadying his expression to avoid more offence. 'It's an exceedingly clever idea: one I may adopt myself.'

'There's no need to mock me,' she answers. 'You are a man: to wit, there are no restrictions placed upon you. You're free to come and go as you please; nobody will stop you.'

He sees now that there is more to her irritation than simple annoyance at having been caught.

'How often do you assume this boyish identity?' he asks.

She doesn't answer immediately, considering how much of her secret to share. At last, she admits that this is her second outing, and the first lasted a mere five minutes before she returned to the safety of her residence.

'It's perhaps not the solution I hoped for,' she reflects.

'Nevertheless, the costume suits you well, young garçon.' McCaulay smiles.

'I'm in no mood for jest,' she retorts, moving to withdraw.

He reaches out, detaining her once more, turning her towards him. She looks up in defiance, but his eyes smile in amusement, and with affection, so she raises her mouth, to take a kiss.

'Now I must leave you, Lord McCaulay. I'm sure you have other calls upon your time.'

She begins to walk away but McCaulay spins her about, and wraps her in a firm embrace, meeting her lips with sweetness, and urgency, as if he might never lay eyes upon her again.

Making no effort to remove herself, she moves her hands within his coat, lifting his shirt so that she might find the bare skin of his back.

Her touch thrills him, sending a jolt to his groin, but he hesitates, remembering that they stand in a public place. Though dusk is falling, obscuring them somewhat from view, were someone to call an officer of the police, confinement in a cell might await him. Being found with a 'boy' would require bribery; even then, he might find the story leaked to the newspapers.

As if reading his mind, she throws forth the challenge. 'My Lord, you're brave enough to accost me in a darkened, foul alleyway, but does your courage take you any further?'

She strokes his growing erection through the serge wool of his trousers, finds the buttons and inserts her hand, cool against the heat of him. What manner of woman is she? At every meeting, he begins under the illusion of having the upper hand and, each time, she so swiftly educates him to the contrary.

She gazes directly into his eyes, and he knows that she sees there the look of a man spellbound, obsessed.

Despite the proximity of passers-by, he moves his hands swiftly, unbuttoning her rough-hewn britches and untying the cotton bloomers beneath. Pushing aside the confines of the fabric, he enters her with his fingers. Her breath is already coming quickly, she being eager to receive him.

He guides his phallus between her legs, its head nudging at her, and places his hands beneath her buttocks. Her movement is restricted, but she angles herself to him, eager to facilitate their union. His shaft presses against the most sensitive part of her, each penetration bringing a wave of pleasure. Her encouragement is loud enough for him to fear drawing attention from busy Audley Street.

The danger of the situation adds great frisson as he spears her, incited by her hunger and his determination to demonstrate that he can meet any trial she sets before him. She clenches and he brings his mouth upon hers, attempting to stifle her cries. His crisis follows close, his cock pulsing.

They gather themselves into a decent state, share a knowing smile, and exit from opposing ends of the alley.

ACHILLES HEEL

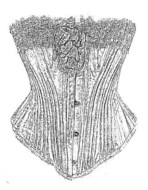

McCaulay takes a short cut through Hyde Park, past the statue of Achilles, created in likeness to some figure on the Monte Cavallo in Rome. It is a sculpture he has always admired, the hero's body appearing too lifelike to be formed merely from stone. Shield upheld and sword in hand, he stands in defiance, ready for war.

McCaulay, vain and egotistical as he is, has never presumed to compare himself with the majesty of the demigod, dipped in the River Styx to render him invincible, but for the heel by which his mother held him. Now, he feels some affinity with the noble warrior, whose pride and courage led him into the thick of danger at Troy.

His battle is less tangible but he feels it nonetheless: an inner conflict, in which his head and heart conduct their own havoc. As for his Achilles heel, her name remains unknown to him, despite her face being etched upon his consciousness. McCaulay stands, for how long he cannot tell, as pedestrians bustle past. The wind has picked up and drizzle is descending. At last, he turns homeward, the final leaves of autumn eddying about his feet.

He passes through Hyde Park. In fine weather, the broad avenue of 'Rotten Row' attracts ladies and gentlemen of fashion, wealth and celebrity. It leads off into the darkness, his own path stretching similarly before him. He rarely thinks of the future, or the inevitable change brought by age but, now, he imagines growing older, dissatisfied, without hope, passionless and withered.

In the summer months, the bridleway is crowded with equestrians, creating a scene of brilliance, pomp and splendour; tonight, it is dank and gloomy. When winter's frost bites, the Park glitters. Then, skaters take to the frozen Serpentine, illuminated by torchlight.

Many a love affair has been nursed in these acres, fair young men seeking out a certain rosy cheek, to be greeted by blushes and downcast lashes. A lady might drop a glove and bestow a smile. Such assignations oft remain furtive, ultimately foiled by a matchmaking matriarch, caring nothing for the secret wishes of youthful hearts.

He has thought to make Mademoiselle Noire his sometime mistress, but he realizes that it would never be sufficient. He must possess her completely. She will be his torch in the darkness: no other exists for him. His ardour won't be thwarted.

A ginger tom shoots past. McCaulay clutches his coat and makes towards the elaborate iron gates. He hurries past Apsley House: one time residence of the 'hero of a hundred fights' – the Duke of Wellington. The monument to his great deeds stands in front of the drawing room windows. If he had, in modesty, forgotten his own greatness, he might have looked upon it, and been reminded.

McCaulay passes out onto Grosvenor Place and through Belgravia.

As he enters Eaton Square, fog is rolling in from the direction of the Thames. The interior of his residence appears less welcoming than usual, although the fires and lamps have been lit. Heading towards his room, to dress for dinner, he stops at his sister's door, knocking gently.

Cecile calls for him to enter, and he finds her at her dressing table, her maid arranging her hair. She would never think to question him, but he feels compelled to explain his hasty removal from the carriage. Sensing that he has something heartfelt to impart, she dismisses Alice and turns to give him her full attention.

'What would you say, sister, were I to tell you that I have fallen in love?'

She is first incredulous, then, seeing the earnest look upon his face, claps her hands in delight.

'Nothing would bring me greater delight, Henry, than to see you happily settled.' She rises to hug him. 'I doubted that the day would ever come. How many beautiful women, of good breeding and charm, have you toyed with? And not one has captured your heart.'

Her words are as he expected, she being so generous of nature.

'That you have taken time to choose wisely is to your credit, dear brother. My heart yearns to meet the object of your admiration, that I might call her sister.'

'What if my bride were not of aristocratic family, Cecile?' he asks.

She gives him the simplest of answers. 'Regardless of her birth, dearest, if she is the other half of your soul she will be a lady indeed. Your good taste and discernment has surely selected a woman of substance, refinement and intelligence. I cannot believe it would be otherwise.'

Her words are a comfort. Certainly, whatever her name or status in society, Mademoiselle Noire lacks neither brains nor imagination. Her conversation is eloquent, her spirit admirable and her bearing noble. Perhaps all may be well.

Cecile, sensing her brother's anxiety, clasps his hand. 'I would receive any you held in esteem with deference and affection, treating her as my closest friend and confidante.'

He returns the squeeze of her fingers; he is blessed indeed to have such a sister.

However, he remains doubtful that his Queen of the Night has any notion of marriage, much less, that she might wish to accept an overture from him.

McCaulay takes leave of Cecile with his customary kiss upon her forehead and promises to join her downstairs in good time.

MISTRESSES

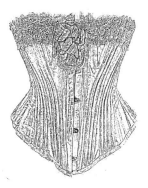

I t is Maud's birthday, for which her great-aunt has been persuaded
to accompany her to the Café Royal: a place not only to dine but
to be seen. The central Domino Room, with its golden goddesses and
garlands, its painted cupids and burnished gilding, is filled with
fragrant perfumes and laughter. The curtains are drawn and the
candles lit, the flames reflected infinitely in the elaborate mirrors. The
air is thick with an atmosphere of Bohemia and tobacco smoke.

Isabella is shortsighted, which is just as well. The far corner is
occupied by a certain set: poets and artists. Isabella, despite her rela-

tive open-mindedness and delight in all that is scandalous, would call them sodomites and rogues. Maud refrains from judgment, thinking them glamorous, and wonderfully amusing.

The hour isn't late but they are so full of absinthe that one of their company is hallucinating, calling out farewell to his mother as he sets off to sea. Other diners look on in bemusement, only a few with vexation. One generally expects such things at the Café Royal.

'What's the commotion?' demands Isabella. She's just begun her consommé veau and doesn't like being disturbed while eating.

Maud is always ready with a story.

'I think they're rehearsing for a new play. They're famous actors, from the Shaftsbury Theatre. Something Shakespearean...'

'Hmmm,' says Isabella, peering in their direction. 'A dining room isn't the place for Shakespeare... Ah, the filets de sole Orly!'

The fish is splendid, accompanied by pommes rissoles and petit pois. Since the occasion is celebratory, she and Maud are also enjoying a bottle of Champagne Perrier-Jouët. By the time their mousse glacée has been devoured and a small plate of cheeses is before them, Isabella is in a state of perfect bonhomie, reminiscing upon her youth, and the subject of dinner guests.

'Such wonderful evenings we had, the Conte and I. Our Torta Barozzi was unsurpassed, making it the greatest torture to resist over-indulgence.'

Maud is familiar with the treat. Her grandmother's cook makes this particular cake every Saturday, rich in almonds and bittersweet chocolate.

Isabella continues, 'Of course, the most difficult task lay in deciding where to seat people. Wives and husbands, naturally, were never placed in close proximity, to avoid curbing their fun. Meanwhile, mistresses, of which some had more than their fair share, had to be located neither too far nor too near.'

Her eyes glitter wickedly.

'One evening, on being quite occupied by the state of the struffoli (as you know, my dear Maud, the citrus glaze for the fried dough must be laced with toasted hazelnuts – walnuts simply won't do) I seated the Duca di San Orvieta between two of his mistresses, with the Duchessa opposite. The trollops fought over his attentions, above the table and below, like squid extracting a mollusc from its shell. The poor man hardly ate a bite.'

Isabella's smile is nothing short of devilish.

'The Duchessa's words to me afterwards were exquisitely colourful.'

Maud squeezes Isabella's hand affectionately; besides her grandmother, there is no one she loves more.

During the carriage ride home, her great-aunt's head begins to nod.

Maud leans over to whisper, 'Now, don't forget, I have the next lecture on Mr Darwin's work to attend tomorrow evening.'

'What's that, my dear?' says Isabella, her eyes fluttering open. 'Another lecture? So soon?'

'They are extremely fascinating,' asserts Maud. 'I'm learning more than you can imagine…'

Isabella's chin is once more upon her chest.

'In fact,' muses Maud, 'I'm having a splendid birthday week.'

IN EMULATION OF MESSALINA

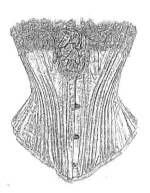

McCaulay returns to his club the following evening, determined that he must speak to Mademoiselle Noire, and make his feelings known.

No doubt she'll refuse, he worries. *I'll entreat her to reconsider. It would be madness to think that she'll lack terms of her own. Naturally, I'll examine any proposal, although her continued exhibition of herself I cannot countenance.*

He finds a place upon a side sofa, away from the main throng.

When Mademoiselle enters, she has never looked more regal,

wearing a dress of crimson velvet, her porcelain shoulders fully exposed, her cleavage displayed to utmost advantage. Her auburn hair appears set with stars, being pinned with diamantes, each catching the light.

She begins her address. 'Gentlemen, you know well the delight of watching a fair bottom wriggle upon a manly piston – your own or that of another!'

Merry agreement ripples among those gathered.

'What joy it is to witness such coupling, spurring on the efforts of others, offering encouragement as you watch appreciatively, waiting your turn.'

She pauses, allowing the rosy image to permeate.

'Some might say that lusts are best inflamed by watching ladies coax one another, with gentle fondles or harsher play. Others prefer a girl to be coy, since modesty has its appeal and men like to hunt. A woman too willing is perhaps no sport. Who among you has not thrilled to overcome seeming resistance? The ladies of our harem know you well, gentlemen, acting the virgin or the whore, as suits the occasion.'

How clever she is, McCaulay finds himself thinking. *She knows us perhaps better than we know ourselves.*

Her voice, low and seductive, continues. 'Tonight, we bid farewell to Evaline, who has been your sporting companion these last twelve months. You have attended to her pleasure as generously as she has to yours, most liberally, and in every manner.'

Mademoiselle here allows the gentlemen to conjure forth their own recollections of the majestic Evaline.

'She is soon to enter the sacred union of marriage and plans to put aside, with some reluctance, her life of adventure within these walls. To mark her departure, she has requested the honour of your participation in a special performance: no less than the reenactment of Messalina's orgy.'

A murmur of approval travels the room.

'The Roman Emperor Claudius' wife, being insatiable of appetite and immensely competitive, challenged the well-known prostitute

Scylla to a contest, to see who might fulfil the lusts of the greatest number of men. Messalina demonstrated herself to be the greater whore, continuing long into the night, obliging the most varied of demands. This evening, Evaline will be without challenge, since we humbly acknowledge her as the foremost lady of this establishment.'

Having received such an introduction, guaranteed to whet the appetite, the lady herself enters, dressed fittingly in a Roman toga, her chestnut hair braided and looped in the style made famous by Messalina of old.

She promenades sedately, appraising her suitors. Satisfied at last that all attention is hers, she reclines comfortably upon the cushioned day bed in the centre of the room. Inch by inch, she raises her skirts, revealing the pale skin of her thighs. She opens her graceful legs, that her forest, lush and curling, might be admired.

Evaline parts the moist entrance to this garden of pleasure. Her fingers are adept and skillful, and it seems that perhaps she has no need of another, her breath ragged from her own touch. It is then that she summons forth her first lover, with a simple crook of her finger.

The gentleman remains fully clothed, taking out only those parts essential to the act, already in a condition ready to conquer. Grasping his organ, he lowers himself upon her, eager to sate his desire.

She tilts her hips, and his rod gains the first toast of the night, pushing slowly, and then with greater acceleration. She closes her eyes, embracing the sensual delight of their coupling, knowing that she will enjoy every man gathered. The night can end in one fashion alone: a feast in which each will enjoy her body.

Within the shortest time, her lover lets forth a groan of satisfaction and Evaline's smile gives proof of her own. She kneels upon the divan, offering her buttocks. Her next suitor pours champagne down the cleft, before bending his head to drink, rubbing his bearded face against the length of her valley, tickling and teasing her with his hairy chin, his nose and mouth. The sucking of liquid from her secret folds makes the lady breathless with desire. She is eager to welcome stricter ministrations.

The gentleman is joined by another, keen to sample her velvet passage. The two share her, stroking with agile tongues, keeping her pleasure simmering, until she is quite beside herself, crying out for fulfilment.

At last, bringing forth their engorged organs, the gentlemen take turns to deliver ever-fiercer strokes, shaking free the lady's breasts from her draping costume.

Her face flushed and radiant, Evaline submits joyfully, reveling in the battle waged at her rump, and letting forth shrieks of encouragement, excited all the more by the knowledge of so many eyes witnessing her arousal, and final culmination of ecstasy. Her cries bring forth those of her gentlemen with due alacrity.

Resting for a moment, Evaline removes her robe, to fully reveal her naked beauty. Reclining, she cups her generous breasts, before allowing her touch to stray to her rounded belly and, once more, to the mount of her Venus.

She teases those gathered, pushing her fingertips inside, so that they emerge glistening with juices. These she sucks, parting her legs wider each time, as she gathers her succulent harvest.

Evaline motions for the gentlemen gathered about her to pleasure themselves. The lady's undulations, most enchanting to behold, summon joyous eruptions from her admirers. These, she rubs provocatively into her thighs, breasts and stomach.

In various states of undress, those about her join in her fondling, lowering their mouths to her nipples, to her arms and legs, holding each limb captive, about the wrist or ankle, each suitor taking care to deliver only the most welcome of sensations.

A cushion is placed under her dainty buttocks, so that her sweet jewel is best able to invite attention. One after another, her lovers take their turn in delighting her, supping at this tastiest of morsels.

Hands and lips continue to rove her body in tender fashion. Her snowy breasts are squeezed and softly pinched while teeth graze her skin. Her nipples ache for those tweaks and bites, just as her inner chamber throbs for the probing of tongue after tongue.

Her ecstasy comes upon her repeatedly and McCaulay wonders at her ability to continue, but Evaline's enthusiasm is far from spent.

Like Messalina, she presents herself for the use of every man, enjoying the knowledge of eyes and hands upon her. She receives their attentions with indefatigable delight.

Mademoiselle has stood unnoticed to one side: unnoticed by all but one. McCaulay cannot help but be drawn into the scene before him, but his eyes continue to seek the one who occupies his thoughts. Seeing his glances, she approaches, coming to sit at his side, so that she might speak quietly in his ear, their conversation unheeded.

'My lord, do you understand the desire for pleasurable oblivion, not knowing who is clasped to you, or whose lips embrace your flesh; the desire to be swallowed deep in an ocean of dark whispers?'

She continues, 'Among my greatest loves is the act of being pinned and invaded – not by two or three, but more, one after the other, losing myself among many, so that my identity exists only as "woman": a goddess of flesh and yearning, given over to base fulfilment.'

The thought of her placed now as Evaline both arouses him and causes him anxiety. Her admission, made so plainly, is both a revelation and no surprise at all.

'On many nights I have availed myself of these very gentlemen, in the adjoining room. Each time, I wondered if you might arrive and see me, as I took my pleasure. There is no part of me that has not been kissed and enjoyed. I encouraged my suitors to bury themselves, to obliterate reserve and find the heart of me: to open doors of one room and the next, until no more obstacles remained, and every lock was sprung.'

The vehemence of her declaration astonishes McCaulay. He seeks words for a reply, but can summon none.

Her eyes have grown dark with hunger. 'There is a wild intoxication in being watched, knowing that every man is waiting for me, their impulse holding them captive.'

Her voice, so close to her ear, is almost a hiss.

'At those moments, I control them, through their eagerness to take possession of my flesh. I satisfy their desires and my own, relishing that which others would consider barbarous.'

McCaulay is uncertain of what to say. His adoration of her is unshaken by her proclamations. The depth of her passion is unexpected, but her sexual preferences don't startle him. Nor does her openness.

Evaline, a little breathless, is now seated upon her knees, taking some sips of champagne. She calls forth another who, until now, has merely observed. She removes his phallus from his trousers, fondling its erect length between her ample breasts, so that juices soon quiver at its tip.

McCaulay turns to Mademoiselle, who sits composed beside him, her hands calmly in her lap, as if listening to a chamber orchestra rather than the grunts and moans of sexual labour.

His desire to convey his feelings overcomes all else.

'Do you never yearn as other women do for the haven of marriage? The security of a husband in your bed? Status as a wedded woman?'

Her voice is almost weary in its reply. 'There is enough conformity in the world, Lord McCaulay. I doubt that mine, or my lack of it, will send the planet from its axis. Meanwhile, my heart doesn't soar for the riches you set before me. Perhaps, one day, I may feel differently. For now, I wish to taste that which most women do not.'

Evaline's suitor spurts bountifully over her magnificent bosom, to cheers of approval, and she beckons another to his place. Her breasts, lubricated well, once more set a man on his path.

Mademoiselle turns fully to face Lord McCaulay, enquiring of him, 'What is it that you desire, my Lord? A meek wife in your parlour, to pour your coffee and soothe your brow? What are you made of? Do your roots hold you fast; or is your spirit free? Perhaps you are no more than a feather, tossed on the breath of others, with no direction of your own?'

'I know that I want you,' he answers, the words tumbling faster than he has intended. 'I think of you every waking moment. You haunt me. There's no escape. You're all and everything.'

His reply is excessively, ridiculously, romantic. It is enough to make her smile.

'For that, I'm not displeased. It would pain me were you to leave this place and never return. You have come to love me, I know. It is the most dangerous game, posing the greatest risk; one I've been ever loathe to entertain.'

Evaline, on her knees, is entered by fingers and by cocks, without knowledge of how many gentlemen are behind her, their attentions freeing the flow of her juices.

Mademoiselle chooses her words carefully. 'If I am capable of loving you, Lord McCaulay, of devoting myself to you, it will never be under the terms to which other women submit, for I am sworn to defy bonds which enslave.'

A gentleman's tongue is applied to the rosette of Evaline's anus, circling before inching within. She takes the engorged member of another into her mouth.

Mademoiselle raises her voice in approval, '*Brava, amici! Magnifico!*'

She turns to McCaulay. 'Observe, my Lord; I'm not the only woman to feel this way. How dull would it be to consume my meat with one variety of sauce alone? My body and spirit would whither, being fed on such limited fare. To sample the delights of a great many women is considered right and healthy for a man. How is it then that the opposite is held true for those of our sex? Where we display undue interest in sexual matters, even within marriage, we are thought immoral. For myself, I conceive of such limitation with horror: a torture for which I have no taste.'

Beads of perspiration drip between Evaline's breasts. Transported to another place, she has no consciousness of vanity. She knows only the sensations within her skin.

'*Mia cara, eccellente! Estremamente provocatorio!*' declares Mademoiselle, standing to applaud Evaline.

Seeking to appease Mademoiselle, McCaulay replies in desperation, 'I swear never to hold you to the covenants binding other women. We can create our own contract. I will be your devoted servant, entrusted with your safety and happiness, sharing your life and your bed, while respectful of your chosen path.'

A phallus, thick and unrelenting, smacks at its target, hefty balls swinging at Evaline's rear. Meanwhile, her mouth laps at the salty secretions offered for her delectation. Her watchers stroke their erections, waiting their turn for release in the confines of her soft body. The smell of sexual heat hangs thick.

Mademoiselle smiles, wryly, at McCaulay's ardent promises.

'Grand words, my love. If they're uttered in truth, I commend you.'

One after another, men claim their fill of Evaline. She has no notion of who impales her, submitting to the anonymity of their lustful cocks, slippery tips gaining easy entry, stroking her to a state between wakefulness and dreaming.

Mademoiselle watches Evaline as if in her own trance, one of remembrance and fantasy, in which she clasps her mouth to the bulbous head of a stranger's phallus, and opens her legs, to be slain by the steel of an unknown assailant.

McCaulay sees her lips part, teeth biting gently upon them and her tongue wetting their dryness. He would scoop her in his arms and carry her to some place of quiet, where he might kiss her heavy eyes and stopper the bottle of her desire, which threatens so dangerously to overflow.

He expects at any moment for her to join Evaline in her choreography of abandon. Whatever her feelings, she controls them for the moment, rising to leave the room.

DISMAL CONSTRICTION

In the dark hours, in the fog, Maud can go where she pleases. She can find her freedom, in the cool night air. It isn't safe, and it certainly isn't fitting, but who is there to betray her?

It is winter, and the year is curling in upon itself, silent and introspective. Clouds bulging with the promise of a drenching render everything still.

London is a city of windows, inviting Maud to ponder what lies within each dwelling: husbands, wives, children, servants; the young and the old; those who have much, and those who do not; those with hope, and those without.

Maud's footsteps lead her where faces are hollow, grey, and the windows unclean. The sun doesn't reach this far, into their tedious lives, lived in joyless constriction. In this foul-smelling maze of filth and fleas, the alleys are turd-strewn and piddle-soaked.

Girls barely budding open their legs to make a living, alongside the toothless and rancid of breath. Hair thick with lice, they all find customers if the price is right, against the wall or on sheets well-soiled. Their holes cost but a shilling. Skins grow thick and claws sharp.

Maud quickens her step but she has no destination. She is seeking but, for what, she is unsure. Time passes and she has no answer. Between tattered linens flapping in the sooty air, she spies a slice of domestic lamplight, and claims a greasy sniff of hissing hot-fat sausages.

Her coat is warm but the chill oozes up through the soles of her shoes. She is drawn to the river, and all its hideous, dead-eyed treasures: rot-bloated cats, and cold-meat corpses of unwanted infants, eels plucking at their tender fingers and toes. So many babies farmed out to gin-soaked crones, who care not if they, nor their charges, sleep and never wake. Rub some alcohol on those young gums. Maggot-damp, life is festering.

Maud has been walking long, almost lost to her place in this vast city. The water is calling her, as it calls to the scratching rats. Dense wreaths of mist collude to hide her. The world is hushed.

And then, she sees him.

The heavy vapours shift and dip, as he passes by, head hunched and coat-collar upturned, walking briskly. She knows him first by the smell of his cologne and by the curve of his nose and forehead. If he looks up, he'll see her too.

His hurried steps suggest he is heading home, having tramped his fill. She follows him, her step in time with his, although it's not easy to match his pace. Fortunately, the grey blanket eats up the noise of her heel. He's uncertain of his path, since one wall looks like another and the curb is quite invisible. Home must be nearby. For a moment, the dirty tendrils part, and he sees his way, taking him more swiftly and obliging Maud to hurry, to remain in his wake.

The night is nearly done. The haggard shaft of first daylight parts the gloom, and they've reached Eaton Square. She keeps him in her sight until the last moment. He mounts the steps, and the door closes behind him.

THE LETTER

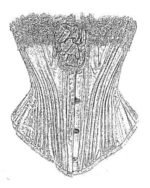

Lord McCaulay sits long by his fire with a large glass of cognac, his thoughts running on the woman who so perplexes him. She must surely endure her own conflict, her head battling her heart.

The next moment, he berates himself for attempting to understand her motives. She is beyond his fathom but isn't it this that makes her alluring? At last, he retires to his bed, sleeping with more reward than has been the case of late.

The following morning, he joins Cecile at the breakfast table for a tolerable repast of kedgeree and poached eggs. His dear sister, dressed fetchingly in dark coral silk, relates her plans for the day. She is to visit her dressmaker in the Burlington Arcade, and meet an old school friend for luncheon at the Savoy; it is to be a most delightful day.

George brings in the morning post and Cecile departs, to ready herself for the carriage. There are several items of correspondence: an invitation to the opening of a new gallery (he will decline); two requests for his presence at dinner (also to be declined); a brief report from his bank, informing him of his current affairs and investments (all most healthy); and a long and exceptionally dull missive from the Oxfordshire aunt, berating the state of her gardens following the wet weather and insisting that she cannot do without Cecile.

She hopes that her great-niece might take the train at her earliest convenience. Of McCaulay himself she makes little mention, other than to add that he might accompany his sister if he has no other business to detain him.

The last is addressed in a hand he doesn't recognize, upon dove grey paper. On opening, he knows who has written, although it is signed briefly, 'M'. That she has discovered his place of residence surprises him not a jot.

> 'We must see how you endure.
> If you have the head and stomach for this particular kind of
>   egalitarianism, between man and woman, we may find
>   a path.
> If not, we shall meet no more.
> Tomorrow, at ten in the evening,
> in the Mirrored Room.'

A MIRROR TO THE SOUL

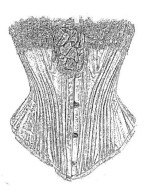

The hours creep slowly until the assignation. The room is unknown to him, necessitating a footman from the dining hall to guide him. Each of its eight walls is covered in reflective tiles, as is the domed ceiling and, even, the floor. Its intent is obvious: to reflect back all manner of activities, and from every conceivable angle.

McCaulay seats himself upon a divan upholstered in dark leather: the only piece of furniture. Long minutes pass before a segment of the wall hinges inwards and Mademoiselle enters. In her hair, upbraided, she wears a long black ostrich plume. She is masked. Silken pastilles cover her nipples, and a satin sash loops through her legs and about her waist, framing her pubis most attractively, as if she were a magnificent gift, for him to unwrap.

Her shoes, too, are decorated with feathers; the heels click imperiously as she walks. She stands before him with legs apart. The reflection from below is most engaging.

'Lord McCaulay,' she purrs, barely above a whisper. 'Why is it that I'm ready, and you remain fully clothed?'

Her request is soon fulfilled, allowing her eyes to appraise him, and her handiwork from some nights past: his groin is now sparsely covered in new growth.

She removes the feather from her hair, touching the tip against his chest, dropping it to brush his legs. She slowly encircles him, letting the feather stroke his back and buttocks. The mirrors afford multiple views of her body as she navigates him: the curve of her breasts, and the glorious roundness of her bottom.

Facing him, she drops the feather to his phallus, its light touch teasing.

'One day, as Shakespeare reminds us, we shall lie with worms as our chambermaids. Until then, should our bodies not enjoy all pleasures? This room heightens the experience of watching, does it not, Lord McCaulay? Every act is magnified back to us.'

In demonstration, she bends forward, her cheeks parting. She whips the feather through her legs, so that it momentarily conceals her delta.

She remains in this attitude, inviting him to touch her. He considers a moment, before raising his hand to deliver a sharp spank. The slap makes her flinch, then sigh: the timbre now familiar to him. He gives another, watching in the mirror as he makes contact. The sting resonates on his palm. He pauses and she remains folded, craving more. Each burning smack causes the peach of her cheeks to ripple.

He feels his majesty rising, the ruby head twitching for her. He gives a final blow to her flesh, before striking with his phallus, assaulting her, embedding his lust. His balls are heavy with ache.

Wishing to show that he can satisfy any urge she cares to inspire, he rides her mercilessly. Her groan of pain and satisfaction spikes his desire.

Watching in the mirrors, he withdraws his cock, pleased at the sight of it, so engorged and powerful. He plunges again, driving his length back into her. She gasps, but pushes back upon him, enjoying the exquisite torment. The sight of their coupling drives him to the brink. He lifts her buttocks high upon his groin, thrusting into her willing flesh, taking her arousal along with his. He ruts his eruption into her, and she accepts her own oblivion, echoing the rhythm of his pulse.

When they have gathered their breath, she stands upright and turns to face him, tilting her head, lips raised and parted, as if to allow him to kiss her. She places the feather between them at the last moment, laughing gently.

'Truly, your prowess cannot be questioned, Lord McCaulay,' she concedes. 'However, if you wish to enter into our contract, I must be convinced that you can honour your part, allowing me to invite others into our bed.'

At this, she returns to the mirrored door and opens it, beckoning two to join them: the huge African and the young Zeus. Both naked, one ebony dark and the other golden, they exhibit strength and beauty such as no man can deny.

Mademoiselle struts between and around them. Knowing McCaulay is watching, she flicks her ostrich feather over her new lovers' bodies, her eyes and touch roving to their tight buttocks, their biceps, and their toned abdominal muscles. She leads them to the divan, kneeling upon it, one seated on each side, her back to McCaulay.

Mademoiselle wraps her fingers around each fat python, caressing to her left and to her right. McCaulay is obliged to watch, envious yet pleasurably inflamed. She catches his eye in the mirror, ensuring that he observes her.

She takes the tip of the African's phallus in her mouth, moving her lips over its head, and her tongue along its glossy length. Her other hand continues its ministrations, until she alters her attention, turning her face to offer kisses to Zeus' generous spear.

So it is that McCaulay is compelled to watch those lips he would kiss and call his own placed upon the organs of other men. Her dainty tongue licks the shaft of another's cock. She takes the greatest satisfaction in her task, an enjoyment heightened by the knowledge of his watchfulness.

Each stroke of her velvet mouth brings forth a grunt of appreciation from the man before her, which serves to increase her fervour. She intends to enjoy those engorged members to the full, not just against her tongue.

She pushes the African onto his back upon the divan, and strides his lap. Her eyes on those of McCaulay, she mounts the giant with care, allowing herself time to accommodate his great girth.

Lord McCaulay is mesmerized as her ivory thighs part. Her hips make a gentle forward caress then tilt back upon the bulk of her lover. His hands span her waist without effort.

Her golden Zeus, oil upon his hands, reaches from behind to cup her ample breasts, as she rises and falls.

McCaulay's cock has never been harder. He is obliged to encase it, tugging his own pleasure in time with hers.

As her motion upon her steed gains in ease, she lies forward, upon the great man's torso, opening wider her legs, keeping the African's phallus firmly within her, while angling her buttocks.

Zeus has rubbed oil liberally upon his organ, so that it glistens in readiness. He caresses the pink bud of her tightest passage, as she enjoys the column impaling her from beneath.

Her puckered bloom is beautifully presented, eager for attention. As his head pushes forward, she utters small cries of anguish and urgency. However, within the shortest time, her golden lover's shaft has entered. He lies partially atop her, moving slowly, purposefully.

McCaulay's view is unhindered as he watches the clenching buttocks of Zeus, plunging into she who haunts McCaulay in wakefulness and sleep. She has chosen her weapons well, and it is evident that her hunger has never been more acute.

Her impending ecstasy is apparent in the energy of her own rhythm, more demanding and faster paced.

Zeus is the first to shudder, surging into her, uttering a great groan of satisfaction.

The music of his orgasm inspires the African below, who shoots forth with a moan long and low.

McCaulay's sweet love writhes, her body held rigid before a shudder passes through her. A flood of passion erupts, as if she were exhaling her soul. Her cry brings tightness to McCaulay's throat, and his own hot spurting. Despite his release, envy burns within him, knowing that others have taken her to such arousal. Meanwhile, his own seed spills unheeded to the floor.

The three are breathless, bodies perspiring. At last, they part, Zeus and the African taking their place either side of the room. Mademoiselle reclines upon the couch, her chest rising with rapid breaths.

McCaulay knows that he must seize the moment, showing her that his feelings of jealousy can be harnessed to other ends, that her enjoyment of other men doesn't lessen his own desire. In fact, that her performance heightens his wish to please her.

He first pulls the ribbon from her waist, so that it unravels, and slithers from between her thighs. He bends his mouth to her breasts, removing the pastilles with his teeth, unveiling her nipples. Her mask he leaves in place. She lies, fully naked, thighs parted, her labia on show: plump and wet from his rival's semen.

Knowing that he is watched, and caring not, he places his own bare body against hers. Their lips meet in a kiss deep and tender. McCaulay enters a world in which she alone exists.

Her nipples brush his chest, and she draws herself closer, his hair against her soft skin. Her belly pushes against his, and her hands snake about his back, at last finding his buttocks, which she draws towards her, wrapping a leg about him. His rod begins to thicken, pressing at her groin.

The moment is exquisite; they lay quietly, knowing that pleasure is to come and savouring this quiet pause before they surrender to the throb of lust growing between them.

When his manhood enters, it is as natural as a fox seeking shelter in its den. Imprisoning her in his steadfast gaze, and cradling her as the most precious jewel, he rocks against her. He keeps his rhythm steady, refusing to rush forward. Her hands clutch at his buttocks, eager to urge him on, to quicken his thrusts and take her with more force, but he refuses to rise to her provocation.

In this one thing he is able to defy her, forcing submission to his pace, wooing her with sweet whisperings of endearment and admiration, and gentle kisses at her neck and shoulder.

At last, she relinquishes her struggle, allowing him to dominate her. His hands clasp the underside of her bottom, thrusting at his leisure, though with focused deliberation. Her eyes, usually so piercing, so taunting, grow wide and dark. Her body is limp in surrender, permitting him to take her as he wishes. He holds her under his spell now, she capitulating to his will.

McCaulay's lips travel down to embrace her breasts and she drops her head back to expose her throat and torso, yielding to his resolve. His kisses are devoutly tender, but still he grips her haunches, so that little movement is possible on her part. He continues his slow momentum of thrusting, ensuring that each stroke is long and deep.

She has never looked more captivating to him: a goddess he is honoured to worship. Her superiority in intellect and wit is as unquestionable as her beauty and desirability, yet she is his, conceding to him, responding to his commands. Her breathing becomes ragged, and her velvet passage grips tenaciously. She wraps her legs tightly, arching in delight. Sucking hard at her breast, and with fingers pressed into her buttocks, he is resolute in his penetration. They gasp together, sharing the exquisite moment, their souls entwined as devoutly as their bodies.

Afterward, they are like dreamers in half-slumber. Eventually, it is he who rises, dressing silently, and departing the room. She is the one who now watches, until the door closes behind him.

AT THE MERCY OF LOVE

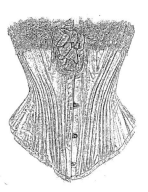

Lord McCaulay knows that he is shipwrecked, without desire for deliverance. His love cannot be denied. Her feelings remain, as ever, mysterious to him; he has no notion if she is capable of returning his esteem.

This matters not; his devotion is set in stone, regardless of how she responds. He must fall on her mercy and, despite his hunger to possess her, accept whatever terms she appoints.

Taking his pen, he writes a simple note, which he sends with all speed, accompanied by fifty hothouse orchids.

My Dearest One,
I assure you of my love and genuine regard,
and my appreciation of your independent spirit.
I am your devoted servant, sworn to uphold
your comfort, safety and wellbeing.
If you will allow me to do so, I will become
your protector, your companion, your lover
and your fellow adventurer.
You are my beginning and my end.
Always
Henry

THE FESTIVE SEASON

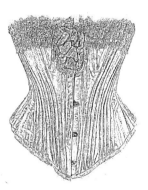

L ord McCaulay hears nothing from Mademoiselle. Each day, he sends fifty orchids but keeps from visiting his club and refrains from correspondence. Once, in a moment of weakness, he lingers nearby, hoping to catch a glimpse of her, either arriving or leaving. He sees nothing.

By day, he walks the streets through which he chased her, wrapped warmly against the wind. Melancholy reflections assail him as he whiles away the hours in Hyde Park.

Winter's icy fingers have entered the city, bringing freezing fog and a damp chill to the air. Those with sense make for Italy or the French Riviera. He feels strongly the urge to leave: to put behind him all torment and find some ease under a warmer sun. He might take a young, carefree girl as his lover, or find release in the arms of a professional courtesan, but he knows such distractions will not suffice. His thoughts will be always with 'her'.

Each evening, Cecile implores him to be merry: to play cards, chess or backgammon. She lures him twice to the theatre and once to the opera: a performance of *La Boheme*, which is hardly likely to bring cheer. He has no taste for dramatic fantasy, his mind being too greatly burdened, and dinner parties he detests. Nevertheless, he agrees to accompany his sister to a pre-Christmas masked ball at the Crystal Palace.

A strange notion grips him that he might see Mademoiselle there, knowing her penchant for concealment. A warm fug permeates the room. As he pushes through the throng of ladies powdered and coiffed, adorned heavily in the latest silks, he sees that they measure their worth by the number of eyes appraising their costume and figure. They are, to him, hollow beasts beneath their trappings. McCaulay unmasks three women with auburn hair, to no avail.

The festive season passes with little pleasure. He purchases the necessary gifts, and makes calls upon those relatives who must be appeased. His smiles he reserves for Cecile, knowing that his unhappiness will otherwise become hers.

After much pleading, he agrees to accompany her to the Barnum and Bailey Circus, for the two o'clock assembly on 26th December. Touted as 'the greatest show on Earth', he wishes very much that the entire company might fall off the globe at the soonest opportunity.

Cecile remains perplexed, knowing that disappointed love must be at the heart of his torture. She evokes the conversation they shared in her boudoir but he asks immediately that they refrain from pursuing the subject.

His custom is now to drink through the late hours, finding oblivion there, and to rise late – usually after Cecile has taken her morning ride in Hyde Park. He lounges at the breakfast table until past midday, scanning the paper (ridiculously reading the small advertisements to see if some coded message might appear for him).

The newspaper holds little to revive him to any interest in the world: the ascension of Queen Wilhelmina to the throne of Holland; the German Emperor's visit to Palestine; the assassination of the Empress of Bavaria; some trifles on the British War in the Soudan; and a snippet on the United States' annexation of Hawaii.

He continues to send orchids, altering his request of the florist only twice: to send fifty red roses on Christmas Day, and fifty white on New Year's Day. Still, he hears nothing, but for the morning he receives a parcel containing a copy of Mrs. Humphry's *Manners for Men*, regarding which the sender directs him towards certain passages, and an illustrated copy of *The Perfumed Garden*, translated by Sir Richard Francis Burton from the original Arabian text.

Lord McCaulay peruses the pages, seeking some hidden message. His eyes alight, in Burton's work, on the thirty-six names for a woman's place of pleasure, each denoting its characteristics: the delicious; the biter; the sucker; the yearning one; the voluptuous; the crested one; the crusher. His eyebrows rise as he reads those words first committed in the twelfth century, concluding that he may have much yet to learn regarding women.

LOST LOVES

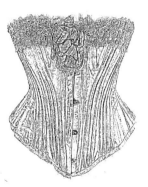

Great-aunt Isabella is in her bed, suffering from chest congestion. Her determined great-niece has donned her plainest clothes for the outing, and a heavily veiled hat, tucking every scrap of hair out of sight. She doesn't need or want attention; she wants invisibility. She slips out through the kitchen and Elsie, the cook, kisses her cheek fondly as she goes.

The Great Wheel at Earl's Court is a sight to behold: 308 feet tall and 270 feet in diameter. There are forty cars, each holding forty passengers. Maud has her heart set upon riding it.

Having purchased her ticket, she stands in line, her heartbeat quickening at the thought of being elevated so far upwards.

Stepping inside, she takes her place by the glass, others pressed closely about her, and they begin their ascent. The urban sprawl is in its first stage of illumination, tiny points of light dotted across London, as the gas lamps are lit.

It's too much to take in. Vast and grimy as the city is, from here, it's pure and beautiful. Below are lone spiders, waiting for their fly-dinners, scurrying centipedes, and foolhardy moths, pretty but fragile. Factories of worker ants: all manner of human life, emulating the behaviour of their multi-legged co-habitators.

The wheel moves upwards, the lower cars emptying and refilling with each stop. Suspended near the top, the view is beyond anything she could have imagined. Her elbow is jogged, as someone cranes to see over her shoulder, and small boy pushes past her skirts, to press his nose to the window. Others move from one side of the carriage to the other, eager to see more, to drink in the marvel of what lies beneath them.

Then, from behind, she hears clipped tones. Turning, she sees him, his collar upturned against the chill. His profile is distinctive.

Not long ago, she saw him speak to a wretch she would have expected him to ignore: an ancient, tattered creature, wrapped in a blanket. He stooped and pressed a coin into the extended, mucky hand, and gave, it appeared, some words of comfort.

Accompanied by two comrades-in-arms (old chums, she guesses) he is refuting a fear of heights, unconvincingly. His companions are tipsy, voices loud and pompous. Far from admiring the glittering firmament below them, they are debating a question most sordid and inappropriate. Women tut in disapproval and their menfolk glare, but they continue unchallenged, being too well dressed and too obviously aristocratic to be confronted.

As the carriage arcs its return towards solid ground, the buffoons elbow their way to her side. She turns her back, avoiding eye contact.

They are listing petty conquests now. The man she is familiar with is far more sober, urging them to desist. To Maud, his companions are

'Toad' and 'Newt', residents of the Serpentine; she imagines long tongues flicking out in amphibious slipperiness.

Suddenly, 'Toad' has clapped his hand upon her right buttock, and is giving it a hearty squeeze. 'Newt' is laughing but the gentleman she knows is horrified, leaning towards her, proclaiming every apology. His lecherous friend is far larger than he: positively robust of gut. He attempts to pull 'Toad' away and they scuffle, the crowd parting about them, in distaste.

Only a few moments have passed, but Maud has slipped a pin from her hat and is now taking aim. As 'Toad' lurches towards her again, she jabs and hits her target. Her stab to his groin evokes a mighty screech and a torrent of ripe language. They jolt to terra firma, and she pushes out through the doors.

There is much commotion behind, and the sound of hearty retching: a cutlet dinner and a full bottle of Chianti are splashing onto someone's shoes.

'Serves you bloody right!' her altruistic gentleman declares.

MAUD AND ELSIE sit in the kitchen with a bottle of turnip wine, as sent by her sister in the country. It is quite vile – but Maud enjoys the intimacy. They eat the remaining third of the Christmas pudding and Maud finds the curtain ring in her portion, signifying that she'll marry in the New Year.

Elsie's spoon scoops the old maid's thimble, which pleases her mightily. She's already had three husbands, and that's quite enough for anyone. The first was a soldier who never returned. The second died in a debtor's prison, leaving her with nothing to her name but the clothes in which she stood. The third was a trader in Petticoat Lane.

'He ignited that in me I thought long gone.' She sighs. 'A grand time we had abed; there's value in that when all's said and done. He came to a bad end, murdered in a brawl over a prostitute, and me at 'ome with the baby.'

Maud, accustomed to the universal assumption that husbands and beds are never mentioned in the same sentence, sniggers. Polite Society can keep its delicate conversation over afternoon tea at the Ritz; she'll take turnip wine and Elsie any day.

The cook says, 'As a young lass, I thought nothing as important as the love of a brave and 'andsome man. Just make sure he's moneyed enough to keep you. The young may think they can live on sweet embraces but they won't fill your belly – or not as you may be intending at any rate!'

Her spluttering laughter brings forth a gobbet of phlegm onto the table.

'It was from my own dear mother, God rest 'er soul, that I first learnt the ways of men and how to catch me an 'usband, as is provident for a young woman. She 'ad advice for every occasion,' admits Elsie.

She takes a hearty swig, and refills her glass.

'An 'usband should be plain enough to sit at his settle, and simple-minded enough to accept the stew on his plate, rather than looking round ev'ry corner for a more succulent chop,' she declares.

Maud nods in agreement. 'She sounds very wise.'

'Aye, she was full of wisdom; but mostly gin!' Elsie shrugs. 'All that advice didn't do me no good in the end, since 'ere I stand ev'ry day, makin' breakfasts, lunches, afternoon teas, suppers and dinners. I'll die in me bed dreamin' of blancmanges an' rhubarb puddings.'

MAUD UNPINS HER HAIR, braiding it into her night plait to control the tangles. Men! She cannot help but struggle against the sweetness of the trap, like a wasp in jam. She has been introduced to any number of 'pleasant young men' and all they do is praise her beauty, feeding her a diet of sugar. It is nothing but poison.

She is convinced that it is only in the bitter moments of desire that there is any truth. There alone do men show their true nature, like a scorpion wielding its sting. This is, at least, real: more real than professions of empty and unfounded love.

What is wickedness? Does the body comprehend good or evil in its writhing dance of pleasure? Maud doubts it.

Rain rattles on the roof, bringing sleep. The night hours slide in and a face comes to her in her dreams: first imperious, then angry but, at last, honest and open. If she were to see herself, she would know that the memory has brought a smile to her lips; a smile that would decry love.

A BREAKFAST SURPRISE

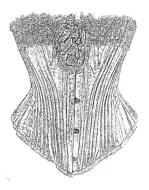

It is often early afternoon before Lord McCaulay bathes, shaves and dresses, and thus it is that he enters the drawing room, on the sixth day of the new year, in his flannel robe, to find there seated, beside his dear Cecile, a woman of familiar beauty and elegant bearing. Her golden auburn hair is arranged in the fashion newly arrived from Paris, and she wears a suit of russet taffeta.

He is rendered speechless, failing to greet either his sister or their guest, rather standing near the doorway in a state of shock.

Setting down her cup, Cecile reaches to shield her guest's eyes, laughing as she does so.

'My darling Henry is the best of brothers. I hope that you can forgive his disheveled appearance. He really smartens up quite nicely when he makes an effort.'

She removes her hand, placing it instead upon Maud's arm. 'Lady Franchingham and I were great confidants at the Beaulieu Academy for Ladies. We lost touch some years ago, when Maud joined her grandmother in Italy, but are now happily reunited.

Maud took me to a meeting of the National Union of Women's Suffrage Societies yesterday. She is determined to improve my mind, although I cannot think that she will have much success. She knows the president, the tireless Millicent Garrett, would you believe, and is keen for me to take up the suffragist cause.'

Maud raises her eyes to his. He presents an ignominious sight in his dressing gown, showing bare legs in slipper-shod feet; his hair is shaggy, his stubble unkempt and his eyes bloodshot.

'What a pleasure to meet at last, Lord McCaulay. I've heard so much about you.' She smiles. 'You should call me Maud and, perhaps, I might call you Henry; I feel that I know you well enough. Sweet Cecile hardly stops from offering up her praise of you.'

He is lost for words, not knowing whether to run from the room in shame or leap forward to grasp her in his arms.

Cecile rises, telling her guest, 'I've promised to run to Penhaligon's for a bottle of Hammam Bouquet. It's for our aunt, can you believe; exotic, I know, all that musk and jasmine! We members of the fairer sex are trying all sorts these days! I've heard Queen Victoria secretly wears it, but people say all manner of things, don't they. Anyway, it's but a short skip to Jermyn Street and I'll be in time to catch the late afternoon train to Oxfordshire.'

Cecile laughs over her shoulder as she departs.

'I know Maud is safe with you; she might even convert you to the notion of women's suffrage, Henry!'

Maud is the first to move, rising elegantly from her chair. Carefully, she takes teacups and plates from the table, placing them upon the side cabinet, next to a covered platter of bacon and eggs awaiting McCaulay's arrival. He watches her, hardly able to believe his eyes, or to accept all that Cecile has told him.

It seems impossible that he should no longer refer to her as Mademoiselle. Despite her modest attire, everything about her remains familiar: her figure, the glint of gold in her hair and her aloof smile. Plush and pink, he thinks of her lips about the shaft of his cock.

'I have the distinct impression we've met before, Lady Franchingham, under entirely different circumstances.'

She perches on the edge of the table, her eyes intently on his. McCaulay moves close, wishing to kiss her, but she leans back. Twining his fingers in the softness of her auburn locks, he presses his lips to her jawline, before taking the lobe of her ear. His breath makes her shiver.

He murmurs, 'I seem to know already, the scent of your hair.'

He fumbles with her jacket; she helps him, until she has shrugged it off. She opens the buttons of her high-necked blouse, her fingers working fast, dropping it also to the floor, leaving her under-muslin and corset. His mouth is on her collarbone, and the upper curve of her breasts.

'...and the fragrance of your skin, here...'

He is more urgent now, his rough chin tearing at her delicate skin. She welcomes him, pulling him to her, encouraging him, her fingers in his hair.

McCaulay reaches behind, to loosen her corset, but loses patience and picks up a knife from the table instead, cutting through half the laces.

It takes but a moment and the abundance of her breasts is in his hands, the loose and flimsy muslin of her chemise barely covering her. Falling upon them, he bites into the generous flesh, burying his torment in the heavy warmth.

Maud's eyes close in the glorious pleasure of his mouth, of his possession of her, of his eagerness to gather her to him.

His hands grasp beneath her skirts and he finds no bloomers, only the top of her stockings and soft thigh above. He could linger there, caressing this tender part, but he lacks patience, bearing down to cup her sex, pushing his fingers within.

'...and the way you shiver when I touch you here...'

Her breath catches in her throat and she surveys him through half-closed eyes. He moves his fingers deeper and she rocks her pubis against him. The warm smell of her makes him slack with lust.

Able to wait no longer, thinking of her hot cunt, he unties the cord of his dressing gown and drops his night trousers, releasing his cock. She takes it immediately, coiling her fingers around the shaft, guiding it to her, as eager as he.

Iron-hard, he drives with piercing pleasure. She opens her legs wider, moving her skirts away and wrapping her legs about him. His thrusts push her roughly against the table, but she rises to meet each one. Her fingers rake his buttocks, gripping him.

Her cries tell him that her crisis is upon her, and he welcomes his own beautiful, shuddering spasm. He clings, his face at her breast, his mouth open in a groan of satisfaction. He assails her with the full weight of his body, pressing down upon her, so that his weapon pins her, immovable. The pupils of her eyes are wide and her breath comes in short rasps.

The table, unsurprisingly, is in some chaos, since she has not removed every item. Her own appearance is in similar disarray: her breasts tossed free and hair tousled.

'Is this how you usually take breakfast, Lord McCaulay?' she exclaims, laughing now and endeavouring to sit upright.

He takes the knife and cuts the remainder of her corset laces, tossing the offending garment across the room, to their mutual amusement, then stops her mirth with a gentle kiss and pushes her back. She doesn't struggle, allowing him to lower his lips to hers. Her hands he places above her head, so that her frame is lengthened, and her exquisite breasts escape her low cut chemise. He holds her wrists there, savouring this moment of physical dominance.

'It was you, I assume, who sent me the books,' says McCaulay, dipping his fingers into a pot of raspberry jam overturned upon the cloth.

Maud only smiles.

'There is an entire chapter in *The Perfumed Garden* devoted to the scents of the body,' he comments, transferring the sticky sweetness first to one nipple and then the other. She chuckles merrily, as he hasn't heard before.

'But nothing on breakfast jellies or marmalades, I'm certain,' she adds, then grows silent as his mouth descends to its task, consuming the jam in long, slow strokes.

He releases her hands to move down her belly, and she opens and raises her legs in invitation, her skirts falling to each side. His mouth sinks to her waiting cunt, his stubble grazing her softness. He laps lazily, as if she were his dedicated plaything, and they had all the time in the world to enjoy such caresses. She surrenders herself to McCaulay's leisure, allowing him to do as he wishes between her legs.

'*Mio amore...*' she whispers, as he presses his nose to her fur, inhaling her sweet smell, intermingled with the saltiness of his recent offering. Sliding his tongue further, she moans, urging him not to stop.

His hands grasp her plump behind, as she rubs the nub of herself against the point of his tongue. Clutching at his hair, she embeds his face in her slit, crying out loudly.

McCaulay hears George's footstep across the marble hall and leaps up, catching the door just as his butler is about to enter, assuring him that all is well and that Lady Franchingham has simply banged her elbow on the edge of some furniture.

'Very good, M'Lord,' says trusty George. 'Should I bring some more tea?'

'Perhaps later,' concedes McCaulay, spreading his arms across the doorframe.

'*Very* good, M'Lord,' repeats George in approval, though his face betrays nothing as he closes the door behind him.

Turning, Henry sees that Maud has secreted herself under the table. She peers from below the cloth, concealing her merriment poorly. He helps her up and wraps his dressing gown about them both, laughing into the crown of her head.

'I seem to spend far too much time in concealment,' admits Maud.

'And following me, I think,' says McCaulay. 'I have seen you, have I not, in the halls of the Natural History Museum? And were you perhaps on the Great Wheel, at Earl's Court?'

Maud strokes the hair upon his chest.

'Do not allow yourself an inflated head, Lord McCaulay. Many of our meetings have been pure coincidence.'

His hands find the hollow in the small of her back. 'And now I have caught you,' he ventures, pulling her closer.

'Or,' she retorts, 'I have allowed myself to be caught.' She smiles again. 'Just for the moment.'

'Then I must take every advantage of this moment,' replies McCaulay, relishing the warmth of her body pressing against him.

He decides one last act must be his. He spins her about, bending her over the table, finding her with his cock. He buries himself, spreading her buttocks, that he might observe his motion. It is a sight to relish, his pounding of the crimson cunt of Lady Maud Franchingham.

With a final pump of his cream-coated shaft, he spews forth his torrent, and she utters her own sob of delight.

When they have recovered, she retrieves her garments from the floor. 'I believe your sister won't be long in returning,' says Maud, rapidly arranging hairpins. 'Having taken my pleasure of you, M'Lord, I shall be on my way.'

PROPOSAL

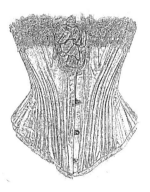

Having assisted Maud into some semblance of appropriate attire, McCaulay falls to his knees, imploring her to make him her slave if she might, but to allow him to always be at her side. Should she wish it, he will be honoured to make her his wife. If she requires time to ponder, he will wait indefinitely (although it is far from his wish).

Her reply is immediate. 'I have no need of a husband, other than as a show of respectability, and fear that I'll never mend my ways, Lord McCaulay; my appetite must be appeased. I hope to have many lovers.

In fact, I'm planning a trip to Europe for this very purpose, since each nation is known to have its flavours and eccentricities. I have no desire to stagnate in a life conceived by others, who presume to know what is right and fitting for me.'

She continues to pin her hair into place, peering at the silver teapot to see her reflection.

'Take heed,' says she. 'I am neither an angel nor a whore but when it pleases me to be so. The same, I am convinced, is true of most women. We are as little worthy of praise as of censure, and often deserving of both. Only those who carve epitaphs over moldering bones should attempt to appraise us with a trite phrase.'

She turns, defiant, but, seeing the look upon Henry's face, at once tender and hopeful, and as sincere as she has witnessed in any man, or woman, she softens her tone.

'It isn't wise to hold me too close,' she warns, her hand now upon his. 'I make my journey soon, and go as an independent woman. However, it would bring me pleasure for you to escort me, as a companion, and your sister, too. She is a sweet soul, who lightens my heart.'

'My darling,' he beseeches her. 'In that case, allow me to take you as my bride, providing a veil of propriety. You may act as you wish once we are abroad, and I may ensure your safety. However, I ask that I be present at each encounter, that you may come to no harm. I have spent my years dallying with trifles; let me now prove myself through loving you.'

His proposal seems so bizarre that Maud cannot but laugh. The notion appeals to her as one both practical and novel. Thus, she accepts, with the proviso that she must, on occasion, be allowed her privacy. With that, he places a napkin ring about two of her fingers, in token of his promise.

They kiss once more and, agreeing to acquire a special license at the first opportunity, part one from the other.

'Who knows how many verses we may play out? We may pen no more than a sonnet, but let us begin,' the bride-to-be declares. 'We may yet write something worth the turning of the pages.'

ITALIAN SONATA

VOLUME TWO - NOIRE

PROLOGUE

Not far from Sorrento, in Southern Italy, where the coast meets the sea in precipitous cliffs, lies Castello di Scogliera, that ancient seat of disdainful nobility. Built upon an island of eternal, wave-lashed rock, the castle is reached only at certain times of the day and night, according to the ebb and flow of the tides, by a cobbled causeway.

Look up at its narrow windows, and you might imagine yourself watched. Perhaps all old buildings watch. How else might they while away the centuries but in observing their residents. They listen, and remember: secrets and deceptions, memories of joy, and pain.

By night, some of those windows wink, lit by candles or chandeliers. Others stand dark, yet with a knowing glint, reflecting the moon's light from their panes.

Take these stone steps, worn smooth from the tread of generations of di Cavours, and all who serve them. Listen to the rise and fall of the sea, and the cold murmur of the granite. Place your hand upon the castle walls, salt-misted damp, where others have touched.

Like the succulent plants which grow on this rock, the inhabitants of this castle are hardy. Tragedy has taught them to be stalwart. It has shaped them in ways we can only imagine.

Come now, and enter, for a fire is blazing in the ancient hearth, and dinner has been set. The wine is poured, and a tale is ready to unfold.

The past does not lie quietly.

SINS OF THE FLESH

B orn with a substantial portion of Toscana in his pocket, the
Conte di Cavour greets the world with the appropriate level of
condescension, and a readiness to take his amusement, regardless of
the cost to others.

Gambling, whoring, drinking and hunting are his birthright; a
legacy he cultivates with enthusiasm. In these pursuits, Lorenzo

prides himself in setting the bar, since all men of nobility require an example before them.

Even the Italian King, Umberto, in his younger years, was inclined to accept an invitation from Lorenzo di Cavour. Certain members of the Russian Imperial family are regular guests at his table.

He is a di Cavour, beholden to nobody on Earth or in Heaven, or (to his mind) in Hell.

His hedonistic ways continue unabashed as the hands of time race to vanquish the antiquated nineteenth century, and usher in the endless promise of the new. Lorenzo may be of ancient stock, the blood of a hundred noblemen galloping through his veins, but he anticipates keenly the awaiting triumphs and entertainments of this brave new world.

Despite, the vast volume of wine and flesh he consumes, the Conte di Cavour retains, at the age of forty-five years, a rakish charm. His hair, silver-threaded, is thick, and his elongated moustache abundant: oiled and curling. Cigar smoke hangs upon his breath and the odour of a thousand cunts upon his cock, though not yet any sign of the pox.

From Siena to Milano to Venezia, he is notorious for the eccentricity of his tastes, which raise the painted eyebrows of even the most jaded prostitute. He is known also for his generosity, and his reputation for debauchery is matched by his renown for bestowing gifts upon the ladies — and young men — who please him.

No matter that, following a soirée to celebrate the fortieth anniversary of Lorenzo's birth, Signora Battaglia had been obliged to entirely redecorate her Yellow Salon, famed for its sumptuous décor, and furniture made by Francesco Scibec da Carpi (as graced the very chambers of Fontainebleau). The evening had been a relatively civilized affair until a band of female trapeze artists he befriended in Orvieto commenced an innovative performance aided by four dozen champagne corks and the salon's grand chandelier (itself a miniature of those hanging in the Hall of Mirrors within the Palace of Versailles).

The Conte compensated Signora Battaglia so amply that the good lady commissioned a portrait in his honour, which hangs still in the vestibule of that establishment.

Similarly, Signora Segreti has readily forgiven him for the ruin of her collection of rare instruments of torture, extracted from the Stanza di Tormenti, located beneath the Dominican convent in Narni. A blacksmith has restored their cruel workings, though they will never be as they were. The cheerfully compliant contortionist duo of Esmeralda and Eduardo should, in truth, be apportioned some share of the blame.

Lorenzo is seldom fully sober, but when he is, the glint in his cold, dark eyes fixes in earnest upon his prey. It is then that his wolf-gaze is at its most dangerous, appraising with devious intent. He is a fallen angel, as devoid of remorse or conscience as Satan himself.

In this, he is the epitome of honesty, making no attempt to conceal his sins. His scandals, each more outrageous than the next, have appeared with regularity in the provincial newspapers, and, on occasion, in journals of international circulation. His exploits, being always worthy of report, might have occupied every edition, but that the wealthier victims of his debauchery have oft bribed silence from those who would make public their shame.

The greediest of matrons, eager for their debutante daughters to marry into wealth and position, yet baulk at placing their tender offspring in his path. How many fair lilies had been plucked from under the noses of the unwary? To deflower these blossoms is mere sport to Lorenzo.

Having cast his carnal spell, even the most demure allow him liberties, transfixed by the touch of his cool hand, which soon finds its way beneath their skirts. The pursuit and rough deflowering of a trembling virgin, aquiver with anticipation and fear, might occupy him for an hour. There is something in that sweet consumption which warms his blood.

The memory of an upturned face, on occasion, returns to send a jolt to his groin. He recalls the gasps and squeaks, from his having pinched an inner thigh, and having let his fingers stray to places untouched even by the lady in question. A firm hand cannot be denied, and his is a hand of experience, and of pleasure and pain, and all that lies between.

How many pretty necks has his teeth grazed, as his thumb has delved and teased? All cunts are hot and wet in the end, however daintily their owners remonstrate. Their arms have curled about his neck and their legs parted in eager invitation, as they've sighed their protests. They've pulled him close while decrying his damnable audacity.

There is something in that single moment, when his cock, the conqueror of so many, forges its path. No woman who has felt his touch has returned to her Mama quite the same. Skirts and hair can be smoothed, and faces composed, but each young "figlia" totters back to her chaperone born anew; her shame as apparent as the semen dampening her drawers, but with new knowledge and a spirit of defiance.

It is his gift to them.

Such a man takes whatever he desires. Nevertheless, the greatest temptation is to possess what is beyond our reach. Such is the paradox of our lusts, to seek delights denied.

What satisfaction there is in seducing a woman whose outward show of respectability crumbles under his tutelage. How often has he sent a wife home to her husband with the sting of his palm, or his whip, upon her buttocks: flesh livid, smarting with the lash, yet thrilling at the humiliation?

It amuses him to see how far he can push their gentle sensibilities. Will they take his engorged phallus between their chaste lips, those lips which kiss their children goodnight? Will they concede as he spreads their buttocks wide and spits upon their anus, to ease his entry where none has been before? Will they consent to being watched by "his man" (his faithful butler, Serpico) as they rut, panting like a stray bitch in the street, welcoming the advances of any dog able to mount?

How many times has Serpico done more than watch? Fine ladies have basked in the degradation of having his servant's organ in their mouth, and wherever else he's chosen to place it.

On a recent trip to visit his mother, at her London house, what fun he and Serpico enjoyed in the company of Baroness Billington and her sister, aided by three stocky dock laborers Serpico collected on his nocturnal wanderings. Lorenzo was quite tempted to send the ladies on their way, at the sight of those firm and muscular chests, and with biceps handsomely inked. His own knees weaken when presented with so much glorious cock. The remembrance still makes his balls ache.

And then, there is his collection of innovative instruments...but these have, of late, lost their allure. Once his subject is willing to be restrained and pleasurably tortured, they're no longer a challenge. Titillation, for the Conte di Cavour, lies more in the conquest than the feast.

PADRE GIOVANNI, of the small town of Pietrocina, has spent a lifetime cultivating his belief in the fiery flames of Hell, and warning his flock, with all due urgency, of the torments that await them for their ungodly acts. He's intimately acquainted with their sinful nature, insisting on every detail via the confessional. Corruption of the flesh he renounces with particular rigour.

As for himself, he feels more concern as to the direction of his final destination than he cares to admit.

How shocked would his parishioners be to discover where his thoughts stray as they bend their heads in prayer? He knows every pretty face and shapely behind, although, he tells himself, these he studies purely with intent to identify which of his female flock might be most cast upon temptation's path.

His own life is one of celibacy, though his hand eases him now and again, when the constant burden of a sinless demeanour becomes too great to bear.

His housekeeper, Maria Boerio, stout of figure and of constitution, has served him ably over the years, fulfilling every duty, from cleaning and cooking to brushing the cake crumbs from his bed. This is, perhaps, his only visible vice: the consumption of heavy fruit pudding in the late hours. It's a duty Maria has performed without remark, having perfected the art of invisibility (a talent honed by all servants worth their salt). Even when the old priest sneezes a quantity of masticated carrot onto her freshly laundered table linen, she says not a word.

Each morning, she checks upon him, to reassure herself that her Beloved Padre, for such he is to her, breathes still. In his slumber, she admires the less weary appearance of his face, and traces the now sagging line of his jaw, the stubble accumulated through the night. That she has oft contemplated stealing a kiss is her greatest secret. No matter that his eyes are cloudy, and his nasal hair grows more abundant with the passing years, or that she knows the state of his bowels by the condition of the undergarments she scrubs. To her, he is all that a man should be: serious-minded and above earthly temptations.

Like all men of his age, he is prone to piles. Even in this, she does her best to soothe him, preparing a tea of butcher's broom, and an ointment of witch hazel and chamomile. Were he to request her to apply the unguent to the pale recesses of his behind, she would do so without question. Sadly, such a plea has never been voiced.

Her adoration is such that, though she knows it to be a terrible and shameful sin, she has, at times, hidden where she might spy upon him, wishing to behold that dear, though aged, body, in its naked splendour. Enfeebled as it is, the elbows and knees at sharp angles, and the stomach flabby; to Maria, the padre's form is a vision.

Her peeping has afforded her, just once, the sight of Padre Giovanni's penis: a sad, flaccid little thing barely worthy of the name. She imagined her own hand coaxing it to life and guiding it, to offer the ultimate comfort. Such wicked thoughts cannot always be avoided.

How fortunate that the padre is a man of God, and above such dissolute thoughts. His purity is her comfort, as she tells herself, her hand cupping her place of warmth betwixt ample thighs. Her stolen glimpses have sustained her through many a long night.

∾

LEAVING Serpico to follow on with the bulk of his luggage, the Conte Lorenzo di Cavour has taken a train from Pisa, through Rome, and onto Naples, before boarding a coach, which has taken him past Vesuvio and Pompeii, arriving in Sorrento by late afternoon. He might have taken a room at the Paradiso Vigoria, to enjoy its lush gardens of citrus and olive groves, looking out over the azure expanse of the bay. In all likelihood, the chambermaids would have obliged him in some amusing manner. He has entertained himself there often enough before.

However, he is eager to reach his destination, the Castello di Scogliera. With the sun dipping into the final quarter of the sky, Lorenzo has boarded a carriage heading to Salerno, via Scogliera and Pietrocina. Already inside sits an elderly priest: an unappealing specimen, to the Conte's eyes. However, he nods in greeting and smiles to himself. He has anticipated sharing the carriage with at least one other passenger, and this white-haired man of the cloth, snuffling into his pocket-handkerchief, has been thrown into his path. Fate will now watch over their journey, if not God (whom Lorenzo has long been convinced looks the other way, if He looks at all).

A few minutes later, the door opens again, hailing the entrance of a third to join them. The woman is dressed head to toe in black, gloved, veiled and hatted with not an inch of skin on show. Nevertheless, the Conte's expert eye, accustomed to appraising a figure at speed and from some distance, easily surmises that the lady is yet in her youth, her waist being narrow, and that she is of some noble birth, carrying herself with a lightness of foot and gentle bearing.

She settles herself on the cushions opposite the two men, spreading her skirts as best she can in the confined spot. There is little space between them, such that their knees will touch, if Lorenzo slouches down even a few inches. She holds her head erect and, though masked by her veil, he would wager 10,000 liras that her look is one of challenge and, even, contempt. Through the fine lace concealing her features, he catches a flash of indignation from her eyes.

It appears that they are the only three traveling. A few moments pass before the driver calls out their departure, placing his whip to the horses. With a jolt, the carriage sways, and they move across the cobbles of the Piazza Tasso, towards the Via Fuorimura, and southwards, past the street-sellers and the first evening promenaders.

Padre Giovanni Gargiullo shifts uncomfortably; his hemorrhoids are paining him more than usual, perhaps due to the heat, and he has a cold coming on. He is returning from his summons to Sorrento by Bishop Cavicchioni, having reported on the declining number of faithful attending his Mass. The Bishop has pointed out that not all of them can be suffering from malady or ill disposition, and the residents of his small town produce children enough between them to compensate for those who shuffle off this mortal coil. Padre Gargiullo is now out of favour, and will not be invited to attend the Bishop's anniversary celebrations. Nor will he be granted a bonus to his stipend.

Feeling thus sorry for himself, he seeks consolation in his Bible, opening it to his favourite passage, in Galatians: *'Now the works of the flesh are manifest, which are: adultery, fornication, uncleanness, lasciviousness...'*

The Conte di Cavour is the first to speak.

'How warm it is this evening, despite the sea breeze. You'll permit me to open the window wider? Perhaps the dusk air will refresh us? It's inordinately stuffy within this carriage.'

Without waiting for a reply, he leans over and does just that, allowing the coolness to enter in.

They pass the very outskirts of the town, gaining a clearer view of the rugged mountain tops ahead.

Padre Giovanni looks up from his Bible, ready to offer his thanks for this consideration, which is most welcome, but the words die in his throat before they can be uttered.

The gentlewoman, sitting so daintily and decorously, modestly veiled and gloved, has loosened the buttons at her neck. Not two or three, but, already, six or seven, such that the jacket of her costume has fallen open almost to her navel. Beneath, where her blouse should be, it is not. Nor is there chemise, nor camisole, nor corset.

There she sits, erect and proper, but with the flesh of her upper torso exposed.

The padre's instinct is to cry out, to voice his alarm, to rage at her indecency. His lips move to shape his protest and yet...not a sound emerges.

She twists a little towards him and, in so doing, her jacket strays open, revealing the inner curve of what swells beneath.

Her skin is smooth.

Unblemished.

He cannot look away.

She reaches to the pins at the back of her coiffure, and removes one, so that a single coil of curled ebony-dark hair falls free. With care, she places it forward, to hang against her chest.

With her eyes upon the clergyman, so that he might know her intent, she moves the fabric of her jacket to one side, to expose fully the sweet roundness of her breast. Hers is beauty indeed: such softness, and youth: her areola the palest pink, and large.

Neither man speaks a word.

Keeping her gaze upon Padre Giovanni, she moves her hand, still gloved, to cup her flesh. She holds the orb against her palm, as if displaying, offering, inviting. Her hair brushes the nipple: satin against silk, midnight against moonlight.

She teases her curled strand against the soft nub, and squeezes gently.

The peak grows pert.

The Conte is tempted to utter some word of admiration or encouragement. It would be most appropriate.

Instead, he holds his tongue.

Padre Giovanni is incapable of speaking, his mouth having turned quite dry. His fingers clutch still at his Bible; in fact, several of the pages have crumpled rather badly.

The lady leans forward, her breasts swinging free of her jacket, bending until she grasps the hem of her skirts.

And then, and then, and then...

She lifts, slowly, inch by inch, the taffeta, and muslin of her petticoats: above the ankle of her boot, revealing the white of her stocking, then past her shin and calf. She pauses at her knee, her eyes flicking to the Conte, to check that he is still observing her.

His mouth twitches a little, as if he might at any moment laugh.

She continues, raising her skirts, revealing legs slender and shapely, until the top of her stockings come into view: stockings fastened with ivory ribbon.

The lady, if such she really is, wears no other undergarments besides her petticoats. Her drawers are noticeably absent.

She moves her feet apart, first a little, and then more, until her legs are wide, the fabric of her lower costume bunched at the top of her legs, draping down either side.

Her gloved hands move across her thighs, where the gauze of her stockings meets her naked skin. She lingers there, playing with the ribbons.

The padre's fingers flutter against the pages of his book, and lose their grip. The volume falls to the floor with a thump, its corner catching his smallest toe, extracting a yelp.

As if growing impatient, she pushes her skirts entirely upwards and reveals, at last, the moist fur of her cunt.

The padre's voice emerges in a single shocked squeak. Lorenzo permits himself a slight shift in his seat, tugging his britches into greater comfort.

She removes one of her gloves: unfastens its buttons, and tugs, until her elegant fingers are free. The lady stretches her hand, as if it were a cat's paw, the claws of which require extension.

With all languor, her fingers find the slickness between her legs. She arches back into the pleasure of that touch, so that her jacket falls fully open. Her breasts push upwards, and her nipples stiffen under the gaze of the two men sitting so very close.

Legs parted. Labia parted. Her secret self, parted.

Her wild and wicked centre, her delicious nub, protrudes from dew-sodden petals. With the lightest of touches, she folds back that rose, wishing to reveal its darkest recesses.

Here I am, she declares silently. *Here is all there is to see. Here is what men desire: the essence of womanhood, from which all life springs. Look and admire.*

The padre feels himself both ice and fire: a pillar of salt and of water. With certainty, he can no longer feel his legs.

The lady's performance is now for herself, as much as for them. Her head lolls back, and she rocks against her fingers, first slow, and then harder. The air is heavy with the sour-sweet stench of her.

No more the tease of a slow reveal. No more feigned innocence. Here is her lust, raw and beautiful.

Her breasts rise and fall rapidly with her quickening breath, and the urgency of her task. Her jaw slackens and clenches, her tongue wetting her lips, parted and panting. She works at her task, eager to extract the honey of her pleasure.

And then her gasps begin, faster than her heartbeat.

Her undulations accelerate, as if a wrathful snake coils and stretches in her womb, commanding her hips to writhe in an exquisite battle. A great jolt shakes her, traveling from her sex, through her belly and spine, erupting from her in fierce proclamation. She is a shimmering raven, taking off in flight, flinging off the trappings of her humanity, becoming one with the air and the night.

Time stops for some moments, though not one of the three can measure them.

Lorenzo has to admit, she has surpassed herself, and he has witnessed some performances in his time.

'Brava, Lucrezia dear,' he commends, raising his hands in applause. 'I should have known better than to throw down such an enticing challenge to one so talented.'

The lady allows herself the smallest of smiles in acknowledgement, fumbling with her buttons, her fingers somewhat numb from the feverish flood bathing her body.

'I'm sure I speak not only for myself but for our good Padre in offering you my heartfelt admiration,' continues the Conte. 'How unfortunate it is that we're almost at our destination, for I feel certain that a second act would have proven most welcome. A good hard fuck does one the world of good, and the padre looks rather in need of a tonic. A rough poke of your delightful cunt, my dear, would have revived him no end, I'm sure.'

Padre Giovanni's eyes blaze, his mouth working to express his outrage, but the appropriate words fail him.

Her locks re-pinned, Lucrezia throws down her skirts, and turns to face the clergyman.

'Take no notice of my half-brother's crude taunts, Padre,' she soothes. 'He's a child you know, always eager for novelty. I imagine that you, more than he, as a man of God, appreciate the true revelation of a woman's passion: a flame lit by Divine God himself, and placed within exquisite flesh, to His own design.'

Having arrived in Scogliera, the two leave Padre Giovanni in peace.

To his great shame, his lap is damp.

BETROTHAL

On a certain Thursday in late March, 1899, between the hours of ten and eleven, a small party has assembled at the church of the Holy Trinity, in the parish of Kensington, just west of Hyde Park Corner, on the Brompton Road.

As the newspapers will report, the bride wears a costume more suited to a fancy dress event than a wedding, in the style of an Indian Mughal. Despite the unconventionality of her choice, those in attendance agree that it suits her well. Her crimson jacket has been embroidered with humming birds and bumble bees, accentuated above the hip by a wide, golden sash.

From its waistband, she later produces a miniature scimitar, surprising those at the Wedding Breakfast with her dexterity in using it to cut the cake.

Emerald drop earrings, a gift from the groom to his bride, peek from beneath titian curls, artfully tucked into a scarlet turban.

The groom's sister, Lady Cecile McCaulay, standing as maid-of-honour, is attired more traditionally, in a green velvet suit, puff-sleeved in the Gigot fashion, tapering to a narrow forearm, worn with a jaunty hat atop her blonde hair.

Both carry a bouquet of orange blossom and white roses.

Standing before the Almighty, the groom bestows upon the forehead of his bride a kiss. It's not too late for them to turn back: to take to their heels. Neither are tempted, however. They are exactly where they wish to be. If Lord McCaulay feels a lurch of uncertainty at the sight of his future wife fluttering her eyes at the handsome young minister waiting for them at the altar, he sets this aside. He is a man besotted, and such extremes of love cause us to make light of those foibles from which, under other circumstances, we might flee.

Lord McCaulay has pursued Lady Franchingham with sufficient steadfastness and ardour, it appears, for her to allow herself to be caught, although those guests closest to the bride might speculate as to the terms under which the contract has been made.

Marriage is a covenant to which Maud had pledged never to succumb, in pursuit of feminine liberation and independence. Yet, here she is, allowing her hand to be held and a ring placed upon it. Their vows are spoken in earnestness, and they shall be true to one another's desires; though the nature of what they mean by this promise is not quite in keeping with convention.

Every inch the blushing bride, her face is flushed with pleasure.

How wonderful it is, after all, to find ourselves surprised by the serendipity of our choices.

Surely, it's of little significance that Maud's wedded state brings her access to a handsome sum, placed in trust at her parents' death, and released only upon her marriage.

As the bride's slippered feet trip daintily up the aisle, she's thinking already of the warmth of her husband's arms, and his strong hands moving up the pale skin of her leg. Perhaps all brides think of these things, however pure and simple and modest they appear.

They emerge into spits of sleet, and a gust takes Maud almost off balance. She clutches at her groom and so taken is he by the surge of joy in his heart, that he lifts her ostentatiously into his arms and carries her down the last of the church steps, into the waiting carriage.

'What a devoted couple they make!' exclaims the priest. 'A true love match, I've no doubt.'

A number of the bride's friends, cheering the newlyweds as they emerge onto the Brompton Road, are unknown to readers of The Times or The Illustrated London News. One might say that their choice of attire is more risqué than is usual for a Society wedding, and the rouge upon their cheeks a little too enthusiastically applied. Among them is the celebrated milliner Ms. Tarbuck, who has supplied the headdresses of the bride and her maid-of-honour for this happy occasion.

The bride's great-aunt, Isabella, remembers the bag of confetti in her handbag, and manages to flutter a handful of rose-petals after the laughing couple.

Eyes bright with happiness, Cecile loves Maud and Henry more than any others in this world; their joy is her own.

Beside her, shaking the wet from her skirts with a grimace of displeasure, is her Oxfordshire aunt. For her, the ceremony holds no allure, far less in such weather, but the marriage of her nephew must be celebrated. How selfish it is to leave children orphaned, she thinks, so that such duties of attendance fall to other relatives.

It won't be long, she supposes, before a match is made for Cecile.

She makes a mental note to speak severely to Henry on the matter, as soon as the party return from their travels. If other suitors are wanting, she believes wedlock to her village parson, newly widowed, might prove suitable. Old enough, and dull enough, to provide a steady, guiding hand.

Yes, thinks the Oxfordshire aunt, it's the least I can do.

HONEYMOON

The newlyweds waste no time in departing for their honeymoon, Lord McCaulay having booked passage from Dover to Calais, across the Channel, on the *SS Mona,* a handsome paddle-steamer.

Henry had thought to leave his sister in the care of his aunt, safely in Oxfordshire. However, at Maud's insistence, Cecile is to make her first journey abroad.

'She has been too much in narrow company,' chides the new Lady McCaulay. 'A tour of the European capitals shall be just the thing, and our little Cecile will return far wiser.'

'In all things, you're right, my love,' Henry concedes. 'I've been remiss in failing to earlier expose her to the elegance of European culture.'

Cecile's final letter of appraisal, sent from the Beaulieu Academy for Ladies, had stated that her genteel deportment was just as was to be most hoped for 'in a dignified young lady of fashion'. There were other, minor, accomplishments: an elegant writing hand, an ability to recite the great poets, and talent with an embroidery needle, alongside her singing voice and her playing of the pianoforte. Beyond this, very little.

Henry finds that he cannot but muse on the contrast between Cecile and Maud, who attended the very same establishment. Maud's broad knowledge of certain aspects of the natural sciences, and the sharp application of her brain to her own entomological studies, are sufficient to put most men to shame.

His sweet Cecile is a model of demureness, patience, and generosity of spirit, readier to think well of others than badly. She is more than willing to look favourably on the world, ensuring a disposition of grace and warmth.

She'll make some chap very happy indeed, Henry has often told himself.

Maud's ability to persuade others to her way of thinking is infallible.

'If she's to find a fitting husband, we must ensure not only her refinement, but encourage her conversation beyond the sensational novels she so admires,' Maud explains. 'Much as we adore Cecile, you will hardly wish her to remain forever in our home.'

'Quite!' Henry agrees, his brow furrowing in alarm. The necessity of marriage for his sister has been playing upon his mind: an issue he has meant to address, but has never gotten around to acting upon.

'Of course, she can hardly be expected to 'discover' a husband for herself,' continues Maud. 'We must, when the time comes, introduce her to those we think suitable.'

Henry nods in approval, reminding himself, once again, how fortunate he is in having chosen Maud for his wife. She possesses not only beauty and charm, but wit and brains. He has married her, in truth, for the blaze of physical passion she evokes in him; however, he has also come to think of her as his intellectual equal.

'With the new century knocking at the door, times are changing,' Maud reasons. 'While a man of notable social standing may not yet expect, or desire, his wife to express *too* strong an opinion on matters of the world, or on those who live in it, he yet requires her to be the engaging hostess at his table. Some awareness and intellectual comprehension must be cultivated.'

It is true, Henry reflects, that no man of position wishes to be known for having a wife with the mind of a child: no matter that such a quality was prized in his grandfather's time.

PRESENTED with the opportunity to travel, Cecile could not be more delighted. How she has longed to see the mountains of Switzerland and the medieval towns of the Rhineland, as described in her favourite novels. Packing her trunk, she has found room for Mr. Wilkie Collins' tales and those of Mrs Braddon, as well as her volumes of *The Mysteries of Udolpho*, and *The Castle of Otrano*. They are faithful friends without whom she cannot contemplate making an extended trip.

What will Europe be like? she wonders, as they board the train from London's Charing Cross, to take them to the coast. *A place of dark-haired, romantic-eyed gentlemen, ancient castles, and gardens filled with lush blooms and exotic perfumes.*

English rain spatters the window but, in her imagination, she is already warmed by the golden, Mediterranean sun.

I might drop my glove and one, bowing, shall return it, meeting my eye for a brief moment. In that mingled glance, our souls will speak.

Her pulse leaps a little at the thought.

He'll press his hand to his heart and promise eternal adoration. Perhaps...

THE SEA CROSSING is not long in duration, which is just as well, since Cecile finds that her stomach is inclined to pitch and heave in sympathy with the boat.

How tiresome, just as she begins her travels! None of the heroines she so admires would suffer from such a weakness, she feels sure.

She retires to her cabin, as do Henry and Maud, voicing a desire to rest from the fatigue of the journey.

Lord McCaulay has barely shut the door behind them before his bride is pulling off her cumbersome underthings and guiding him to the bunk.

'My love,' she murmurs, sitting astride her husband's lap.

'My love,' he sighs.

To the heaving sway of the boat, she rocks, the occasional jolt of a wave thrusting her upon him.

BY THE TIME they board the train from Calais to Paris, Cecile has recovered her appetite, and is keen to partake of afternoon tea. Announcing themselves indisposed, the newlyweds lock themselves into their compartment; from the ensuing moans, Cecile guesses that the motion of the train is afflicting them.

Luckily, her own constitution is restored, and Cecile is emboldened to search out the dining car. Not wishing to sit alone, she places herself at the table of two elderly ladies, who make her most welcome. A pot of Darjeeling and a selection of eclairs and fondant fancies are soon placed before them, and the time passes pleasantly. Old ladies, Cecile finds, are always eager to recount tales of their youth, and to share gossip on notable figures of their own sex. The Browne-Huntley sisters are no exception.

'My dear, do look!' declares the first Ms. Browne-Huntley, indicating a rising figure at the far end of the car: a woman in a travelling costume of stiff brown cotton, her jacket and skirt bearing an extraordinary number of pockets.

'It's the intrepid Ms. Flora McTavish,' says the second, tapping Cecile's hand excitedly.

'Is it?' says Cecile, doing her best to catch a glimpse. 'I've read about her in *The Lady*. I thought she was traversing the Wadi deserts of Jordan and Syria, dressed as a man and riding a camel.'

'She was indeed,' replies the first, 'But she's lately been in London, delivering a series of lectures on the Bedouin tribes. No doubt, she's now setting forth again, to new adventures.'

'How marvellous,' says Cecile.

Her skin is far darker than is seemly for a lady, ponders Cecile, *but that is the foreign sun, of course. I must be careful to always wear my hat.*

The great Ms. McTavish straightens her hat, and removes a last crumb from her mouth.

If I truly were an adventuress, thinks Cecile, *travelling to remote jungle villages, in the Congo, or to obscure places of spiritual mysticism, in the mountains of Tibet, perhaps I wouldn't care if my nose came to be covered in freckles. I might, even, not mind wearing such drab colours. One must be practical I suppose, when travelling by mule and rickshaw.*

'Ah!' announces one of the old ladies, 'We're approaching the outskirts. Time to ready ourselves.'

Cecile makes her way down the dining car, still musing on where she might like to travel, were she to follow in Ms. McTavish's footsteps, and how large one's baggage might conceivably be under such circumstances. Entering the corridor to their compartments, she looks out, avidly, at the Paris skyline. How glorious it is, at last, to be in the city of which she has read so much, filled with chic Parisiennes, and their handsome beaux.

Meanwhile, another passenger is approaching, from the opposing end: a passenger so tall that his hair, golden and curling abundantly from the crown of his head, brushes the ceiling, and so broad that his shoulders fill the width of the passageway. There will be no space for one to pass the other.

His nose is pressed not to the view beyond the window but to a map, so that, as they draw level, and the train lurches, Cecile finds herself up against the solid, unyielding chest of this man. Stumbling, in her lost balance, she treads most heavily on his toes.

To her surprise, the voice that speaks is American, and though Cecile has been brought up to consider her cousins from across the Atlantic to be vulgar and noisy, she finds this voice to be caramel-buttered, the vowels drawn out like the promise of summer.

'Pardon my clumsiness, Ma'am,' says the voice of sugared sunbeams. 'Let me help you up.'

And two great hands are suddenly beneath her arms. lifting her through the air to land once more on her feet.

'You're not injured, I hope,' asks the honey-mouth. It's a voice unlike any Cecile has heard before and, as she looks up at the man to whom it belongs, she finds that *he* is unlike any she has met before.

'The name's Lance Robinson. Pleased to meet you,' says the handsome giant, and extends his hand to shake hers. Cecile's teeth rattle a little in her head.

'Short for Lancelot. My mother's choice. She loved those tales of King Arthur and all those gallant knights of the Round Table, off doing good deeds. S'pose she hoped I'd turn out just the same.'

'And have you?' she asks, then blushes. 'I mean… I'm sure she's very proud of you.'

Cecile finds that she's craning her neck to look at him.

'She is that,' nods the American.

If I were to marry, thinks Cecile. *You're the sort of man I might like to be married to.*

'My Pa, too,' continues Lance. 'He's looking to expand into South America, to link the wide-open plains of Argentina with their capital, via railroad. It's my duty, as a good Texan son, to help him in that great plan, and my honest pleasure too. I'll be taking the SS *Leviathan* to Rio in three months' time, and then onwards, to Buenos Aires.'

'What a grand adventure that sounds, Mr. Robinson' says Cecile.

'I'm headed down through Europe, travelling the railroads, to meet various bigwigs. I'm learnin' all I can.'

'No galleries or museums? Not like a traditional 'Grand Tour'?' comments Cecile.

He shakes his head and gives her a smile that sends her pulse into a most perturbing rhythm.

'It's all work for me, but I'm havin' a mighty-fine time anyways.'

Cecile looks at his lips as he talks, and wonders how they might feel pressed against her own. She can't help but notice, he's looking right back at her.

They stand, just like that, until the door of Lord McCaulay's compartment opens, and Cecile hears Henry's voice, calling to her.

'Well, it's been so delightful to meet you, Mr. Robinson,' she says, offering him her gloved hand. It's upon the tip of her tongue to ask where he might be staying in Paris, but such forwardness is beyond her. No lady would ask such a thing…

He gives her hand another solid shake.

'Ma'am, the pleasure was all mine.'

Paris!

The same sooty rain that commits London to sit in mud and dripping grime, bestows this city with glistening streets, which infinitely reflect the dazzle of its evening illuminations. Perhaps, it has the same perils and filth, the same overflowing sewers and excrement-smeared cobbles. And yet, our merry party sees only its glittering entertainments, and daring triumphs.

Determined that his bride shall enjoy every comfort, Henry has booked the Suite Impériale, at the newly opened Hôtel Ritz, in the 1st arrondissement. Conveniently, there is a modestly-sized adjoining room for Cecile. It's a home from home indeed, with endless hot water in the bathroom. From the ceiling of its grand salon, upholstered in red and gold, hang large chandeliers, their illumination reflected in the Baroque mirror between the windows, which look down upon the Place Vendôme.

'This bed is said to be identical to that used by Marie Antoinette, in the Palace of Versailles,' remarks Maud, in the early hours of their first night in the city, the coverlet drawn up to her chin. Sumptuous as the room is, the windows do rather let in a draught.

'And we all know how Marie Antoinette kept herself warm,' murmurs Henry, his hand moving to find the small of his wife's back. As their hips meet, his mouth closes upon hers. His chin is bristling from the day's growth. Rough on her cheek, rough on her collarbone, rough across her nipple. He descends beneath the covers and, with a contented sigh, Maud opens to take that rasping, hungry mouth between her legs.

MAUD BEGINS by taking Cecile to the Paris ateliers, provisioning them both with a wardrobe suitable for the warmer weather into which they are headed: dresses in light muslins and silks, their waists narrow, accented with a sash or belt, and broad-brimmed hats to keep off the sun, trimmed with ribbons and artificial flowers. Cecile looks longingly at those adorned with exotic feathers. Henry, being firmly against the slaughtering of birdlife, would be enraged.

Afterwards, they lunch at the Café Anglais on the Grands Boulevards, ordering briny oysters and snails dripping in garlic-butter.

How stylish the French are, muses Cecile. *The women manage to look elegant even while eating with their fingers.*

In the evening, they venture to Voisin, on the rue Saint-Honoré, feasting on lobster thermidor and incomparable sole meunière, before taking their seats at a performance of Donizetti's *Lucrezia Borgia,* at the Paris Opera.

'A woman worthy of the name,' Maud whispers in Cecile's ear. 'Intelligent, *and* cunning.'

However, it seems that cunning is never enough. Cecile can't help but wonder why women in such tales always come to a tragic end.

Does any opera end happily for the heroine? she muses. *If I were to write the libretto, I'd ensure a better outcome. Surely, every woman's story doesn't need to end in misery.*

The next day, after touring the Louvre, they drive down the Champs-Elysées, taking the air in Le Jardin des Tuileries. Cecile sees that, as in London, the parading of one's fashionableness is the prime intent. At L'Arc de Triomphe, Henry insists that Cecile have her photograph taken, a young man being ready with his photographic apparatus.

She stands rather shyly. Cecile has had other portraits captured but none so publicly. She feels the eyes of passers-by upon her as she poses, directed to stretch out her arms, as if pushing against the pillars of the arch.

Maud whispers in Henry's ear and it's suggested that the man bring his equipment to the hotel one evening.

'I shall hire some oriental costumes and we shall play-act,' she declares, her eyes twinkling, Cecile notices, with their customary mischief. 'A tableau, Henry, don't you think? Just as you saw once, in London? We might capture the fun upon this gentleman's camera.'

Cecile turns away in some embarrassment as her brother draws Maud to him and they engage in the sort of kiss that, Cecile feels certain, is not seemly in public.

MAUD HAS INSISTED that Cecile be allowed to accompany them as much as possible, and be encouraged in new experiences.

They spend an evening at Le Café du Dôme, where the famous (and soon to be famous) eat plates of Saucisse de Toluouse and mashed potatoes for a few Francs. The room is thick with cigarette smoke, and with Bohemians: sculptors and painters, poets, and writers. Models recline on purple velvet banquettes, profiles displayed to advantage.

Another night, they dine at Maxim's on La Rue Royale, and drink absinthe at Le Casino de Paris, on la Rue de Clichy.

'Made from the flowers and leaves of *artemisia absinthium*, and sweet fennel,' Maud explains, stirring with a spoon and adding a little water.

Just like liquorice, Cecile thinks, sipping at the green liquid, and doing her best not to show she doesn't like it.

Henry kindly intercedes, ordering her a glass of Calvados instead.

On a rainy Saturday evening, Cecile takes a table with them at Les Folies-Bergère, her eyes widening at the sumptuous and grandiose spectacles, of acrobats and jugglers and fire-eaters, not to mention at the lack of clothing on the beautiful young women parading past.

'My goodness, they must be chilly!' she remarks, but Maud assures her that all the dancing keeps them warm.

For comparison, they try the Moulin Rouge, in the Jardin de Paris, with its red windmill on the roof and monumental elephant in the garden, around which tipsy revellers Can-Can, in emulation of the dancers in their titillating costumes.

'Heavens!' declares Cecile, her eyes even wider. 'Who'd have thought one's legs could do that!'

It's all diverting... though she cannot help but wonder at the ostentatious artificiality of these amusements. Both evenings, she surveys the audience, to see if she might recognize a certain tall gentleman, with golden curls, but there is no sign of Lance. She is part disappointed, and part relieved. For some reason, she wishes not to imagine him here, looking up the skirts of the audacious dancers.

On their fourth day, Cecile begins to question whether she really likes the French capital.

They ascend the Eiffel Tower and, while marvelling at the view from the top, Cecile is startled to feel a hand grope at the underside of her bustle. She spins about, and the perpetrator, face impassive, fades into the crowd. By the time she finds her voice, her assailant has truly disappeared.

What use will it do, now, to make a fuss? she decides. *People will only think that I'm drawing attention to myself, and it will be most distasteful.*

Again, in the Basilique du Sacré-Cœur, on Montmatre, with Christ and all the saints and adorers looking down, her head cast upwards to take in the detail of the frescoed ceiling, Cecile finds herself assaulted by a hefty pinch upon her *derrière*. This time, she turns to find no-one nearby but an elderly priest, clutching his prayer book.

He smiles benignly and walks on.

Europe, or what I've seen of it so far, Cecile thinks, *is distinctly lacking in gallantry. By far the nicest man I've met is my Texan.*

Except, of course, that he is not *her* Texan.

If it had been love at first sight, Cecile laments, *he would have torn off the edge of his map and written me a note, before we parted: some address, or a meeting place. Now, we shall never see each other again!*

As her head rests on her pillow, she finds that her thoughts turn to Lance, wondering where he is, and what adventures he's having. There's no doubt in her mind that he *will* be having adventures. The question, now, is what sort of adventures are in store for her?

It's without much regret that she waves off Maud and Henry on their penultimate evening in Paris. She's content to eat a light supper in her room, and spend time with the novel Maud has passed to her: an exciting read by Mr. Stoker, set in the dark mountains of Transylvania.

Here is what she has been hoping for from their trip. She desires the mysterious unknown, and the grand, unmapped landscapes of remote regions. City life, as lively and surprising as it is, is less engaging than she'd hoped, and she feels the unwanted press of the city's residents upon her.

'Don't tell Henry,' Maud had said, leaving the edition on Cecile's dressing table. 'He doesn't need to know everything.'

'REMEMBER,' Maud tells Henry, as they pass out of the doors of L'Hôtel Ritz, 'You're my escort, leading me by the hand as I indulge my wicked nature. Here to protect but not to subdue.'

'Of course, my Mademoiselle Noire,' he replies, dropping his kiss upon her hand. 'Whatever amusements you seek, it's my pleasure to assist you, and my honour to keep you safe in that pursuit. Few men are so fortunate: to marry not one enchanting woman, but two.'

'Lord McCaulay!' Maud laughs. 'We each possess more than a single face. Dig a little, and you'll find you've married a whole harem!'

He takes her dancing, and buys her roses and orchids, so many that, in the morning, the hotel has to send out for more vases to accommodate them.

They laugh, and dance, and, arm in arm, explore the glittering streets of the moonlit city.

I'm in love, thinks Henry. *I thought I was before, and I was, but, now, it's something different.*

She smiles at him through eyes half-closed from too many glasses of champagne, sitting in a quiet corner booth, in la Brasserie de l'Espérance, on the Rue Champollion.

'What shall we do tonight, my husband? Shall we pay for some company?

Her fingers twist in the curls that rest upon his collar.

'How many women would you like, my love? How many soft mouths?'

He stiffens in his seat, wary that they may be overheard. However, the room is full of chatter.

Maud leans closer, her voice seductive.

'Or would you like a man to join us? Would you like strong hands on your body, his desire pushing against your stomach, his erection rubbing yours?'

Henry's mouth grows dry when she speaks like this, and her eyes darken. Then, he remembers her as the taunting Mademoiselle Noire, appearing again, to seduce and bewitch him.

'Would you like him to grip your cock alongside his, and stroke both together?

He shifts in his seat and lowers his eyes.

'Do you want hands that will be rough with you?'

Henry waves away the waiter who comes to refill their glasses.

'When he's ready, he'll push you down and order you to kneel, to spread your legs.'

Maud's breath is on his ear.

'From behind, he'll push apart your buttocks, feeling with his fingers, his tongue…'

Her hand creeps over.

'You'll beg him to do whatever he wants.'

Maud's fingers deftly unbutton Henry's trousers and she drapes the edge of the tablecloth to conceal his lap.

'To push that tongue inside you, until you open, like a woman.'

She reaches inside the fabric, her hand encircling him.

'Beg him to enter you. Beg him to stretch you.'

Maud strokes the thickness in her palm.

'You'll ache for him to thrust deeper.'

Henry has grown so large that Maud's fingers, long and elegant as they are, no longer meet around the circumference.

'When you think you can bear no more, he'll groan and judder, piercing you all the harder as he spurts. He'll pull out, and the thick, salted cream will run between your cheeks.'

She works more rapidly, working Henry's slick tip, and he is reminded of another hand, gloved, lingering upon his body, to inflame him: the hand of Mademoiselle Noire, provoking and awakening.

A few moments more and Henry's eruption covers her hand.

Everything she says is true. He does wish it, and he loves her for knowing.

THEY PAY the bill and head to Le Chabanais, where the Prince of Wales has been known to spend an evening. In the Japanese room, where delicate bamboos and willows fill the pale green walls, Maud removes her crimson taffeta evening dress. She lays back upon the bed, naked, Henry watching, as one girl after another is sent up, each given their turn to please her. He watches her arching back, her legs parting, opening to receive pleasure.

His cock aches for her but he knows he must wait.

'Find me a man,' she says, at last, her voice low and her eyes at their darkest.

Henry knows what Maud wants.

Not him. Not yet. Nor an evening-suited diplomat or financier, though there are plenty of those to be found at this establishment.

It doesn't take him long, just a few minutes' walk.

He brings back the most uncouth he can find. As broad as a shire horse and provisioned, it turns out, with an organ worthy of the same. Rough in speech and manner, and foul of mouth. Hair thick upon his chest, back, groin and buttocks. Eyebrows and beard matted, like a pirate king. Hands as large as dinner plates and teeth rotten, displayed in a lecherous grin. His breath reeks of cheap rum.

'I'm here to fuck you, slattern,' he says, staggering towards the bed, and taking out his sweaty cock. The man keeps his clothes on, filthy as they are, with the grease of mutton chops, and the lingering odour of urine.

He pulls Maud's legs, bringing her closer to the edge. Pushing them wide, her lips, poppy-red in their engorgement, split for him, and her excitement trickles onto the embroidered silk coverlet.

Three fat fingers enter her; enough to make her gasp.

'Good and ready, ain't yer, my lady?'

He gives her a lecherous wink, then turns his head to Henry, leering.

'Not enough for her, eh? Needs a real man.'

He grasps his meat, a hefty sausage as thick as Henry's wrist, already bobbing eagerly, and gives it a few tugs.

'Dunnat you worry. I'll do the job good and proper.'

Henry makes to rise from his seat, itching to give the blaggard a black eye, but Maud shakes her head.

Laughing at Henry's ire, the ruffian turns to the job at hand, widening his stance so that he can get a good grip under Maud's body. He pulls her up, towards his groin and, obligingly, she wraps her legs about his hips.

Gripping his erection, he guides it to her, lining himself up before making his thrust. His cock slides in like a spade through sodden peat, buried in one fluid motion, despite its size. He holds himself there, his hands under her buttocks, fingers pressed into her flesh.

His groan is that of a man finding where he wants to be.

'That's a nice welcome. Warm 'n' wet.'

He smirks, pulling himself out slowly, to allow an extended thrust once more, clutching her to him as he re-enters, giving her the full benefit of the invasion.

Maud's face is impassive, her pupils wide, lips parting with each drive of the man's cock. Her breathing is coming in shorter gasps already.

Henry, nails pressing sharply into his palms, can hardly bear to look. At one word from Maud, he'll land a blow on the villain's nose. He boxed for his university club. He knows a thing or two.

'Washing my dibber in your ladyship's juices. Fancy that, eh!' says the rogue.

He throws his head back in laughter, pulling Maud further upwards, so that only her shoulders and head remain upon the bed, her long hair flung behind her.

She takes his strokes in silence, as if in a trance-like state, watching his member enter and withdraw, sticky with her complicity.

'And what are yer like from behind?' he grunts, turning her.

He peels off his braces, dropping his trousers to his ankles, but keeps on his shirt, and his boots.

Henry sits, as he knows he must, watching as the other's hairy buttocks clench and relax.

Maud turns her head to one side, a golden hummingbird beside her on the quilt. Her eyes are open, her head turned towards the chair Henry sits in, but he doesn't think she sees him. Not now.

It's not long before the man has built a rhythm, entering Maud with progressive speed.

Henry looks away, to the curtains, but he can still hear: the man's heavy breathing, and the slap of his flesh against Maud's. Also, another sound. A soft, budding whimper, a plaintive cry.

Henry turns in time to see his wife's mouth open in full wail, her face pressed into the quilt.

He is half-disgusted, half-aroused, as the man chokes out his eruption, holding Maud rigid, pumping into her. Afterwards, coughing
with the exertion of his labours, he gobs up a lump of phlegm, spitting
it onto the rug.

He's dressed again soon enough, wiping his nose on his sleeve and
pocketing the two Francs Henry passes him.

'Best coin I ever earned,' says the rogue, giving Henry a final wink
on his way out.

~

FROM PARIS, they travel to Strasbourg, onwards to Munich, then
Prague, and southwards to Vienna, until they reach the darkly myste-
rious Budapest, where Gothic turrets and Baroque palaces vie with
Byzantine architecture.

Cecile finds herself most enchanted by the Hungarian capital.
Here, at last, is a sense of inscrutability. She feels the presence of the
past, of interwoven centuries, offering glimpses of their secrets.

The weather grows warmer, as the weeks pass, and they venture
further south.

Cecile has lost count of how many galleries and museums she's
visited, how many cathedrals. It astonishes her that so many churches
are filled with the voluptuous. Paintings and sculpture of earthly flesh,
in close proximity with the divine. There's something compelling in
those outstretched hands, which reach, upwards, to the Heavens.
Hands of sinners and saints, seeking something beyond themselves.

Finally, they head towards Italy, via Zagreb. In Venice, a gondola
takes them down the Grand Canal, and through the maze of smaller
waterways. They visit the gilded Palace of Ca' d'Oro, with its courtyard of ancient marbles, and ornate balconies, then take a tour of the
Doge's Palace. As the sun lowers to the last quadrant, they take a table
at a café in Piazza San Marco, drinking coffee and watching passers-
by: young men walking out with their sweethearts; mothers shep-
herding their children, who throw breadcrumbs to the birds; grand-
mothers selling posies of flowers from brimming baskets. Maud

points out a pickpocket in the crowd, one she has seen sidling up to people in the throng.

'He brushes against them as lightly as an insect pollinating a flower, taking what he needs, while leaving nothing in return but the promise of dismay,' she observes, sipping from her cup of rich, dark coffee.

'How dreadful,' exclaims Cecile. 'We should alert the *polizia!*'

She is a little testy today. So many hands, always reaching to touch her, to stroke the white-blonde of her hair, to take some ownership of her person. She is irritated by old women presuming to pinch her cheek, so fair in comparison to the olive tones of Southern European skin. In truth, Cecile is dissatisfied with herself. She had hoped to feel changed by these travels, to have her mind opened to new possibilities. Instead, one city tends to seem much like another. They each have their monuments and their beauties but, everywhere, there is the same congregation, the same grasping, pressing confluence.

'Everyone must make their living, as best they can.' Maud shrugs.

Cecile looks to Henry for his opinion, but he keeps his eyes lowered to his copy of Baedeker's *Handbook for Travellers.* She is left to fume in silence.

Maud and Henry continue to include Cecile in their excursions, and her every comfort is accommodated, yet she cannot help but feel a strange discomfort, a sense of exclusion that has grown with the passing weeks. Henry is content in his marriage, she's sure. He's happy, she feels certain. And yet, at times, there's something feverish about him.

Having read in a story by Mr. Doyle, about Sherlock Holmes, of addiction to opium, she wonders if Henry has fallen into this habit. Sometimes, she wakes in the small hours, hearing her brother, and Maud, return from some performance, or entertainment. She roused herself, one evening, soon after they had crossed into Hungary, to knock on their connecting door. Henry, opening it to her, was so unlike himself, eyes huge and dark in his pale face, as if a spectre were upon his shoulder.

Some unknown force sits between them, separating her from

Henry, and from his bride. She'd hoped to become closer to Maud during their travels, yet their rekindled friendship, in London, seems an age away. Maud, now a wife, and privy to things Cecile cannot imagine, occupies another universe.

Cecile cannot fathom it, but Maud appears to have a closer affinity to Claudette, her new maid, hired in Paris, than to Cecile, her own sister-in-law.

All things change, Cecile tells herself. *Perhaps, one day, when I am married, and wise, I shall look back on myself, and not recognize the girl I was.*

THE WAGER

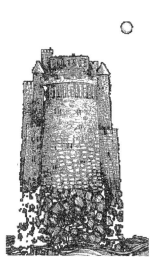

Within the Castello di Scoglieri, two sit by candlelight. The woman's eyes are strangely bright, as if the twinkling crystals of the chandelier had dropped into those dark pools. Her fingers raise her glass, her lips drinking deeply.

'Do you have a conscience, brother? Or were you born without the capacity to feel guilt, or shame?'

'You know me better than anyone, sister dear. If you say it's so, I must believe you,' he replies, raising his own glass to hers.

'I'd declare you the blackest villain, were it not that I know your sometime softness towards those of your own blood. The paradox is that you derive such pleasure from tormenting us. There are many types of prison, and you appear a master in their creation.'

'My dear Lucrezia, what form would your rebellion take, had you not my little cages to rail against? I merely feed your desire to disobey. In this, I know you better than you know yourself.'

The matter of their argument is for the moment set aside, as Vittoria has entered, bringing with her the chocolate tartufo.

'A letter arrived this afternoon, sister, from my dear aunt Agatha. It seems she's invited a guest to spend her honeymoon at the villa, and requests a room with us for a few weeks, to allow the newlyweds their fun.'

'A guest?' interrupts Lucrezia. 'Her grand-daughter, isn't it? The same Maud, a renowned beauty, who was staying with your mother — in London?'

Lorenzo's knife slices into the tartufo with more aggression than is necessary.

'A handsome marriage to a young aristocrat, I hear...' Lucrezia adds.

Lorenzo waves his hand in dismissal.

'My time in London was brief. I barely spoke to the lady in question. She was tolerably attractive,' he admits, 'Though I fear will not age well.'

'I wonder at your forgetting her so easily,' asserts Lucrezia. 'A little bird told me that Isabella had hopes that this pretty thing might ensnare you.'

'I do not say that I forget,' replies Lorenzo, his eyes narrowing.

'Agatha requests accommodation for the groom's sister also, a girl barely presented to society. No doubt, she will be a bore, with no conversation or other talent to recommend her. I must leave her to you Lucrezia. Your tolerance for dullness exceeds my own.'

Lorenzo finds the cherries within the tartufo, and lifts them to his mouth so that, when next he smiles, the stain of the scarlet syrup is evident upon his teeth.

'I'll do as you wish, as always,' answers Lucrezia. 'But I must be rewarded. I've kept my side of too many bargains, and I'm yet to see the benefit.'

Lorenzo licks his spoon thoughtfully.

'I'm listening, though you're hardly in a position to make demands of me.'

'You know perfectly well what I want,' hisses Lucrezia, her fists clenched tight upon the table. 'A larger income, so that I might make my own way, and leave here. Away from you!'

'The money is easily arranged, of course,' sniffs Lorenzo. 'But you would miss me, would you not?'

Lucrezia, for once in command of her temper, declines to answer.

'Perhaps we might play a game, to while away the tedium of entertaining our young houseguest. My aunt, I know, will amuse herself, but young women are so… needy.'

Lucrezia knows Lorenzo's games of old.

'I wonder, sister dear, which of us might first make a conquest of this squeaking mouse? Show me the little pet, tamed and compliant in your paw, and I will fulfil your request: an allowance of a million Lira a year, in whichever currency you prefer.'

He pauses to allow the sum to hang before Lucrezia, laden with possibilities.

'If her soft fur finds its way between my teeth, I'll devise an amusement of my own choosing, to which I will expect you to comply.'

Lucrezia has grown a little pale. There are few things she has denied Lorenzo, grateful to him for his having claimed her, his halfblood, from the orphanage in which she was raised, but she is wise to the intricacies of his thinking, and the paths of his cunning.

'I know how well you rise to a challenge. Your performance for the padre passed the carriage journey most pleasurably. You have a talent for play-acting, like your mother before you. Sleep on it, my Lucrezia,' he offers. 'And may your dreams be sweet.'

LUCREZIA REMOVES the rubies from her ears, and fingers the expensive bottles upon her dressing table. Her wardrobe is filled with the latest fashions, from Rome and Milan. He has been generous, and where would she be without that generosity?

However, the price to be paid, she finds, is too high. She is as much a prisoner here as… any other. All under his roof are his to command, not just the scullery maids. The yoke is becoming heavier than she has the will to bear. His torment of her, devising new ways in which she must bend herself to accommodate his whim, is insufferable.

The fate of the young woman soon to join them is nothing to her. What does she care for some spoilt and silly English girl, who cannot begin to imagine the life Lucrezia has endured. It will be easy enough to win her trust. She shall extract a kiss from her within the week. Perhaps more.

Harder shall be the task of keeping Lorenzo from her girlish fancies. His roguish charm, when liberally applied, rarely fails.

Her imagination envisions well the forfeit she will pay if he wins this wager. It is the one thing she has refused him, though not on grounds of morality or fear of the Almighty. To offer that part of herself to him would be to give herself in entirety, and this she cannot allow. No man, she has decided, will have her so utterly in his power.

SITTING ALONE AT THE TABLE, Lorenzo clicks his fingers and, from the shadows, a dark figure emerges. It is Serpico, who hears all, and says little.

'I have unfinished business with the new Lady McCaulay,' the Conte explains. 'We'll bide our time, but —be ready to act when the opportunity presents itself. Go to the villa, Serpico. Watch, and listen.'

GOOSEBERRY

Cecile joins Henry and Maud in taking a *vaporetti* across the viridian waters of the Venice lagoon, to the isle of Murano, where Henry orders fifteen chandeliers of hand-blown glass, each tiny crystal droplet threaded with gold, for delivery to his London residence.

'So many, my love?' comments Maud. 'We've barely four reception rooms at Eaton Square.'

'Ah, but we shall require something bigger, will we not, Lady McCaulay?' Henry smiles. 'A married man requires a larger home, most certainly, and there must be space for children.'

'Indeed?' Maud's eyebrows rise. 'And how many are you hoping for?'

'One to start with,' answers Henry quietly, dropping a kiss upon her glove.

Cecile's cheeks grow warm, at this mention of private matters. She is feeling, more than ever, that to live as a supplicant under the roof of her brother and his wife is a state she cannot long endure. She is the gooseberry, set against their wedded ease. As kind as Henry and Maud have been, her place is untenable.

What choices await? Marriage to someone 'sensible', of Henry's choosing? Or spinsterhood, living with her aunt, in Oxfordshire? Both visions cause her to shudder. Her daydreams of emulating the noble Ms. McTavish, in her exploration of the wild territories, are no more than flights of fancy. Her spirit, she likes to imagine, is willing, but the practicalities of such an existence are beyond her, even were Henry to allow it, and release funds to indulge her independent travel. He never would allow it, she is certain. Her own pocket-book income is too small to conceive of true independence.

Cecile must marry. There can be no way around it. But where are the suitors of her star-gazing? Where is her brave soldier? Her dashing prince? Her noble knight?

As THEY SIT at breakfast in the dining car, Henry hungrily consuming kedgeree, Maud sips from her teacup, looking at the passing country-side, the terrain growing more mountainous.

How many trains have they taken since leaving Paris, slicing through the miles, and the hours, by day and night?

She is thinking of Henry, inside her, moving in syncopation with the engine's forward motion, and the rhythmic rocking of their carriage. Henry staring intently into her face, eager to possess her, which he does, if only for that moment. His hands are full, of her breasts, of her buttocks, of her hair, long and silken. His mouth also, full of belly and thighs, his teeth biting gently, wishing to devour her. His tongue is sweet between her legs.

She can see him, wrapped in her, inside and out, flying through the dark.

His kisses tell her everything she wants to know. They can be as reverential as those of an angel kissing the hand of God, but they can be something else too. She prefers the latter. Henry is apt to be tender, when what she needs is a little brutality.

Beneath the table, she kicks off her slipper and touches her stockinged foot to his leg, eliciting a smile from her husband. Cecile, sitting beside Henry, begins to make conversation on the weather, speculating on how hot it might become. Pointedly, she turns her face to the window.

We've been discreet... or discreet enough, Maud thinks. *It's too tiresome to be always checking my behaviour, and with my own husband! Really, it will be as well when Cecile has a husband and home of her own.*

Most nights, Maud lies awake until late, watching Henry sleep, just as she knows he watches her in the morning. Exhausted by their love-making, his cock spent, and Maud's thighs damp with the evidence, his face is noble in repose, eyelids fluttering as he dreams.

She dreams too. Dreams of the living but, also, of the dead. Haunted by her past as severely as if the ghosts of the departed sat upon her bed. She'd wondered if the nightly presence of Henry might drive those ghosts a little further off. Perhaps, but not yet.

THEY TRAVEL SOUTH, to the marvels of Florence. After trips to Pisa and medieval Siena, their journey takes them onwards, to the attractions of Rome, and the sultry heat of Naples.

The summer has arrived in earnest, the midday heat obliging them to make early morning excursions to view glowering Vesuvio and the ruins of Pompeii.

They arrive in Sorrento on the late afternoon train, to a waiting carriage, sent by Maud's grandmother to collect them. They progress slowly, up the winding coastal path, under hanging trees, as the sun begins to relinquish its hold on the day, sinking reluctantly, that dusk may creep in its place. Cliffs loom above, as they climb, the rock face closing in as they travel higher.

The carriage continues through the dwindling light, navigating the twists of the road, which snake onwards, until their heads are nodding sleepily.

After some time, a jolt wakes Cecile. The moon has risen and, as it emerges through rolling, black clouds, she sees clearly, in the centre of the bay, the brooding silhouette of a castle, perched high upon an island of rock. Its jagged turrets are too numerous to count, but one dominates all, creating a pinnacle from which lights wink.

A strange pull tugs inside her, of exhilaration and dread, a force physical in its potency, as if something within those walls were calling to her, inviting her in.

Cecile looks down from the window, down the steep cliff face, down to the waves below. The sea stretches onwards, vast and inscrutable, yet, she feels the presence of something that has been waiting for her, all this time. Waiting for her to arrive.

As they clatter through the entrance to the Villa di Scogliera, home to Lady Agatha, the occupants of the carriage are thinking of welcoming beds and the pleasure of laying their heads on soft pillows.

The hour being late, the party are taken to their rooms. Cecile is ready to submit to sleep, and does little more than remove her outer travel clothing, laying herself down in her under chemise.

She drifts into dreams, of a dark tower, and a spiral staircase, and a voice calling to her. Of course, it's no more than the sound of the sea, swimming through the open shutters.

CONFIDENCES

What pleasure it is, after many weeks of travel, to find ourselves settled for a longer stay. Where trunks may be properly unpacked, and the body permitted to rest, without thought of which galleries must be toured, or which monuments admired.

More delightful still, when the location of our sojourn is as beautiful as the Villa di Scogliera, and our host requires nothing from us but that we allow our constitution to be revived. In this respect, the hospitality of Lady Agatha, Maud's grandmother, is exemplary.

Henry and Maud love her dearly, she knows, but, observing them, Agatha intuits Cecile has been too much in their company, for her own comfort, at least. Agatha's suggestion that they leave the love-birds to occupy Villa di Scogliera alone for some weeks is a most welcome suggestion.

She has arranged all with her nephew, Lorenzo, whose home, the ancient seat of the di Cavour dynasty, lies but four miles hence, standing upon a great outcrop, in the centre of the bay.

The Castello, and its Conte, are known not only to the humble villagers who provide victuals for its tables, and their sons and daughters to work in its grand halls. The Castello and its occupants are known to the grandest in the land, and beyond. Tales of the Castello di Scogliera reach the ears of noble families residing in the foothills of the Pyrenees, and those living in the shadow of the great Carpathians.

Perhaps because of this, few venture within its walls willingly.

Cecile has heard no such stories but, as Agatha's carriage clatters across the cobbles of the causeway, her heart's pace quickens. For here are towering turrets, the very same as whispered to her on the night of her arrival. Here is the imposing prominence, rising to dominate the bay and the simple fishing community of Scogliera. Here are the windows, dark and narrow, the panes of which catch the early morning sun. Glinting, like so many eyes, looking down upon those who approach.

Sitting beside her elderly companion, Cecile feels again that uncanny tug, somewhere beneath her ribcage, as if an invisible thread were attached there, drawing her, inevitably, closer.

They pass beneath a mighty arch, onwards, up a steep track, barely wide enough to admit them. The horses plod their ascent, through lush foliage, the wheels of the carriage skimming nodding lilies. Branches of oleander brush the roof.

At last, the path opens, and the horses stop before the great doors of the castle itself.

From here, so high above the waters of the bay, the Mediterranean stretches, a shimmering vision.

'*Benvenuto!*' calls a voice.

'*Mia cara!*' replies Agatha. '*Bello per vederti. Come va?*'

'*Molto bene grazie,*' answers the person emerging from the castle to welcome them.

Cecile stands shyly, but the dark-haired beauty wastes no time in embracing her, clasping her arms about Cecile as if they have known each other always.

'*Benvenuto, nuova amica.*'

'Oh! Good morning!' says Cecile. 'It's lovely to meet you. But I'm afraid I really don't speak Italian.'

'Ah!' exclaims the young woman, surveying Cecile with a twinkling eye. 'But now you are here, in our *bella Italia,* you will learn.'

'Really, Lucrezia! You must know that it's too forward to jump upon a new acquaintance,' berates Agatha. 'Cecile won't know what to make of you!'

'*Scusami,*' begs Lucrezia. 'You will learn Italian, Cecile, and perhaps I will learn manners.'

'Impossible girl!' says Agatha, giving her an admonishing smack upon the hand.

'I shall improve myself,' promises Lucrezia, bestowing Agatha with a kiss upon both cheeks. '*Adesso!* Let us go in, and take English tea.'

CECILE DECIDES that her room is by far the loveliest she's ever seen. There's a small sofa, upholstered in golden yellow damask, before the hearth, unlit on this warm day. Also, a lady's writing desk and chair.

Meanwhile, the bed is of dainty size, draped on all sides with muslin, upon which orchids are embroidered in violet thread. Carved into the pale wood are all manner of creatures. Frogs and beetles, moths and worms nestle between creeping ivy, curling about the bedposts.

'Like fingers about a lover's neck, yes?' says Lucrezia, her own hand tracing a tendril of ivy upon the polished surface.

Cecile nods in mute assent. What things Lucrezia says!

And how she dresses! Lucrezia's day-gown, like Cecile's, is made from fine white cotton, but the cut is far more daring, revealing the swell of her ample bosom. A design of interwoven snakes encircles her waist, created from tiny beads, in all shades of green.

'I sewed this belt myself,' says Lucrezia, proudly, seeing Cecile's eyes upon her costume. 'The serpent is an emblem of the di Cavours.' Her tongue flicks out, to touch her upper teeth, and she gives a playful hiss, laughing to see Cecile's startled expression.

'Do not worry, *mia cara*. I promise only to lead you into pleasant temptations.'

Blushing, Cecile turns away, not knowing what to say.

The room is not at all as she imagined it might be. There is nothing stark, or dingy; the dust and cobwebs of past generations do not hang from the bedstead. Rather, dazzling sun pushes through the window, the shutters of which have been folded back.

Below, she can see a terrace, and the slope of the garden, exquisitely lush, leading down, out of sight. Beyond is an expanse of blue, the water mirroring the undisturbed azure of the heavens.

From the pale-wash upon the wooden floors, to the white pillows and linens, a brightness fills the room. The walls too are painted white, though far from bare. A garden of butterflies, thick among bougainvillea, have been conjured upon them, fluttering beside berry-eating birds.

'Do you like my work?' asks Lucrezia, seeing Cecile admire the walls.

'It's marvellous!' exclaims Cecile. 'How clever you are!'

Cecile has spent many hours with a paintbrush and canvas, under the guiding eye of the art master, at the Beaulieu Academy for Ladies. Never has she created anything a fraction as magical.

'You should see the jungle in my room, with tigers! But this gentle garden I made for you.'

'It's the most beautiful gift,' says Cecile, and by some strange impulse, she traverses the few steps between them and gathers this dark-haired beauty in an embrace. One of gratitude, but something else too.

Who is the young woman standing before her? One obliged too much to keep her own company? One similarly frustrated, despite the luxuries with which she is surrounded? One who, though she may not know it even herself, seeks a soulmate, someone she can trust?

'Come,' says Lucrezia, 'Now we must show you a real Italian *giardino.*'

'WE HAVE SOMETHING IN COMMON, you and I,' says Lucretia, leading Cecile into the sunshine.

Skirts brushing dahlias as large as saucers, cheerful marigolds, and the fat heads of peonies, they descend from the upper terrace, following steps cut into the granite upon which the castle stands. Bees flit back and forth, dipping into brimming cups of pollen.

Cecile presses her handkerchief to her forehead; it's a blazing day, and she's forgotten to put on her hat. Fortunately, as the path winds down, they enter the shade of a pergola, tumbling with a profusion of egg-yolk honeysuckle, and clusters of wisteria, blooming in deepest violet.

'I'm sure we have many things in common,' Cecile replies. 'We must share the same dreams for the future: of discovering more about the world, exploring new places, and experiencing all the things we cannot yet imagine... and finding true love, of course, and our place in Society.'

She pauses to inhale the scent of a lush pink rose, unfurled to its full-blown beauty.

'Perhaps,' says Lucrezia, 'But I was thinking more of the past than the future. She pauses. 'Agatha told me that you lost your mother, long ago.'

Lucrezia stoops to pluck the head from a lily, resting the pollen-rich stamen against her chin, where it leaves a yellow powder stain.

'You lost your mother?' exclaims Cecile.

'She was one of Milan's most celebrated *Diva Operativa*,' Lucrezia answers. 'No one sang Violetta in Verdi's *La Traviata* better than she. The old Conte, Camillo, pursued her, and won her in all respects, though she was no more than a dalliance for him. By the time I was born, her heart was broken.'

Lucrezia's face is still. The story, though true, she knows, must be told with sufficient pathos. She keeps her gaze upon the lily in her hand, twirling it slowly as she speaks.

'She placed me in an orphanage, writing to Camillo to tell him of my whereabouts, then threw herself from the roof of La Scala.'

With these words, she lets the flower fall from her fingers. Cecile cries in horror.

'What a terrible story! Oh, Lucrezia!'

'Yes, and a lesson to all young women, I like to think,' adds Lucrezia, with brittle laughter. 'To his credit, my father paid generously enough to ensure that I was never ill-treated. Nevertheless, his interest extended no further than to read an annual report of my continued presence in the world.'

She allows herself a wry smile as they walk on.

'It was upon his death that Lorenzo sought me out, and brought me to live with him, though his mother, Isabella, was less than delighted.'

Cecile lays her hand upon Lucrezia's arm.

'When I think of her, my mother, I imagine that she's in another room.' Lucrezia pauses, pinching the underside of her wrist sufficiently to make her eyes water. 'A locked door separates us. Except that, one day…the door won't be locked anymore…'

The two stand in silence for a moment.

'And what of you, *mia amica?*' she asks, with an attempt at brightness, as Cecile supposes. 'Tell me of your mother.'

She beckons Cecile, and they emerge from the shade of the arbour into a flood of sunlight and a clear view out, over the sea. On all sides, there is an abundance of lavender and camomile, threaded with purple irises, and a profusion of wild garlic. Thyme pushes up between the flagstones. Piled in happy heaps and jumbles, soft and lush, the garden is perfect in its chaos.

The breeze is salt-scented, like a top note over the mixed fragrance of a thousand blooms.

'I was so young when she died, of influenza, that I don't recollect much about her. I do wonder what it would have been like if she'd lived, and my father, too. Perhaps, had they stayed here, with me, I'd have had a sister,' says Cecile.

Lucrezia, though curious, knows there are limits to how far she may politely probe. Cecile will tell her what is pertinent in her own time. Meanwhile, Lucrezia decides that diplomacy is the best strategy and the adoption of a tone of intimacy.

As if struck by a blinding notion, she declares.

'*Mia piccola*! We have been sent to one other! You and I shall be sisters!'

In this place, so bright and bursting with life, anything seems possible, and Cecile finds her heart leaping.

'You can't know, really, how I've longed for a sister,' she says, returning Lucrezia's enthusiasm. 'I thought, perhaps, that Maud might... but I can't seem to know her properly. She's generous and often great fun, but I don't think she ever tells me, truly, how she's feeling.'

'*Sì, mia sorella*,' replies Lucrezia, slipping her arm through Cecile's. 'We shall now call ourselves sisters. And we shall begin by telling each other all our secrets.'

'Oh! That won't take long at all. I've never had the opportunity to do much of anything that would warrant keeping a secret.'

'Whereas, I have a great many,' returns Lucrezia, offering Cecile a conspiratorial smile. 'But I shall be wary of frightening you off,' she teases, 'So don't expect to hear all of my misdemeanours.'

'Whatever you say,' answers Cecile, giving her arm a companionable squeeze. 'We've plenty of time to get to know one another. Of course, I shall forgive any wickedness you might reveal. I might even make some up, for myself, or you'll think me most dull.'

Lucrezia is obliged to turn her head, that her face may not betray her. How completely without guile the child is!

'I love the wildness of this garden,' proclaims Cecile. 'The wisteria, tumbling as it likes, and the roses, too. So much untamed beauty. I can hardly decide where to look first, and everything framed by this never-ending sky and the open waters stretching away.'

'You're exactly right,' agrees Lucrezia. 'It's free in a way that we are not. Perhaps that's why it inspires us.'

'Oh! I've a great many freedoms,' admits Cecile. 'My brother's very generous, and more forward-thinking than most men, I'm sure. In London, I attended meetings of the National Union of Women's Suffrage Societies, with Maud. Henry's a great believer in women having their own voice.'

'I'm delighted to hear it,' says Lucrezia. 'I fear we are not so far ahead, here, in Italy. A woman has no voice unless she is married, and then her voice is that of her husband, rather than herself.'

'I suppose it's always the way,' sighs Cecile, brushing her palm against a swathe of daisies, their faces filled with the sun. 'All husbands seem to want their wives to be obedient...'

'Even our clothes are designed to rein us in,' continues Lucrezia, giving the same daisies an irritable swat of her hand. 'As if our bodies were something to be feared and subjugated! Restrict the body and subdue the passions; that's what men say. We're corseted to control our chaos!'

They continue down, each set of steps leading to a lower terrace, past arches overgrown with wandering vines and trailing passion-flowers, and the sweet, thick breath of jasmine. The path tumbles with scarlet geraniums and blazing nasturtiums.

'We couldn't not wear them though, could we?' says Cecile. It's only half a question.

'Let's take a stand,' counters Lucrezia. 'Think how lovely it will be to just have your muslin chemise against your skin.

'It *is* hot,' admits Cecile.

They pass figs and the citrus-sharp tang of lemon trees, and branches laden with ripening cherries. Lucrezia twists a peach from its stem and takes a bite, letting the juice run down her chin.

'From tomorrow, no more corsets,' she announces.

Lucrezia imagines her constriction lifting already. Liberated not only from her tiresome stays but from the confinement of Lorenzo's power over her. Why should she not win the wager he has thrown down?

THEY HAVE sat for some time, perched on the smoothest of the rocks, petticoats tucked up, to dip their toes in the lapping waves. The tide is at its highest, and most still. A serene warmth embraces them.

'Do you ever sail from here?' asks Cecile.

'Sadly not. No boat can be launched, as the rocks sit jagged, not far beneath the water's surface.'

'Ah yes, a hidden danger,' says Cecile. 'Waiting to shipwreck the unwary.'

'Sì, mia piccolo,' says Lucrezia, quietly.

Having taken enough sun, they lie on the terrace above, tucked under the shade of an olive tree, eating peaches to slake their thirst.

Cecile cannot recall ever being as happy as she is now, lying on the grass, looking up at the underside of a swathe of poppies, the light revealing the veins within the petals.

This is what a garden must look like when it's consumed centuries of warmth, thinks Cecile. *It's nothing like the Castle of Otranto, or Udolpho. There's nothing sinister here. Only sunshine and happiness.*

As if in agreement, from behind, comes the sound of cheerful whistling, towards which Cecile twists her head.

Up above, someone has climbed an olive tree, to better cut a crossed branch... and perhaps to admire the view, which is particularly lovely on this summer's day.

'Who's that?' whispers Cecile, giving Lucrezia a nudge.

Lucrezia doesn't need to open her eyes to answer.

'Raphael. Our gardener; Piero, is really too old now to manage on his own. Raphael is his grandson,' she says, twitching a grass stem between her teeth. 'He's a great help here. He looks after Agatha's gardens, too. He's most obliging, and will do anything you ask. Anything at all...' murmurs Lucrezia.

'Well, that's jolly handy,' says Cecile. 'These gardens must need a lot of watering.'

'Yes, lots... Every day is ideal. Twice sometimes,' sighs Lucrezia, rolling on her side.

The two fall into quiet contemplation, although their thoughts do not, perhaps, follow quite the same path.

'You know,' says Lucrezia, raising herself upon her elbow, and choosing her next arrow with care. 'I do wonder what it must be like to be with a man.'

'Lucrezia!' exclaims Cecile, sitting up in surprise.

'Not Raphael of course,' adds her Italian friend, rolling once more upon her back. 'That wouldn't do at all, would it?'

'I should think not,' answers Cecile, although, from the corner of her eye, she is looking at the strong arms of that young man, who is wielding his saw with great mastery.

'I mean that I wonder what it must be like when you're married,' says Lucrezia.

'Well,' admits Cecile. 'I do know a little.'

'Do you truly, Cecile?' asks Lucrezia, giving her all her attention. 'Then, I must beg you to share your knowledge with me. It would shame me to admit the extent of my innocence.'

Cecile's eyes lower in modesty.

'I've heard that, when a wife embraces her husband, there's a little bell inside of her that starts to ring, just like the one inside a church tower,' says Cecile, 'But smaller of course.'

'A bell?' says Lucrezia, 'Well, I suppose anything's possible...'

She begins to laugh, which becomes a sneeze.

'*Scusami!* It's the pollen, *mia cara*. Only the pollen.'

'Oh!' says Cecile, 'Hang on, I've a handkerchief in my pocket. I found it in the drawer beside my bed. It may be a little dusty, I'm afraid. Perhaps it's one of yours?'

The linen, when Lucrezia unfolds it, bears an elaborately embroidered monogram of the letter 'L'.

'Ah yes,' she remarks. 'Possibly. Though the castle has seen many guests in its time. It could belong to… anyone.'

THE CURSE OF THE DI CAVOURS

'I hope you find yourself comfortable, Lady McCaulay,' the Conte enquires, as they sit to dine. 'And that our little piece of Italy agrees with you.'

'Oh yes! It's wonderfully peaceful here, and most kind of you to have me,' Cecile answers.

The Conte is older than his sister, but just as handsome, his

features pronounced, and carried in that manner which comes naturally to all of noble blood.

His waistcoat, of purple silk, embroidered in gold, and the
billowing sleeves of his shirt, like poured cream, would make a dandy
of him, but for the dark tunnel of his gaze. Lucrezia has changed into
a dress of scarlet hue, though her belt of emerald snakes is still about
her waist. Cecile suddenly feels her own gown, in palest apricot, to be
rather gauche.

Dishes of soup are laid before them, vibrantly orange. Tomato,
Cecile guesses, lifting her spoon.

'It's our delight to share our home with you,' adds Lucrezia,
passing Cecile butter for the warm bread rolls.

'I'm sure that I'll have far more fun with you, than with Maud and
Henry,' Cecile replies, passing on the butter to Agatha.

Under the Conte's penetrating eye, Cecile finds herself gushing,
saying what she will later find ridiculous.

'My brother will think of nothing but birds while we're in Italy.'

'Is that so!' Lucrezia laughs.

'Oh yes!' asserts Cecile, wishing now to explain herself. 'He took
me once on a trip to the Norfolk flats, near Cley, to see the curlew
sandpipers on their migratory path to warmer climes. I stood in the
briskest of winds, a mist of drizzle descending, while Henry peered
through field glasses for the longest time. He passed them to me at
intervals, with a look of suppressed ecstasy, indicating some remote
creature paddling through water.'

'His wife, I'm sure, can divert him to other pastimes,' muses
Lucrezia, her lips twitching.

The room falls quiet for a moment, in contemplative mastication,
before Lorenzo turns once more to his guest.

'We enjoy the isolated splendour of our island, but we sadly lack
many of the modern comforts of this age. We do without electricity,
we wrap ourselves against draughts, and live with floors which creak
as if we were at sea.'

Lorenzo shrugs in acceptance.

'However, the causeway is open for some hours each day, so you may venture into the village, though there is little there to amuse a young lady from London, I would think.'

'Please do call me Cecile, and I'm so pleased to be here. City life, while exciting in its way, is filled with multitudes of people. Here, I feel I can breathe, and that something special is waiting for me. Although, I admit, the castle looked intimidating when I saw it from afar, like Bluebeard's fortress, or Thornfield, except surrounded by water, rather than forest, or moors.'

Lucrezia smiles. 'And who is your Bluebeard? Who your Mr. Rochester?'

Seeing Cecile blush, Agatha pats her hand.

'She's only teasing, my dear. Castles such as this make everyone feel that way, as if there are secrets in the walls. Real life is not generally made of the stuff of sensational novels, but I fear this place, perched between civilisation and the vastness of Neptune's empire, has history enough to fuel an entire library of sordid tales.'

Lorenzo's eyes have been upon his knife, the pad of his thumb pressed lightly on the blade. He looks up; not at his aunt, but at Cecile.

'And would you wish to find danger here?

'No... no! Of course not,' says Cecile, her tongue too fat and clumsy for her mouth. *He must think me very silly*, she berates herself. She so wants him to find her other than a simpering schoolgirl.

A magnificent dish of hot spaghetti is brought to the table, steaming, and slippery with oil, and the Conte nods for a little more Chianti to be poured into Cecile's glass. His man, Serpico, does so without spilling a drop onto the crisp tablecloth, though, Cecile notices, he lingers perhaps a little too long over her shoulder.

'May I say how much I admire your costume, Lady Cecile. The floral decoration at your neckline is most becoming.'

Lorenzo makes no pretence of hiding the direction of his gaze, which rests upon the generous swell of her bosom beneath delicate fabric: shimmering lilac, trimmed with rosebuds.

'The flower is a symbol of awakening nature, of renewal, and youth,' remarks the Conte. 'In Japan, the cherry trees blossom for just one week of the year, inspiring admiration not only for their flowers' beauty but for their very transience. In beholding them, we're reminded of the brevity of human life, of our own fragility.'

'How fascinating,' replies Cecile, glad for the change of subject. 'Have you travelled to the Orient?'

'I have,' says Lorenzo, his eyes capturing those of his sister for a moment. 'Though the greatest mysteries, and joys, are often close at hand, rather than in places far abroad. The wisest among us appreciate what is right in front of them.'

At this, his gaze moves from Lucrezia, and fixes so intensely on Cecile that she is quite taken aback, unable to manifest a suitable response.

'My goodness, Cecile, you're feeling the full charm of my nephew this evening,' remarks Agatha. 'I hope you know enough of men to take such effusions of admiration with the pinch of salt they deserve — although it's true that you deserve the compliment.'

'*Brava*, Agatha,' declares Lucrezia. 'Cecile, I'm sure, is not so foolish as to believe every word she hears from men.'

She shoots Lorenzo a look of great smugness, but he continues, unabashed.

'My sister, as you see, is wearing scarlet: a colour which suits her well, representing the wilder aspects of her nature, and serving to warn the unwary. She is a work of human artifice, carefully cultivated, in ways you cannot imagine, while you, Cecile, are truly nature's creation, pure and simple.'

'I'm sure you're too harsh upon Lucrezia,' asserts Cecile. 'Meanwhile, I've no wish to be worshipped as anything other than I am.'

'How sensible you are, dear one,' agrees Lucrezia, giving her brother a sharp look. 'Men, I fear, are quite the opposite, wishing to be adored regardless of morals or prowess or intellect. It's enough, in their eyes, to be a man!'

'Now, children! No arguments, please. You'll spoil our enjoyment of Magdalena's cooking,' reprimands Agatha. 'Lorenzo, you must allow us to defend our sex and, in so doing, be somewhat hard upon yours.'

Lucrezia leans across the table to touch her wine glass against Agatha's, her eyes bright with mischief.

'You see, brother. You're outnumbered. We women are taught from birth to follow rules. To smile just enough, but not too much, to look a certain way, and behave a certain way. Really, you cannot be surprised that, on occasion, we rebel.'

'In that, dear sister, you seem to excel,' answers Lorenzo, retaining a tone of amusement rather than chagrin.

Cecile finds herself looking at him more closely. *He's old enough to be my father, except that, I'm certain my own father was nothing like the Conte.*

She has, before sleeping, let her thoughts wander to Lance, her Texan, from the train. If she has imagined anyone's arms about her, they have been his. Now, she feels the stirring of something different altogether. A feeling of dread and excitement as she looks at the Conte's thin lips, beneath his moustache, and the small, white, even teeth revealed to her in his half-smile.

She searches for some topic of conversation. Something to say that will make him look at her again. Except that, she now sees, he *is* looking at her, without her having said a word, and her own eyes, which should lower, in modesty, look back at him.

'Although,' adds Lucrezia. 'I recall, on his last birthday, my brother dressing as Marie Antoinette, chest hair curling above his bodice. How was that, brother? Did it enlighten you to the disposition of women, to be corseted, struggling for every breath, as society insists we must?'

'Indeed it did!' answers Lorenzo. 'I wouldn't for all the world be born a woman, knowing the indignities to which your sex is subject.'

Lucrezia leans towards Cecile, speaking in a confiding whisper. 'His skirts were lifted more times than the French Queen's ever were.'

'Really, Lucrezia!' admonishes Agatha, whose hearing is still acute. 'Too crude!'

Cecile is most shocked, but finds herself, nonetheless, disposed to giggle. She cannot meet Lucrezia's eye.

'Not that I disapprove of people having their fun,' adds Agatha. 'I had suitors enough in my time, and my husband was not the first man to kiss me, nor the last… A good lover can make you sing, even when you believe you have no more songs in you.'

'True enough,' remarks Lorenzo, 'Virtues carried to excess become vices, I believe.'

'The saddest part of aging is the setting aside of vices we no longer have the energy to pursue,' sighs Agatha. 'These days, I content myself with novels.'

'Ah, the cheese!' declares Lucrezia, as Violetta brings in a large platter. 'The grapes are from the vines in the garden, Cecile. And we have *formaggio di capra* — cheese from goat's milk. You must try some.'

'Indeed you must, Lady Cecile,' agrees the Conte. 'It's made to an ancient recipe, such as was enjoyed by my great-great grandfather, and probably long before that.'

'How long have your family lived here?' asks Cecile.

'The castle was built in the thirteenth century. The original cannon remains upon the roof, directed out to sea, through the battlements.'

'However,' his face takes on a sudden sternness, 'I advise that you do not venture there, since I believe the roof is no longer sound, and the tower staircase which leads to it is certainly dangerous. Several of the steps are crumbling. Better to avoid it altogether.'

'No one uses that staircase,' adds Lucrezia, for once in agreement with her brother. 'Far too gloomy, and full of dust and cobwebs. Cecile shall admire the sea from the garden. No need to make herself dizzy on the roof.'

'Besides which,' the Conte continues, pouring himself more port. 'There is the White Contessa, who walks the upper corridor by night, and climbs the tower.'

'A ghost?' exclaims Cecile.

'There are many, but she is the only one who haunts that part of the house. You may hear her, perhaps, in the dead of night, sobbing for her lover. Her husband had him flayed before her, then hung his body from the window of the tower room, a rope about his neck, his flesh for the gulls to peck.'

Oh! The horror! A strangled gasp escapes Cecile.

'It's said that the Contessa cursed him, and all males of the di Cavour line, before slicing her own wrists. She was found the next morning.'

Lucrezia dips her finger into the camembert upon her plate.

'Every time he recounts the tale, the details become more obscene. But, I suppose we must all be allowed our little fantasies.'

'The di Cavour blood is strong,' answers Lorenzo. 'Dark, and furious, and sublime.'

'And not without a hint of madness,' adds Lucrezia quietly.

'In the light, there is always some darkness,' he replies.

'No doubt, extended bachelorhood produces an excessive imagination, and a tendency to the morbid, Lorenzo,' chides Agatha.

'Perhaps that's part of the curse. I don't believe the di Cavour men ever find true love, or true happiness,' says Lucrezia, staring pointedly at her brother. 'Isabella would enlighten us further, I expect.'

'Least spoken on that subject is best,' suggests Agatha.

Lorenzo's face has grown pale, as if mention of the curse has touched some place of sensitivity.

'If Hell resides anywhere, it's in the dark recesses of the mind. Perhaps this is a curse all men suffer, to live under 'mind-forged manacles', as Blake writes in his verse.'

The candles upon the table have sunk low, but there is flame enough for Lorenzo to light a cigar.

'Forgive me, ladies. Let us retire. Serpico shall walk with me in the gardens. Evening is the most beautiful time, when the divine eye is half closed. The blooms are different, by night, their scent more intense, more vivid. The night, we might say, brings a clarity impossible in the blaze of day.'

The corners of the room flicker in shadow. The candles are guttering but what light there is illuminates Lorenzo, who is looking at Cecile, her blue eyes raised to him most prettily, her expression one of pleasing reverence.

'You never can tell who you'll meet by night. It's a different realm... one in which we may wear a different face.'

As the women leave, Lucrezia walking arm in arm with Cecile, Lorenzo watches.

His eye is upon Cecile's neck, where blonde wisps curl against the soft whiteness of her skin, and upon the slope of her exposed shoulder.

She is a canvas not merely unpainted, but newly stretched upon the frame, and his appetite, lacking of late, is awakened.

Perhaps, this conquest will offer more than amusement. Might he, in her, find a woman worthy of bearing the next generation of di Cavours?

In the dark hours, the cold fingers of mortality reach closer to him. Not yet, of course, but waiting. Waiting.

He recalls his father's skin, at the last, like the crust on cooling wax; his hands nobbled, age spots dappling the skin. Those hands, shaking as they held a glass. The hands of a dying creature, near bloodless, nails ridged and horny, pipe-yellowed. His eyes, clouded, caring no longer to see, nor his mind to remember.

Will he, Lorenzo, end this way? He has memories enough to keep him company, but they do not soothe him.

Cecile stands at her window, listening to the sounds of the night: the rhythmic song of friction-legged crickets and the throb of toads, above the rising tide. Moonbeams ripple across the olive grove, shivering the trees, and a tiny golden glow moves through the darkness. The glow of a cigar.

It's past midnight when she succumbs to sleep. The house is still, but for the scratching of mice, and the quarter-hour chime of the great clock.

There are footsteps beyond her door, and the knob turns, slowly, opening enough for fingertips to curl around the heavy oak. A face, pale, eyes intent, looks long upon the sleeping figure.

SHE AND HE

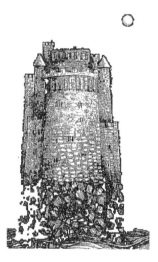

Beside him, Maud is still asleep, her eyelids trembling, as if thoughts trouble beneath them.

He pushes down the coverlet and takes the soft flesh of her exposed breast, finds her nipple with his mouth, squeezes it between tongue and teeth.

She twists towards him, sighs.

His cock is rigid, pressed to her belly, ready to slip into the ancient rhythms of skin on skin.

He lifts her leg, and guides his hardness between her lips. Cupping the underside of her buttocks, he draws her closer, driving through all that separates them, until there is no divide.

Even in sleep, she responds to his body, her pelvis tipping to his entry. His lips, against her ear, whisper his love, his promises.

She wakes with a gasp, like a swimmer breaking through the surface. Waking to the heat of his palms, pulling her onto his thrusts, his stubble grazing her neck. His hipbone grinding hers.

There is nowhere to go but within each other. No more he and she.

~

THE ROOM IS as she remembers it: the walls painted pale green, the bedspread patterned with oranges and lemons.

She watches as he dresses, pulling on his costume for bathing, towel over his shoulder.

'Come and join me,' he says. 'Come and swim.'

When he's gone, she seats herself at the dressing table. Her musical box is where she left it.

Someone is only dead when all who knew them are dead.

That's what people say.

The musical box plays still, although the hand that once turned the key is no longer here to do so, or to touch her forehead, or stroke her hair.

She always vowed not to be like the ballerina. Each time the lid is lifted, she's obliged to perform, to display the elegance of her pirouette. How often beauty conceals pain…

Of her father, Maud remembers less: his moustache brushing her cheek; the smell of pipe tobacco; her pressing of her palm against his, stretching her fingers in a childish attempt to align with that larger hand, warm against her own.

She was staying here when they set off, into the mountains; it was here she remained, since they didn't return. The desire to seek out danger must be in her blood. Climbing, after all, is a hazardous pursuit.

The pillowcase on the bed might be the very one upon which she shed her nightly tears.

She leans forward and mists the mirror with her breath. How quickly it lifts, and vanishes.

Folding back the shutters, Maud sits on the window seat. Henry has almost reached the cliff steps.

She raises her hand to wave, although his head is turned away, and he's too far away to see.

Someone else is close by though, someone whose back and arms are strong, and whose skin is dark from the scorch of the sun. Someone with soil beneath his fingernails.

He looks up, and she smiles.

PIETY ABOVE AND DEVILRY BELOW

The Conte, having consumed the last sliver of his crisped breakfast ham, dabs his lips.

'We should begin today by giving our guest a tour of the castello, should we not?'

Lucrezia inclines her head.

'Of course, brother. Though I hope you'll spare us from climbing every staircase. Cecile will better enjoy the sun and the open spaces of the garden than these gloomy corridors.'

'We shall see,' says the Conte. 'Too much sunshine is not good for the soul.'

They commence in the library, the windows of which face the open sea, illuminating books ranged from floor to ceiling.

Such strange titles, muses Cecile. The shelves in Henry's library are heavy with illustrated editions on birds, and collections of maps, beside works by the great poets and playwrights, and volumes of the ancient classics: Sophocles and Plato, Livy and Cicero. Here, the spines reveal English and Italian publications, and on such peculiar topics: *The Extraction of Toxins from Botanicals*; *Madness: a study in hereditary affliction*; and *The Art of Trepanation*.

Her eyes seek out what's familiar to her. There will be some poetry perhaps. Tennyson or Browning? Rossetti or Arnold? She finds them, at last, beside works by Manzoni and Carducci.

'*Goblin Market*, I think,' says Lorenzo, reaching above, to hand her a slim volume.

'Like pretty Laura, in the poem, you have gold enough upon your head. Enough to purchase whatever your heart desires.'

Standing close, he bends, lifting a stray lock of her hair, as if to inhale the scent. Blushing, Cecile steps to one side, tucking the errant curl behind her ear.

'Thank you,' she murmurs. 'Ms. Rossetti's verse is beautiful. I won a prize, long ago, for its recitation, at the Beaulieu Academy for Ladies. Sadly, I've mislaid my own copy. The illustrations in this edition are enchanting.'

'Ah yes,' says Lorenzo, 'They are by the great lady's brother, the infamous Dante Gabriel Rossetti. Such lips he draws, such eyes...'

The drawings are, indeed, sensual, causing Cecile to bow her head in modesty.

'I make a gift of this to you, fair Cecile. It will give me pleasure to think of it in your possession.'

To refuse would be discourteous, so Cecile accepts with a shy smile.

'You are too generous, but I thank you for it.'

Clutching the volume to her chest she walks on, stopping at a large, leather-bound edition, which lies open upon the desk.

'My Goodness! What *are* they doing? It looks dreadfully awkward!' remarks Cecile.

Lucrezia's hand moves to close the pages, and she glares at her brother.

'Don't be a prude, Lucrezia,' admonishes Lorenzo. 'Cecile is no schoolgirl. She may look if she wishes. My collection is at your disposal, Signorina McCaulay.'

'That's... very kind.' Cecile is determined not to betray her discomfort but is at a loss as to how best to respond.

The Conte's eyes follow where hers linger, as if to gauge her daring.

'Ignore my brother,' interrupts Lucrezia, folding Cecile's hand over her arm. 'He takes delight in provocation.'

'As you please,' he answers to their retreating backs. 'I judge no man, nor woman's, curiosity. Too many waste a lifetime justifying their own sins, while condemning those of others. An exhausting occupation.'

The carvings within the dark wood of the shelves are even more surprising to Cecile. Each narrow section depicts creatures she recognizes from mythology: the gorgon Medusa, and the multi-headed hydra, Cerberus guarding the gates of Hell, leaping satyrs and rearing centaurs. Twisting, eyes ablaze, hooves and hands and necks reach forward, as if to escape the confines of the wood. So many monsters and demons, and angels too, entwined in a Bacchanal, frozen in their macabre dance.

The ceiling, too, is intriguing: Cecile has never seen so much naked flesh, hands clutching, grasping, claiming. In the frescos of Florence's churches, and those of Rome and Venice, the faces of saints and sinners were contorted in similar states of agony and ecstasy. However, these are different; there's violence in them, and lascivious hunger.

'The theme is Zeus' seductions,' explains Lucrezia, seeing Cecile's upward gaze. 'Leda with the swan, and Europa carried off by Zeus as a white bull. So predictable! Men always the ravishers and we the ravished!'

Cecile opens her mouth to speak, but no words emerge.

THEY COME next to a long corridor, portraits spaced evenly along either side. Here is something more familiar: an extended acreage of ancestors, lined up for inspection. Or, perhaps, to inspect; faces stern and formidable look down from the frames. Cecile feels the lingering presence of those long-gone.

'This is our father,' says Lucrezia, indicating a handsome man, the very image of Lorenzo, with the same air of disdain and pride.

'Don't be fooled by his good looks, Cecile. Our eyes are not always to be trusted in leading our heart on the wisest path.'

'Nor, always, our ears,' adds Lorenzo, pointedly, coming to stand behind Cecile, so close that she feels his breath upon her neck. It's most uncomfortably disturbing, and yet she cannot bring herself to move. Lorenzo's hand touches briefly upon her waist and he moves past them, leading them onwards, along the passageway.

There is a series of the young Lorenzo: with his dogs, with his first horse, on Isabella's knee.

'And who's this?' asks Cecile, stopping at another portrait, recessed into an alcove. 'Is it you Lucrezia? But, it can't be. The expression is too sad, I suppose...'

Lucrezia eyebrows arch.

'My father sent money to the orphanage in which I was raised, but he never visited me. Sons born far from the marriage bed may find a place, but rarely daughters. I doubt he had any image of me, not even a sketch in a forgotten drawer.'

'We should remedy that,' says Lorenzo, appearing again at their side. 'A reclining nude, I think. You have a body worthy of immortalization, *mia sorella*... or so I would imagine...'

Lorenzo presses his finger to his lips, as if to still his laughter.

'*Diavolo!*' reprimands Lucrezia, giving him a forceful pinch upon the back of his hand. Cecile observes that it makes him wince, but he returns her look of concern with a wink.

'Have you any other siblings?' Cecile asks, thinking to divert the conversation.

'Probably, many.' Lorenzo shrugs. 'But I am the only legitimate heir.'

~

THE TOUR TAKES them next into the courtyard, within which stands a tiny chapel.

'How beautiful,' remarks Cecile, as they enter to a view of marble saints, clasp-handed. Above the altar, in stained-glass, Jesus stands in the desert, tempted by Satan, his face turned away in steadfast repose.

'It's remarkably tranquil. There's no sound of the sea here,' says Cecile. 'I suppose it must be the thickness of the walls.'

'Indeed,' says Lorenzo. 'There are many places in the Castello where all is not as it seems. As in life, piety above and devilry below!'

Cecile doesn't know what to make of Lorenzo's comment. Really, he says so many strange things.

Smiling at her puzzled expression, he moves to a heavy door, studded in iron, turning the key. It opens near silently, the hinges well-oiled for an ancient egress surely seldom used.

He makes a sweeping gesture.

'Follow me...'

A lantern sits nearby, and a box of long-stemmed matches. Lucrezia lights the wick.

Steps spiral down, taking them beneath the chapel, the flame casting a dull glow, swallowed by the darkness. Even with her hem lifted, Cecile fears she may trip and tumble. The air becomes still, subterranean dank, while the walls are damp to the touch. Her heels scrape stone, step by step, until they emerge into a space too large to be lit by the puny lamp. From somewhere beyond, there is a subdued, rushing sound, as of water moving.

The cold creeps over Cecile, in her flimsy muslin gown.

'We're almost level with the sea,' explains Lucrezia. 'The tide is coming in.'

There are other sounds too. Squeaks in the shadows, and the scratching scamper of small feet.

'Our crypt,' declares Lorenzo, his voice resonating. He leads onwards, his lamp illuminating the hard edges of tombs, until the room narrows, and ends at solid wall.

Lorenzo raises the lantern, passing it slowly over what hangs there: iron hooks and tethers, leather straps and chains.

'And what do you think happened here, sweet Cecile?'

He lifts her palm to the dank wall, holding it there with his own, his skin warm and dry, pressed to the back of her hand. She stands immobile, as if her arm and hand were no longer part of her, and she were only observing them. And then, her hand is passed through cold metal, a circlet closed about her wrist. Her breath stops with the heavy clunk of the bolt through the cuff's clasp.

'You're a captive of the crypt, now,' says Lorenzo. 'No one will find you.'

His words drop, one by one. 'Scream... and no one... will hear you.'

In the velvet dark, Cecile feels his fingertips brush her collarbone, and quivers, in the uncertain space between fear and yearning.

Would his single hand span my throat? What if his fingers were to move lower? How quickly would he reach beneath the bodice of my dress? His hands on my skin, his mouth, his tongue...

Cecile's head is spinning. She has entertained such thoughts, reading to candlelight, covers clutched to her chin. Never before have they come to life so vividly in the presence of a man.

Can he tell what I'm thinking? It's as if he sees to some secret place, thinks Cecile. *And has God seen my thoughts? Doesn't he see everything?*

Lorenzo's voice is no more than a murmur, so that Cecile almost wonders if her own mind is conjuring the words.

'Can you hear them? Those who were manacled?'

His breath is on her cheek.

'…and stripped?'

His lips brush her ear.

'…and beaten?'

'Really, brother!' declares Lucrezia, her voice awakening Cecile from her strange reverie.

Lorenzo's face, shadow-flung by the dim light, smiles, thin-lipped, eyes half-closed, as if in his own trance.

'What fierce horrors! Have I frightened you? Do you strain and protest to be freed? Perhaps you're less reluctant than you imagine.'

'Pure wishful thinking!' says Lucrezia, freeing the weight from Cecile's wrist and rubbing where the metal has left its mark. 'Poor Cecile will pack her bags and leave us!'

She leads Cecile back, past the mouldering remains of ancestors, and spiders scuttering, until their eyes see the staircase once more.

Lucrezia has not thought to see Cecile so easily brought under her brother's spell. She will, she realizes, need a more direct approach in claiming Cecile's affections, and allegiance, for her own.

SECRETS

Cecile closes her book.

She still thrills to read of Dracula's visitation of Lucy, making her, night by night, his blood-bride, visiting her bedroom while mortals sleep, to suck forth her soul. And, at last, transformed, his willing victim rises from her grave, beautiful in her undead state, driven by lusts no living woman may speak of.

It's the fourth time she has read the tale but, tonight, she cannot concentrate.

Her thoughts are not here, on the page, but deep beneath the castle. Her body is warm beneath the covers, while the di Cavours lie in cold splendour, in their ancestral tomb.

All must die, of course, but Cecile is too young, and her pulse too strong, to envision her own end. How can flesh so alive imagine itself dead. Impossible!

∾

THERE IS a creak beyond the door, and a gentle knock, as of one who does not wish to disturb the sleeping house.

Cecile pulls the covers a little tighter to her chin.

The knock comes again, louder this time.

'Mia cara,' whispers a soft voice. 'It's me! Are you awake?'

Cecile watches as the handle turns, and the door inches open.

A white-gowned figure enters, hair dark about her face. Not Lucy or Mina, nor Dracula himself, but Lucrezia!

'You *are* awake!' she says, closing the door behind her. 'Quickly, make room for me, it's too chilly to stand about.'

She pulls the drapes around the bed, against the draught, and wriggles beneath the embroidered quilt. Her icy toes touch those of Cecile, making her start.

'How jumpy you are!' declares Lucrezia.

She sees the closed book, still upon the coverlet.

'Ah! No wonder!'

Lucrezia gives Cecile a smile.

'Are you not glad to see me?'

Cecile shuffles a little closer.

'Of course,' she answers. 'I wasn't expecting you, but I'm glad you're here.'

'I knew you would be,' asserts Lucrezia. 'We're sisters now, and sisters share everything.'

She picks up the book and settles it on the night-stand, smoothing the quilt, and nudging closer to Cecile.

'You remember, in the garden, I told you I'd share my secrets... ,' says Lucrezia.

Her fingers steal to find Cecile's.

'Earlier today, you thought the portrait in the long gallery might be me.'

'And who is it?' asks Cecile. 'Not your mother?'

'No, not her,' concedes Lucrezia. 'Another, whose story is more tragic by far than that of my mother... though her story is sad enough.'

Cecile gives Lucrezia's hand an encouraging squeeze.

'A girl was born to the family before Lorenzo: Livia, older than him by two years. You recall the handkerchief you gave me? It was one she'd embroidered, with her own initial.'

Cecile's face displays every bit of the curiosity Lucrezia has anticipated.

'This was once her chamber.'

Cecile sits up in alarm.

'She slept here... in this bed?'

Lucrezia nods.

Cecile draws back, as if the mysterious Livia might appear suddenly, her head on the pillows, beside them.

'I hope she won't mind, wherever she is now, that I'm occupying her room.'

'She's in a place where I doubt she minds much about anything,' whispers Lucrezia, dropping her voice to a more confiding whisper.

'She was never happy... I'm told. Never a happy child.'

Lucrezia hesitates.

'She became unwell, increasingly subject to fits of violence, her mind distracted.'

'How awful!'

'Awful, as you say, but some people are not born to happiness.'

'She was troubled from an early age?' says Cecile.

Lucrezia lowers her eyes.

'Trouble visited her in the night, and she was unable to escape it, until her own mind chose to escape through a tangled garden of madness.'

The hairs upon Cecile's arms prickle with horror.

'She's a warning to us,' says Lucrezia. 'That the act of love is not always sacred, and not always desirable.'

Her voice is barely a murmur.

'She was sent away... to an asylum, Lorenzo tells me. They discovered, soon after her arrival, that she was with child.'

'Oh!' exclaims Cecile. 'But, but...' Her modesty makes her reluctant to form the words. 'She wasn't married!'

'Indeed not,' says Lucrezia.

'What happened?' asks Cecile, her eyes wide.

'Apparently, she lost the child, and her own death followed soon after. A blessing, we might say.'

The two fall into reflective silence, but Lucrezia glances up through her lashes, to look at Cecile.

Such an innocent, she thinks.

'We'd never wish to fall into trouble, would we?' asserts Lucrezia, her voice firmer now.

'Never,' agrees Cecile.

'Men see our virginity as a prize, and they wish to conquer it. So, we must resist,' adds Lucrezia.

'Absolutely,' Cecile agrees.

Even to Lucrezia, she dares not reveal the thoughts which come to her by night, as she dreams, and those which bear down upon her as she reads.

'Do you want to know what happens? When a man and woman lie together?' asks Lucrezia. 'I've been talking with Magdalena, and she's told me everything...'

'Really?' asks Cecile.

'Oh, yes!' answers Lucrezia. 'And it's most shocking! Close your eyes, and I'll tell you, as best I can, of what happens to brides on their wedding night. Then, you shall know, and be prepared, and if a man who is not your husband attempts to seduce you, you shall know straight away, and be armed to rebuff him.'

Lucrezia's voice is soft as she relates the journey of skin upon skin, and flesh within flesh, and the words take on a rhythm of their own. Cecile keeps her eyes shut tight and, beneath the quilt, her hand creeps low.

No details are spared in Lucrezia's telling of the tale. Cecile feels the weight of the words, pushing and pressing upon her, as if the power of them would enter her. She shifts beneath the covers, her fingers between her legs.

Imagine! She thinks. *Just imagine!*

Lucrezia smiles to see her bite her lip, to catch her breath and gasp.

Later, when sleep comes, Lucrezia's hand rests upon that of her English friend, Lady Cecile McCaulay.

BIRDS AND BEES

Maud has been in the clifftop garden of the villa since late afternoon, bathed in the ruddy golden light of Italian summer. She's observing the slow buzz of dragonflies, gossamer wings catching the light. On the baked rocks, lizards sun themselves, until the shadow of a bird causes them to dart for cover. It would be too warm for comfort, but that the breeze likes to play in such high places, lifting petals from their blossomed bowers and shivering the leaves, leaving its whisper as it passes.

Today is one of many days on which she has recorded not only the variety of life crawling in the dust, but upon the trunks of olive and fig trees, and within the curtains of bougainvillea and jasmine.

As in London, she observes where eggs are laid, and how emerging maggots chew and wriggle. She has sought the ordering principles of trailing ants, as they work together, using their feelers to pass messages as they forage, and their collective strength to claim fallen fruit.

The hours have passed in note-taking and sketching, doing her best, with water-colour paints, to capture the iridescent shine of blue-backed beetles and the flaunted flare of caterpillars, blazed in yellow, lime and crimson. She has captured every dazzling pattern.

There are yet a million unexplored places, and unnumbered creatures, their habits unknown to her. How far, she thinks, do they act from instinct, and how far from intelligence, from learning: the termites designing their mound, and the wasps their nest, each with its intricate geometry. Not to mention the bees' endless obsession with the hexagon.

Beside her, Henry sketches tiny finches and White Wagtails, remarking on their gleaming plumage and jaunty tail feathers, recording, by means of his own onomatopoeic shorthand, their airborne melodies. Beneath their glorious top notes, are the hums and clicks of Maud's realm of study.

She's reached into the wells of lilies, to pluck out flexing earwigs and bent to look under the shading leaves of succulent aloe plants. So many plants offer shelter, as if their residents had a hand in the almighty design, requesting the necessary corridors and chambers.

As she stretches out, peering at the veined petals from below, attempting to see the world through those insectile eyes, her body is heavy with sunshine, and the drowsy, contented slumberous stillness that comes from having lain long in the warmth.

Legs bare, shoes set aside, underthings rolled up and folded — it's glorious to feel the sun upon her skin, the prickle of the grass against her ankle, her heel, her toes.

Buzzing insects land upon the fabric of her skirt, attracted by the bright colours of its floral sprig.

Henry has long since put aside his notepad. He lies, long and lean, next to her, shirt-sleeves pushed up, to reveal his lightly-haired fore-arm, cast over his face, to shade his eyes. His hand rests, upwards, on his cheek.

She can smell his perspiration, and her own.

She'd thought he was asleep, but he shifts, and turns his head. He watches as her fingers unfasten the small buttons of her blouse.

'Here,' she whispers, lying on her side.

She takes his hand, draws it inside her blouse, inside the under-chemise, his palm to her full flesh. As their lips and tongues meet, he reaches for her nipple, soft between his fingers, then tight and hard, each squeeze sending the familiar, warm ache to her cunt.

He raises her skirt, bunching it behind her waist, exposing not only the length of her leg, but the abundant hair between her legs. His hand is warm, running up the back of her thigh, to the delicate skin beneath the curve of her buttock.

Her cunt is wet with yearning for him, pressed to the bulge of his trousers. Raising her leg, she invites him to free himself, to guide the fatness of his erection into her, and he groans as he pulls her onto his groin. She likes the roughness of the fabric against her nakedness, the scrape of his buttons against her lower belly, the constriction of his clothing, and hers, which must be overcome.

Henry moves over her, and she opens herself to the weight of his body. He draws down her chemise fully, to expose both her breasts, his mouth finding them, sucking hard, to make her cry out.

She never asks him to stop.

Instead, she says, 'More.'

He frees himself fully from his trousers, baring his buttocks, in their clench and thrust.

They writhe, limbs entwined, sweat-mingled, as if she were of his rib and, with relentless intent, wished to fuse again with her Adam.

She rises to meet him, and the world contracts to mouth and tongue and hips.

VISIONS BY NIGHT

What dreams Cecile has!

Like Jonathan Harker, in the book she has read so many times since Maud gave it to her in Paris, she is a prisoner of the castle, her innocence the meal upon which her captor preys.

Each night, she wakes, her skin clammy, her heart threatening to break from her chest, recalling visions of a creature dark and threatening: a creature which scales the sheer granite beneath her window, to enter her room.

No matter that she secures the latch and the shutters in her waking state. When she feels the presence of her demonic visitor, she rises, mesmerized, to welcome him, opening to his embraces.

Though she may retreat to her bed, recoiling from the hunger in his eyes, there is no escape.

Hand by hand, he crawls up the coverlet, peeling it back, to expose her, shivering in her nightgown. His nails are long, and fingers slender, about her ankle, and then her shin, upwards, past her knee.

Each night, these dreams grow more vivid. The beastly hand taking further liberties with her body, finding the fur between her legs, stroking it, until, like a cat relaxing under the caress of its master, her legs fall to either side, revealing her inner self to that creature's hand.

She has felt the wicked talon extend, to enter the velvet chamber of her womanly self, as if to draw forth some secret truth. And, all the while, those mocking eyes blaze. She has woken with her own hand upon her sex, her own finger buried in the place no lady should speak of.

What power does Castillo di Scogliera exert over her in those sleeping hours, that it moves her to so debase herself? From what place in her imagination does this creature emerge, to paw and seduce her body, to thrill and terrify her?

She hears it breathing.

And, in those first moments of waking, she remembers whose face it is that looks upon her, who sees beneath her skin. It is the face of one who sleeps within the castle walls.

ON ONE SUCH NIGHT, she rises from her bed, lighting the stub of her candle, determined to shake this disturbing spectre, venturing to the kitchen, where jugs of fresh milk sit on the cool pantry shelf, alongside Magdalena's peach tart.

Passing through the great hall, the clock chimes the half hour past midnight. The doors to the ballroom are flung wide, revealing the floor of gleaming black marble.

The room is still, but the echoes of the past are calling to her. As the clouds part, a silver crescent shines through the windows and she sees herself in a dress of billowing purple, dancing across that dark-water surface, spiralling on turbulent waters, on an expanse midnight deep.

It is then the door at the other end of the room opens and a tall, silver-haired figure enters, his hand clasped firmly about the arm of Vittoria. Cecile does not yet know the name of every maid in this vast dwelling on its granite island, served by so many silent feet and nimble hands, but Vittoria has the charge of Cecile's wardrobe. It is she who launders and presses the delicate muslins and silks worn by Lucrezia and Cecile. It is she who heats water for Cecile's bath, and places a warming pan in the bed. Her dark head, its hair plaited and pinned, is now almost as familiar to Cecile as her own.

There is a large cabinet at the side of the room, behind which Cecile crouches, blowing out her candle. Though she understands little Italian, it's obvious that Vittoria is being admonished. The Conte's voice has a hard edge that has not been previously revealed in Cecile's presence.

Vittoria's sobbing rises, imploring, and someone falls against a table. A vase topples from its placement, smashing upon the marble floor.

Cecile leans forward to look, hardly caring now if she's seen. No servant should be disciplined by force, she feels, no matter their misdemeanour. Lorenzo's behaviour is unpardonable.

However, the commotion has ceased. In fact, there is no sound at all from the far end of the room. As Cecile looks, she does not see Vittoria prostrate upon the floor, picking up pieces of broken glass, nor Lorenzo towering above her, his hand raised to strike.

Instead, to Cecile's astonishment, Vittoria's face is upturned to her master, and his lowers in a kiss. Moreover, his hands do not rest lightly upon her shoulders or back, or clasp her about the waist. They grasp at the fleshiest part of her, through her skirts, and Vittoria, far from objecting, appears to sanction this liberty, her own hands reaching brazenly to the Conte's neck, drawing his mouth closer to her own.

Cecile is unable to look away.

Whatever argument there has been is clearly mended, and whatever relationship exists between the two, it is far beyond her comprehension.

As she watches, the Conte drops to his knees and reaches beneath Vittoria's skirts, drawing down her bloomers.

These she steps out of and, as Lorenzo takes a seat, he lifts her dress, and bends her over his knee, legs slightly parted, the pale orbs of her buttocks displayed.

What dissolution is this! More indecent than any Cecile has conjured in her dreams.

The Conte raises his hand, holding it aloft for a moment, before descending with unforeseen force, delivering a crack upon the waiting cheek.

Vittoria cries out and Cecile's conscience insists that she intervene, it being impossible that Vittoria should consent to such humiliation and ill-treatment.

But, as a further smack reaches its target, and another, Vittoria's cries no longer speak of pain but of some other need, some desire which Cecile half recognizes.

Vittoria squirms but makes no attempt to extricate herself. Her voice beseeching, Cecile senses, not for her punishment to end, but for something else to begin.

The Conte ignores these supplications, continuing the ruthless dispatch of his hand. Vittoria's bottom has grown pink beneath his fierce ministrations, her voice fainter in its pleading, as if in acceptance of whatever Lorenzo should choose to deliver upon her.

Cecile is transfixed, her mind telling her that she should depart, that the scene unfolding here is not for her eyes. Her body, meanwhile, refuses to obey her.

All grows quiet again; the Conte's hand no longer raised in

savagery, but resting between the cheeks he has so harshly assaulted. That hand, moving between the lady's parted legs, his voice murmuring to her, in measured tones.

If Cecile were to know the actual words spoken by that gentleman, she would blush indeed.

Vittoria, meanwhile, has ceased all sign of struggle, and the sounds which emerge from her are the sighs and gentle moans of a woman desiring more, rather than less.

Lightheaded with all that she has heard, and beheld, Cecile resolves that she must return to her room. For her to remain is unconscionable.

She is unsteady as she rises from her crouching position, and casts one final glance at the dissolute scene. The Conte is no longer looking at the ample bottom provided for his amusement, but to the opposite end of the ballroom, where the illumination of the moon betrays Cecile's flushed face.

To that young lady's dread dismay, he smiles, and, to her shame, she knows, without the slightest doubt, that he has been aware of her presence long before she stood.

SHAME

'What a sight you are!' exclaims Lucrezia, taking a bite of her breakfast roll. 'Have you not slept any winks?'

Cecile does her best to summon a smile but she's too weary to appear cheerful.

'Something is bothering you, *mia cara*.'

Pouring coffee from the pot, Lucrezia adds cream and sugar.

Cecile so much wishes to confide, but what should she say, and where should she begin?

'Tell me,' urges Lucrezia, putting aside her own cup. 'I am your friend. I will help.'

Cecile takes a sip of coffee. The sweet warmth is a comfort.

'I woke from a... disturbing dream, and wanted to distract myself, so I came downstairs,' Cecile begins. 'And then...'

'I hear you, *piccola colomba*.'

'I saw something...'

'Ah...' says Lucrezia, nodding her encouragement, her nail tapping against her tooth.

'Something I shouldn't have seen...'

At just that moment, there is a knock upon the door and a tray enters, of steaming eggs and slices of cured ham.

It is Vittoria who carries the tray, placing it carefully at one end of the table.

Cecile feels a sudden constriction in her throat.

As Vittoria glances up, Cecile observes something familiar to her. She is reminded of Maud, as she has seen her sometimes, in the morning, with a look of serene satisfaction about her. As Cecile looks at Vittoria, there is no shame, only slight surprise at being so scrutinized. The shame, rather than being Vittoria's, is perhaps Cecile's own.

'*Scuzi, signore,*' says the young girl, bobbing her curtsey.

When Cecile lifts her cup, she finds that her hands are shaking.

'I believe I can guess,' says Lucrezia, her own eyes upon this fleeting exchange. 'Say nothing more, *mia cara*. I know my brother, and his fondness for the young women in his service. Vittoria has not been long with us. She is a novelty to him.'

Lucrezia spreads jam thickly upon her roll.

'He's no worse than most men. We women must keep our wits about us. Don't judge him too harshly, but don't trust him either.'

Cecile nods mutely.

One question preys upon her mind.

Can I trust myself?

SURRENDER

Henry's feet are bare on the grass, the dew wet and cool between his toes.

The summer house, Maud had written, the note delivered on the tray, with his customary glass of whisky, taken before bed.

The moon is alive. Not hazy or softened by passing clouds but dazzling, bright. Henry follows, through the garden, through the fragrance of ghost-white, smoke-sweet lilies.

Other feet have trodden here; other hands than his have brushed the half-closed blooms.

He hears their voices, before reaching the final bend in the path. They are inside, but the doors have been left wide. Maud sits upon the edge of the table, legs parted. A dark head is between them, his hands holding her bunched skirts on either side. Kneeling, he is rousing her to the final movement of her song.

When her gasps ebb, Raphael rises, lips wet with her pleasure.

Seeing Henry, he unbuttons his shirt.

For what does our human soul hunger but beauty? Raphael's is carved from daily labour, his abdomen hard against Henry's palm, hard beneath the waistband, hard, down to the silken curls and thickened cock. When Raphael's trousers drop, Henry's mouth opens, to consume all that he is himself.

Maud unfolds a lounge chair and reclines, her eyes half-closed, but watching. Henry looks back at her, at his Mademoiselle Noire. The stage is his tonight.

Beauty is in every act that shows us how vividly we live. We are born from the substance of this world, and we yield to it when we die. And, between, there is flesh and pleasure.

Raphael's mouth meets his own, with kisses ginger-sweet. Kisses rough and hands rougher, pressing Henry to the floor, his hands unfastening Henry's trousers. Raphael's weight bearing down. Belly to back.

Day has surrendered to the liquid of the night.

Surrender, thinks Henry. *I want to surrender.*

His body accepts Raphael's teeth and tongue, Raphael's hands, Raphael's cock. One body, slick with sweat, they slide into one another.

∼

THE NIGHT IS MADE from stars, as much as from the darkness. They look down from above, their eyes glittering, watching as Maud watches, and someone else too. There is another pair of eyes, unseen. The eyes of one who will report to his master.

WARNINGS

I
t's early when Cecile knocks on Agatha's door, but that lady has been long awake. She finds her sitting at her dressing table, brushing out her soft, silver hair.

'Does Isabella still dye hers that improbable shade of blue?' asks Agatha, plaiting the length, before coiling it in place.

'Lilac,' answers Cecile, with a small smile. 'It suits her, I think.'

'Of course, my dear.'

Agatha pinches her cheek. 'What a kind girl you are. Now, come and sit with me, and tell me what's bothering you.'

What a relief it is for Cecile to be guided to the sofa, to sink into its soft cushions. Agatha strokes the faded green brocade.

'I remember sitting on this seat, years ago, when Isabella was newly married and I came from London, to visit. We met during our year of coming out, and I'd danced and chatted with Robert, her older brother, at various balls and other events that season. However, it was at Isabella's wedding that we fell in love. How could we not, in such a place, under the Mediterranean sun?'

Cecile smiles. It's the sort of romance she's always dreamt of for herself.

'We can have anything our heart desires. The tricky thing is determining what that is exactly. Are you having trouble deciding, Cecile?'

She does not trust herself to speak, but Agatha seems to sense, at least in part, the anxieties of love.

'I knew Lorenzo's father well. What poor Isabella endured! He was a reprobate and a gambler, and a seducer of women. Look at our young Lucrezia, born of his affair with that Milanese singer.'

Agatha gives a sniff of disapproval.

'Talented she may have been, but no good sense at all, abandoning her baby and throwing herself from the roof of the opera house! It's the stuff of those Penny Dreadfuls!'

Cecile wonders, faced with the same situation, how she would behave. The thought of such a thing brings a flux of bile to her throat.

'The old Conte paid to house Lucrezia in a place for… unwanted children, and she was conveniently kept away from polite society,' continues Agatha.

Cecile shifts in her seat, uncomfortable in discussing the details of Lucrezia's upbringing. Though, she knows that her new friend would care not a jot. It's one of the things Cecile most admires about Lucrezia: that she rises above the commonplace need for approbation.

'I must warn you,' Agatha adds, 'Lorenzo has followed the same path of riotousness as his father before him. He's charming, of course, when he chooses to be. Enough women have fallen at his feet. Some even fool themselves into thinking him besotted.'

Cecile picks at the embroidery on a cushion.

'Still, we must give credit where it's due,' concedes Agatha. 'Lorenzo took up Lucrezia's guardianship on his father's death, and has kept her close ever since. She's become quite a lady. One would never guess...'

She gives Cecile's hand an affectionate squeeze.

'It's best to know something of the world, my dear, and navigate it wisely. Young women are too often brought up with their heads in the clouds.'

'Are all men like this?' asks Cecile.

Agatha hesitates to answer.

'Not all,' she replies. 'Maud tells me that Henry worships her. A true love match, it seems.'

'Yes,' agrees Cecile, remembering her many hours alone on their travels through Europe. 'Maud understands Henry, better than me, I sometimes think. She makes him happy, at least.'

Agatha is right, that she has much to learn. Cecile shall begin by taking up Kipling's *Indian Tales*.

They're written by a man so they must have some wisdom to impart, she decides.

Moreover, they appeal to her desire to know of foreign places. Above all, she has set her heart on understanding more, feeling she knows so little.

TODAY, Lucrezia has decided they are to have a breakfast picnic. She sends a note to Cecile's room, instructing her to come to the second terrace, where a table has been set. 'No corset!' she has written in her large, looping hand.

'How comfortable you look,' says Lucrezia, when Cecile appears in her muslin dress, descending the steps with evident ease. 'Now, you may eat as many pancakes as you like, warm from the griddle. Nothing to hinder you!'

She passes the honey, having poured it liberally onto her own plate.

In the bold sunshine, the events of the night seem but phantasms. Cecile determines to put her schoolgirl silliness behind her. Her imagination has been unruly, and she has invented absurdities.

Still, she cannot help but probe a little. Lucrezia will know, surely, who it is that so startled Cecile. The servants cannot all be in the habit of midnight-wandering, scratching at doors.

'Ah yes,' replies Lucrezia, spooning the last of the fig compote from the jar, directly into her mouth. 'There is nothing to worry over, my Cecile. It is only Vittoria. She sleepwalks, and is apt to much strange behaviour.'

'Still,' she adds, with more seriousness, 'It's better not to disturb such people when they wake in the night. Keep your door locked, and ignore whatever you hear. Doors are best locked in this castle anyway. My brother is fond of the company of young women, and the temptation of your unlatched door may be too much for him. Do not allow yourself to become his plaything, Cecile. Remember, if you will, the fate of my mother. Remember, poor Livia...'

Really, thinks Lucrezia, taking up a peach, and a knife to peel it with, *if she chooses to ignore me, she deserves all that falls upon her head!*

However, Cecile readily gives her assurance. She is yet to decide how she feels about the Conte. His passion is flattering, but she must be the stronger party in this question of propriety. Perhaps, this is how it is with all men, before they accept the soothing regularity of the wedded state. How can she judge?

It would not be unpleasant to call myself a countess, muses Cecile, *and to be mistress of this garden, and the castle. I could travel, seeing countries I know only from the atlas. And, once wed, would he not give up his flirtations? Surely, I would be enough, as his bride...*

For a moment, she is no longer sitting at her breakfast but is in her marriage bed. Something within her thrills to the thought.

'I was speaking to Agatha, earlier,' admits Cecile, 'She told me that I shouldn't fall in love too easily.'

'You're not in love at all, I should hope,' says Lucrezia, looking quite stern. 'For you to consider the overtures of my brother is one sort of foolishness. For you to believe yourself in love, or that he is in love with you, is quite another.'

Cecile isn't sure what she's feeling. Not love, no... Something else. Perhaps it doesn't matter. The one thing she could not bear would be to marry a man who bored her. Lorenzo, whatever his faults, does not weary her with dull conversation.

'People marry for other reasons than love, don't they?' says Cecile, feeling the remark to be such as a woman of the world might make. 'Besides which, if I were to marry him, you and I would truly be sisters, together always.'

'This I would dearly love,' answers Lucrezia, 'Though it would be a high price to pay, I fear. When daylight ends and night has not yet fallen, you cannot tell a dog from a wolf. Be careful, my Cecile, for you are looking into the twilight, and in pursuing my brother, you would have not the faithful dog about your skirts, but the greediest of wolves.'

'Agatha said much the same to me,' admits Cecile. 'As my chaper-one, she's keeping her eye on me, as Henry told her to, I suppose.'

'She's a funny bird, I think you say,' replies Lucrezia, rising from the table, and beckoning Cecile to follow. They stand where the terrace falls away, admiring the unhindered view of the sea beyond. 'Have you seen her photographs? All of the dead people of her youth: writers, artists and musicians. I wonder, sometimes, if any were her lovers.'

'Lucrezia!' admonishes Cecile. 'Even if you think such things, you shouldn't say them.'

The warm breeze is delightful, lifting the delicate fabric of their dresses, to billow behind. Cecile feels the strength of her body, standing in resistance to the moving air. How marvellous it is to have only the muslin against her skin, and to relax into the natural rhythm of breathing, without the constriction of whalebone stays.

'Nonsense,' smirks Lucrezia. 'I see Agatha, as Flaubert says, her 'dry bones quivering with joy' at the remembrance of passion past. At least, I hope it's so. How sad it would be to reach such an age and have no memories to call upon.'

'Well, perhaps...' concedes Cecile. 'But there must be more to look back on than love affairs. There are all sorts of things I want to do, besides...' she is unsure quite how to end the sentence.

'In this, we agree, *mia piccola*,' declares Lucrezia, taking Cecile's hand. 'We shall know our own value, and we shall make our own happiness, without relying upon a husband, or any man. And, we shall do whatever is necessary to gain such independence.'

Cecile laughs. Lucrezia's wild declarations, outrageous as they are, fill her with a surge of excitement.

Whatever is necessary, Lucrezia tells herself.

From his tower, Lorenzo looks down upon them. Lucrezia's arm slips about Cecile's waist and their heads, dark and fair, are held close. The breeze moulds the flimsy fabric of their dresses to slender curves. He lingers upon the image; the swell of breasts, and legs parted to the teasing wind.

VIOLENCE

'I fear you must prepare yourself, my dear, for my winning of our little bet.'

Lorenzo sits before the dying embers of the fire in his private sitting room, cigar in hand. Lucrezia, in her dressing gown, her long hair plaited for sleep, stands, warming her back to what heat remains. It has been raining, and the night has grown unseasonably chill.

'Her terror at the prospective assault on her virginal state offers more entertainment than I'd foreseen!' he observes. 'She positively pants to be seduced, while tormenting herself with her own wickedness.'

'As you say,' admits Lucrezia. 'But don't be so sure of your victory. She's as liable to submit to my kisses as yours. She'll take my embraces as sisterly affection before realizing to what she commits herself and, then, in the heat of the oven, will rise to me as sweetly as new-baked bread.'

'Of course, it may be that she requires a rougher hand than yours to lead her astray,' he counters. 'One inclined to force, rather than teasing pleasure. How deliciously she would struggle at being punished over my knee, and how rapturously she would beg for more. The anticipation of it is most diverting.'

Lucrezia rolls her eyes.

'You're nothing if not predictable, brother. Meanwhile, if you wish to play your games with Vittoria, it would be prudent to do so behind a locked door. Our virginal Cecile, no doubt, thrilled to her unexpected act of voyeurism, but I fear you may frighten her off altogether if she finds you too engrossed in the charms of our serving staff.'

'But perhaps I wish to begin as I mean to go on,' answers Lorenzo. 'Let her see that she must compete for my affections. In point of fact, I rather fancy that she would put up with a great deal, if the enticement were sufficient. As the next Countess, I believe she would do very well, and endure whatever dalliances I pursued as those due to a hot-blooded nobleman of the di Cavour line.'

'You are shameless...' says Lucrezia. 'Though I'd expect nothing less.'

His attitude gives her pause. Once he has truly set his mind to the acquisition of a prize, Lucrezia knows, he will not step aside.

'She might be persuaded into all manner of sport, once the family diamonds are at her disposal,' muses Lorenzo, drawing thoughtfully on his cigar. 'She appears particularly disposed to being restrained, which makes things a great deal easier. It's always interesting to see how far a 'lady' will surrender herself when she feels her own will is no longer an obstacle. All the trappings of defiant struggle may be observed, while the body submits to the true spirit of debauchery.'

Lucrezia, for all her exasperation with Cecile's naïvety, cannot help but pity her. To marry Lorenzo would be a harsher sentence than she would wish upon any woman. Far better for the coddled innocent to succumb to Lucrezia's embraces, and escape with her liberty.

She knows well Lorenzo's darker inclinations, and that her own avoidance of submission cannot be infinitely extended. Lucrezia must find another path, away from his guardianship, and the power he holds over her.

'I'm quite taken with our fair Cecile, I admit,' Lorenzo continues. 'My inclination is to marry her without further ado, which might be most speedily achieved by compelling the necessity of a ring upon her finger.'

He stretches out his legs and leans back, drawing deeply upon the cigar.

'I lack the patience for a prolonged courtship. I might take my prize, and sire the next heir to the di Cavour title in one swoop.'

His exhaled smoke plumes between them.

'It would be a pretty piece of work for one evening, would it not?'

Lucrezia turns away, refusing to be goaded.

'No doubt, Lady McCaulay will positively run to the altar once her maidenhood has been lost. I might even allow her to believe herself in love.'

'You're too kind, I'm sure,' replies Lucrezia. If she but knew for certain that provision existed for herself in Lorenzo's will, she would swiftly arrange his demise — the fact of which is not lost upon the Conte. His machinations, and his tastes, have long been repugnant to her, and she feels the leash tightening upon her neck with each day that passes.

'Of course, no wife should bask too long in the unconditional love of her husband.'

Lorenzo has risen from his chair, tapping the ash from his cigar into the hearth.

'True devotion is best inspired by a desire to please, isn't it, my dear.'

Standing close, he wraps the length of Lucrezia's dark plait around his fist, pulling firmly upon it, so that her neck bends back.

'Naturally, there will still be a place for you,' Lorenzo says, his lips almost upon her exposed throat. 'I can think of plenty of ways in which you may be party to the merrymaking, sister dearest. And, Serpico, you know, is very fond of you. Such a faithful servant, and deserving of sharing in the same pleasures enjoyed by his master.'

He pulls aside the collar of Lucrezia's dressing gown, and tugs her nightgown, beneath, to expose her collarbone. It is his mouth she expects to descend there but, instead, she feels a sudden heat. He tugs the gown down further, his fingers hovering above her breast. He has raised the glowing tip of his cigar, holding it almost to the tender flesh. She winces, straining to release herself, but his grip upon her hair is firm.

'I've plans enough for you, my dear, when the time comes. But we may taste a little of your fine wine tonight. It's a simple matter to uncork the bottle.'

Taking a final draw upon the cheroot, he exhales the smoke against Lucrezia's face, then throws the stub into the fire.

As his hand moves to unbutton his britches, Lucrezia raises her knee, catching him abruptly in his sensitive parts. Another twist and she has hooked him from his hold upon her plait, and drawn his elbow up, behind his back.

'You may find I have a bitter aftertaste,' she hisses, pulling his arm a little higher.

'You enjoy pain, do you not, brother?' she taunts, pressing his head to the hard marble of the mantle. 'In this, I shall oblige you.'

Lucrezia takes the side of his hand between her jaws. The flesh yields to her determination to inflict injury.

With his blood in her mouth, she leaves.

PLEASURE

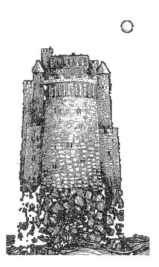

Twilight has descended, and the first stars are visible, the breeze carrying scents more extravagant than by day. Lilies and jasmine, Cyprus and pine. The air is thick with the salted-brine of the ocean, weaving between floral notes.

Following the rain, the grass is damp underfoot. There is a subtle chill to the air.

Nevertheless, Maud insists that Henry remove his clothing, until he stands naked.

'We exist between the Earth and the Heavens,' she tells him. 'Part soil and part starlight.'

She ties the sash to close his eyes, and another to bind his hands behind him.

'We tread the bridge between this world and the Divine and, at certain moments, we feel ourselves closer to one than the other.'

She guides him, until his back feels the rough bark of an olive tree.

'Tonight, the other world is calling to you.'

He hears the swish of her skirts retreating and is reminded of another time, long ago it seems, when she passed behind her seated audience, her gloved hand touching briefly the back of his neck.

He is alone, exposed. The cool air makes him shiver.

Some time passes, in which he listens to the cicadas and the staccato squawk of a night heron.

As a nightjar lands close by, adding its low, churring call, he hears footsteps on the path, and the brush of skirts, female voices, hushed, speaking rapidly in Italian. How many, he cannot tell. Maud does not seem to be among them.

'*Guarda!*'

'*Lui è bello.*'

'*Sembra freddo,*' says another.

'*Lo riscaldiamo,*'replies her friend, and the voices descend into giggles.

They draw close, bringing with them the scent of their bodies.

A hand, tentative, touches his chest, stroking the golden hair, moving outward, to brush his nipple.

Another alights upon the muscle of his upper arm.

They are close enough that he can hear the intake and exhalation of their breathing.

He understands now, and his pulse quickens. A flush of excitement fills his groin, and that which had lain dormant between his legs gives a small leap.

'*Guarda quello!*' says one of the women.

Fingers rest upon his lower belly, moving lower, into the thatch of his pubic hair, moving to grasp the root of his cock, until it is encompassed in a small, warm hand. Henry's voice catches in his throat.

'*Cosa sciocca!*'cries the next.

The hand moves back and forth, experimentally. The woman before him whispers encouragement.

'*Crescere per me... fammi vedere*'

Her breathing is as rapid as his own. She stands closer, her skirts either side of his knee, leaning in, the fabric of her blouse skimming his bare chest.

'*Vogliamo anche un po 'di divertimento!*'exclaims another, to his right.

The hand upon his arm moves behind, to settle upon his buttock, giving a gentle squeeze.

'*Buona e ferma...*'

The women giggle again, but they quieten as the woman in front removes her hand. She has brought him to full erection, and Henry is a man amply endowed. His understanding of Italian is insufficient to understand all, but he recognizes admiration, and a note of urgency in the exchanges that follow.

'*Lo voglio...*'

'*Devo essere il primo!*'

'*E io dopo.*'

Whatever argument is afoot, it ceases as a mouth lowers, taking him inside. There is no hesitation; tongue and soft inner cheeks caressing him, sucking hard along his length, releasing him, and taking him again. Here is the enthusiasm of a woman devouring what she wishes to claim as her own. Moans of satisfaction escape him.

It serves to inspire his devotee to further effort.

'*È delizioso,*' she murmurs.

Henry's head has grown light, so that he can hardly register the movements of the women either side. There are kisses upon his shoulders, and playful pinching, the nipping of impatient teeth, and fingers stroking...

A great squeeze upon his buttocks makes his cock leap again, deep inside the woman's mouth. She hums with pleasure, and cups the weight of his testicles in her hands.

'*Lo voglio,*' whines the woman to his left.

She raises her skirts, pressing the smooth flesh of her inner thigh to him, straddling his leg. Petticoats pushed aside, she is naked beneath, her hot cunt rubbing above his knee.

'*Il mio bel uomo inglese,*' she sighs, and her lips close upon his nipple.

The night swims as Henry becomes lost, his cock achingly hard, his skin warmed by silken mouths and cooled by the night air.

Belly, rod and scrotum, they feed on him, greedy consummations, sucking, biting. Where one leaves off another takes her place. Breath sweet and hot, demanding.

He pulses to satisfaction, a willing slave to their fingers and insistent mouths. Then, brought to fullness again, they guide him to lie upon the dewy grass, untying his hands briefly, only to secure them again, above his head.

They take turns to straddle him, to draw him inside their velvet lips.

'*Mio Dio!*' cries the first, as her own delight overtakes her.

'*Cazzo a me!*' exclaims the second, clenching his girth with contractions of pleasure.

'*Mi trafiggono!*' sighs the last, as she grinds her longing upon his length.

Henry is moving away from his past, towards something else, unknown, and unchartered.

While he breathes, there are certain things he cannot help but yearn for.

BLOOD

It's past midnight when Cecile wakes, her pulse quickened by her dreams.

She has imagined herself a bride, in a gown of white silk, wearing a tiara of pearls and sparkling gems. The ring is upon her finger and she the mistress of the castle. Except that her groom does not lead her to the comforts of his bed, but straight from the chapel, down the dank steps, to the obscurity of the crypt.

Her husband's clasp upon her wrist is firm, dragging her to the manacles, in the deepest shadows of that foul place.

'And, now, my Contessa,' says the voice both seductive and cruel, 'How shall we spend our wedding night?'

Strong hands rend the virginal bridal silk, until her pale body quivers before him, exposed. Her arms, outstretched, ache from the constraint of their imprisonment, as she submits to his desire.

WAKING WITH A START, Cecile is relieved to find her covers warm about her, rather than the oppressive chill of the crypt.

She rises to open the shutters and unlatch her window, looking out at the dark sky and sea. The waves churn below, at their height upon the rocks, and the breeze brings the faintest sound of keening. A night-bird flaps past with a baleful screech.

She cannot yet return to her bed, fearful of what her mind may next conjure. Cecile unlocks her door, telling herself that she must escape the confines of her chamber. She lights the wick of her candle and considers descending, to breathe the freshness of the garden.

What then moves her to venture to the end of the corridor, and continue, to the wing where Lorenzo's apartments are located? Does some inner voice urge her to seek out what she knows is forbidden?

If I'm discovered, I'll pretend that I'm sleepwalking, she decides. The door to his solitary tower looks like any other and opens easily. There is no squeak from its hinges. Nothing to betray her.

She climbs the stairs, one foot in front of the other, until she reaches a door. It's ajar, so why shouldn't she look inside?

It's a well-furnished room, the floor covered in fine rugs, and thick drapes at the window. The room is dominated by a bed. His bed. A bed that rises high from the ground, away from the cool air about her feet. Its canopy is hung with a heavy swathe of amber fabric, while purple velvet curtains, embroidered in gold and secured by thick cord, adorn each corner post. They aren't yet closed, for there is no head upon the pillow, despite the late hour.

Cecile looks back, the way she has come. What if he were to appear, and find her? A shiver catches through her spine. Fear, and something else…

Her feet should take her away from this place but she allows them to lead her upwards, through another two rotations of the curving stair.

There is another door. Another room. This time, locked.

A chill draught descends upon her, and the far-off murmuring of the sea. There must be a window open above.

She presses her ear to the door. Are there voices? Muttering? From within the room, or from the wood itself?

Cecile pushes away, her back finding the cold stone of the opposite wall, and flinching at the touch of it.

It's as if the castle were a living thing, the air drawn through its passages like breath.

She hurries away, down the stairs again.

No more madness, she resolves.

But, as she passes the bedchamber, there is a tug inside her chest.

Would not the key to that door be in his room?

Entering once more, she sets her candle upon the nightstand and opens the drawer. Nothing there but papers. On top is a small box. Her heart races for a moment, but it contains only cigars.

Where else to look?

There are several wardrobes, filled with suits and hats, drawers of gloves and cravats. She cannot possibly search them all, and time is passing. Has she returned with the intention of being discovered, and caught in wrongdoing? Her heart races at her remembrance of the manner in which the Conte punished Vittoria.

And then she sees it.

A key, upon a ribbon, hanging in plain sight, from the centre of the canopy above the bed.

It takes but a moment and she has climbed up, her fingers reaching for what she seeks.

~

CECILE OPENS the door only a little; enough to admit her entry, closing it immediately behind. It's extraordinarily dark and her candle is burning low. There's a chest in the corner, a chair, horse tack and riding switches on the wall. The room is being used for storage, perhaps.

A strange place to keep them, she thinks. *And how peculiar for such a place to be locked. There's nothing here of interest.*

To one side is a table, upon which several wooden objects are arranged. Most are bulbous at one end, sometimes both. Some are subtly curved in shape, others are straight. She picks one up. Smooth, polished, and heavier than she imagined, made of oak, or walnut. It sits well in her palm. Her fingers close about it, naturally.

The Conte is well-travelled. Tribal items from Africa, or totems. She has read of such things.

Cecile rests upon the chair for a moment, heavily padded, and upholstered in a dark, velvet fabric. How unusual its shape is, with slender, golden-gilded arms, protruding upwards. *Perhaps for invalids,* Cecile muses, *that they might grasp these and pull themselves upright.* And there is a little platform beneath, perhaps to aid in mounting the chair. *Like climbing upon one's horse,* Cecile decides, endeavouring to understand the design. Although why there should be a significant hole in the seat, she cannot imagine. *No wonder that it's been put away, for it would make a most peculiar addition to the drawing room.*

Cecile has a vague memory of having seen something similar in the book in the library; the one that Lucrezia closed before she could look properly.

Behind the door is some strange contraption, with cogs and wheels. She turns its handle and a chain link moves noisily. A most peculiar device, and she cannot begin to imagine what use it serves. Perhaps no use at all, since it has been relegated to this out-of-the-way location.

What had she expected to find?

It's all rather disappointing.

At the far end of the room is a picture.

Some out-of-favour relative, thinks Cecile, relegated to this forgotten storeroom.

As she draws close, she sees that it's no di Cavour depicted, but a woman from the Orient.

A souvenir from the Far East, of course, where Lorenzo has travelled.

Cecile raises her candle.

The background is filled with Oriental script, and there is the lady's face, upturned, a little octopus sitting beside her ear. A peculiar choice, thinks Cecile. She's used to seeing dogs and horses in paintings, birds and cats, on occasion.

The octopus is whispering something to her. How fascinating are the Chinese; or is this Japanese?

She moves the candle across, and her hand begins to shake.

For the lady is quite naked, and there is a delicate tentacle wrapped about her nipple. Another, thicker, encompasses her thigh. Several curl around her arms. One drapes possessively across her stomach. Between her open legs is the head of a terrifyingly huge octopus, its beak lowered, as if to devour her. And yet the woman appears not to struggle, or be in distress.

Cecile cannot help but look, and look again. So many tentacles. Caressing. Constricting. Engulfing her.

Her eyes return to the horse tack, except that she sees, now, that it's no such thing. This metal and leather was never intended to bridle a mare, and while several of the switches are, undoubtedly, horse whips, some are not. Their handles are too short, and their tails too long, and thick, stained crimson-dark.

She looks again at the chair, and at the mangle, and recalls her brief glimpse at the book in the library. Figures, half-clothed, contorted awkwardly.

It's too strange. There's something here she cannot comprehend, and yet she knows. Her imagination places her over the end of the chair, bending, the Conte raising her gown with the tip of a switch, her face burning with shame as his hand finds her bare flesh.

~

SHE LOCKS THE DOOR, hurries down, and climbs up to replace the key upon its ribbon. The mattress creaks under her feet, threatening to topple her.

Looking down at Lorenzo's bed, her chest constricts. This is where he sleeps, beneath the soft coverlet. She sees her own head on the pillow, and he above, his body pressing heavy, and his tongue teasing. Tentacle-like, reaching to find her, leaving a wet trail on her skin.

Her legs are weak, as she descends from the bed.

If she were discovered by him, in her intrusion... She moves swiftly to the door.

Cecile's footsteps are light upon the wooden floor, darting to avoid the places where she knows it squeaks. She reaches her door and her fingers find the handle, but her heart is hammering so rapidly that she fears it will rupture.

She must calm herself. A tonic is needed. A strong drink. Isn't that what's recommended?

Henry has never permitted her to take spirits. A little wine, or a glass of sherry, only. In the library, there are decanters. Brandy, perhaps. Doctors give it to calm the nerves.

The clock chimes one as she crosses the hall, lit by pale moonlight through tall windows.

Passing the shelves of books, she moves directly to the table upon which the crystal decanters are kept, unstoppers the first and sniffs. The liquid is pungent, reminding her of smoking bonfires and aniseed. She pours a little into a glass and raises it to her lips. It burns, and makes her splutter, but the warmth is quickly inside her. There is comfort in it, despite the vile taste.

A little more, and she shall be calmed enough to return to her bed.

With the glass emptied, she rubs at the rim with her nightdress and replaces it upon the tray.

Her pulse is steadier now and her eyes roam upwards, to the ceiling, where fleeing women run, mouths agape, in terror, and in warning, pursued by the beasts of Zeus' seductions.

She pauses to look upon the ancient volumes, touching the old leather.

One is embossed with a golden serpent, coiled through the spine. Its small, bronze clasp opens easily, loose on its hinges. *Efficacious and Undetectable Poisons.* The book is dirty, inside and out, with the grease of many fingers. It falls open at 'Ridding the Body of Unwanted Pregnancy'. The ink is smudged, as if from something spilled.

Cecile snaps it closed. She has no desire to think on such things.

The monsters of ancient mythology, carved into the shelves, look down on her, eyes sharp and mouths sneering. The whole room, she might imagine, is mocking her. She does not belong here. There are secrets in these books, as well as within these ancient walls, and the castle's many rooms; they are best left undisturbed.

As she turns to leave, there is a shift in the shadows. Someone is approaching, carrying their own small source of light.

There is just time for Cecile to blow out her candle, and hide behind the curtains.

With a firm footstep, the person crosses the room, striking a match to ignite the oil lamp upon the desk.

She hears the pouring of liquid from the decanter, and a grunt of satisfaction. The tumbler is refilled and knocked back once more, and a third time, the glass landing heavily.

'*Cagna di coraggio. La farò pagare!*'

Cecile has no need to peek from her hiding place and no desire to do so. She knows this cursing voice. The thought of Lorenzo discovering her twists a coil of fear in her stomach.

After he has left, she creeps out. The decanter is almost drained.

The lamp's flame remains lit and, in its pool of light, Cecile sees the glass, the very one from which she drank. Bloody fingerprints are upon it. Something dark has dripped across the rug.

It is not only the gentleman on the pale horse who comes for us in our bed in the ripeness of old age. The villainous may lend a hand, delivering souls into the rider's embrace. Poison, blade or the quiet dispatch of the pillow on a sleeping face: the tools of those doing amateur business for the Reaper.

Violence is apt to dwell just as readily in the sedate parlour or over the cooking of a mutton leg as on the battlefield. Newspaper columns long and short catalogue grisly misdeeds of the everyday. She knows violence exists beyond the flights of fancy in her novels, and that poison lurks in human veins, as potent as any administered into a pie-crust or pot of tea.

With shaking hand, she lifts the lamp, and makes her way back, through the darkness.

TEMPTATION

In the days that pass, Cecile is plagued by memories and strange images. Though his manner is always polite, the Conte's courtesy appears but outward show. When he smiles, she feels the points of his teeth upon her skin. Cecile wonders what it would be like, to submit to those teeth.

Strange that she sees so little of him during the day.

'Like all nocturnal creatures, he prefers the cool of his tower rooms,' explains Lucrezia. 'Or his library. The sun doesn't agree with him.'

Each evening, dishes arrive at the table, and Cecile's mouth opens to each delicious sensation: succulent crab and lobster, rich Ossobuco, served with risotto alla Milanese, ricotta-stuffed cannelloni, and zesty lemon gremolata. There are meringues and panna cotta, topped with sweet raspberries, creamy zabaglione and tiny apricot pastries.

As they dine, the Conte asks about her London suitors. Shyly, she admits there are none. About her desire for children. She cannot answer. Does she ride, and hunt to hounds? Has she ever suffered weakness of constitution, or serious illness. Does she enjoy travel? Could she live in Italy, perhaps…?

'Have done with it and present Lady McCaulay with a ring,' exclaims Agatha at last. 'Although it would be courteous to approach her brother before you enquire any further as to Cecile's readiness for marriage.'

Lucrezia drinks more wine than is good for her, and blazes silently.

The mirror over the mantel, in the dining room, reflects the flicker of the chandelier, small points of light, quivering in that cavernous room, with its pomegranate-red walls.

Is Lorenzo her Hades, her dark temptation?

Her mind wanders, from the dining room, out, through the chill corridors, to subterranean places; down to the damp, dark dungeon. She feels again the weight of a metal cuff about her wrist and cool hands touching where she longs to be touched. A face; impassive, imperious, close to hers.

Beneath the covers, she listens to the far-off rush of the waves and the rattle of the windows. Sometimes, she hears a distant wail, but it's only the rising wind, she tells herself. Then her dreams take her, and she tosses on her own inner sea, lost in thoughts disturbing and arousing.

∾

It is long past the hour when she should be sleeping but, tonight, Cecile is awake, reading to the last stub of her candle. *Jane Eyre* has called to her, as if the answer to something lies within those pages. So many secrets and half-concealed truths.

Page after page, her fingers turn, though her eyes are sleepy. When she hears footsteps run past her room, she looks up. Again, there is the sound of running feet but, this time, they do not pass by.

There is a long scratch at the door, as of a fingernail drawn slowly across the wood.

'Who's there?' Cecile's voice trembles.

There's no answer, but for the further clawing of the oak, and a splintered laugh. The footsteps run again. Then quiet.

Could it be the phantom of the White Contessa, roaming the castle to mutter her curses?

Surely not!

Cecile dons dressing gown and slippers. Dare she venture into the corridor, to see who terrorizes her? She's afraid, but will not be intimidated. She'll unbolt the door, and, no matter what she sees, she shall stand firm and confront this creature of the night, be it real or a thing from her imagination.

The cool night-breath of the corridor slides past her cheek, threatening her candle's meagre illumination. Little enough light, but sufficient to see that a door is ajar. One she knows is usually locked. In her idle hours, she has tried almost all of the doors in this wing of the castle. They lead into bedrooms, and a linen cupboard, a room for bathing, a storage place. This door belongs to one of the towers, leading to the rooftop ramparts: forbidden to her, for its crumbling stairs, and its hidden dangers.

It's open, thinks Cecile, *and I must see.*

The stairs are narrow but her feet are dainty. She keeps to where the tread is widest, though her sleeve brushes against the cold stone.

She has reached the second curve in the upward spiral when she hears the rapid movement of feet following where her own have trodden. From below, the face of Lorenzo looks up at her.

In a moment, his body is pressing hers to the wall, head and shoulders above her, his hand grasping her wrist.

'All good girls are in their beds.'

He holds her arm at an angle so awkward, she cannot help but cry out.

Cecile knows she should struggle. Instead, she is limp.

His eyes are shuttered. What manner of sentience moves inside, she cannot guess. She knows only that his nails dig into her flesh, hard enough that she will later find the scabbing of half-bloomed blood.

'Let me go,' she says, in a voice so small she can barely hear herself.

'Let you go?' he answers. 'You were looking for something... What shall you do, Lady McCaulay, now you have found it?'

At any moment, someone will come, she thinks, in horror. *Someone will come.*

'Your head is full of hysterical fantasies, my dear. I'll give you something to dream of, in your bed, if you wish it.'

With a twitch of his fingers, he has loosened the ribbon which closes her dressing gown, and pushed it aside, so that there is nothing between his hand and her body but the thin fabric of her nightdress. To Cecile's surprise, her legs part to the force of his thigh.

A groan of pleasure escapes his throat.

'*Mia amore.*'

His nose is in her hair, his breath in her ear.

'I am a man undone. It's no sin to desire. Struggle if you wish, but I see your feelings, your passion. Your every look betrays you.'

He has found her breast, pushing down the flimsy muslin. He leans over her, his tongue, warm, tracing the curve of her skin.

Half-heartedly, she twists away, but he holds her firm.

Molten pleasure is welling within, commanding her to open to him.

A dream-like state overcomes her, and she succumbs willingly.

She knows not how much time passes.

When he kisses her, she is compliant, her lips yielding to the pull of his teeth, until the taste of metal fills her mouth.

The wall is no longer hard against her spine; it almost feels as if it is melting, enveloping them inside its granite embrace, extracting the essence of this moment. Cecile images them as two flowers, pressed between the pages of a book, preserved for eternity in stone.

Is it a growl she hears, below them on the stair? Someone or something else is close by, and the surprise of it is enough to rouse her, so that she wriggles free, pushing past the dark figure.

Does she imagine the wretched cry which follows her stumbling feet? Inside her room, she fumbles with the bolt, pushes her spine to the solid wood, giving in to the sob rising in her throat.

In her dressing mirror, she sees a pale face staring back at her. She dreads almost to look, fearing what she may find in that reflection. Even now, she feels his lips on her skin. She hangs her head in shame, but her body is alive with sensations. Why did she not struggle harder? To what would she have submitted, had not someone interrupted them?

Her mind skitters away from the answer; yet her body knows.

THINGS LEFT UNSAID

'It's nothing, I'm sure,' answers Lucrezia, to Cecile's impassioned outpouring. 'My brother is many things, but he's not a murderer.'

Cecile cannot bring herself to speak of the locked room upon which she has intruded. However provoking the contents may be, she cannot escape her shame at having behaved underhandedly, stealing the key and entering where she has not been invited. She shall endeavour to forget that she ever crossed its threshold.

'But... the blood!' implores Cecile.

'My dear one, his horse, perhaps, bit him. He whips it most cruelly, you know. My brother is only happy when tormenting some creature. I live in hope that the beast may yet aim a kick to Lorenzo's head.'

Lucrezia has no wish to relate the events of the previous evening, nor her part in them.

Cecile cannot set aside her agitation so easily, but she allows Lucrezia to distract and entertain her, in her usual way.

They discuss plays they've attended, and books they've read, places they've seen, and those they long to see.

How much easier it is to relax, without the constant pressure of a corset about my ribs, thinks Cecile.

Through the heat of the day, they lie in the shade, in the lightest of their gowns. Lucrezia wears green silk chiffon, the bodice and skirt embroidered with purple foxgloves, the dainty capped sleeve accentuating the slender elegance of her arm. Cecile's lemon muslin, hand-printed with daisies, is soft against her skin.

She opens her *Jane Eyre*, while Lucrezia has a copy of the newly released playscript of Mr. Wilde's *An Ideal Husband*. Cecile has seen the performance, at the Criterion Theatre.

'Do you think there is such a thing — as the perfect husband?' asks Cecile.

'Undoubtedly not!' replies Lucrezia, 'Unless we may find a man happy to leave us entirely to our own inclinations.'

Her expression takes on a sudden seriousness.

'None of us are perfect, Cecile. We're human, so can we ever be? We're too full of fear and frailty to avoid wrongdoing. I only wonder if, sooner or later, we pay for what we've done...'

'Why so serious, Lucrezia? You've committed no sin, I'm sure, that the Almighty would be unable to forgive.'

The clouds are gathering above, casting a cool shadow over the late afternoon. A sudden chill has passed over the two, and Lucrezia closes her book, standing, and offering Cecile her hand.

'As Mr. Wilde would say, perhaps, none of us should be entirely judged by our past...'

ABDUCTION

Nature is remorseless, random, brutal and beautiful; logical and yet unfathomable. If Maud studies the ants and bees and beetle-life, each with its own purity of purpose, will she find clues to a hidden purpose in her own life?

There is a spiral staircase in the villa, leading down from the bedrooms. Maud finds herself standing, often, at the top, looking

down through its curving descent. It makes her think of the theories
of Mr. Gaudi. How fascinating it is to ponder the power of the
cosmos, the movements of which combine with gravity to generate
the spiral motion of water on Earth, from the swirling stir of the
greatest oceans to the propensity of her bathwater to funnel down a
plughole.

The same inward, spiralling movements, she knows, are found in
the animal and vegetable kingdoms, from the snail's shell to the falling
motion of a winged sycamore seed.

And what of me? she thinks, stroking the as yet imperceptible swell
of her stomach. *Am I spiralling in ever smaller circles?* Despite all her
efforts to forge her own path, is this how it ends, eased into the role of
breeding queen?

~

THE VILLAGE IS STRUNG with flickering lanterns, through the trees and
down the cobbled alleys, golden-gleaming. The day's humidity is
lifting and, far off, dark clouds are gathering, over the heaving waves.
A storm is approaching, but there is time yet.

Masked and costumed, Maud leads Henry by the hand. She is
Columbina to his Pierrot.

They duck through the crowds, past revellers dancing in the fountain of the market square, trousers rolled up and skirts tucked into
bloomers. The residents of Scogliera have painted their *bauta* masks
themselves for the festival of Sant' Andrea, the patron of all fisher-
men. They cannot boast the grandeur of their Venice counterparts,
but their disguises do well enough, freeing them from their everyday
selves, left in their kitchens and their fishing boats. Accordions and
violins, playing whirling tunes, beget a frenzy of riotous behaviour.
Dresses slip from shoulders, and men's shirts unbutton.

Maud is looking for something. She'll know it when she sees it,
like a beast prowling by night, in search of what it requires to live:
flesh, pulsing warm. The savagery of it thrills her. Tonight, the heart
of Mademoiselle Noire beats in her chest.

There is a dark side to every coin, even if it appears to shine brightly. Though her face is hidden, Henry can sense the tension in her body, and the strangeness of her mood. She's been too long in an abundance of warmth. Now, she yearns for chill breezes. The rising wind threatens to blow the lanterns from their ribbons. One escapes its tether and blows down towards the harbour, heading for the open sea.

As they reach the far end of the street, the illumination grows dimmer. The carousal of the main square seems suddenly far away. Hazy. Here, there is a charge in the air. On this night, of chaos embraced, little is as it seems.

A group of five sit at a table on the street, with a flagon of wine and glasses near emptied. Unlike the revellers in the square, these men are taciturn; without laughter. There is an underlying hunger in the hunch of their shoulders, as they swill their wine and wipe their thin lips.

Henry attempts to steer Maud back, towards the glitter and the music and the dancing, but one of the men calls out, and raises his glass. He is Harlequin, in a half-mask, painted black. His eyes gleam beneath arching brows, and the bump of his devil's horn.

'*Siediti!*' he says, rising from his chair, to allow Maud to sit.

She converses in fluent Italian, while Henry is obliged to listen, understanding barely one word in ten, but comprehending all. The men laugh at her flirtation and jokes, and all the glasses are refilled.

Maud loosens the ribbon on her bodice, smiling at Henry as she does so.

'These gentlemen are from Sorrento, and have a carriage, as you see. They've asked if I might like to lie down for a little while. Later, they'll drive us to the villa, and stay, if we wish for company...'

She kisses his cheek before rising. Henry watches as she walks away from him. He remains at the table, his eyes fast upon her retreating back.

~

As she steps up to enter, Harlequin places his gloved hand lightly upon her ankle, and she is struck by a distant memory, of another hand upon her, grasping the same place, in the house of her great-aunt, Isabella.

She looks down at that half-masked face, and sees, now, that it is he. The realization makes her laugh. He may grasp as tightly as he dares, but she will never be his.

'I believe we've met before,' she remarks, 'Though we're yet to gain an intimate acquaintance.'

'And shall we rectify that, sweet cousin?' he replies, in perfect English.

She has stood upon the brink many times, knowing that a chasm lies before her, yet unable to resist the precipice. No matter that some things are better only dreamt of than lived, and some best avoided altogether.

As she lays back upon the velvet banquette within the carriage, she has no desire to know what may happen next. There lies the excitement of anticipation, in uncertainty. She wishes to lose herself in the possibilities, while there is still time.

His hands reach beneath the petticoats of her costume, to lower and discard the frilled pantaloons of her Columbine.

There are many forms of prison. Some endure physical incarceration. Far more are held captive by their fears. Maud has no desire to conform, or to hide. A rejected suitor may yet prove an adept lover.

She's ready to throw herself into the jaws of the wild hunt. Her sex opens to his tongue, and the beauty of her freedom surges through her belly. Her desire spirals outward, upward, fusing with the night.

She thinks of the other men, waiting their turn at the table, eating her, teeth and tongue. Henry infiltrates her thoughts only fleetingly. This moment is not for him. It is for her, and her blood, burning black.

≈

THE LIGHT IS GROWING DIMMER, and Maud's head lolls, at last, to one side, sent into slumber by the powder artfully blended with her wine.

Returning to the table, Harlequin nods to three of his companions. It only takes one to master the reins; the other two find accommodation inside.

'What the deuces do they think they're doing!' shouts Henry, as the horses are spurred into a canter, taking the carriage not towards the villa, but onto the clifftop road.

Harlequin and his man block Henry's path, the larger of the two placing a robust hand in the centre of Lord McCaulay's chest.

'Your lovely wife has found her entertainment elsewhere, it seems,' says Harlequin. 'We shall return her when she is tired of us... or when we have tired of her, *signore*.'

'The devil take you!' answers Henry, bunching his fist to give the fellow a crack upon the nose. He does not see the arm raised against him until it is too late. He is rendered unconscious by that single blow, delivered to the rear of his skull.

'*Complimenti*, Serpico,' says Harlequin. 'You are always to be relied upon.'

SEDUCTION

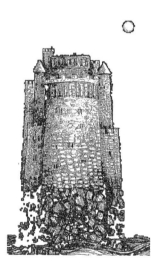

Lucrezia and Cecile dine with Agatha, consuming Magdalena's crispy calamaretti fritti, in honour of the festival of Sant' Andrea, and sweet tiramisu. Cecile can hardly believe her memories of the previous evening. Isn't so much of what occurs in the late hours, by candlelight, an exaggeration of events, the result of her inflamed imagination?

Lorenzo is absent, taking a plate of cold meats in his room, as Lucrezia explains. Cecile, nodding with feigned neutrality, is inwardly relieved.

Once Agatha has retired, Lucrezia leads Cecile through to the library.

'While the tiger is away, we little rabbits shall play,' says Lucrezia, pouring two generous measures from the decanter discreetly refilled by one of the many servants. None would guess that, the very night before, Cecile helped herself from that same crystal bottle.

She blushes at the remembrance and then shivers, recalling the bloody fingerprints left upon Lorenzo's glass.

'Come outside, *mia cara*, and see the beautiful sunset. We shall sit and welcome the twilight as we drink my brother's expensive brandy.'

The sun's warm fingers are retreating, while those of the moon are yet to reach.

'I love this time of evening, so full of promise, before the dark embraces you,' says Lucrezia, touching her glass to that of Cecile. They sit on one of the middle-terraces, with a view across the water, back to Scogliera. Lucrezia closes her eyes as the burning warmth of the alcohol enters her body.

'You see the lights, dear one? They're celebrating. It's the festival of the *calamaro*, of the squid, thanking the sea for its rich harvest. They begin by carrying the icon of Sant'Andrea to the harbour, and blessing the water, but the rest of the day is spent in feasting, drinking and dancing, until they can barely stand up. If the wind were to change, you'd hear their music.'

'Andrew the fisherman apostle,' muses Cecile, her head already hazy from alcohol. 'Have you been to the festival many times before? I mean, wouldn't you like to be there, enjoying yourself?'

'How sweet you are, my Cecile. I prefer to be here with you. I've seen enough drunken carousing to last a lifetime. Besides which, the causeway is covered by the high tide. We couldn't go even if we wanted to. My brother asked, most particularly, that we did not go. He says that such festivities are for peasants, and that we, as noble *ladies...*' At this, she stands to conduct a mock-curtsey, 'should hold ourselves one step removed.'

'And do you always do as he tells you?' asks Cecile, allowing herself to be a little mischievous, and taking another sip from her glass.

Lucrezia's laugh is one of genuine merriment.

'My darling,' she cries, giving Cecile a kiss upon the cheek. 'Come! We shall be disobedient in other ways, and he shall never know.'

She leads Cecile through the wisteria walk, and down the steps, past daisies and briar roses and wild mint, descending carefully, releasing the scent of thyme as they tread, brushing past hanging honeysuckle. The air tastes of orchid and oleander.

At last, they emerge through the olive grove, reaching the place where they're hidden from view. The sea is close, lapping at the rocks, and there is a slight mist on the water.

'There's nothing to fear, little dove,' says Lucrezia. 'Help me. I'm going to swim.'

And she turns, indicating the buttons on her dress. Cecile is hesitant, but does as she's bidden.

When it's loosened, Lucrezia withdraws her arms and steps out, to stand in her shift.

'There's no one to see,' coaxes Lucrezia.

She removes her underthings too, and pushes the slip from her shoulders, until she stands bare, arms open to the breeze on her skin.

There's hardly any moon, but Cecile can see the swell and curves of Lucrezia's body; much like her own, yet different.

'You'll catch cold,' remonstrates Cecile, 'Or someone will come!'

Lucretia places her finger to her lips.

'Just you and I, my Cecile,' she says, and takes her hand, so that Cecile faces her, nose-to-nose and chin-to-chin.

'Come in with me.'

The tide is at its highest point, not rushing up to send its spray flying, or receding with great, sucking breaths, but gentle, its sound dark and deep; a lovely, liquid undertone to the night.

I'm dreaming, thinks Cecile, as she allows Lucrezia to help remove her gown. Once naked, she looks down at her arm, at the pale glimmer of her skin. Without her clothing, she hardly feels like herself. Instead, she's a creature of the night. Like a snowy owl, she might shake out her wings and fly away, over the water and down the coast, swooping over rooftops and forests and mountains.

Lucrezia moves to sit on the edge, slips into the water, dives, then emerges, lashes wet, water dripping from her nose.

'Come and join me, my little seal. The sea is eager for you,' she calls, cupping water, and sending an arc to wet Cecile's feet.

Cecile follows, perching on a rock, smooth and cold against her bottom. The sea is mackerel-silver in the moonlight, slippery and cool as she enters.

She gasps and then laughs, finding her balance, kicking her feet, and sculling, until she bobs in one place.

'That's better,' says Lucrezia. 'Ladies shouldn't stand without their dresses in the evening air. We have our modesty to think of!'

They both giggle at that.

Lucrezia reaches for Cecile's hand, guiding it to her body, hidden by the water.

Only a dream, thinks Cecile, as her palm is placed against Lucrezia's breast, and the heartbeat is strong beneath her hand.

The air is charged, with the heat of the day, and humidity waiting to break into rain, with a thick excitement, a palpable anticipation. The night seems to hold its breath.

Their lips are so close that it takes no effort at all for them to meet and Cecile finds that Lucrezia's mouth is as warm as she knew it would be. The waves move over their shoulders as they kiss.

Cecile is unfurling into the promise of the unknown.

She accepts Lucrezia's hands upon her body, where her own have touched. She both fears to speak, and finds that there is nothing she needs to say. Under Lucrezia's touch, she melts into the water, swirling deeper, gripping Lucrezia's fingers, contracting in strange, quivering thrills. A rippling, swelling force is devouring her, one she cannot fight. Lucrezia's eyes have become fierce and brilliant, as Cecile's voice rises in small gasps and half-swollen cries. Her blood is singing, and the sea is lifting her, in the murmur of the moonlight.

Afterwards, they are two, among the many waves in that wide ocean, breathing in the darkness, which blooms, enormous, around them.

Cecile no longer feels that she's dreaming. Rather, she is awake, and the water is full of stars.

～

LATER, having dried themselves with their petticoats, they put on their dresses, and lie on the grass, listening to the night and all that is in it. To the water's rhythm and the click of crickets.

Cecile closes her eyes, so that the stillness may cover her. The world, in its infinite complexity, is reduced to the sea breeze and the light touch of leaf upon leaf, tiny creatures moving in the under-growth, and the soft rhythm of the sleeping sea.

REVENGE

It is late, as Cecile and Lucrezia make their way back, up through the terraces, to the castle. The library doors onto the terrace are no longer ajar, but one of the windows has been left on the latch. Cecile's arm is slender; she might reach through and open it wider.

The curtain is partially drawn, muffling the movements within:

creaking hinges, and the scuffle of footsteps, laboured breaths, and the heavy thud of a closing door.

'Be still,' warns Lucrezia, placing herself where she may peer around the edge of the curtain.

'Brandy, Serpico,' commands a voice Cecile knows well.

There is the sound of cursing as boots are thrown upon the floor.

'*Lasciate courier la cagna,*' says Lorenzo, sinking into his armchair, and gulping his restorative. His gloves and mask he discards, putting on his smoking jacket over the gaudy costume. '*La goderò nel mio tempo.*'

'What are they saying?' whispers Cecile.

Lucrezia shakes her head, unsure of how much to reveal.

She is not party to every plan conceived by her half-brother. Nor does she wish to be. There are some wickednesses of which she would prefer to remain ignorant.

'He has someone waiting for him,' Lucrezia explains. 'I don't think he likes her, but he's going to see her tomorrow. He says that she'll be ready by then. She's slighted him in some way, and he's angry.'

Cecile nods, and beckons Lucrezia to duck beneath the window with her.

'I don't like being here, Lucrezia. We should try another door. Perhaps the kitchen?'

Lucrezia nods and moves silently along the wall. She has no inclination to linger. Cecile raises herself into a crouch to follow, when a certain name catches her ear.

'*Avrò la mia vendetta contro la Signora Maud,*' hisses the Conte. '*Se lei non sarà mia moglie, lei sarà la mia puttana!*'

His tone is unmistakably that of a man intent upon misdeeds. Cecile stumbles, and catches her sleeve against the edge of the window, tearing the fabric, and grazing her arm.

'Serpico! *Chi è là? Qualche spia?*'

The words have no sooner left Lorenzo's lips than his man has sprung to the curtain and drawn it back. Cecile stands in horror as the window is flung open and she is dragged through, into the room, like a scrap of rag.

It's rare for Lorenzo to be taken aback, but so he is on seeing Cecile, deposited crudely upon the floor by his faithful manservant. For a moment, he ponders the best approach. To his knowledge, her Italian is rudimentary.

'*Che male hai sentito?*' the Conte asks in Italian, assessing how far Cecile has understood what she has overheard. Her countenance assures him that all is safe, and his expression becomes more amused than angry.

'What a pleasant surprise, Lady McCaulay,' he says, helping her to her feet, but keeping a firm grip upon her arm. 'Though I cannot begin to speculate on why you're eavesdropping at my window, like some secret spy. If you desire my company, you have only to enter, in the civilized manner, through the door.'

Cecile has never been so roughly handled. She is both indignant and deeply shamed, for what can she say in her defence? As to her appearance, she can only begin to imagine what state she presents, her hair salt-wetted and tumbled from its pins, and her pale pink dress, grass-stained and crumpled.

The Conte steers her towards the desk, until she feels the wood hard against the back of her legs, and he looms above her, looking down through eyes half-closed.

'Whatever you think you have heard has made you breathless,' he observes.

He lifts a tendril of hair from her neck and she shivers at his touch, despite all that her mind tells her.

'So predictable, my sweet one,' he sighs. 'Women are all just the same, protesting more for show than through modesty. For all your restraint and chastity, if I tore the gown from you now and laid you across this desk you would part your legs and allow me anything.'

'Indeed I would not!' answers Cecile, provoked at last into a response. 'I understand why you're yet a bachelor if you believe this to be the way to woo a lady.'

With a cruel laugh, he grasps her about the waist and lifts her body onto the desk, his hands making quick work of throwing up her skirts, his hips forcing her legs apart.

'Tell me that you'll marry me and I shall spare you,' he declares, as she struggles against his coarse advances.

'You would not dare, Sir! Even your servant would not permit it, I'm sure.'

'How quaint you are, my dear,' answers the Conte. 'Serpico, as you can see, is in no hurry to come to your aid. If you squirm, I may ask him to hold your down, while we endeavour to conceive an heir. Perhaps, then, you shall be less coy. Even your brother, I imagine, would entreat wedlock on your behalf, under the circumstance of a fruitful belly. I wonder if he hadn't that very plan in mind, in allowing you to reside so unprotected under my roof. The Lady Agatha is a poor chaperone against such a suitor as I.'

Lorenzo's legs push further between hers, and his hand rises towards her neck. It is then that she sees the bloody bandage. If she refuses him, will he bring violence upon her? Might he strangle her, or knock her unconscious, and then have his way? In that moment, an image flashes before her of the strange contraption in the secret room. Could it be that it's an instrument of torture?

He sees the terror in her face, her eyes upon the crimson-seeped cloth and his teeth reveal in a slow smile.

'A wildcat stronger than you bit me, and she shall be sorry for it yet. Now, madame, tell me. Shall I call the padre to attend us at his convenience, and you may plan a wedding as pretty as you please, or shall we see how delightfully you submit under duress?'

Cecile feels the bile rising in her throat. Whatever madness possessed her, permitting her to entertain the idea of becoming the next countess, it has passed. The scales have fallen from her eyes, and she sees before her the devillish countenance of a man who would rule her rather than worship her.

However, she nods her head, and stills her body under his hand, despite the rapidity of her pulse. Her only hope, surely, is to accede and escape.

Agatha will never allow the marriage to take place, nor Lucrezia. I'm not alone, Cecile tells herself.

'Ah, my sweet!' smiles Lorenzo, receding from his assault with serpentine speed. He raises her hand and kisses it lightly, his moustache twitching with suppressed mirth, taking pleasure in this show of mock-chivalry.

'You had best find your bed, Lady Cecile. There will be time enough for love when we are wed.'

He bows as she finds her feet, allowing her to pass unmolested. She crosses the room unsteadily, but with as much dignity as she can muster. Though her legs threaten to fail her, she reaches the door, and passes through, closing it quietly behind her.

The low chuckle of the Conte's laughter follows her out.

REACHING THE STAIRS, Cecile takes them as quickly as she is able, tears of shame smarting in her eyes. How foolish she has been, like a fly enticed into the spider's web, bound by her own illusions of romantic love.

She wishes only to find the safety of her room. Yet, as she turns into the gloomy corridor in which her chamber lies, feeling her way along the wall, she sees that Lucrezia is waiting for her, dressed now in her nightgown, trying the handle of Cecile's door, pushing it open to enter.

Cecile calls to her, ready to fling herself upon the shoulder of her friend, to seek her comfort. As the name leaves her lips, the figure turns and Cecile's heart ceases, for one brief moment, to perform its function. For the woman, barefooted, her long, dark hair loose down her back, stark against the white of her gown, is not Lucrezia.

It is as if Lucrezia were to have been summoned from the distant side of some dark mirror, and have been made flesh in changeling form. Her eyes burn with the same intensity, yet contain a wilder ferocity.

'Who are you?' demands Cecile, her voice louder, in its fear, than she would have thought possible.

The woman turns towards her, mouth moving, as if to speak. A keen desire to impart some message is apparent, though no words come. She is impotent, her voice lacking the power to make itself heard, and her face crumples, at once transformed, downcast in misery.

A rush of compassion overwhelms Cecile, to see this creature so troubled, and she calls out once again.

'Don't be afraid. Tell me who you are.'

The woman turns and Cecile sees, now, that she clutches a bundle beneath her arm.

The corridor is dark, in the absence of a candle, but before the woman takes flight, Cecile sees a small face tucked within swaddling. A face delicate enough to be that of a child. Of a baby. A face unmoving, as if the poor mite had ceased to belong to this world.

The tormented figure runs into the darkness beyond and Cecile, seared by dread, pushes through her door, bolting it behind.

As she flings herself upon her bed and presses her face against the pillow, a thunder crack rends the sky, and the first rain begins to fall.

IN PURSUIT

Henry wakes in the alleyway behind the bar, his face pressed to the dirt, and his jaw aching. He is alone, and a cold fear grips his heart.

He must find her.

At the harbour, the tide has reached its highest point, and is now on the turn. The revelries have subsided, most having succumbed to alcohol-induced sleep, wrapped in the arms of friends and lovers. Masks lie discarded on the cobbles.

From the villa, he locates a gun and a horse, and heads back through the main street of Scogliera, and onwards, taking the coast road.

The sky is a bleeding bruise of ink and purple, seeping and spreading, covering the moon, and obliging Henry to set an agonizingly slow pace. His eyes strain to make out the edge of the cliff, and to keep his horse safely guided. It is eerily quiet, without a single birdcall. Below, even the incessant rush of the waves is muffled, and their movement is concealed by an ascending mist, creeping from the sea, inland, rising to climb upwards, and drift across the road. Were he to ride blindly, he might find himself straying to the precipice.

Dear God, he prays, *may the carriage containing Maud not have fallen from this path.*

The air is damp and heavy, acrid almost, smelling of metal, swaddling him as he plods on. The toss of his horse's mane and its snorting breath are more tangible than his own hands, deathly white, numb upon the reins. The first fat splashes of rain break from above, hitting the baked dust of the road.

Too much time has passed, thinks Henry. *She might be in Sorrento by now, hidden somewhere I'll never find her, or placed on a boat. Who knows what dastardliness those curs have in mind... And here I am, barely able to see two steps in front of me. What hope is there!*

His mare stumbles against a rock, causing Henry to pause, and in that moment, he hears a voice calling to him, faintly, on the mounting wind. A voice of pain and fear, and so distant that his ears must deceive him. It is his imagination, surely. He listens again, but hears no more, and is about to continue when something catches against his lip. A hair has blown across his face, one which, as he removes it, he sees is long and auburn gold. He winds it about his finger, that thread binding her to him, and he to her.

She is not in Sorrento. She is close.

With uncanny conviction, he feels it, and he knows that her life is in danger. Whatever dread trembles beneath his skin, fluttering like a living thing, he must find her.

He looks about him, scanning the trees to his right, moving closer to peer through the shadows. The clouds part briefly, allowing the moon's illumination, and Henry sees that there is a break in the line of the cliff rising sheer above him. A crevasse. Wide enough for two horses. Wide enough, perhaps, for a carriage.

With his hand extended to touch the side of the passage, he nudges his horse onwards, with the press of his heels. The overhang above offers shelter from the rain, but allows no strand of moonlight to reach. Far off, thunder has begun to rumble.

Gradually, the trail opens and rises through the hillside, lemon trees and pines on either side. Without cover, Henry is soon wet through, but he can think only of where the path may lead. He is drawn, inexplicably, upwards, certain that Maud has called him to her.

Rounding a bend, he sees two horses, turned loose to graze, and behind them, the carriage, its door left carelessly ajar.

She is here. Somewhere close.

The track has ended, the trees closing in, preventing Henry from riding further. He dismounts, leading his mare through the narrow trail, pushing past dense foliage.

Ahead, there is a small flicker of light, and the outline of a wooden cabin. Henry ties his mare, and creeps forward, skirting the side, to peer through half-closed shutters.

What he sees chills his blood.

A NEW COUNTESS

Does Cecile sleep? How can she?

No matter that the key is turned in her lock, and her trunk placed before the door.

What does she fear most?

The return of that creature in torment, clutching her pitiful babe, or the knock of he who would call her wife, demanding permission to enter?

She lies awake, listening to the castle's creaking bones, steeped in the sea's embrace, and the sigh of wooden boards stretched by the salted wind.

She hears the clock chime each quarter hour. Time is not her friend, for it brings with it the inevitability of what must come. Will Henry countenance the Conte's suit of her hand? If he hesitates, will Lorenzo declare that he has already seduced her, obliging a marriage to save her honour? What escape can there be?

As soon as first light breaks, Cecile creeps to enter Lucrezia's room. How strange it is. What has passed between her and Lucrezia seems, once more, to have been no more than a fantasy, yet her body is warm, and Cecile wishes, more than anything, to remain enfolded in that dear embrace.

Lucrezia has pulled back the covers, gathering Cecile to her, holding her tightly. She too has spent the night in a troubled state, for what she believed she knew has twisted upon her and she finds that her intent now wears a different face. More than ever, she wishes to escape her jailor, but not at any price. For the friendship she has enacted with such care has become its own truth.

With sobs and sighs of despair, Cecile relates the events of the previous night.

'Lucrezia, you can have no idea of his true nature.' Her voice is quivering as she forms the words. 'He intends to visit Henry today, to agree terms for my hand, and he will say the most terrible things, to convince my brother of the necessity of a wedding. I have little idea why his mind is so set upon me, when he might surely choose any as his bride. Perhaps he thinks I shall be more biddable. Perhaps he's right, for I feel that my will to decide my own fate has been taken from me.'

Lucrezia finds that her fury burns even brighter than before. She will not betray Cecile, nor leave her to the machinations of her brother.

Together, they must escape.

~

WHEN CECILE HAS CALMED HERSELF, she steels herself to say what she knows she must.

'There is someone else in this house, Lucrezia... Someone we must help. When I returned to my room, I thought you were there, at my door, but it wasn't you.'

'And who was it?' asks Lucrezia.

'I don't know,' wails Cecile, her courage crumbling. 'And I was so terrified, Lucrezia! The woman looked wild, and sorrowful, and savage. And, in her arms, she carried...'

Cecile cannot bring herself to say more. She is stricken.

'There, there, my love. Soon, we shall be away from this place, and you need never think of these things again.'

At that moment, the door to Lucrezia's chamber opens, and another enters the room, the sight of whom rouses a stifled cry from Cecile.

'*Mio Dio*! You look at me as if I were Lucifer himself, risen from Hell!' remarks Lorenzo, seating himself upon the foot of the bed.

'Do you smell sulphur?'

'*Buongiorno, fratello,*' says Lucrezia, fixing him a steadfast eye.

'*Buongiorno, sorella,* and good morning my Cecile. How is my bride-to-be this morning? I see that you have been sharing confidences, and that my sister is the first to hear our joyful announcement. She will be delighted, I know, to hear of my victory... in claiming your hand.'

At this, Cecile buries her head upon Lucrezia's shoulder, stifling her tears.

'One of the maids has been walking in her sleep again, and has given Cecile a fright, as you see,' counters Lucrezia, with an arch to her brow. 'Everyone must lock their doors, and we should supervise more closely, do you not think? We cannot have so much wandering in dark corridors, and the rattling of doors that are not our own.'

'Ah yes,' says Lorenzo. 'I believe I saw Lady Cecile wandering herself, last night. One never knows who, or what, one might encounter. I'm sure that our young guest has too vivid an imagination. In the half-light, we see what we wish to see, as well as what we fear. Sometimes, of course, the two are the same. Then again, perhaps it was the White Countess, though the castle has many ghosts, and doors are no hindrance to them.'

With a sniff, Cecile raises her head. She must be braver, she knows.

'I have warned against these night-prowlings,' continues Lorenzo. 'Lady Cecile has been reading her novels, I suppose, and her fancies have taken flight. Women's minds are too impressionable for such stories.'

At this, Lucrezia comes to her defence.

'I find that life can be just as provocative as fiction. More so! Tales are not summoned from thin air. They are inspired by real events, often filled with more misery than the brain can fathom.'

Lucrezia spits the words at her brother.

'Men only rile at us reading such stories for fear of us emulating the transgressions within their pages.'

'I, for instance, might suddenly take a notion to be guided by my namesake, she who used her knowledge of chemistry to poison her rivals, and avenge lovers' deceit or insult, without fear of detection.'

'Quite true, my dear,' replies her brother. 'There's nothing of which we're incapable, if only we set our minds to it. Yours, I know only too well, is capable of great adaptability.'

'I'm sure that Lucrezia would never commit such an atrocity,' declares Cecile, an inner force driving her to speak. 'What do we have if we lack our code of morality, our good name, and the respect of society?'

'We might say we have our freedom,' adds Lucrezia, with some fierceness.

'No! I refuse to believe it,' cries Cecile. 'Your conscience would feel it too heavily. Whatever you feel, you must allow your nobler feelings to rule.'

'*Cara mia*, you think too highly of me. I am many things, but I'm no saint,' replies Lucrezia, a little wearily.

'My sister is also clever.'

Lorenzo reclines further upon the coverlet.

'If she chooses to poison someone, no one shall suspect her but the worms, who may suffer indigestion at second-hand from her efforts. Fortunately, she knows that were any such malady to befall me, Serpico would avenge me with all alacrity.'

'If I do poison you,' sneers Lucrezia, 'It will be to save Cecile from becoming your wife.'

'The next Contessa di Cavour will gain not only status and wealth, but a husband able to satisfy her. What more does a woman want?'

Saying this, the Conte reaches for Cecile's hand, raising it to his lips.

It is all she can do to avoid turning in disgust.

'Wives must take their husbands as they find them,' he muses.

'And why should a woman take a husband at all?' retorts Lucrezia.

'Women are mortal flesh, just as men,' he shrugs. 'And the flesh must be clothed, and housed, and warmed through the long hours of the night. Many, I find, are only too happy to place themselves in the power of another. The rest must endure their shackles, regardless of discomfort.' He raises his eyes to Lucrezia, '... or desire for escape.'

'Now,' continues the Conte, rising to leave. 'Cecile should speak to Magdalena about preparing a wedding feast. While the causeway is clear, I shall ride over to the villa, to tell my future brother-in-law of the happy news. I shall let him know that I'm not one to insist upon a virgin bride, and that I found you to be all that you should be, my dear, to the very point of your acquiescence. He will, I've no doubt, agree that the marriage should occur without delay. Servants do gossip and I have a feeling that he shall wish to secure the honourable reputation of his sister.'

'*Diavolo!*' hisses Lucrezia.

'The devil is always in fashion. Though I'm told one has to have been good in order to appreciate being bad. The devil is a fallen angel after all.'

He smiles at Cecile as he opens the door.

'I doubt that I shall join you at dinner, my love, for some other business awaits me. An old friend with whom I have an account to settle. I fear it may take some time to reach satisfaction, and I plan to drive a hard bargain.'

BETWEEN LIFE AND DEATH

Any man of reason has pondered that, perhaps, there is no Heaven, nor Hell, no eternal bliss nor damnation. In which case, our actions are of no significance, for good or bad, but that we must live with the memory of them.

What consequences are there for taking a life? For leaving a man with a mortal wound?

He'd been tempted to shoot them all dead. Three bullets for three heads. There are few practical skills associated with his class but, at least, he's used to handling a gun. He knows how to take aim, and gently squeeze the trigger. He can thank his father for that, though it's years since he's been obliged to put his marksmanship to the test.

He's not one for violence, but how should a man behave when the woman he loves is in danger. What scruples can possibly apply?

His first bullet had passed clean through a shoulder, the next shattered a knee. The third was never fired. His fury burned no less fiercely, but Henry found himself unable to injure a man who'd prostrated himself upon the floor. It was easy enough to tie them with rope.

He dares not think what Maud endured in those hours before he found her. Placed before him on his horse, his cloak wrapped tight around her bruised and bloodied body, her back leaning into his chest, she was barely conscious, subdued by her injuries and the potency of her sedative.

The return journey had been perilous, the steep track turned to mud by the rain. His mare lost its footing more than once, sliding its descent, with rolling, panicked eyes. The obscuring mist lay thick along the coast road. Henry had hugged the cliffs, plodding at a steady pace, and avoiding the worst of the rain by keeping close. To do otherwise would have been too treacherous. And all the while, his hand had lain upon Maud's heart, comforted by its abiding beat.

Reaching the villa, he'd slid her from the saddle and carried her in, to the warmth of their bed. She'd roused a little at the removal of her wet clothes, her arms rising to defend herself, yet too weak to open her eyes.

'There, my love, you're safe now,' he'd whispered. 'I'm here, and I shall be here always.'

~

THE HOURS HAVE PASSED, Henry fearing to leave her side. The fire has been lit, but still she shivers. Too long in the wet, and her body weakened by its ill-treatment, a fever is consuming her.

Her pulse falls to barely a flicker, and her breathing is shallow. She is waxen-pale, more sculpture than living woman. Her lips are paper-dry, though he wets them, before passing the sponge about her neck.

He takes her limp fingers and kisses each one. Slowly, so slowly. He pauses before he reaches the smallest. He presses her palm to his cheek, wanting to hold the moment still. Whatever is to come, he won't let it in.

He lays his head upon her chest, seeking to hear her heart, but she's so still, as if already departed. He speaks her name, but she cannot answer.

His tears come then, a distillation of his rage and sorrow until, face wet with all he cannot say, he falls asleep, the coverlet damp under his cheek and Maud's chill fingers still clasped in his.

∾

HER SCENT IS HIS SUSTENANCE. Her lips. Her body.

The sun rises, bringing with it all the vitality of the day. He opens the window, so the sounds of the garden may enter.

'Be careful when you love something wild,' she'd said. 'You may wake one day and find that it has flown, or crept or scampered away, leaving a space which can't be filled by anything tame.'

'Maud, don't leave me,' he pleads. 'You can't leave.'

His love for her claws at him, fills him with terror.

He has spent his life looking for her. How can he bear to lose her, now that she is found?

∾

MAUD DREAMS that she's climbing a ladder. Something, or someone, is pursuing her. She must reach the top, without knowing where the ladder leads. She dreams that she is on the mortuary slab, dissected.

Her organs are removed, one by one. Nothing is hidden. She is laid in the cold earth, in a hole where the worms are waiting for her.

When she wakes, it's to the sensation of heaviness on her chest. Her fingers move to push it away but she finds soft curls and the shell of Henry's ear. His face is rough, stubbled.

She is thirsty and her body aches, but a feeling of strength is within her too. Her hand has touched the veil which separates us from the next world, and she has lingered long in that dark place. In a slumber deeper than usual sleep, she has tossed between life and death, but she has not surrendered.

WHEN THE CONTE DI CAVOUR arrives to seek a meeting with Lord McCaulay, he finds the gentleman to be indisposed.

'What a pity,' Lorenzo remarks to the maid who takes his card. 'No matter. Give his Lordship my felicitations on his marriage. I have some acquaintance with his charming wife, and will now be delighted to enjoy the same with his sister. I'll return another day. Perhaps I may join his Lord and Ladyship in taking afternoon tea. Such a civilized custom.'

The Conte can barely contain his merriment as he mounts his stallion.

No doubt, he sits in his room and wrings his hands for his abducted darling. Fear not, Lord McCaulay, for she is in my firm custody, and I ride to visit her now. I shall give her every attention, and ensure she remembers the day she spurned the advances of a di Cavour, in favour of the milksop love of an English lord.

A FOUL PLOT THWARTED

'*I mbecilli! Sciocchi! Li maledica!*'

So many plans carefully laid, conceived over months. And to have them foiled by a mere foppish aristocrat! It's intolerable!

Lorenzo's desire for revenge over the imperious English woman has been long-awaited. No doubt, despite her rescue, she will forever remember her experience as an unpleasant one. However, he has been denied the climax of his own entertainment in the unfolding of this 'three-act play'. And Lorenzo is accustomed to gaining satisfaction, in all things.

Damn those peasant imbeciles I engaged to guard her and damn this tunnel!

Muttering more curses, he tears at a cobweb brushing his neck and returns the lantern to its hook, with a brusqueness that causes the glass on one side to crack.

Both hands are needed to open the door which leads from this passageway beneath the sands into the dank crypt of the Castello. The tides have fallen particularly inconveniently of late, covering the causeway just at the hours when he needs to move on and off the island. Privacy, like all things, comes at a price, but his bones are not growing any younger. The subterranean damp discomforts him.

The door has become stuck again, the wood expanding in its frame with the flow of water above. Serpico, walking behind his master, is obliged to put his shoulder to the oak to heave it open.

'I shall block this passageway and have done with it. Better to return to my Siena residence and leave this place altogether. Returning here after so many years travelling has been a mistake,' grumbles the Conte. 'Only the contents of the library and my private collection of curios have given me amusement, besides the occasional girl from the village, and such women are to be found anywhere. Serpico, you must arrange transportation. Have them sent on. My artworks too, of course.'

'Sì, maestro,' nods his manservant.

He passes by the staircase which would lead him to the chapel, taking instead the third door in the chamber, one hidden in a corner recess.

'Lady Cecile looks fertile enough. Once she is with child, I shall confine her to these walls. As the new Contessa, I may entrust her in watching over what is most inconvenient to me,' muses Lorenzo, leading the way. 'It will do very well, and I might visit once or twice a year, to ensure the addition of other di Cavours to the succession.'

As for this marriage, I shall need to act quickly. If Lady McCaulay real-

izes my part in her abduction, and confides in her gallant knight, he'll not only remove Cecile from under my roof, but may call me out in a duel.

He smiles. The more he ponders on the plan, the greater its attractiveness. He has no desire to have his habits hindered by the presence of a wife and, once he has enjoyed the novelty of her body, he knows well enough that his interest will wane. Her intellect is insufficient to engage him, and her conversation too lacking in sophistication. On state occasions, perhaps, he might have her brought to him, to appear before the royal court. She would do well enough.

Lucrezia is another matter, he thinks, climbing narrow steps.

She, I cannot spare. Where I go, she must accompany me. Her defiant outbursts of invective are most appealing. She'll make a satisfying mistress. Her acquiescence is inconsequential. If offspring are the result, they may be raised alongside my legitimate heirs, here, at Castello di Scogliera.

'Some housekeeping is in order, Serpico,' says the Conte, stepping over to pour himself a restorative from the decanter. 'Our guest in the tower has been making herself increasingly meddlesome, and Vittoria is too often careless in securing the bolts. I take no pleasure in the decision, but we must change her accommodation.'

Sitting in an armchair, he eases off his riding boots.

'Fetch her, Serpico, and secure her in the crypt. The key to the manacles you may place upon the hook at the foot of the stair, alongside those for the other doors. Bring down her bed and other comforts. I fear I cannot trust her with a candle, but you may fix a small lantern high from the ceiling, to be kept lit only during the day. Her mind, I fear, has fallen to such chaos that no recreation may alleviate its suffering. She has no solace in reading or other pastimes, so the lack of greater light may be of little consequence.'

'*Naturalmente, maestro,*' replies Serpico.

'I've been too soft of heart, and I see it is a failing. I'd hoped to return her to some civilized version of herself, to make amends for the abuses of my father, and calm her troubled spirit. I see that my hopes were in vain. Some wounds cannot be undone, the scars running too deep. A woman's mind, as well as her body, lacks the strength of a man's. It is one of life's truths, is it not Serpico?'

With a concurring bow, his vassal departs.

Lorenzo's eyes alight on the pair of ancestral pistols mounted above the fireplace.

In the event of a duel, my aim is true enough, but I dislike uncertain outcomes. Better to settle all, with my bride's signature upon the register, and oblige the English milksop to call me 'brother'.

Pouring another large brandy, the Conte finds his spirits lifting. How satisfying it is to see events turned so amusingly to his advantage.

ENTRAPMENT

C ecile wakes to the shutter banging and finds the window ajar. Fresh air is what she needs, and she gives the window a great push, leaning out to let the breeze catch her hair. The open sea is below, glinting with the reflection of a thousand scattered stars. Her eyes traverse the wall, which drops straight onto the rocks, forming part of the sheer cliff. If she were to be locked in this room, there would be no escape.

She has an image, suddenly, of Lorenzo scaling the side, like a creature of the night, unnaturally, as in that story by Mr. Stoker, of wolves and devilry and eternal damnation.

Perhaps she does read too many novels, or novels of the wrong sort.

But I'm sure that those who write such things draw not only from their imagination. The wickedness of those supernatural characters must be inspired by the true, baser nature of man.

The sea is rough, carrying a salted mist even as far as her window. The gulls have tucked themselves in the nooks of the granite, out of the way of the wind's whims.

She breathes deeply, then reaches to pull the window in. Her arm being not quite long enough, she's obliged to fetch her dressing table stool and, with one hand holding the frame, stretches for the handle. In doing so, she catches sight of the terrace below, where two stand together.

The hands of one are about the other, pushing away then pulling close, voices raised and then quiet. She cannot make them out, but one is a man and one a woman.

A midnight tryst? wonders Cecile. Raphael and Vittoria are courting, Lucrezia tells her. Perhaps they've stolen out to share a kiss.

Not wishing to intrude, Cecile reaches once more to tug the window handle, but the wind carries those voices upward, and she recognizes the tones of brother and sister.

Cecile picks out fragmented words, having learned a little Italian since her arrival. Enough for her to understand that she overhears an argument.

'... cannot go on.'

'...wicked...'

'...do as you're told.'

'and if I won't?'

The sharp slap of hand upon flesh cuts through the night, as if the blow were upon Cecile's own cheek.

Tumbling from the stool, the window pulls shut behind her, and Cecile finds herself upon the floor, the breath knocked from her body.

As if in a trance, she returns to lie beneath the coverlet. How foolish she has been, entertaining notions of playing the grand Contessa. She knows well that she has permitted herself to be flattered, ignoring the realities of the man before her. Has she encouraged, where she should have remained aloof?

Yet I have resisted his advances to the point that I retain my virginity. How far can he carry this empty threat that I carry his child?

Will the Conte's words have already poisoned her brother's ear, convincing Henry that she is a 'fallen woman'? For all the modern-thinking he has adopted of late, will her brother look sternly upon her?

I must get word to Henry.

She cannot have him believing such unseemly lies about her character. Cecile reminds herself of Henry's love and regard for her. Surely, he'll believe her assertion of her unmolested state, over any claims made by the Conte.

If I marry the Conte, it will be of my own free will, in good conscience.

I am not alone, she reminds herself. Agatha will speak for her, she's certain. Maud, too, will support her, being of such an independent nature, and Lucrezia. She must strategize, insist upon delay, appealing for time to organize the wedding in a respectable fashion. The Conte could not reasonably refuse her.

In spite of all she has witnessed, some part of her thrills, still, to imagine Lorenzo's hands reaching to possess her, his mouth claiming ownership of her skin, his eyes penetrating her very soul.

May it not, even now, turn out for the good, she wonders.

A man mellows under the influence of a wife, so they say. Once married, would he not grow to love me? I would be the mother of his children, his Contessa, his lifetime companion... and I would have position, and wealth, and Lucrezia would be always with me. What wonders we might discover together, all the world at our feet.

Even as she paints the scene, she knows it to be an illusion. She closes her eyes, in semblance of sleep, but is unable to quieten the fierce revolutions of her mind.

The wind continues to whip around the fortress walls. The worst excesses have left the terraces scattered with fallen blooms, flowers torn from their stems. The vivid beauty of the garden has been battered, cowed by the weight of raging rains. She listens to the hollow mistral-moan, pressing on all sides, as if to seek ingress.

At the window, the wind keens, and the castle responds with its own creaking of wood and plaster, shifting internally to meet the mournful lament. Hewn from the same granite as the island it stands upon, the ancestral stronghold of the di Cavours has withstood the centuries. Its occupants awake, and surrender, through the cycle of birth and death, but the castle walls remain unchanged, holding captive the souls within them, until they find repose in the depths of its vault, in those cold tombs.

The wail of the wind seems amplified, echoing inwards, carrying down the passageway, ever louder, until she begins to think her mind plays tricks on her. The weeping howl might be outside her very door, so magnified it seems. And then, to her shock, there is a kick upon the door, and the uttering of execrations.

'Sta 'zitto! Non lottare! Donna del diavolo!'

In reply, only an animal-whine, as of one held in the jaws of the huntsman's trap.

Cecile cannot close her eyes and pretend all is well. Instead, she rises, and lights her lamp, turning the flame low, and when the ululation has receded, moving past her chamber, onwards, she draws back the bolt and peeps into the corridor.

It's dark, but her lantern shows her the outline of a tall figure, broad of back, carrying a woman in his arms, her hair hanging loose, her head lolling.

Pulling her door closed with a quiet click, Cecile follows.

At the top of the staircase, she looks over the bannister, through the gloom, watching the pair descend. The woman's face, cast upwards, is pale in the darkness, her mouth slack. Her voice has folded in upon itself, until it is only a whimper.

Feeling for the edge of the steps with her slippered feet, Cecile takes each with care.

At the bottom, the moonlight from the tall windows shows her the profile of Serpico, with his hooked nose, and prominent brow. The woman clutches a bundle, close upon her chest.

Serpico crosses the hallway and enters the library. Having left her lamp upon a side-table, Cecile creeps to peek through the door left open behind him. The library is empty but for he, and the wretched woman he carries.

He walks directly to the right-hand side of the room, and looks along the shelving, as if seeking a particular title. Cecile sees him reach to touch the spine of a volume, and the wall moves. A dark space opens and Serpico, bearing his human burden, enters.

Cecile darts forward, but the shelf has slid back into its former position before she has reached even a third of the way. Looking at the books ranged before her, she cannot begin to guess at which unlocks the mechanism. Her hands trace the leather, pushing randomly at the height which appears most likely, without success.

The door has closed, and there is no hope of her following.

IN THE DARK

'Good morning, my dear. Now, I've no intention to slight where your heart has chosen,' begins Agatha, rising from the breakfast table, as Cecile enters the room. 'But I cannot hold my tongue.'

'My godson tells me that you've accepted his proposal of marriage, and that we should expect a new Contessa before the week is out.'

She pauses, as if searching for the right words, and seats herself again.

'My dear, it's all most sudden! Am I to believe that a proper courtship has taken place? That he has won your heart? That you are convinced of his suitability as a husband?'

Cecile finds that she must sit too, for her legs will no longer support her.

'Of course, the Conte is undeniably handsome and a man of status, and no inconsiderable means...'

Cecile looks across at Lucrezia but her friend makes no contribution, her eyes downcast to the rim of her coffee cup.

'If you're sure that this is the path to your happiness, I'll be the first to congratulate you,' adds Agatha, 'But I wish you to assure me that you've given the matter proper consideration, my dear. To act in haste is folly, as the marriages of so many demonstrate, and the Conte, for all his attractions, is not one to be tamed.'

Agatha sips from her cup.

'It's true that wives choose, often, to be blind to the indiscretions of their husbands, but is this what you wish for yourself, Cecile? For I cannot believe that the tiger will be turned from its nature.'

Agatha's plate is laden with ham and eggs, glistening in oil. As she raises a sliver of meat to her lips, Cecile feels, suddenly, quite sick.

'I understand that your suitor's eagerness has led to his early departure, crossing the causeway as soon as it became safe, to meet with the padre to acquire a special license. I must say that his hurriedness is unseemly. People will talk, Cecile.'

Agatha raises a toast soldier to attack her molten-yolk, looking sharply at Cecile. Her face is not that of an excited bride, Agatha cannot help but notice. In fact, she looks decidedly wan. Agatha lowers her voice, speaking with more gentleness.

'Forgive my indelicacy, my dear, but I must ask. Is there reason for this celerity? Have you permitted the Conte... freedoms? You are young, I know, and the passions of a whirlwind courtship can lead us astray. You would not be the first young woman to find herself in a difficult situation.'

'Lady Agatha,' Cecile begins, feeling that she must find her voice. 'The Conte's ardour has been difficult to keep at bay...'

Her eyes brim with tears.

'But I have not succumbed to any action obliging marriage, no matter what the Conte may infer. I fear that I do not know my own mind, and I do not know the Conte as well as I would like.'

With a little cough, Agatha dabs her napkin to her mouth.

'I see that I am right. You are not ready to be married.'

She hesitates.

'You wish to delay, my dear?' coaxes the old lady.

'I do,' admits Cecile, her hands trembling upon her cup. 'I don't understand his urgency, and I am fearful of what the Conte may have said to Henry to persuade him of the necessity for a hurried ceremony. That Henry has not visited, to discover my own feelings on the proposal, pains me.'

She finds that she cannot look Agatha in the eye.

'Of course, my dear. Say nothing more. I shall write this moment to Henry, and I shall speak to Lorenzo on his return. If he values your hand, he shall wait for it. It's indecent for him to bully you into marriage, and improper to fail to observe a courtship of adequate duration. He is too used to having his own way.'

Cecile once more cannot speak, but her eyes show her gratitude.

Lucrezia has sat in silence, but her own voice is added now to that of Agatha.

'Like all men!' she scoffs. 'They think only of their own desire, assuming reciprocity, and that everything can be accomplished in the twitch of a tail. Cecile shall not be manoeuvered into marriage. We'll tell him that she shall not wear some dusty relic of a dress, handed down from his grandmother. We shall take ourselves to Sorrento, and ensure Cecile is properly attired, with a trousseau as befits the next Contessa di Cavour. With all the items that must be purchased, and tailored, it will allow Cecile several weeks to decide her mind.'

'Marvellous, Lucrezia. Your tenacity does you credit,' admits Agatha, rising from the table.

She places her hand upon Cecile's shoulder. 'What it is to have good friends. As a married woman, you'll find them just as important as you do now. More, perhaps...'

With that, Agatha sweeps from the room, calling over her shoulder, 'I shall show you my letter for Henry when we meet for luncheon, my dears, and we may send Raphael to deliver it this afternoon.'

Cecile has risen and flung herself into Lucrezia's arms in a moment.

'There, there,' soothes Lucrezia, 'We shall not allow anything to happen unless it's your wish. Don't despair, *mia piccola*,' says Lucrezia. 'Together, we shall be stalwart, as the English say. Lady Agatha's letter will set all to rights. And we may prevail upon your new sister-in-law. She has some acquaintance with Lorenzo, I believe, and will speak for you, I'm sure. She may convince your brother that the match would be ill-fated, if that is your desire.'

'You're right, of course...' accedes Cecile.

Lucrezia holds Cecile's hand tightly.

'And, if you wish it,' ventures Lucrezia, 'We may suggest a modest income for you. I have jewellery that will fetch enough to live on, for some time. We might be our own selves, and not think of marriage just yet. We may rent a small cottage, in your English countryside, play music, paint and write, and turn our faces to the sun.'

'Could we really do such a thing? Might we?' asks Cecile.

The picture is suddenly an attractive one.

Feeling herself grow stronger, Cecile recalls something else that her conscience refuses to ignore.

'Last night, Lucrezia, I saw the strange woman again. She looks like you, except filled with wretchedness, as if carrying some terrible grief.'

Lucrezia diverts her gaze. There are many secrets, and she has concealed the truth for so long that she doesn't know where to begin revealing it.

'Not only that, Lucrezia,' Cecile continues. 'Serpico took her into the library and a wall opened. They stepped through, and I couldn't follow, but I fear something dreadful is afoot. I've been so caught up in myself that I've neglected to see what may be happening under my own nose. I don't know what's taking place here, but I can't ignore it and leave. How would I ever rest easy, having procured my escape, if this woman remains here in distress? We must find her and help her.'

Lucrezia has thought herself strong and this English lady weak, but admiration wells within her, and something akin to shame. Her own inclination is to flee, and not look back. No doubt, her principles are ill-formed. A childhood of manipulating others to ensure her comfort has given her little compunction to act otherwise than in her own interests.

'We must look Lucrezia, and find this passageway, and where it leads to,' urges Cecile. 'We must be brave.'

Lucrezia has long known who resides in the tower, and the story of why she's there.

'For her own good,' Lorenzo has told her. 'What life would she have? She's a danger to herself, and all around her.'

Lucrezia has allowed herself to believe this to be true. It has been convenient to do so, and Lucrezia would rather not bring complications on her head. However, she feels some shift in herself.

'*Sì, mio dolce*,' she nods. 'We shall look.'

LUCREZIA KNOWS ALREADY which book must slide back, to engage the mechanism. Her fingers find it easily, and the gloom of the stone passageway is revealed to them. A cool draught rises from the opening, and the smell of damp stone.

'Where does it lead?' asks Cecile.

'You know the place. Where the di Cavours lie in their tombs. There's more than one door to that chamber,' explains Lucrezia. 'We should take a lamp.'

As they descend, the dark is palpable. Cecile's hand finds the rough granite of the wall, cold to the touch, using it to feel her way. The lamp, held aloft by Lucrezia, throws little enough light, making it difficult to see the edge of the steps. Cecile fears that she may stumble, but some force draws her forward. Something is here that she must discover.

At last, she finds the flat of the floor, and they stand together. Water is dripping. Small bodies scuffle and scuttle.

'*Ratti*,' says Lucrezia. 'Let's move.'

Their breathing is so loud that it seems to fill the space, but there's someone else too, Cecile is sure. Another's breath in this subterranean cavern; inhaling, exhaling.

Lucrezia holds their lamp higher, illuminating the tombs down either wall. It's cold, here, in this buried place. The skin on Cecile's back prickles, as if something unearthly touches her from the shadows, something wild and terrible. She feels eyes upon her, beyond the meagre pool of light in which they stand. Eyes which have watched long, seeking her out, wishing to communicate.

The flame of their lamp sputters, eaten by the darkness, and a mournful wail begins to rise. It curls from the walls in an unravelling ribbon of grief and pain, as if the stones of Castello di Cavour bemoaned the long, dark hours of silence, and their own centuries of suffering.

Lucrezia clutches at Cecile's arm.

'*Così terribile! Preservami Dio!*'

'I'm here,' says Cecile. 'We're together. We'll do this together.'

She doesn't feel brave, but she must convince herself to be so.

The wail subsides, replaced by a scraping sound, as of nails against stone.

'Can you hear it?' asks Cecile

The sound comes again. A scratching, ahead of them, deeper in the crypt. As they move forward, there is the smell of decay, of old meat, of sour flesh. And a faint glow, as from a lantern turned low.

At the far end of the chamber, a figure crouches upon a bed, hair long and tangled, face turned away. Her nails drag across the stone, lifting periodically to renew the motion, hands cuffed and chained. When the woman raises her head, her eyes are sunken and her face deathly, in the flicker of the oil lamp.

'*Mio Dio!*' exclaims Lucrezia. 'Livia!'

She jerks at the utterance of her name.

Cecile's instinct is to draw back, but this is no monster, and there is no malevolence. She is flesh and blood and her nails, though blackened and broken, are those of no demon, but a human wretch.

'It's alright,' Cecile whispers, whether to herself, or Lucrezia, or this poor creature. 'It's alright.'

Cecile takes the final steps towards the woman, bends to take her hands in her own, refusing to be deterred by the unwashed smell of her body.

The woman's mouth moves, as if to speak, her voice rasping, but the sounds she wishes to make are unable to leave her tongue. They remain half-formed, dying in a stutter.

'These are like the manacles Lorenzo placed about my wrists that day...' says Cecile.

The remembrance of it, of her own quickened pulse, of the strange excitement it roused in her, now makes her feel nauseous. For who can be responsible for this but the Conte. Nothing happens in the Castello without his direction.

'There are keys, near the staircase. Wait here, Cecile, and I shall fetch them. One may open these cuffs.'

Before Cecile has a chance to answer, Lucrezia has moved away, taking their lamp with her. Despite the dim glow from the lantern suspended overhead, the darkness seems to flood into her eyes, her nostrils, her ears. All the horrors of that place whirl about her within that rushing dark. Her consciousness sways inside her.

To be left here alone, without sufficient light or warmth, without anyone to care. What mind would not be disturbed by such imprisonment, such isolation?

Livia's fingers press tightly to her own.

When Lucrezia returns with the lamp, Cecile's own face turns towards its welcome light.

It's the work of moments to fit the key into the lock and slide back the bolt, revealing the skin of Livia's wrists, rubbed red. Her mouth trembles again, but words still will not come.

'Come with us,' says Cecile.

'Cecile,' warns Lucrezia. 'We cannot!'

Cecile stands, attempting to raise Livia to her feet, but she cowers away, reaching for the bundle beside her on the bed.

'Come with us,' says Cecile again. 'We can't leave you here.'

But the woman who was once Livia has closed her ears, turning her face to the wall.

As she pulls the bundle towards her, Cecile sees again the tiny face, with its open, upturned lips. Not a baby, but a doll.

'I WILL TELL you all I know. But not here,' says Lucrezia. 'In the garden.'

How long ago it seems, that first day, when Cecile explored the fragrant terraces, and delighted in the cascading of lush blooms.

They close the door, returning to the light.

'You told me that she'd died,' admonishes Cecile, as they hurry down the steps. 'But you knew all along... knew she was here.'

'I didn't tell you all of the truth,' Lucrezia admits. 'What good would it have done for you to know everything?'

'I might have married him,' says Cecile, 'Not knowing what he'd done!'

Lucrezia looks behind them, as if to check they are unheard and not followed.

'I told you most of the story. You remember that Livia had a baby? It was Camillo who visited her in the night, her own father. It's no wonder that she began to lose her wits. Lorenzo tells me he remembers hearing her crying, often. She would never speak of it.'

Lucrezia looks again over Cecile's shoulder.

'Perhaps Isabella never knew. They say that mothers do not always, or that they cannot allow themselves to believe.'

Cecile looks out at the sea, upon which the sun catches brightly.

It seems so cruel that we feel the warmth and light, while one who might sit with us, had life treated her more kindly, remains in darkness.

'They hid her away, in the asylum, not just for the wild behaviour she began to exhibit, but to conceal the pregnancy. The baby died, but she did not, and whatever remaining sanity she possessed ebbed away. Through grief I suppose, and being put in such a place. I'm sure that we'd lose our reason too, under those circumstances.'

'It's too barbarous,' says Cecile.

'When Lorenzo first brought me here, he showed me her tower. Her room was simply furnished but she had a window, and Vittoria would sit with her. I believe him that, when he claimed her from the asylum, he'd hoped to offer her a life of some comfort. He was brave in some respects, for his own mother believes Livia to be dead. Lorenzo could have lived with the same lie. Instead, he found her, and returned her to her family home.'

Cecile cannot help but frown.

'And what now? She's too inconvenient, so is parted from all humanity, confined in that dark, dreadful place. This I cannot forgive him.'

'I agree that we cannot leave her there,' concedes Lucrezia. 'But I don't know what we may do. The strings of the mind, like those of a violin or piano, easily run out of order, and I fear Livia can never be mended.'

Lucrezia takes Cecile's hands in hers.

'I'll speak with Magdalena. It may be that we can take her from the crypt. There's a passageway from that chamber, which runs under the sand, to Scogliera. A relative of Magdalena may agree to look after Livia. Money can always be found. Lorenzo is generous in the purse he allows the kitchen. We might say that she escaped and drowned, if we leave her clothes upon the rocks.'

'Yes...' says Cecile, wiping a tear from her eye.

'And then we too must disappear, *mia cara*. We aren't safe here. Despite these plans of marriage, my brother is not content. I fear that, as his wife, he does not intend to do kindly to you, and that, soon, his spite will turn on us.'

The sun is warm, yet Cecile cannot help but shiver.

'*Mia bella*,' says Lucrezia, placing her arm about Cecile's shoulders.

'I've been wandering in the dark but I've found you. Let's leave this place. It's too full of others' history, reaching into the present. We should make our own history now.'

CONSUMED

Lorenzo has been drinking for many hours, having begun before dinner: a solemn affair, in which neither his bride-to-be, nor Lucrezia were able to return his conversation.

Hell take them!

Lorenzo is tired of waiting. In the morning, the padre will come, early, as soon as the tide recedes and his horse may cross the sands.

They'll speak their vows in the chapel, without guests, or wedding gown, or flowers. He'll drag her from her bed if necessary and hold her upon her knees before the altar, but he'll have his way.

She's of the age of consent. Once we're joined in the eyes of God, no one shall have the power to challenge our union. She'll do as she's bidden, and her brother may gnash his teeth all he likes, without authority to interfere.

He raises the decanter once more, but it's empty.

How long has he been plagued by this hopeless longing? He's yearned for something, but known not what, wasting time and energy in pursuit of endless distractions. Now, he knows what he wants. An heir! She'll bear him fine children, he's certain, and they'll be his legacy. Sons! This is what he wants.

The seas are eternal, as are the wind, and thunder and all elementals, but not human flesh. It withers and fades. The body is finite. Even the brightest light may be extinguished, and he is weary to the bone.

Is it the curse of the White Contessa, bringing down her ill-wished prophecies on the men of his line, or is it his own wickedness, that leads him on devilish paths?

His heart is a night garden of buried deeds, in which virtue has been strangled by rambling, venomous creepers, poisoned by the serpent's fang.

His head is growing heavy, nodding to rest on his chest. His cigar droops from his fingers.

Quietly, the shelving in the wall slides open. Someone is standing silently, watching, having emerged from the darkness.

Lorenzo dozes, and dreams that the crushing hand of mortality is at his throat. He wonders, as he has on other nights, who or what may await him when he crosses from this world to the next.

It's Livia who grips his neck, her eyes alight as she squeezes her brother's last breaths from his chest.

The cigar is still glowing, its heat catching easily at the papers on the desk. How beautifully they flare, curling to ash at her touch. Such a little thing, but look what it can do. She holds it to a newspaper folded on the table, to a book lying open, to the curtains.

Flames lick upwards.

DEATH

A room full of paper makes a feast for crimson tongues. Hot and hungrily, they consume. The flames are undiscerning. All volumes are to their taste.

The leering devils carved into the shelves find they dance more merrily in the heat of fire. Swooping down the chimney, the wind blows encouragement on the blaze.

Livia drops the cigar onto Lorenzo's lap and runs from the room, her bare feet taking her up the stairs. It's dark, but she knows the way. Along the corridor and up to her tower room. It looks larger, without her bed. She takes a cushion from the armchair and hunches behind.

Best to hide, she thinks. Hide where no one will find me.

CECILE WAKES to the smell of smoke, and a fist beating upon her door.

'Quickly!' Lucrezia implores. 'We'll take the servants' stair, down to the kitchen.'

Agatha stands beside her, holding an oil lamp, looking frailer than usual, her face grey with fear, coughing at the fumes drifting around them.

Holding her between them, Cecile and Lucrezia have almost reached the end of the passage when they hear a long and melancholy keening.

'It's the wind,' says Lucrezia, but Cecile knows better.

'Not the wind,' she says. 'It's her!'

A sorrowful, spiralling note drifts down the corridor, from the direction of the tower.

'We must leave,' insists Lucrezia.

But Cecile is already turning back the way they've come.

'Take Agatha to safety. I'll try to find Livia.'

Lucrezia calls Cecile's name, but she's already gone, feeling her way through the dark, her fingers keeping contact with the wall, following the wailing lament, until she reaches the door to the tower.

It's open.

Lifting the hem of her nightdress, she takes the stairs as quickly as she can, groping for the edge of each step above her. The air clears as she ascends, the smoke being yet to reach this part of the castle.

The room appears empty, but for a chair that's seen better days, its rose-brocade faded, threads loose and puckered. Tattered braiding trails from dusty curtains, hanging forlornly from their crooked rail.

A simple chandelier, empty of candles, moves in the draught, its few glass beads tinkling faintly.

Apart from this, the room is silent.

There is little enough light. The moon, barely at half-strength, shines weakly through the window.

'Livia,' urges Cecile. 'We must go. Come with me.'

There's a mirror on the wall, mottled with age. Cecile sees herself in its dingy reflection. For a moment, it's as if she's the occupant of this pitiful room; she the one who must be saved. Then, behind her, something moves. The mirror shows her a crouching figure. A ghost from the past, with a face bone-white, and eyes beetle-dark.

She is whimpering.

'It's me. You're safe,' coaxes Cecile.

I'll never be safe, thinks Livia.

She almost knocks Cecile to the floor as she rushes past and takes the stairs again. Not down but up.

'Livia!' Cecile calls, following close behind.

Lorenzo's warning had some truth, for the steps have deteriorated badly. Her feet are small, yet twice she slips, grazing her shin.

Smoke has begun to enter, rising, the smell acrid, but at last, having climbed the curving spiral, doing her best to judge the distance from one step to the next, Cecile reaches the upper door. It is cast open, the brisk night air sweeping in, with refreshing coolness.

Coming out onto the flat of the roof, Cecile sees, ahead of her, the wind whisking Livia's long hair. Torn strips of cloud are streaming across the moon. Livia runs, climbing onto the battlements.

'Wait!' Cecile's voice is taken by the swiftness of the breeze.

She races to her, placing her own foot on the stone's edge.

They stand, nightdresses billowing, looking down at the tumbling froth, and the straining sinew of the sea.

There is the sound of glass shattering, and flames begin to leap from the windows, fumes belching out from the fiery belly of the library.

Cecile reaches for Livia, who hugs her bundle closer to her chest.

The small face is visible, the face of the doll who is not a baby, but represents the baby who might have been.

For a moment, Cecile imagines how easy it would be to hold hands, and step into the air together.

There is the sound of coughing behind them, as Lucrezia stumbles onto the roof.

'Quickly! You must come now!' she exhorts, her voice rasping.

Cecile looks towards the sloping gardens, where the leaves shimmer, wild, on the whipping arms of dark branches. From this corner point, she can see both the harbour and the open sea, the terrace on one side of the library — where she crouched, eavesdropping on Lorenzo — and the castle wall, sheer beneath them, upon its granite plinth.

As she turns, she sees the flutter of white fabric.

Livia di Cavour has flown free, down, to the welcoming glow in the darkness.

She disappears into the night. Into the sea.

THE WHITE CONTESSA watches over the two young women as they flee through walls of billowing smoke and blazing cinders. As they pass, through crack and spit and roar, she blows back the flames and fumes, that would scorch and choke them. In their wake, the fire leaps once more, fuelled by her molten anger. She watches the demise of the ancestral home of the di Cavours, who made each other what they were, and are.

Cecile and Lucrezia stumble, at last, from the kitchen door, faces blackened with soot, clutching one another. Their feet take them to safety, where Agatha and the loyal servants of the household stand, beneath overhanging oleanders, faces raised in awe, and fear, and lit by the fierce heat.

The castle remembers, as it burns.

AWAKENING

Henry had long dreamed of unravelling the mysteries of the universe, as if they were a puzzle to solve. To this end, he has studied the classics of Greek and Roman literature, attended dissections of the human body, and wandered the streets of London, seeking to understand human nature through the observation of each face. He has believed that time will bring ultimate wisdom. Now, he realizes that these mysteries will only ever be partially understood. They are not to be solved, only to be experienced, and the greatest mystery of all is our ability to love another more than our own self.

Certain forces drive us through this life: hunger, the need for comfort and shelter, for warmth, and curiosity for learning, but one drives more forcefully than all the rest: the desire for love, the desire to find a kindred spirit.

Why did he marry? What did he hope for?

He'd long realized that perfection, as the world defined it, bored him. Instead, he has chosen a wife who's unbiddable, unfathomable. She possesses elegance and manners but demonstrates them not for the benefit of others, as much as for her own ease.

They are husband and wife, yet she remains a mystery to him in many ways. How far do her kisses reveal her thoughts? He thinks of his hands sliding over her body, his body sliding into her. What does he learn from the small, indefinable sounds that escape her, that he listens for?

She is like the sea, the depths of which are inscrutable. He sees what she allows him to see, reading the small clues that float occasionally to the surface.

And how much he loves her, not just with passion but with steadfast love. What happiness he feels at the sight of her, the sound of her voice, and the scent of her body.

Maud's eyes are closed in sleep beside him, her breathing regular. The fever has passed. It's been many days since her kidnapping, and the fire at the Castello. What fearsome alignment of the stars there must have been. He might have lost two, dearest to him in all the world. His Cecile, and his Maud. Both are safe now.

She shifts beneath the sheets, stirs, and sighs, and wakes. Her eyes are moist with tears.

'My darling,' he whispers. 'There's only you and me. Nothing bad. Nothing to harm you.'

Maud's eyes meet his for a long, sorrowful moment, and her lips attempt to form words. She is a scorched moth, drawn to the deadly flame. Fragile. Mortal. The soft beauty of her body will be its downfall.

Her mouth on Henry's is soft and compliant, opening to him. Her body, too, wishing to be taken charge of, and cherished. She takes his musk-scented strength inside herself.

'I love you,' he tells her, and she knows that he speaks the truth.

His love is not for an idea of what she might be but for herself, in spite of all that she is, and because of it.

NEW BEGINNINGS

'Oh! *Scappa!*' cries Lucrezia, startled by a plump and hairy caterpillar investigating the crook of her elbow. 'What a vile thing!'

'Don't be scared,' says Maud, lifting it from her arm and placing it upon a nearby leaf. 'From the unpromising caterpillar comes the butterfly. It retreats temporarily into its cocoon and transforms, born to beauty, and the freedom of the air.'

'I like the idea of freedom,' muses Cecile. 'Maud, can one marry and be free do you think?'

'History tends to show us otherwise,' Maud replies, with a half-smile. 'But, it's up to us to write new rules. Perhaps it can be done...'

'Of course, there's no need for you to wed yourselves to men and the predictability that entails,' asserts Agatha, lifting the teapot. 'I am deeply sorry, my dears, for your loss, and I cannot begin to imagine how Isabella will take the news of her son's death. I shall travel to London, I think, to spend some time with her. She will be distraught. Though Lorenzo's behaviour was not always as she would have wished, the bonds of blood cannot be denied. The loss of a child is inevitably painful.'

She visits each cup.

'I shall not presume to probe your heart Cecile, but I hope that any wound may soon be mended. The Conte, I fear, would never have made you happy.'

Cecile, her eyes upon the honeysuckle pattern of her teacup, finds that her heart is strangely untouched, and the realization shames her.

'If you do decide to marry, one day,' Agatha continues, 'There will be other suitors. Meanwhile, you may be whatever you choose and, my darlings, you'll always have a home here, at the Villa Scogliera.'

'Thank you, Lady Agatha,' answers Lucrezia. 'I may well be in need of your hospitality.'

Cecile rises to give the old lady a kiss upon the cheek.

'I shall write to Isabella,' says Maud, 'Offering my condolences. She was very good to me, during my stay with her in London.'

'She thinks of you with great fondness, my dear,' says Agatha. 'There was a daughter, but she died. A frail girl, I heard. No doubt, Isabella found great comfort in your company.'

Cecile and Lucrezia's eyes meet, but they say nothing.

'Such a terrible tragedy,' remarks Maud, 'For that ancient castle to be left in ruins. I visited often, as a child. The gardens are beautiful, I recall.'

She takes a sip of hot tea.

'I never met Lorenzo there. He was always away: at university, and then travelling, or residing in Siena, I believe.'

'Did you not meet in London?' asks Lucrezia, 'Not so long ago…?'

Maud's eyes flash, but she composes herself. The question goes unanswered.

'And sad, also, to lose one's home. I understand that there's little provision for you, Lucrezia, in your brother's will, and some distant cousin inherits the title…'

'We were only half-siblings,' admits Lucrezia, 'However, my jewels were in my pockets when we fled. My brother was generous in his gifts. The gems are real… as far as I know.'

'My condolences for your loss,' adds Maud, almost as an afterthought, her expression somewhat distracted. 'I hear that Lorenzo was apt to smoke cigars, and he seems to have fallen asleep while doing so. I'm pleased that the servants escaped unharmed.'

'Yes,' comments Agatha, 'All but his man, who is unaccounted for. Serpico was seen entering the library, to rescue his master, despite the heat of the flames. Terribly brave. It speaks for some worthiness in one's character, to inspire such loyalty. Sadly, neither body has been recovered. The ceiling has collapsed and the room is quite destroyed. Better to leave them resting in peace.'

'Peace was something my brother struggled to find in life. Perhaps he may do so now…' confesses Lucrezia. She hesitates, as if to say more, but changes her mind, and looks away.

'Cecile was so brave,' adds Agatha. 'Turning back to save one of the staff she thought was still in the upper part of the castle.'

Lucrezia shakes her head slightly, as her eyes meet Cecile's.

'It was more foolish than brave,' says Cecile. 'For the cry for help I thought I heard was only the wind, whistling down an open staircase. An illusion. Nothing more.'

Agatha places her palm against Cecile's cheek.

'Courageous and modest!' she avows.

'Padre Giovanni Gargiullo, from Pietrocina, is coming to say prayers at the site.'

Agatha looks wistfully, towards the sea.

'I'll do what I can for the staff. Raphael is to work here now, and I'll employ Magdalena, if she wishes to come. I'll write references, that all may seek employment in Sorrento.'

She gives a sniff.

'They might find it suits them better, in the end. A modern hotel offers more opportunities than a private home. Times are changing, after all.'

When Maud turns her head, Henry is there, come to bring her shawl.

'It's starting to feel like autumn, my love, with this chill in the air and leaves chasing each other about the garden. Perhaps it's time for us to leave,' he says.

Wrapping the shawl about Maud's shoulders, he places her arm upon his.

'Walk with me,' says Henry, nodding at the others before leading her away, through the olive trees, where the breeze shimmers the slim, silver-green leaves.

'I wish to discuss something alone with you, my love. There's an expedition heading to Brazil, organized by the Ornithological Union and the Natural History Museum. I've been invited to join them, and must telegraph soon.'

He turns to face her.

'I'd thought to decline, as the expedition will require us to put aside many of our comforts, but I think the trip is just what's needed. A fresh page, putting aside all that's happened here. If we're to join them, I must telegraph soon.'

Henry pauses, endeavouring to read her expression.

'Don't think that I make this suggestion lightly, Maud. It's my duty to ensure your happiness, and I believe the adventure will revive you, offering opportunities for your own study. You might present a series of papers on your return, or find a publisher for your work. Your illustrations are more than fine enough. The work of the Royal Entomology Society would be enriched by your efforts.'

She sighs, before allowing herself a tentative smile.

'We can, I suppose, live as many lives as we like…'

She touches his cheek.

Driven by curiosity, and by grief, seeking to punish and lose herself, she has embraced those extremes, wishing to awaken parts of her nature as yet undiscovered. She has taken herself to the brink, seeing the chasm, yet stepping into it. She cannot live without folly and danger it seems, but perhaps there are other ways to court them. Some winds keep us awake, while others lull us to sleep, and some blow out the old, leaving room for fresh approaches.

'How pleasant it is to bask in your adoration, husband,' says Maud, leading them towards the clifftop steps. 'To know that you seek my own happiness in equal portion to your own.'

Her tone is suddenly playful.

'I think you'd love me even if I ate nothing but garlic and cabbage.'

'Probably,' he muses, while crinkling his nose in an expression of distaste.

'And will you still love me when my skin wrinkles like an over-ripe apple, and my teeth come loose?'

'Even more then, for my skin and teeth will be the same - and we'll have grown old together.'

Maud pauses, smiling with pleasure at Henry's answers.

'And what if I spoke only of the latest fashions in hats and shoes?'

'I would, although I might have to stop your lips more often with my kisses.'

She raises her face to his, and they stand for some moments, his arms wrapped closely about her, his embrace both tender and passionate.

It is she who breaks away.

'And will you continue to worship me if I grow fat, so that I waddle more than glide?'

Henry laughs.

'I might urge you to eat less cake, my darling,' he admits. 'But I'll love you no matter how you're embellished.'

'And what if my belly swells not from cake, but from your love?'

Henry looks at her directly. Is she in earnest? He sees in her face a strange excitement.

'My darling!'

Falling at once to his knees, he presses his cheek to her stomach.

Maud has been looking for so long while unsure of what she sought or how to find it. She has been scared, of herself, and of the changes coming, but the rules are changing.

Isn't this how it is? The world changes a little every day and so do we? The world can be fearsome, but no more so than the unfathomable space inside.

Maud is ready to enter a new incarnation, in which she's lifted by the wind, and carried to new places. She'd thought them too far away for her wings to reach, but it's only a matter of flying to where she wishes to go, towards the points of light in the dark.

She's still mistress of herself. She always will be.

She holds her face to the sun, and feels its warmth not just on her skin but inside too. Henry's lips join hers once more and so light and joyous are their kisses that they float upwards, drifting through the air, over summer-bathed lawns; swooping through the Cyprus trees, where they shiver and shimmer in the branches. Out, out, out they go, to the open sea.

EPILOGUE

Whom among us would not be tempted by the wild luxuriance of barely discovered lands? By the vast, lush jungle? A place of violence and beauty, in its endless, devouring cycle, and home to untold species, waiting to be looked upon by human eyes: joyous parrots and gaudy toucans and others perhaps yet without names.

The night before their departure, Cecile dreams of the sinister night howl of monkeys. She cannot content herself with a quiet life. Not for her a tranquil existence in a provincial English town, or days of ease at the Villa Scogliera. The world awaits her.

And she will not be alone.

How kind her brother has been, and Maud too. Henry is to pay not only for her passage on the SS Leviathan, taking them across the Atlantic, but for Lucrezia's too. A young woman must have company, and she cannot bear to be parted from Lucrezia. They shall make a jolly party.

It's without regret that Cecile stands on the deck of the great steamer, looking down at the bustling harbour. Among the many heads below, Cecile spots one whose golden curls rise above those of his fellow passengers, as he makes his way towards the wooden plank bridge.

Her eyesight would need to be better than it is for her to read that his luggage bears the initials L.R. Nevertheless, when he raises his face to look upon the vessel destined to take him across the high seas, Cecile has no difficulty in recognizing those bold features.

And she smiles.

Of course, this story has no ending. The words stop here merely because this is where we choose to leave... for now.

REVIEWS

If you've enjoyed this work, Emmanuelle would love to receive your review.
Reviews are essential in bringing new reader eyes.
Find 'The Noire Series' on Amazon

With sincere thanks

MURDER ON THE SS LEVIATHAN

VOLUME THREE - NOIRE

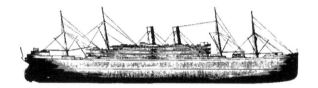

Coming Summer 2018

Henry and Maud, Lucrezia and Cecile are not alone.
No one is safe.
No one can be trusted.
Beware the shadows, for someone lurks with evil intent.

FURTHER WORKS, BY EMMANUELLE DE MAUPASSANT

Highland Pursuits

It's 1928, and defiant debutante Lady Ophelia Finchingfield has been banished to the Highlands of Scotland. A bizarre selection of suitors soon present themselves, but Ophelia remains one step ahead, until she begins to harbour feelings for Hamish, the Castle's estate manager. To Ophelia's annoyance, he's already spoken for, and glamorous French coquette Felicité has no intention of letting ruggedly attractive Hamish slip from the service of her bed. Intrigue abounds, as Ophelia discovers that there's more to her rival than meets the eye, and that the Castle is a hotbed of illicit cavorting.

Highland Christmas

Castle Kintochlochie is hosting a wedding, but malicious forces are at work. Is the castle really haunted?

'Highland Christmas' is the sequel to 'Highland Pursuits', featuring 1920s debutante Lady Ophelia Finchingfield.

A riotous romantic romp, with a mystery to solve.

Cautionary Tales

The boundaries between the everyday and the unearthly are snakeskin-thin. The trees have eyes and the night has talons. Demons, drawn by the perfume of human vice and wickedness, lurk with intents malicious and capricious. Tread carefully, for the dark things best left behind in the forest may seep under your door and sup with you. The lover at your window or in your bed may have the scent of your death already on their breath.
Is the shadow on the wall, really yours, after all?

'Funny, brutal, and irreverent' – Bustle.com
Twelve tales inspired by Eastern European and Russian superstitions and folklore; darkly delicious imaginings for the adult connoisseur of bedtime stories.

Viking Thunder
'We all struggle. We all desire.'
Elswyth is faced with the prowess of Eirik: a giant of a man who lets nothing stand in his way. She cannot deny her sexual attraction and, ultimately, the satisfaction she finds in Eirik's bed.
As Elswyth explores her true identity, she is torn in her loyalty. If she returns with the Northmen to their distant lands, what dark secrets await?

Baby Love
8 months pregnant and still sexy!
Delphine's rat-fink husband has packed his bags and abandoned her for the charms of their neighbour, leaving Delphine struggling to cope. Delphine's sisters insist that the best remedy for a broken heart is a dose of pampering. Cue a spa break, where handsome Texan Jack and suave Marco await. Will there be more in store for Delphine than a hot stone massage and a spell in the Jacuzzi?
A romantic comedy from Emmanuelle de Maupassant, set in British Cornwall.

Short stories by Emmanuelle de Maupassant appear in the following anthologies

Best Women's Erotica of the Year Volume 3 (Cleis Press)
Big Book of Submission Volume 2 (Cleis Press)
For the Men (Stupid Fish Productions)
Dirty 30 Volume 2 (Stupid Fish Productions)
Amorous Congress (Riverdale Avenue Books)

BONUS MATERIALS

Included at the end of this edition are the initial chapters of 1920s romance romp, *Highland Pursuits.*

HIGHLAND PURSUITS

It had been in the back of a taxi, in the summer of 1928, that Lady Ophelia Finchingfield had first realized her views on the wedded state. Perhaps it was his awkward, overly lubricated kiss, or the inept grope upon her breast that brought the revelation. Perhaps it was the conviction that her suitor lacked the brooding depth of a Heathcliff, or a Rochester. Whatever the substance behind her discovery, she accordingly turned down an offer of marriage from the Honourable Percival Huntley-Withington who, at the tender age of twenty-two, had recently succeeded his father as Earl of Woldershire.

Some months earlier, just after Easter, Ophelia had begun her debutante season. She had since attended twelve balls, nineteen cocktail parties, and eleven dinners. Most mornings had seen her riding in Hyde Park, along Rotten Row and Ladies' Mile, returning to a formal breakfast of kippers, omelettes and grilled kidneys.

She had attended polo and cricket matches, had played croquet and lawn tennis, and had tried her hand at archery and at bowls. Her attendance had been sought at intimate concerts, garden parties and picnics.

There had been nights at the opera (where no one listened), and nights at the ballet (where no one watched). It was apparent that the real purpose was to be seen. Ophelia had become accustomed to falling into bed, exhausted, often no earlier than two in the morning.

Her little Cairn terrier, Pudding, was most affronted by her mistress' new social habits. Ophelia had scarce time to bestow the tickles that Pudding's soft little belly had come to expect. In the hours of Ophelia's absence, Pudding would bury her nose upon her mistress' pillow, feeling the passing of every minute, and ruminating sorrowfully on her neglect. Only the sincere embraces of Ophelia's return convinced Pudding she was not altogether forgotten.

Barely halfway through the marathon of endurance, at the end of May, Ophelia had wondered how she would maintain the pace. Her own debutante ball had been scheduled for the first week in August, and she'd begun to feel that her feet would be worn to stumps before the date arrived. It being her own dance, she'd have no choice but to endure the clutches of every decrepit old wart and every young toad wishing to shuffle her about. She would have a moldy time of it.

There had been little need for her mother, Lady Daphne, to court favour on her behalf, since the family's wealth alone inspired others to solicit her presence. The Honourable Sir Peter Finchingfield, MP for King's Lyppe, was heir to a successful turkey farming business. Moreover, he was a rising star in the Conservative party, tipped for a cabinet position, having recently led a vital debate in the House on subsidization of root vegetable growing, with particular reference to swedes and turnips.

What Sir Peter lacked in charm was provisioned by Lady Daphne, herself the daughter of a noble family, though one of constrained means. She believed in her own infallible taste: in clothes, literature, art, music and interior décor. It was of no regard that her acquaintance with them resembled that of a bee flitting from flower to flower, without collecting a grain of pollen.

Those confident in the marvel of their own brilliance are never shaken by the criticisms of lesser creatures. In her eyes, all things connected with herself were highly sought after. Since social standing and money happily met in the Finchingfield household, the world at large was disposed to agree.

At the birth of her baby daughter, Lady Daphne was confronted with the uninspiring option of naming her after Sir Peter's mother, Edna, or his grandmother, Elsie. Pretending a great love of Shakespeare, she landed upon Ophelia, a name that she hoped would bestow her (as it turned out) only daughter with a love of literature.

For all her espousal of the arts, she'd never read a word of the Bard, though she had once attended a performance of *Hamlet*. In the dark, none had noticed that she'd dozed from Act Two through to the final bloody end. Naturally, she was much congratulated on her originality and, since neither of the grand matriarchs were alive to see injustice done, the matter was settled.

Lady Daphne had been preparing at least twelve months for this momentous occasion in her daughter's life, though obliged to honour the wishes of Ophelia in delaying her 'season' until she had finished her studies in art history at Girton College, Cambridge. In this, Ophelia was supported wholeheartedly by Sir Peter, who saw no reason for a modern girl of intellect to be without education.

The preceding summer and autumn months had been spent in Paris attending the Louvre, the Philharmonie de Paris, the Musée d'Orsay and the Palais Garnier, so that Ophelia might improve her knowledge of music and the fine arts.

To Ophelia's delight, her mother had at last conceded that they should both visit the renowned Antoine in the Galleries Lafayette to have their hair styled *a la mode*, in the boyish manner. In matters of fashion, Lady Daphne could not bear to lag behind, and she emerged with a sleek bob. Ophelia, who, in all things, was more unruly, found that her curls refused to sit demurely, even under the expert hands of Monsieur Antoine.

She emerged with hair springing wildly about her dainty face, heightening her wide-set eyes. Her mother was unable to hide her dismay, but the cut gave Ophelia great satisfaction. Not only would it be easier to wash, but it well-matched her mischievous attitude. The overall effect was delightfully impish.

They had been outfitted lavishly, as regular visitors at Maison Worth, and at the atelier of Madame Vionnet, on L'Avenue

Montaigne. How many hours had she stood, in one pose and then another, as satins, tulles and velvets were draped and pinned, and silks held to her face. Her mother had insisted on several suitably virginal evening gowns in white, embroidered in diamante and silver thread, georgette crêpe day dresses in cornflower blue, apricot and apple green, new riding attire, head-dresses of ostrich feathers, and shoes dainty of heel, destined to be danced to their graves upon the polished floors of London residences. Ophelia had embraced the novelty, having been previously confined to sensible wool for winter and summer cottons.

For Lady Daphne, as chaperone, the season would be almost as onerous. In gold brocade and lamé, diamonds glittering against pale skin, she had every intention of rising to the occasion. Even had she worn the rough serge of a nun, her elegance would have marked her as superior among her sex. Her dark-haired beauty had been admired in her youth, and was admired still.

Upon her return to London, Ophelia completed a course of instruction under the Vacani sisters, going thrice weekly to their studio in South Kensington, to learn the waltz, foxtrot and polka. In preparation for her presentation at Court, she was also schooled on the finer points of the deep curtsey she would perform, first to King George, and then to his consort, Queen Mary.

'Keep your back straight at all times,' commanded the first Miss Vacani. 'Bend at the knee, your eyes ever upon the King,' urged the second. 'Smile as you rise, and you may receive a returning smile of approval,' continued the first. The two always seemed to be finishing each other's sentences. Ophelia thought of them as a pair of budgerigars, contentedly preening and casting a twinkling eye on those about them.

It seemed to Ophelia that the whole experience was designed to subjugate her: to place her neatly in a box, from which she should seek to charm without uttering a single original thought. Speaking at all, it appeared, was to be undertaken with caution.

'Say as little as is needed. Absence of conversation is no impediment to success in gaining a man's interest,' Lady Daphne had advised, on the evening before it all began.

'Moreover, it is best never to meet a man's gaze directly. They find it intimidating, as if we were probing their mind.'

Ophelia wondered what she might be expected to find there...

Lady Daphne's advice appeared unending.

'Remember too that it doesn't do to let others know of your cleverness Ophelia. Men fear that a woman who is too clever — by which they mean the slightest cleverness at all — is not theirs to control.'

Lady Daphne had given an arch smile. 'Better to put that cleverness to covert use; once married, a woman can achieve a great deal behind the scenes.'

Ophelia didn't see why her achievements, whatever they might be, shouldn't be celebrated in the same way as a man's. Nevertheless, she bowed to her mother's wisdom in matters relating to the 'handling' of men. Her own father, she knew, acceded to Lady Daphne in all matters of Society and the household. Moreover, Ophelia was convinced, he considered himself fortunate in being able to do so.

It could not be said that Ophelia hadn't tried with Percival, although she had vowed never to lose her senses over a man. She had no intention of her life imitating that of her Shakespearean namesake.

Early on in the season, adorned in palest mauve silk, with cornflowers embroidered from shoulder to hem, Ophelia had taken her place among thirty strangers for a soirée, all but a second cousin on her father's side perfectly unknown to her. A portly gentleman, seemingly with some standing as a manufacturer in the northern counties, had been describing to her, at some length, the procedure for making clothes pegs, when Percival had presented himself, to escort her into dinner.

Well-mannered and agreeable, though sporting the pimples of youth and an over-fondness for hair oil, Percival was perfectly pleasant. Sadly, he lacked intellect: the result of interbreeding by certain

old families. Nature had bestowed upon him a brain never intended
for strenuous exercise.

Following her mother's tutelage, Ophelia had smiled more than
commented in reply. Largely, she had held her tongue, assuming an
expression of rapt fascination, as Percival inventoried his January
'bag' of hare, duck and goose, partridge and pheasant. By all accounts,
it had been the most successful of shooting seasons.

They had next met within the marbled and mirrored halls of
Grosvenor House, Ophelia wearing sequinned dancing shoes,
fastened with diamanté buttons, and a shimmering silver gown.
Percival had rescued her from a retired major whose toupée, in vivid
tangerine, would have looked quite at home in the jungles of Borneo.
Percival had swooped in, taken her hand, and led her into the throng
for a foxtrot. She'd been more than willing to overlook a few crushed
toes.

By their third meeting, Ophelia, demure in white silk with a silver
lace overlay, had begun to view him as a good egg, despite his limited
conversation. He had partnered her at supper, eaten without spilling
anything over her or himself, and had given her a chaste kiss upon the
forehead on departure, uttered with a cheery 'toodle-pip'.

The following evening, they had taken lemon ices on a balcony at
the Connaught Hotel, where tulips, apple blossom and rhododendrons
spilled from vases on every surface, and arum lilies and climbing roses
swathed a glass wall, floodlit from behind. Ophelia, wearing buttercup
yellow chiffon embellished with tiny violets at the neck and hem, had
allowed Percival's aristocratic hand to creep about her waist. She'd
prepared herself for a 'lunge' and had been all too ready to engage him
on equal ground, but he had merely given her a playful pinch and
licked, somewhat provocatively, the cherry from the top of her sorbet.

In truth, it was Percival's lack of sexual guile, his very inexperi-
ence, that soothed Ophelia. She'd had her fill of sly weasels and ebul-
lient stags. She was not a rabbit to be caught in the mouth of the most
daring, nor a common wild flower to be trampled underfoot. Her
enthusiasm had quickly waned for evenings spent among a hundred

other guests, crammed into a first-floor drawing room in Belgravia or Mayfair, converted into a ballroom for the night.

Ophelia was not the only debutante for whom the relentless requirement to be cheerful was wearing thin. In fact, if each young woman, so carefully outfitted and scented, were to peek into the thoughts of those about her, she'd find that few take pleasure in having their every action, word and article of costume dissected. Such are the rigours to which debutantes are subject.

To Ophelia's slight chagrin, it was obvious that Lady Daphne drew a great deal more admirers than she. Other chaperones sat quietly dozing over their knitting. Lady Daphne, statuesque, and resplendent in her Paris fashions, attracted not only an assortment of middle-aged fathers but several of the most eligible young men.

It had been on the fifth evening of Ophelia's acquaintance with Percival that he had escorted her from pre-dinner drinks at the Ritz to Devonshire House. Her mother had intentionally removed herself to a cab directly behind, whispering a hurried reminder to Ophelia that she be intelligent enough to conceal her intelligence.

Percival had indeed seized the opportunity to make known his ardour. He'd clamped his wet lips to hers, tongue probing at her upper molars and, despite her utmost readiness to surrender to the moment, to allow Percival to prove himself masterful, she'd been struck by a sense of absurdity.

She knew that wives were obliged to put up with things they found distasteful, and that a woman's passions were secondary to those of her husband, if they existed at all. Moreover, Ophelia was not averse to wedlock as a means to further her social position, to secure her financial future, and to access a lifestyle that would include regular trips to the Continent, and attendance at soirées hosted by the elite of her class.

She held hopes that her life might amount to more than choosing clothes and menus, and entertaining people who bored her silly, but she also viewed marriage as a contract; in signing it, she was determined to acquire the very best terms.

As Lady Daphne would say, 'You were born, and you will die. What you make of the middle is your own affair.'

Her reluctance to commit to the wedded state might have been attributed to her age. In no more than the twinkling of an eye, Ophelia, like the rest of her cohort, had been transported from gawky childhood to the realms of eligible womanhood. 'Ah!' we might say. 'What could be more fitting then, that Lady Ophelia Finchingfield, a radiant example of the innocent feminine, would cast down her eyes, and resist the eagerness of her suitor.'

Were we to reach inside the mind of our young heroine, we'd discover that far from being averse to physical intimacy, it was a subject she'd examined most thoroughly, and with regular indulgence, often while daydreaming in a long, hot bath. Rather than being coy, she looked forward keenly to her place at the lovers' table, in anticipation of sampling all its dishes.

Ophelia hoped that she would be proven correct in her belief that marital comforts were an important aspect of marriage. She believed there were all sorts of lovely things you might do with a husband, if he was amiable enough to experiment, and not treat you like a statue of the Virgin Mary.

As Percival had withdrawn his tongue, dabbing saliva from the edges of his mouth, he'd extracted from his pocket a ring, and an alarmed repugnance had welled within, surprising her in its vehemence.

It was at that moment that the placement of her head within a noose became apparent. If she failed to wriggle free, she'd find herself being kissed by Percival Huntley-Withington for the rest of her miserable life.

Ophelia's rejection of marriage to the Earl of Woldershire so incensed Lady Daphne (the opinion of Sir Peter was of no matter) that Ophelia had been placed on the next overnight sleeper to Scotland, to stay with her grandmother until she saw sense.

If Lady Finchingfield could overlook Percival's mother expelling cigarette smoke from her nostrils in the manner of a horse snorting steam on a chilly morning, then Ophelia could put up with marriage to a man lacking sex appeal. In fact, thought Lady Daphne, the less pizzazz on that front the better; in her experience, less appealing husbands were rather easier to manage.

Unceremoniously banished from the social whirl of London, Ophelia reclined upon her bunk, rocked by the rhythm of the Scotch Express to Inverness, accompanied by the warm snuffling creature that was her beloved Pudding. She had insisted that where she go, her Cairn terrier follow.

Ophelia had never met Lady Morag MacKintoch but she feared her grandmother feeding her nothing but bread and water (physically and sexually) until she relented and threw herself back upon her mother's mercy.

Cabbage too, thought Ophelia with a shudder. *No doubt, there'll be endless cabbage, and spinach, cooked for hours and spooned liberally onto the plate. The servants will have been thoroughly trained in the over-boiling of vegetables, and the very walls will be impregnated with the smell of Brussels sprouts.*

This sorry contemplation inspired her to extract her Cadbury's Milk Tray, hastily purchased at King's Cross station for such a possible crisis. Pudding sniffed hopefully as Ophelia tore the seal and chose a strawberry crème.

Despite these forebodings, Ophelia could not deny a certain excitement. Scotland, she decided, would be the place to run into an artist, the sort who would be expertly experienced: a marvellous kisser, and much besides.

In fact, she mused, *wild Bohemians are probably thicker on the ground in the Highlands than they are in Bloomsbury. They'll be everywhere, painting grand views and sighing for a muse, from which to draw inspiration and upon which to pour their passion...*

Ophelia closed her eyes, and wriggled under the covers, sucking thoughtfully on a caramel. Hugging her faithful terrier, she drifted into delicious dreams. Reclined upon a chaise longue, draped in nothing but a wisp of chiffon, her imagination conjured for her a brooding, Byronic artist, eyes seared with yearning. Overcome with desire, he crossed the room in a great bound, and tore the chiffon from her, crushing her lips to his. His mouth then ravaged her breast, and the hardness of his thigh forced her legs open to him.

Her belly fluttering in delight, Ophelia squeezed Pudding a little tighter.

RECIPES

In the footsteps of Isabella and Maud, you may like to try some of the recipes from 'The Gentlemen's Club'.

Both serve 8 to 10 persons

TORTE BAROZZI

A flour-free dark chocolate and nut 'cake' – suitable for those who are gluten intolerant

Melt 250g chocolate and 150g butter in a bowl set over hot water. Set aside to cool slightly

Beat four yolks with 150g sugar until fluffy, before stirring in the chocolate mixture, along with 150g of toasted, crushed almonds, a dash of your chosen liqueur (brandy or rum for example) and 60ml of rich coffee.

Beat the four egg whites in a separate bowl, to soft peaks, and fold into the chocolate mixture.

Pour into pan, oiled and dusted with cocoa powder, and with a sheet of parchment paper in the base. Use a sprung pan if you have one.

Bake for 35 to 40 minutes (until a cake tester inserted in the centre is slightly damp) – at 325F / 160C

Remove from the oven and set the pan on a cooling rack, removing the torte once completely cool (run a butter knife along the inside edges to release).

Dust the top of the cake with icing sugar.

STRUFFOLI

Deep-fried balls of dough about the size of marbles: crunchy on the outside and light inside, glazed with honey and other sweet ingredients.

In a food processor, pulse together 700g of flour, zest from one lemon and orange, three tablespoons of sugar, half a teaspoon of fine salt, and a quarter teaspoon of baking powder.

Add 55g of unsalted butter and pulse until the mixture resembles breadcrumbs.

Add three large eggs, a dash of white wine, and a teaspoon of pure vanilla extract. Pulse until the mixture forms into a ball.

Wrap the dough in cling-film and refrigerate for thirty minutes.

Divide the dough into four, rolling each on a lightly floured surface, until about a quarter of an inch thick Cut then into half inch wide strips, and each strip into half-inch pieces.

Roll each piece of dough into a small ball and dredge lightly in flour, shaking off excess.

In a deep frying pan or saucepan, pour enough oil to be able to submerge the dough balls, which you will fry for only two minutes each, in batches (test the temperature by browning a piece of bread).

Drain on a paper towel.

When your frying is done, use another pan to boil about 250ml of honey, about 100ml sugar, and a good slosh of lemon juice stirring until the sugar has dissolved (about 3 minutes).

Remove the honey syrup from the heat, before adding the fried dough balls. Stir in also some toasted, crushed hazelnuts (place in oven for about 8 minutes, on a baking sheet), and allow the mixture to cool in the pan for a few minutes before transferring your struffoli to your serving plate.

To create a traditional wreath, place a water glass at the centre of your plate, coated in oil or butter. Arrange your struffoli around the glass and drizzle over any remaining honey mixture.

Allow to set for two hours (or make a day in advance) – before removing the glass.

ABOUT THE AUTHOR

Emmanuelle de Maupassant lives with her husband
(maker of tea and fruit cake) and her hairy pudding terrier
(connoisseur of squeaky toys and bacon treats).

If you enjoy this story, you may like to read the sequel - Italian Sonata

For behind the scenes chat, access to 'advance reader copies' prior to
release, and secret giveaways, join Emmanuelle's Facebook 'Boudoir'
group.

www.emmanuelledemaupassant.com

ABOUT THE EDITOR

Adrea is a Melbourne-based freelance writer, editor and former stage director. She holds a BA (Hons) in theatre studies. Through her fiction and non-fiction writing, she engages with themes of the feminine, often focusing her lens on the rich diversity of feminine sexuality. She is also deeply interested in myth and fairy tale re-tellings. After many years interpreting play-texts as a theatre director, Adrea is now applying those skills in deepening the "theatre on the page", enhancing the writer's voice through developmental editing.

Adrea's erotic short stories and poetry appear in various anthologies, including *For the Men* (2016), *Coming Together: In Verse* (2015) and *Licked* (House of Erotica 2015), *The Mammoth Book of Best New Erotica 13*, and *A Storytelling of Ravens* (Little Raven 2014). Her provocative flash fiction and short stories feature on many online sites. In another guise, she has published a feminist creative essay in *Etchings* literary journal (2013), and her short memoir story was published in an Australian anthology the same year. Adrea is working on acollection of themed erotic short stories *Watching You Watching Me* and her first novella, a mythical re-telling.

To discover more, visit her at:
https://koredesires.wordpress.com/about/
https://www.facebook.com/adrea.kore
https://twitter.com/adrea_kore

32679284R00223

Printed in Poland
by Amazon Fulfillment
Poland Sp. z o.o., Wrocław